MEDUSA
IN THE
GRAVEYARD

TOR BOOKS BY
EMILY DEVENPORT

Medusa Uploaded
Medusa in the Graveyard

MEDUSA
IN THE
GRAVEYARD

EMILY DEVENPORT

A TOM DOHERTY ASSOCIATES BOOK

NEW YORK

MEDUSA IN THE GRAVEYARD

Copyright © 2019 by Emily Devenport

Edited by Jen Gunnels

A Tor Book
Published by Tom Doherty Associates
120 Broadway
New York, NY 10271

www.tor-forge.com

Tor® is a registered trademark of Macmillan Publishing Group, LLC.

Library of Congress Cataloging-in-Publication Data

Names: Devenport, Emily, author.
Title: Medusa in the graveyard / Emily Devenport.
Description: First edition. | New York : Tor, 2019. | "A Tom Doherty
    Associates book."
Identifiers: LCCN 2018057725| ISBN 9781250169365 (softcover : acid-free paper) |
    ISBN 9781250169358 (ebook)
Subjects: LCSH: Artificial intelligence—Fiction. | Space ships—Fiction. | GSAFD:
    Science fiction.
Classification: LCC PS3604.E8846 M425 2019 | DDC 813/.6—dc23
LC record available at https://lccn.loc.gov/2018057725

Our books may be purchased in bulk for promotional, educational,
or business use. Please contact your local bookseller or the
Macmillan Corporate and Premium Sales Department at
1-800-221-7945, extension 5442, or by email at
MacmillanSpecialMarkets@macmillan.com.

First Edition: July 2019

Printed in the United States of America

0 9 8 7 6 5 4 3 2 1

Acknowledgments

For Jen Gunnels, for suffering through the various incarnations of this book, and for Martha Millard, for suffering through the various incarnations of my career.

There is a crack in everything.
That's how the light gets in.

—Leonard Cohen, "Anthem"

MEDUSA
IN THE
GRAVEYARD

PROLOGUE

Itzpapalotl is a goddess of nightmares.

She's also a ship belonging to the Weapons Clan, but there's no reason she can't be both. Especially once you've seen her. A beautiful thing, of inexplicable design (at least to me), she is the home of Bomarigala, a scion of his clan. Medusa and I have come to find him. I'm not sure what we'll do with him—we'll cross that bridge when we get to it.

We move through that unfamiliar space under Medusa's power, on biometal tentacles that flex and release silently. Her face covers mine like a mask. Together, we see. We hear. We look for the man who almost destroyed everything we have worked for.

We're not on our home ground, but we haven't been for some time. We have a secret weapon up our—well, sleeve, though Medusa would require a lot of those. Yet I would be lying if I told you everything is going our way. I have never been so exhausted in my life. I have quite a few old grudges weighing me down. Bomarigala is no easy prey—he is a remnant of the old Empire of Clans. He's got a lot of syllables in his name, and he earned every single one of them, in places I would not care to tread under *anyone's* power, Medusa's included.

Bomarigala is as old as Gennady Mironenko, the man who made us. He may be older. He persists in a youthful state, with all his powers, all his faculties intact and humming along with dreadful efficiency.

Though we're expecting dire consequences for our invasion, he takes some of the wind out of my sails when we find him, because Bomarigala is just sitting there, pouring tea into *two* cups, as if he's expecting company. When he looks up at us, he smiles. It's a thin smile, but I'm impressed anyway. Most people would have screamed and tried to run.

"It's a black tea," says Bomarigala. "Not very subtle—I like the ones that have some kick to them. If you want cream and sugar, they're on the tray." He motions for us to sit with him on his dais, to pick up the antique cup.

I feel grateful that Medusa's visage covers mine. She is a beautiful predator, with much better focus than I can muster. At this moment, when I should
have enjoyed the most clarity, I can't help pausing to admire the scene he has
set for us, in a room as grand and expansive as the court of a Chinese king.
He looks like a figure from an ancient silk painting, dressed in Hanfu, his hair
a black curtain.

I think Medusa expects me to say something pertinent at this point. When
I miss my cue, she steps into the breach.

"You just *had* to wake them," she says. "With no second thoughts about
the consequences."

Bomarigala lifts one eyebrow. "Oh, I assure you, there have been *plenty* of
second thoughts about the consequences of waking the Three—but we committed ourselves long ago, and we can't afford to have doubts."

Medusa pauses, waiting for me to make my own commitment. I fail again.

Bomarigala, an ancient person wearing a young face, sees right through
me. "So tell me, Oichi—what are *your* doubts?"

Oh—that is the right question. My doubts. I have a lot more of them now
than I did when I started.

Let me tell you all about them.

PART ONE

WATCH OUT—THEY BITE

1

Establishing Normal

My name is Oichi Angelis, and I shall always be a worm, regardless of where I go, because of where I have already been.

I was born and bred in the endless tunnels of a generation ship. All my life I have plotted and maneuvered. I have killed and I have avoided being killed. I have communicated with three ancient spaceships on a planet called Graveyard. Now I will have to negotiate with the powerful Weapons Clan who made us.

What seems like negotiations to some, plays out more like war to others. Perhaps that's why I told the emissaries from the Weapons Clan to dock their ship in Lock 212. It has seen more than its fair share of bloodshed.

She was a sleek little craft, called *Merlin*, probably named after a bird of prey rather than the wizard. She sat complacently while our scrubbers removed toxins generated by her thrusters. Medusa and I abided on opposite ends of *Olympia*; our link allowed us to spy together on *Merlin*'s crew, through their security systems and their intercoms, even through the big view window on her bridge. They hadn't seemed alarmed about where we told them to dock. That was because they didn't know what Medusa and I had done to other people inside Lock 212.

The name *Merlin* had me thinking about sorcerers, so the score for *The Sorcerer's Apprentice* played in my head as she was towed into Lock 212. I loved the music by Paul Dukas, and its accompanying images from the animated movie *Fantasia*—the marching brooms and their unrelenting bucket brigade. Two flutes and piccolos, two oboes, two soprano clarinets and bass clarinet, and three bassoons and contrabassoon (instruments that are underused, in my opinion). Four horns, two trumpets, two cornets, three trombones, and a collection of timpani, glockenspiel, bass drum, cymbals, triangle, harp, and strings. Do I imagine the perfect tones of a celesta in there? Lending bright magic to this sorcerous collaboration? All of them marching together with a *tum-te-tum te-tumpetty-tum*?

The scrubbers, our version of the ensorcelled brooms, scurried from their cubbies to clean every inch of *Merlin*'s surface. It was a job they had not done very often, so I imagined they wanted to be extra diligent.

People peered out of *Merlin*'s view windows and into our lock, but I doubted they could see much. A few emergency lights were on; I kept the main lights off for the time being. That made it easier to see into *Merlin*, whose interior was brightly lit. Communications Officer Narm spent the most time looking out, along with a pale young man named Wilson, who was one of the engineers, and a tiny woman with white hair and skin the color of dark plums. The lady was named Cocteau; the ship's roster identified her as another engineer.

<Two engineers,> I remarked to Medusa.

<Do you suppose Cocteau is a descendant of Jean Cocteau?>

Medusa referred to the director of another of our favorite movies, *La Belle et la Bête*. That bumped Dukas's apprentice out of my head and replaced him with Georges Auric's score for Jean Cocteau's film, which was far more romantic but still appropriate. The score is played by a full orchestra, including a choir, and it lends *La Belle et la Bête* an emotional potency to complement its gorgeous images. <There may be thousands of Cocteaus,> I mused. <Millions . . . >

<They should have their own planet,> said Medusa.

When the last minute of the decontamination period expired, Narm sent a message. "Our captain and Representative Lee are standing by for your directions as to where and when the meeting will take place."

"This is Oichi Angelis," I replied. "I will rendezvous with your captain and your representative inside the lock."

I messaged Medusa. <It's time.>

<Coming.>

Merlin's crew sat in front of the observation windows as if engrossed in a movie, watching *Olympia*'s scrubbers take one last spin over the exterior of their ship. I continued to surveil them and listen to their conversation through the open link. Perhaps it would get more informative, now that our meeting was imminent.

"Anyone show up yet?" said Captain Thomas.

"Nope," said Mirzakhani. She was a medical tech whose roster profile stated she could also do *field surgery*. "It sure is dark out there."

"Maybe they have better night vision than we do," said Narm.

Engineers Wilson and Cocteau both shook their heads. "These folks thought they were alone out here," said Cocteau. "They conserve energy where they can."

I heard a rustle in the hall behind me and turned to see Medusa moving around the corner. She was the Prima, the Queen of the lightning-fast death blow, my superstrong biometal friend.

She joined me at the pressure door and flowed over me. Her suit sealed around me, her face settled over mine, and we became one. Now I could hear with her sensitive ears. I could see with eyes that could stare into the heart of a sun without blinking, yet also see the movement of a bee gathering pollen on a distant flower.

I stretched her tentacles luxuriously. <I've missed you. We don't do this as much as we used to.>

<You would prefer to go back to the days when we skulked together on *Olympia*'s hull, plotting the downfall of the Executives?>

I felt an unexpected stab of longing.

<Oichi?>

<It's showtime,> I said.

The scrubbers crawled off *Merlin* and scurried to their cubbies. I opened the pressure door.

Inside *Merlin*, Mirzakhani let out a little gasp. "There's a light!"

We stood in that bar of light, and because the source was behind us, our dark twins stretched far ahead of us.

"Are those *tentacles* . . . ?" said Narm.

Our shadows moved toward *Merlin* like a sea monster reaching for prey.

<We may have overdone it a bit with the shadowy tentacles,> said Medusa after we had been waiting for a while and no one came out of *Merlin*'s air lock.

I sighed. <I should have killed the lights in the hallway first. Oh well. Lesson learned.>

The outer door of *Merlin*'s air lock opened.

"It smells okay." I heard what I assumed was Representative Lee's voice. "Feels drier than I would have thought, considering they have a big habitat for crops in here."

Captain Thomas peered down the ramp and past the light that lit a path into the air lock. We had moved out of it, trying to diminish that whole tentacle-monster effect. Medusa waggled the tip of an appendage, hoping to capture her attention.

Thomas whispered to Lee, "Did I ever tell you how much I admire your calm?"

"It's a complete sham," he replied sotto voce.

"I admire that even more."

It wasn't a sham. We could hear Lee's heartbeat. It remained slow and steady. Captain Thomas started to move down the ramp, but Lee put a restraining hand on her arm. "Some things I say or do may not make sense," he said in the same low voice that he apparently didn't know we could hear.

Thomas kept a straight face. "And that's different from the usual—how?"

"Good point." Lee withdrew his hand.

The two of them descended the ramp. Lee's heartbeat continued steady, while Captain Thomas fought to stay the same. She used her breathing to get control. I admired her for that.

When they were within ten paces, I stepped into the light again.

They stopped abruptly. The captain spoke in a steady voice. "I'm Epatha Thomas, captain of *Merlin*, and this is Representative Lee. Thank you for allowing us to dock."

I selected a voice from my database that resembled the tone and cadence of Captain Thomas's speech patterns. "I'm Oichi Angelis. And this is Medusa."

I didn't realize how baffling that sounded until they frowned.

"I'm wearing Medusa," I explained. "We are two people, though at the moment, we appear to be one."

Medusa pulled her tentacles in closer. Fully extended, they can stretch six meters in all directions. They could have broken our visitors' necks before either of them had a chance to register alarm.

"You came from the Weapons Clan ship?" I said. "The one at the outer edge of the Charon system?"

"Yes," said Captain Thomas.

"How long did it take you to get to us from there?"

"About three weeks."

"*Weeks.* We don't use that term. My records indicate it's from Old Earth. It took us a year to cross the same distance. Our drive is primitive compared with yours."

"If it is," said Thomas, "nothing else about *Olympia* is primitive. Your ship is a marvel."

I didn't answer. Medusa's tentacles coiled and uncoiled languidly. We watched Captain Thomas's autonomic system wreak havoc with her pupils.

Yet her voice remained steady when she said, "*Merlin* is locked down according to your security specifications. As we discussed when you gave us clearance to dock, my crew numbers six people, including Representative Lee and myself."

I focused on Lee. His pupils, heartbeat, and respiration betrayed no nervousness. I wondered what made him so confident. Was it experience? Or did he have some advantage we weren't guessing?

Medusa's lips curved in a faint but perceptible smile, and we heard Captain Thomas's heart stutter.

"I will introduce you to the Security Council," I said. "You may relay your message to them. Do not attempt to share it with me as we make our way to the House of Clans. Please follow me."

Medusa and I pivoted and walked to the outer door. Thomas and Lee followed in our wake.

When our backs were turned, we heard Captain Thomas taking another deep breath. I suspected she would need to do so again.

Because she was about to see more tentacles.

If dreadful things have happened inside Lock 212, you could say the same thing about the House of Clans. True—blood had not literally been spilled there, but if you knew the long history of outrages Executive clan leaders had legislated therein, you could understand why it had been shed everywhere else.

Despite its history, Order and Law are personified in the graceful lines of the House of Clans. One could almost believe it had grown naturally inside the Habitat Sector, along with the garden that framed it. I escorted the emissaries up its expansive central aisle. At the far end, the Security Council knelt on low daises, in a semicircle. The tentacles of each of their Medusa units towered overhead and moved as if stirred by a gentle tide. The members wore fine but austere clothing woven from a blend of cotton and silk.

The whole scene made me feel as if I were an actress who had stepped into a Japanese Noh play. That's normal on *Olympia*. Protocol dictates every step we take in here. Courtesy and decorum comfort us. I led our guests past empty rows, where clan leaders sit when debates are held and votes are cast, and halted when we were within ten paces of the council members.

The Council Prime sat near the center of the group. Kumiko covered his face, her expression serene. "I am Terry Charmayne," he said. "Please tell us why you have come."

Merlin's captain seemed to become more poised under pressure. "I am Epatha Thomas, captain of the Union Ship *Merlin*, and this is my colleague"— Thomas gestured—"Representative Lee. We come as messengers for Bomarigala of the Weapons Clan."

Perhaps that was the only thing Thomas had planned to say to the Security Council, but Terry asked her a question before Lee could begin his spiel. "What is the *Union*?"

"The Union," said Thomas, "is a collective of worlds, governments, and entities that share laws and treaties. In particular, Union worlds have agreed to base their laws on a Bill of Rights."

"The Weapons Clan also follows this *Bill of Rights*?" said Terry.

I thought he had zeroed in on an awkward point, but Thomas answered confidently. "The Weapons Clan does not consider itself to be a member of the Union. They observe Union laws when doing business with members of the Union."

"Are *you* a member of the Union, Captain Thomas?"

"Yes. I am a contractor, sir. I am not a member of the Weapons Clan."

Kumiko's eyes shifted to regard the representative. "And you, Lee. Are you a member of the Weapons Clan?"

"No," said Lee. "I am a professional courier. My delivery of this message will fulfill my contract. My role is to be a messenger of the Clan, not to act as their spokesperson."

That was an interesting distinction.

"What is the message?" said Terry.

Lee did not possess a fine voice, but he spoke clearly. "The Weapons Clan regrets that indignities were suffered by the people of *Titania* and *Olympia* during this voyage that has brought you to the Charon system. They wish you to know that events beyond their control separated them from you. If their agents had awakened when they were supposed to, they would never have allowed the destruction of your sister ship, *Titania*."

He paused as if expecting questions at that juncture, but we waited to hear the rest.

"The Weapons Clan regrets the loss of life from *Titania*," he continued. "They invested enormous resources into *Titania* and *Olympia*. They wish to propose a contract with the survivors on *Olympia*. If you will accept employment with the Weapons Clan, all debts will be paid. You will find their patronage beneficial. You need fear no reprisals for any destruction of property belonging to the Weapons Clan. You may show your good faith by declaring *Olympia* to be an outpost of the Weapons Clan when you establish orbit around Graveyard. Details of your employment will be negotiated once you have done so."

Lee dipped his head. "That is the full message."

The Security Council studied Lee and Thomas. Each Medusa unit wore her own expression. Some of them looked amused. Others seemed concerned. One of them curled her lips in a scornful smile. Their tentacles continued to move to the same slow current.

"Did you memorize the message?" Terry Charmayne asked at last. "You spoke it exactly as it was delivered to you?"

"Sir, I did," said Lee.

"Do you endorse it, Representative Lee?"

"It is not my place to endorse the message," said Lee. "Most Union officials would advise you to think carefully before you sign any contracts."

I wondered how the Weapons Clan would react if they learned that Lee had added that caveat. They might not be so eager to pay him. At least—not with credit.

Did he imply that the Union was more honorable? I doubted the Weapons Clan placed their highest value on that quality.

"We will consider the offer," said Terry Charmayne, "and the advice of Union officials. Oichi will take you back to your ship now."

"Thank you," Thomas and Lee said together. We pivoted and walked back up the central aisle.

The aery Habitat Sector contrasts starkly with the narrow tunnels that riddle the hide of *Olympia*. Movers can take you far, but quite a lot of worming is required to travel between the House of Clans and Lock 212. Our passages are lit only at intervals. Darkness pools between the lights, and I wondered each time Thomas and Lee followed us into another shadow, did they think it might be their last?

When we escorted them into a mover, Lee cleared his throat. "I'm assuming the people responsible for the destruction of *Titania* were prosecuted, according to your laws?"

"You could say that," I replied. *If you don't mind stretching the definition a bit.*

Thomas and Lee didn't look at us the rest of the way back. They seemed preoccupied. Representative Lee wore his bland expression as comfortably as I wore Medusa. Captain Thomas had frown lines between her brows. I thought I should do something to ease the tension, and I doubted my conversation would do the trick, so I played Rachmaninoff in the mover. I'm not sure the music made them feel any better, but it certainly improved *my* mood.

A few suites and one piano concerto later, we emerged near the pressure door of the air lock that housed *Merlin*.

"I will see you to your door," I said.

Even Lee's heart rate jumped at that prospect.

Nostalgia buoyed me as we walked them in, traveling on my feet. Medusa's tentacles towered over us, casting serpentine shadows on *Merlin*'s hide. Their movement calmed me. I felt prepared for the task at hand.

I let myself savor a few memories as we walked past seldom-used equipment and tow cables. Just over *here* we broke Percy O'Reilly's neck. Over *there*, we pulled Ryan Charmayne off his feet and had a nice (if brief) conversation with him.

When we had reached *Merlin*'s ramp, Captain Thomas paused and turned to us. "Thank you for letting us deliver the message."

"You're welcome," I said, my tone warm.

Perhaps a little *too* warm. Thomas frowned. We suffered an awkward moment until they finally turned and walked up the ramp.

That left us at their backs. We watched them for a moment, then started up after them.

Startled, they looked over their shoulders at us. Lee said, "Medusa— *please . . .*"

<Ah-hah!> Medusa stopped dead. Without her, I couldn't move, which was awkward. <Oichi, we must rethink this.>

I didn't want to rethink it. Once again, I tried to move forward, to thrust her tentacles at the emissaries of the Weapons Clan, but Medusa wasn't budging—at least not in *that* direction. She had no problem with reverse.

"We'll talk again," I said, and made the most dignified exit I could.

Thomas and Lee stayed frozen while we moved away. The pressure door spun shut behind us, taking our light with it. We used the Security surveillance cameras to watch them as they backed up, all the way into *Merlin*'s air lock.

Through their intercom, I heard Lee say, "We almost got killed."

Captain Thomas closed their outer door. I imagined her typing the security code as fast as her fingers could go—that's what *I* would have done. She said, "Her tone was too friendly at the end, there. That mask over her face made it hard to tell what she was thinking."

"That mask is Medusa," said Lee. "I think that mask talked Oichi out of killing us."

Except that Medusa *hadn't* talked me out of it. She simply hadn't cooperated.

<Medusa,> I said, <what the hell just happened?>

2

Itzpapa-whozit

In the cycles before *Merlin* made her first approach, we expected to encounter someone else entirely. An asteroid belt stretches midway between the gas giants in the outer solar system of Charon and its rocky inner worlds. We had been told that the belt hosted an extensive colony of miners. Such an intrepid vocation must attract adventurous people. Could they fail to notice us? How long would they wait to say hello? How long should *we* wait to do so? We debated the protocols.

<We mined asteroids ourselves, about thirty years ago,> Medusa told me. <We got a lot of water ice, some metals, and other useful elements. The gold used in the decorations on the House of Clans are from one of those asteroids.>

She referred to the fish and flowers embossed on the doors. I wondered if the Belters of Charon made similar use of the materials they mined. I would ask them, once we made formal contact.

Olympia had been in-system for a year by then, on a course that would allow us to assume a parking orbit around Graveyard, the fourth world out from Charon. We had passed four gas giants on the way in, gorgeous monsters with moons that were small worlds in their own right. We marveled at the visible storms on two of those giants, cyclones large enough to swallow ten Graveyards.

Would we seem a marvel to the Belters? Had they seen a generation ship before? Was *Olympia* just another wonder in a place already swamped with them?

Judging by the warning beacons we passed, it might be more amazing that the Alliance of Ancient Races who guarded Graveyard had decided to allow *Olympia* to travel so far in. The spare communications we received from system officials informed us that everyone else from out-system had to wait years for permission—and when that was granted, they could visit only in small, unarmed ships.

Merlin had been that sort of ship. She didn't approach *Olympia* until we neared the occupied space of the asteroid belt—but she hadn't come from the belt. She came from out-system, from space through which we had already passed.

I was pretty sure which clan had sent her.

"This is Union Ship *Merlin*," Narm hailed *Olympia*, calling the language we had used all our lives *Standard Dialect*. "Requesting permission to dock. Our captain and a representative would like to meet with your clan leaders. We will comply with your security and medical protocols. Do you copy?"

He repeated his message in more dialects, including two labeled *Tagg* and *GenParl* that included some recognizable words. We sent our reply in *Standard* before he got all the way through them.

"We have received your message. Stand by."

Stand by was a bit of an understatement. We argued for hours while *Merlin* maintained a steady distance from *Olympia*.

<*Merlin* is a famous wizard,> said Nuruddin Jackson, our cinema expert. Movies and music play oversized roles in our lives on *Olympia*, so Nuruddin's opinion always carries weight. <He appears in several of the movies in my database. Sometimes he is a virtuous protagonist; other times he is a mischievous trickster.>

Nuruddin's Medusa unit, Nefertari, disagreed. <This *Merlin* is a ship, and in all of our movies, ships are given female personae. Therefore, she may be named for a falcon. According to our nature database, merlins are clever and swift. This seems a good name for a small ship.>

Our visitor might be a powerful trickster or a clever little raptor. Either way, she should not be underestimated, but I wasn't sure everyone on the Security Council grasped that.

<She's tiny,> said Jonquil Schickele. <How much harm could she do?>

That provoked a flurry of opinions concerning spies, germs, and gravity bombs, yet I doubted *Merlin* was on a mission of destruction. She had come to establish contact. Such things are better done in person.

You could say the same thing about assassination. It's possible I was letting my curiosity get the better of me. I decided to ask the opinion of a person whose life was consumed with ensuring the survival of our generation ship. I paid him a visit in Ship Operations (the location of which is still unknown to most of my fellow citizens).

"Nemo, you are captain of *Olympia*," I said. "If you are opposed to these visitors, I won't allow them to set foot on our ship."

Nemo didn't have to ponder it for long. "I can list pros and cons either way. If you want to allow the visit, specific protocols must be observed. I can communicate those protocols to *Merlin*, if that's what you decide, but if you're asking me what I think—I vote for letting them visit. Once they've linked with our auto-approach system, we'll have access to their docking history. We can find out who they are and where they've been. We can get quite a lot of information out of them without asking, just because of that link." He shrugged. "We may also be subject to security breaches, but sometimes you have to sacrifice information to gain information."

To me, that was the real point.

That's not what I told the Security Council. You can argue with officials for only so long before it becomes circular.

<Nemo votes yes,> I said. <He'll convey the Security protocols.>

<We'll prepare for a formal meeting,> Terry Charmayne replied.

I remained in Operations while Nemo and his crew handled the approach. Barring Weapons Clan operatives, these were the first outsiders I had ever seen. The prospect of meeting them was both exciting and disturbing.

"What are your decontamination procedures?" our communications officer asked *Merlin*.

Narm responded with a list.

"That should be sufficient," said Nemo. "Permission granted. We're sending auto-approach guidelines."

Merlin accepted our link. Nemo was proved right when we were able to access a ship's roster of biographies and profile pictures of the crew. For outsiders, they looked remarkably similar to us.

Narm's full name was Narm Ha-neul. From his picture, he appeared to be twenty-something, and he reminded me of a Weapons Clan operative who once tried to kill me—Tetsuko. Unlike Tetsuko, Narm wasn't wearing a perpetual smirk. At least, he wasn't wearing one in his profile picture.

As to other information we might gain, Nemo was proved right again when we heard Narm exclaim, "Wow!" in what sounded like genuine astonishment.

Along with the auto-approach link (and our spyware), we had sent a general diagram of *Olympia* and her specs. "*Wow*," Narm said again. "Cap, come look at this."

There was a pause while Epatha Thomas joined Narm at his display. In her profile, she appeared to be in her midforties. When her picture had been taken, her hair was carefully coifed. Her expression suggested she thought something was funny or possibly strange—she couldn't decide which.

Later I would see quite a different expression on her face, but this one intrigued me.

"Have you ever seen a ship this big?" said Narm.

"Not a ship," said Captain Thomas. "Sunbusters are that big. See those towers on the leading edge? That's where the injectors would be on a sunbuster."

<They don't sound as if they're aware they're on an open mic,> I said.

<They're not aware,> replied our own COMMO. <When they accepted our auto-approach, they didn't look to see if anything else was attached to it. If they're not already suspicious, they won't know until they run a detailed Security check.>

"You're sure they're *not* weapons?" Narm said, presumably referring to our research towers on the leading edge.

"I'm sure they're not *injectors*," said Thomas.

"They're not weapons," said another voice, this one bland. "They could be *harboring* weapons."

This third person turned out to be Representative Lee. I thought his tone suggested he knew more about us than Narm and Cap. "The scale of *Olympia* is like nothing you'll see outside a city-class space station, and it beggars most of those."

I don't know if Narm found that information useful. I certainly did.

Olympia spins to simulate gravity, so *Merlin* would have to match the speed of the spin, fly into an access canyon, and pivot so the top of her fuselage turned toward *Olympia*. Once they linked with the tow structure, *Merlin*'s belly would be exposed to the stars until we towed her into an air lock.

<Which lock do you want them to use?> said Nemo.

<Lock 212,> I replied.

My order was executed without a ripple of awareness of the mayhem that had occurred inside (and outside) Lock 212 in the past few years. Only Medusa and I shared that knowledge. I wondered what she would say when she found out which air lock I had chosen.

I didn't wonder for long. <Naughty,> said Medusa.

<I'm sentimental.>

<We shouldn't kill the messengers. We must practice diplomacy.>

<Lock 212 was available,> I said. <We know it well, so if there's trouble, we'll be able to respond confidently.>

<Have you ever known me to respond otherwise?> said Medusa.

Her tone was mild, but I think she was a little annoyed with me. Before I could compose an answer, Nemo said, <According to her specs, *Merlin* generates a light gravity field, just enough to let them walk around with their mags switched off. It could take them seventy-two to one hundred twenty hours to adjust to the conditions of *Olympia*.>

<Let's give them forty-eight,> I said.

<I'm putting this on-screen.> Our communications officer sounded excited. One of the large displays hanging over the center lit up with an image. <This is the last place *Merlin* docked. She's called *Itzpapalotl*.>

We all stared at it. I'm not ashamed to say my mouth was hanging open. <That's a ship?>

<Some might say that about *Olympia*,> Nemo reminded me.

I stared at *Itzpapa-whozit* a little longer. <Well,> I said at last, <it looks as though the Weapons Clan is accustomed to building on a grand scale.>

Size was the only thing that ship had in common with *Olympia*. She looked like an alien cathedral that had somehow become spaceborne. Our generation ship had gigantic engines on our Aft Sector, but *Itzpapalotl* had nothing remotely like that. She possessed structures that defied explanation.

Medusa interrupted my survey. <I found the word *Itzpapalotl* in one of our databases. It means *obsidian butterfly*. She was an Aztec goddess of nightmares.>

That did not put my mind at ease.

<Is there a ship's roster for *Itzpapalotl*?> I dutifully pronounced the name. <Although that would be a pretty big file.>

<It would,> agreed our COMMO. <Unfortunately, *Itzpapalotl* has way better security features than *Merlin* does.>

Better security features than *Merlin* *appeared* to have, I could have said, but I saw no reason to cast more suspicion on our visitors than we already entertained. After all, I wanted to meet them, to learn everything I could about them—and about the people who sent them.

"Look at the tow structure," we heard Narm say over the link.

I frowned. <What's wrong with our tow structure?>

"It looks new," said Captain Thomas.

"I don't think it's new," said Representative Lee. "I think it hasn't been used very often. I'll bet it's spent most of its time retracted, waiting for ships that never came."

Well, now! Wasn't he Mr. Know-It-All?

He was right about those ships, though. I wondered what other insights he might have.

<Did a ship just dock with *Olympia*?> Nuruddin's son, Ashur, called.

Ashur was part of my inner circle, so I answered his question truthfully. <The Weapons Clan have sent messengers. Once they go through decontamination, they will meet with the Security Council.>

<Will you have to kill them?>

I'm sorry he had to ask that question.

<Medusa will assess the situation, too,> I assured him. <There will be a consensus.>

<Will I be part of that consensus? I don't know if I want to make life-or-death decisions.>

<You won't be making them today,> I promised. <If we establish a useful dialogue with them, I will ask you to meet them.>

<What do they look like?>

I showed him Security footage of the newcomers as they docked. He watched the process long after most people would have gotten bored with it. <Interesting,> he said. <I've never seen a ship towed into one of the locks before.>

Once it was in the lock, I gave him a look through *Merlin*'s view windows at the people moving inside.

<They look like us,> he said. <Except that big fellow is so pale.>

<His name is Wilson.>

<He's as light as Gennady Mironenko was.>

I felt a twinge of pain when I remembered Gennady. True, he had blown me out of an air lock, but I don't think that was personal. I hoped Wilson wouldn't turn out to be quite so scheme-y.

The visitors fascinated Ashur, but his mood changed once he got a good look at them. Perhaps he knew what circumstances might force me to do to them. <Let me know if I can meet them later,> he said as he bowed out.

I felt disturbed after he left. Maybe I had insulated him too much from the hard realities of my responsibilities. Someday, those responsibilities would be his, and how would he cope if I protected him from the harsh choices? I brooded on this as I watched *Merlin*.

<Nemo, what are the decontamination protocols?> I asked when I hadn't seen Captain Thomas at the windows for a while.

<Various agents are squirted up their noses, and their bodies and clothing get sprayed,> he replied. <If we visit the Belters, or if we use our shuttles to visit Graveyard, we'll have to undergo the same sort of process.>

<Do you think it works?>

<Never forget Murphy's Law.>

On *Olympia*, we may have forgotten who Murphy was, but we were unlikely to forget his law. *Anything that can go wrong, will go wrong.*

With that in mind, I continued to watch the view window and study the ship's roster. We listened to the ambient conversations that took place near comm units inside the ship, but they did not seem edifying. Either *Merlin's* crew didn't know anything incriminating, or they were accustomed to holding their tongues about it, even in private.

They spoke of inconsequential things, calling each other *Wilson, Cocteau, Mirzakhani*—they liked to use their last names instead of their first. They had that in common with our Security personnel. They told jokes I didn't get and spoke in sentence fragments that left me scrambling for cultural references.

The g's from our spin took a toll on *Merlin's* crew. I saw Narm and Wilson stagger a few times, though their faces showed no distress. Cocteau seemed to shrug it off without a hint of effort. Perhaps because she was so small? Her center of gravity must be lower.

Two engineers, I thought as I watched that elfin lady. *There's more to you than meets the eye, Cocteau.*

I harbored my suspicions. I have to admit, by then I had already decided what I should do about our visitors once they delivered their message. I thought there was nothing these people could tell me that would change that. As it turned out, they didn't change *my* mind.

They changed Medusa's.

3

The Long Game

Captain Thomas had apparently invested in quite a few security features on *Merlin*. She spent a lot of time activating them after Medusa and I lunged at her in Lock 212. "I think I know where Bomarigala can stick his bonus," she said, her voice shaking.

Bomarigala. They had mentioned that odd name before.

"The Weapons Clan sent us on a suicide mission." Lee's tone was no longer bland. "Those SOBs thought we were expendable."

"Are you saying they knew the *Olympia*ns wouldn't like their message?"

"I'm saying what we delivered isn't the real message. We just got sent in to stir the pot. Now I don't trust our so-called employers to let us go home in one piece." Lee paused. "Because now we've seen what they made. I'm betting they'd rather keep that a secret."

"Great," said Thomas. "So now we have to make our own deal with the *Olympia*ns, or the Graveyard Belters—or both."

Join the club, I thought.

Some time passed while the air in their lock must have been cycling. Their inner door opened.

<*Merlin* has gone on high alert,> reported our COMMO. <Everything okay?>

<Everything is fine,> I lied.

Thomas must have finished typing in Security protocols, because Lee said, "Will that keep her out?"

"I sure as hell hope so," said Captain Thomas.

<*Will* it keep us out?> I asked Medusa.

<There's no reason to find out.>

Previously, she and I had always been on the same page. I had expected we would continue to be. This was a rude awakening. <Why not? What's to rethink? We should send a firm message back.>

<My dear,> said Medusa, sounding more annoyed than tender, <in the

past, when we wanted to accomplish our goals, we had to be calculating, secretive, and—well, somewhat murderous.>

<Yes,> I hoped to remind her, <it was *very efficient.*>

<These people are not Executives. They require a new approach.>

<Only Executives are worthy of murdering?>

<That would be lovely. I doubt it. My point is that we may be shooting
ourselves in the foot if we always respond the way we used to.>

She had a point. Perhaps I was more upset that I hadn't seen it on my own.
Yet I couldn't help feeling thwarted. <You don't even have a foot.> I pouted.

<They are head-blind,> said Medusa. <They can't communicate the way
we do. I tried several times to interface with them, but the tech wasn't there.
I'm guessing they have no brain implants at all.>

Terry Charmayne interrupted. <Is it done?> He sounded unhappy.

<No,> I said. <Change of plans.>

<You're going to kill them later?>

Medusa answered. <We're not going to kill them at all.>

<I can't say I'm sorry to hear that.> To prove it, his tone improved consid-
erably. <I want to know more about the Union.>

<Well, it looks like we will,> I said. <Especially since we've got them
trapped in an air lock.>

<We've had the formal meeting,> said Terry. <Let's try another approach.>

<Agreed.>

When Terry had nothing further to add, I said, <Medusa—why does their
head-blindness matter? Isn't it technically head-*deafness*?>

<Semantics,> said Medusa. <There is still so much we don't know about
them. You heard what they said—now they have to bargain with us. We have
an unparalleled opportunity to ask questions of people who have nothing to
lose by telling us the truth.>

I still felt that sending their messengers' bodies back to the clan would have
been a satisfying response. For me, at least.

In this case, a cooler mind had prevailed. It had been frustrating, but with
each passing moment, I felt more persuaded to explore other possibilities. <Do
you really think they'll open up to us?>

<Maybe,> said Medusa. <Representative Lee was candid when Terry
questioned him. I'd like to see if he will continue the trend.>

<What if he doesn't?> I flexed my hands.

<Then they should remain our guests. We don't know anything about the
Union, or—if we're going to be honest—the Weapons Clan, and they do.>

Her tone had veered from annoyed to impatient. Perversely, I felt on the edge of tears. Was I a child, ready to pitch a fit if I didn't get my way? That sort of display wouldn't convince Medusa to see my side of the argument. I took a deep breath. <I see your point. Before we calculate our next step, let's get some expert advice.>

Captain Thomas and Representative Lee needn't have worried that we could break through their pressure door. Medusa and I were already moving away from Lock 212. What Thomas and Lee had said to each other about the Weapons Clan made me realize I needed to confer with someone who knew more about them.

On *Olympia*, the one who knew the Weapons Clan best was Captain Nemo.

"You and I have a lot in common," Captain Nemo told me the first time I met him, a year before *Merlin* came to visit. "We had to play the long game."

"That's why you work for the Weapons Clan?" I accused.

He was unmoved. "They followed us for one hundred years. Do you believe they never did anything but watch us?"

I'm sorry to say that I did.

He nodded. "They were willing to sacrifice our lives, but they also saved our lives on several occasions. Oichi—*Olympia* has never operated independently of the Weapons Clan. Do you recall learning about the wheat plague that wiped out eighty percent of the crop about fifty years back?"

Every kid on *Olympia* learned about the Great Wheat Plague. "They had to destroy most of the remaining plants," I said. "Then our scientists engineered—"

"No," said Nemo. "They had to destroy *all* the remaining crop. Yet here we are." He signaled to one of his staff, and she enlarged a picture on her screen, of endless rows of wheat, thriving in the Habitat Sector.

"Oh . . ." I said this a lot in that first meeting. Then I rallied. "They were protecting their investment. That doesn't mean we have to be their assets."

"I agree," said Nemo, "but do you see my point? We aren't one hundred percent self-sufficient on *Olympia*. The next wheat plague could wipe us out. We need allies. Who are they going to be?"

Not the Weapons Clan, if I could help it, but I'm not in charge of *Olympia*. Even I had to admit, there are times when you need to leave politics to the politicians and negotiations to the ambassadors.

So a year later, when *Merlin* showed up with her obnoxious message from the Weapons Clan, and I overheard Captain Thomas saying, *Now we have to make our own deal,* I considered a new possibility.

The crew of *Merlin* might make a deal with *us.* Others might do the same—who knew what the Belters had to offer?

I was about to find out.

Captain Nemo called me before I could call him. <Someone has sent you a private message.>

<I'm on my way to see you,> I said, though his Security overlay would already have shown him that. <Is there an identifier attached to the message?>

<She's calling herself Fire. Here's the header that goes with the message.> He sent it, and I viewed it in the virtual display all *Olympia*ns have inside our heads, thanks to our brain implants. Beneath the header, an icon represented a communications link.

I recognized the icon. I had seen it on warning beacons, the same ones that had been blaring, "YOU MUST RECEIVE PERMISSION FROM THE WORLD AUTHORITY ON GRAVEYARD TO VISIT THIS SYSTEM. TRESPASSERS WILL BE DESTROYED. YOU WILL RECEIVE NO FURTHER WARNING," since we had entered the Charon system.

Had our permission just been rescinded?

Medusa and I doubled our speed.

If you're wondering what it's like to have a brain implant like mine, just visualize something in your imagination, a thing or place. Add sounds to that. Add odors, taste, possibly even a sensation of touch. (Those last three are optional.)

Are you doing that? Now clarify it until the scene you're picturing has as much definition and detail as the real space in which you exist. Overlay it with tactical grids and numbers, to let you know temperatures, velocities, distances, heart rates—any information you think you might need.

Yeah, that's not fair. I couldn't do that without my implant, either—but with it? You'd be amazed at the possibilities. Inside my head, Fire's header looked like this:

Origin: Queen's Fire, Special Agent, the Alliance of Ancient Races;
Recipient: Oichi Angelis, Generation Ship *OLYMPIA*

<Have you read the message?> I asked Nemo. It wasn't an accusation; I knew his Security clearance gave him access to any communication that came through that link. I had never disputed that right.

<Just the first line,> he said. <That's how I know her name.>

<Queen's Fire in the header,> I mused. <Fire in the message.>

Medusa said, <That sounds like poetry.>

Oichi, said the message, *my name is Fire. I think it's time we began a dialogue. I would like to establish a communications link with you. Will you add me to your directory? You can grant permission by using your private comm system to call the main directory on Graveyard, and then selecting my icon.*

"I'm concerned about the icon she's using," I said to Captain Nemo.

"It represents the Alliance of Ancient Races," he said a bit stiffly, and I wondered if it bothered him that I was wearing Medusa. I had never brought her to Ship Operations before. Did Nemo consider that a breach of protocol? "You may recall it from the first warning beacons we passed as we entered Charon's solar system."

"I remember." I examined Fire's message from top to bottom. "I don't see a time stamp on this. How come its arrival wasn't recorded?"

"We don't know how she managed it," said Nemo. "We suspect she found a way to send us a message that wouldn't be detected by the Weapons Clan. Maybe that's why it doesn't have a time stamp."

We assumed the clan were monitoring our communications to and from Graveyard. We didn't know what we could do about it. Maybe Fire knew. If so, she might prove to be a useful ally.

I copied the message.

"You should be careful," said Nemo.

"I will," I promised, though I was planning to be the opposite. "Have you learned anything more about *Itzpapalotl*?"

"No," said Nemo, "but we've studied *Merlin,* and we believe she is built for more than just space travel."

I didn't quite get his drift. "You mean—she has time-travel capabilities?"

He didn't laugh. "I mean she can fly in atmosphere. Her tail has a swept-back delta wing design. If we had any doubts about that, the landing gear in her belly would dispel them."

That I did get. "She could take our delegation to Graveyard—and land there."

"Yes," said Nemo.

"That's good to know. By the way, have you ever heard of someone named Bomarigala?"

"No," said Nemo.

"He seems to be a luminary in the Weapons Clan."

Nemo didn't blink. "If the Weapons Clan is anything like the Executives, they've got quite a few luminaries."

"Are they?" I asked. "Anything like the Executives?"

He paused, and I wondered if he resented the implication that he knew more than he was telling. I had hoped to get a lot more information out of him this time around. Instead, he seemed to be erecting barriers. "My interactions with them were at a distance. They were always concise and efficient. They created our society, Oichi. They must have based it on something."

"One would think," I mused. "Well. Our guests on *Merlin* have had a scare, but we'll try to negotiate with them. I'm going to send our best ambassadors to patch things up. I'll keep you posted."

He nodded.

As we pivoted to leave, I stole glances at Nemo's officers, all working diligently at their stations. They seemed unconcerned to see Medusa in the Command Center.

I wondered if I were reading Nemo wrong. His heart rate and pupils had indicated no deception. Why did I get the feeling he didn't want Medusa there?

When the pressure door had been sealed behind us, Medusa said, <I don't think he likes me.>

<We should look up the protocols for the Ship Operations center,> I said. <Maybe we violated them.>

<We *can't* look them up.> Medusa tapped the controls next to the door of a mover, and it slid open. <They don't officially exist.>

I tried to look at it from Nemo's point of view. If I were a captain, what would my first priority be? <Weapons aren't allowed in Operations. Technically, he may see you as a hazard.>

<*Technically*, he has a point, but Medusa units are well established on *Olympia* now. We are linked with high-ranking clan members. It should be moot.>

<I'll ask Security Chief Schnebly if he knows why—and if—Nemo doesn't want you in Operations.>

I should have done that immediately. Instead, I got busy, and I forgot—

which was a shame, because Nemo's attitude about Medusa units may have been more important than we realized.

Medusa and I parted ways. <Fire's message is encouraging,> she said when she had dropped me off at my quarters. <If we're going to be living here, we should get acquainted with our neighbors.>

<I'll send a courteous reply,> I promised.

<Keep me posted.>

She left me without a glance back. That was abrupt for Medusa. If I hadn't been so preoccupied, I might have wondered about it. My thoughts were already shifting as I closed the door to my quarters.

<I hear the *Merline*rs are still alive,> Ashur said without preamble, further complicating my preoccupation.

*Merline*rs. I liked that. <They shall not be harmed,> I promised.

<Then let's invite them to a tea party. In your quarters. With cakes and so on, and pretty music playing. I'd like to be there, too—with some Minis.>

<An interesting idea.> A tea party might break the ice a little better. I had thought to have Terry Charmayne present, but maybe Ashur was just the person who could set the *Merline*rs at ease. In his own way, he was as charming as the Minis he had made. <I see no reason why you shouldn't be there. Which Minis?>

<Kitten, of course. I don't think Dragonette would forgive me if I didn't send her, too. Let me ponder it.>

<I'll leave the final selection to you.>

<Let's all get a good night's sleep, then.> Ashur sounded happier than he had in a while, though *happy* might be the wrong description. Perhaps—*positive? Motivated? Upbeat?*

<Father,> he called Nuruddin without breaking the link with me. <Good night. I'm going to sleep.>

<Good night, Son,> Nuruddin answered. <Please don't stay awake thinking half the night.>

<I'll try.>

That was the best Ashur could promise. For the past year, he had been trying to adjust to new family circumstances. He spent most of his waking hours working on his immersive music programs, investing so much energy, he may as well be an adult with a full-time job. Nuruddin respected that, because his own projects consumed so much of his time, and for the same reason.

If I tell you that I'm the reason Ashur and Nuruddin have had their lives upended, it may sound grandiose, but it's also true. I've never regretted the decisions that led to their pairing with Medusa units. Possibly I'm not capable of that sort of remorse, even though my actions led to a chain of events that provoked Nuruddin's husband into divorcing him. Many families were disrupted by our revolution—some clans were decimated. Compared with those consequences, Nuruddin and Ashur got off relatively unscathed.

That's what I like to tell myself. Now I wonder if I pulled them into my inner circle out of pure selfishness.

Then, I congratulated myself for listening to Ashur's good idea and put the matter aside in favor of different (if related) matters.

I followed Fire's directions to select her icon and sent her a short message:

Hello, Fire. I'm pleased to make your acquaintance. Why do you wish to speak with me?

She answered within half an hour:

We can tell that Olympia *was built using ancient tech from the spaceship graveyard. Even more important, Oichi—we can tell that you were, too.*

That was an interesting way to put it. We were *built*. An accurate description, but painfully so.

I took a breath. My reaction seemed a bit prickly. I was a mover and a shaker on *Olympia* now, but I had begun my life as a lowly worm. I liked to think I was over that. Maybe I had overestimated my own resilience.

I would have felt more inclined to say that we were *engineered*, since DNA was involved—but I didn't grow up in the shadow of the Three, the entities who tower over the graveyard that defines the world toward which *Olympia* is bound. I had yet to lay eyes on that landscape, so I could only guess how crowded it might be with ancient machinery. Quite a few things had probably been *built* from those odds and ends. Possibly even intelligent things.

After all, the Three were intelligent things, and someone had *built* them. They had been in communication with me for years, before they finally shut down the conversation and resumed a sleep that must have lasted millennia.

Yet even now, I could sense those ghosts. On some level, they were still aware of us. The *sleep* they had imposed on themselves was not the illogical, insensate thing that it was for humans. I had no idea what to expect from them, whether they would decide to wake once we assumed orbit around Graveyard or to stay asleep.

What could they expect from *us?* Maybe that was the bigger question. A year had passed since their last communication. Now there were other people from Graveyard who wanted to talk. I'm no expert on trade, but Fire's communication seemed like the sort of overture you make when you want to do business with someone. My prickly reaction would be useless if I wanted to cultivate our new neighbors—so I put it aside.

How can you tell we have that sort of connection to Graveyard? I asked.

Because you're here, she said, *and nobody has tried to blow you up, and things are stirring that have not taken notice of anyone in a very long time.*

These things, I sent back. *Are they three things? Three very big, old things?*

Indeed, said Fire. *At your current speed, you will pass through the Belt long before you reach Graveyard. You will contact the Belters. They will want to barter. What do you have to trade?*

Perhaps we could trade the food and textiles we grow in our Habitat Sector. We had many resources that might prove valuable.

How much of that should I reveal to Fire? I decided to keep it simple. *We grow food crops and have a textile industry.*

She took longer to respond to that one, and I wondered if I had made a tactical mistake. Did our industries sound paltry? Had I just torpedoed our first contact? I should have conferred with Terry Charmayne and Ogden Schickele before I answered that query.

Yet when Fire responded, the tone of her message was enthusiastic. *The Belters would like to meet you. Please visit Maui on your way past. Let us know when you think that will be.*

I breathed a sigh of relief. If my reply had been ill informed, at least it hadn't done too much damage. I sent an acknowledgment and promised to get back with the details.

At that point, I should have notified Medusa, and then Terry and Nemo, possibly even Ogden. Instead, I sat there and reviewed Fire's messages multiple times. I'd like to tell you I was thinking about the best way to pursue trade with the Belters.

I'm not sure I was thinking about anything at all. Across from me stood one of the few objects I can claim to love, a painted silk screen depicting a tiger at the edge of a lake. It had been gifted to me by a member of an almost-dead clan. Full disclosure: I killed the man who gave me the screen. While he deserved it, that doesn't make the gift any less sentimental.

My tiger eternally worries that the waves breaking against the shore of his lake might get his toes wet. I relate to his anxiety.

Finally I stirred to look for information. <Captain Nemo, how long before we reach the asteroid belt?>

Though I called him by name, he wasn't always the one who answered. This time, it was his second-in-command. <Six decacycles,> she said.

That was more than twice the amount of time it had taken *Merlin* to reach us, though we would be traveling a fraction of the distance.

We were approaching Graveyard at an oblique angle to its orbital plane. We had made no plans to visit the Belters. We could use a shuttle to make the side trip, but our window of opportunity for getting there and getting back to *Olympia*, before she was too far away to catch, was narrow. Like the tiger on my screen, I worried about the unknown.

I worried for quite a while.

When I got tired of that, I used a Security camera to look at our visitor in Lock 212. Figures moved behind her view windows. They peered into the lock, undoubtedly searching for shadowy tentacles.

How long had it been since a ship had used that lock? When *Olympia* was built, supply ships had probably docked there. When Sheba and Baylor Charmayne plotted to destroy *Titania*, Baylor had used the shuttles to raid our sister ship of supplies. They must have used the big locks to unload their loot, possibly even this, my favorite lock.

Percy O'Reilly and Ryan Charmayne were killed inside Lock 212 for very good reason, not for petty revenge—but now I found myself questioning my motives for directing *Merlin* to dock there. Had my resentment of the Weapons Clan clouded my judgment? I think maybe it had.

Merlin traveled the distance it had taken *Olympia* a year to traverse, in a fraction of the time. She had structures, arranged in three pairs around the craft. Those structures belonged to her star drive.

She also had a main thruster at her tail, with her center of mass aligned above it, closer to her nose. Captain Nemo said she could operate in atmosphere; *Merlin* could land on Graveyard.

How well would *Merlin* navigate in the asteroid belt? She had small thrusters, too. She had used them to dock with *Olympia*, so one must assume they would help her avoid bumping into asteroids. She might be quite versatile.

I watched our visitors in Lock 212, through the Security cameras. Again, I saw movement behind *Merlin*'s windows, and I considered the questions Captain Nemo had asked about who would be our allies. They had sounded rhetorical, but really—they were practical.

My painted tiger always looked worried, but he still dared the edge of that lake.

Bearing that in mind, I composed another message. *Fire—what if we could meet you sooner? Say, in a few cycles?*

4

Crow

I stayed up late, exchanging messages with Fire and congratulating myself for finessing what I felt sure would be the next stage in our introduction to the Charon system, the establishment of trade and cultural exchanges with the Belters. The possibility that I might be doing so by hijacking the emissaries of the Weapons Clan gave me particular satisfaction. True, I had almost killed the *Merlin*ers, and that would present a challenge when I tried to talk them into working for us, but I felt optimistic we could come to some agreement.

It's a little sad to look back on that moment of irrational exuberance.

Ashur also remained wakeful, far longer than was good for him. When he finally closed his eyes, he thought it would take him forever to drift off, but the whirlwind in his mind settled quickly. Looking back, he realized he should have been suspicious about that.

How do I know he felt all those things?

Because I ended up in the same dream.

That business about mental whirlwinds isn't just poetry. Knowing that Ashur felt responsible for making peace with the emissaries from the Weapons Clan provoked a similar sort of storm in my own head. Back when I had thought I was the only one engaged in sedition, I had enjoyed a moral clarity that eluded me now that I could see the results of my actions on my comrades, some of whom were very young.

When Ashur said good night to his father, I didn't break my link with him. I meant to, but I wanted to let him do that first. I thought he might have something more to say to me. Once I got to talking with Fire, I forgot about it.

Hours later, I closed my eyes, probably at the same time he did. We both felt as if we had gone to sleep—until we opened our eyes again.

Ashur and I stood together. He blinked, and any notion I had that he could explain what we were doing there together was quickly dispelled by the expression on his face. Looking around didn't clear up the mystery. Our surroundings were strange—though not *completely* unfamiliar. We have no cities on *Olympia*, but we've seen plenty of them in movies.

"Am I dreaming?" said Ashur.

"I doubt it," I said. "This is what it was like when the Three talked to me. They looked real."

Indeed they did, but they hadn't shown me anything as odd as this. The stark and jumbled city in which we stood was nothing like *Olympia*, inside or out.

"This isn't one of your immersive programs?" I said, though I knew that was a shot in the dark.

"Not one of mine. Maybe it's somebody else's? It's like the city in *The Nightmare Before Christmas*."

"Yes! And who could forget the wonderful score by Danny Elfman?"

"Which isn't currently playing in our heads—otherwise, this would be a lot less scary."

What our situation lacked in music, it made up for in other effects. The air felt warm and dry, a new sensation for we who were accustomed to the chilly tunnels of a generation ship. I smelled plants, as if we were in the Habitat Sector. Stars crowded the sky.

I barely noticed them, because I couldn't look away from the scarecrows.

Probably they were why Ashur had thought of *The Nightmare Before Christmas*. Though there were also a couple of brief-but-memorable scenes in *Jeepers Creepers* and *Jeepers Creepers 2* where the monster pretended to be a scarecrow. Last but not least, Scarecrow was one of the main characters in *The Wizard of Oz* (one of Kitten's favorite musicals).

All those straw men would have been lost in this crowd. This City of Scarecrows stood or hung or sat or reclined on every side in various stages of construction or decay. Their heads were made of pumpkins, and those that had eyes glowed with an inner light. I considered the lyrics from Danny Elfman's song "This Is Halloween": *Pumpkins scream in the dead of night. . . .*

If *these* pumpkins started screaming in the dead of night, I might feel inclined to scream right along with them.

"Are they going to talk to us?" Ashur said. "Like the Three talked to you?"

Good question. Somehow, that seemed like a bad idea, as if speaking to one of these entities would be making a choice we couldn't take back.

"We shouldn't stay here," I said. "They're getting too interested in us."

Ashur offered his arm, and I took it, glad for the contact, even if it was just virtual. The scarecrows watched us go. They seemed interested in our progress.

We watched them, too, worried that they might try to approach us as we passed. If some carved faces looked malign, their neighbors were comical—or friendly or serious or bemused. Many were just weird, and the shape of the pumpkins contributed to their character. They grew in patches linked together with vines that snaked up and over fences.

We turned down a crooked lane between contorted houses. The streets that branched from our path sometimes twisted at painful angles, and I sensed that if we followed them, we would see something very different.

Whether we would survive that exploration was another question. With so many bright eyes watching us, I felt inclined to be careful with my feet. *You can talk to us, if you like*, the scarecrows seemed to be thinking. *Will you see us? Will you wake us? What will we do if we become aware of you, Oichi? What will we make of each other?*

"Pretty intimidating, isn't it?" someone said.

We were confronted by a scarecrow who leaned against a fence post, his thin arm propped on his hip and one leg crossed over the other. He wore a spotted shirt, a red vest, and faded blue trousers over a body made of long sticks of wood. On his neck sat a round yellow pumpkin with a face carved on it. The face reminded me of Jack Skellington, the Pumpkin King of Halloween Town. The light that shone behind his eyes glowed steadily. "How do you do?" he said. "I'm Crow."

Ashur squared his shoulders. "I'm Ashur. This is my friend Oichi."

"Can you guess what it is you're seeing?" Crow's carved mouth moved stiffly, though his words were clear. "It's okay to guess wrong. I won't think less of you."

Ashur kept his eyes on Crow. "I may have seen it in a movie. My subconscious is turning it into a dream."

Crow turned his head in negation. "This is not a dream, Ashur. We are speaking to you."

"We?" said Ashur. "Are you one of the Three? Is this the graveyard?"

"No," said Crow, "and yes. I am *not* one of the Three, though I will be your emissary to them should you chose to approach them. This is the graveyard you see around you—or its analogue, to be more accurate. As you can sense, there are entities here—not just the Three—and you may choose to speak to these others. You may bargain with *any* of them—and *they* may try to bargain with *you*."

"Some of them seem so—" Ashur let his gaze travel to other scarecrows. "—odd. Dangerous, even."

"Oh yes," said Crow. "No doubt about that. Some are dangerous because they're so different, some because they're evil. Some are dangerous because they have so much to offer, and who knows what will come of that? After all, the Empire of Clans created powerful arsenals from this ancient technology. Their children almost destroyed the far-flung colonies of humans, right along with those of other species, though they aren't the only ones to have engaged in mass destruction."

This was the first that we had heard of human colonies, far-flung or otherwise. I wasn't sure if I should be thrilled or sad.

"So," Ashur said, "the graveyard is full of weapons?"

"Yes, but not just weapons. In fact, weapons are a small part of what you can find here."

"If that's true, then why is the Weapons Clan so interested in the graveyard?"

Crow's smile stretched wider. "That's the question you should ask. Keep it in mind when you come here. *You* should do so, as well, Oichi." Crow turned to me. "I can't answer it for you, but you'll find some sort of answer. That's definite."

"How do you know we'll go there?" said Ashur. "I mean, *here*?"

Crow didn't budge from his casual pose, but his eyes glowed brighter. "We know whom we want to talk to. You'll get an invitation soon."

I couldn't let that go unchallenged. "Ashur is twelve years old." I tried to ignore the outraged expression on Ashur's face. "If they invite him, can we refuse?"

Crow's lantern face assumed lines of dismay. "You shouldn't do that."

"Will they be angry?" I said. "Will they try to hurt us if I leave Ashur out of it?"

"Oh no." Crow waved his hands. "Quite the opposite. If Ashur isn't in your delegation, things will turn out differently. You'll make connections, and *they* will improvise. Only—take a look around you, Oichi. Do you want any of these entities to improvise your fate?"

To Ashur's credit, he didn't smirk at that. He was going to get his wish, though I would not relish explaining that to his father. Because I *didn't* want those entities to improvise our fates. Not even a little bit.

"I'll let you get some real sleep now," said Crow. "I just wanted to say one more thing before we meet again. It's not just about whom you chose, *Olympians*. It's about who chooses *you*."

I woke in the dark. Ashur's presence had evaporated in my hands, like smoke.

I called him. <Are you all right?>

<We shared a dream!> he said. <It was amazing!>

It wasn't a dream, but I didn't want to burst his bubble. Besides, who was I to say what we had experienced? It was a lot like what I had felt when talking to the Three, but it wasn't *exactly* like that.

<What if I really go to the graveyard?> said Ashur. <What if I talk to the Three?>

What the hell am I going to tell your father? I wondered.

<If they invite me—I'm going,> said Ashur.

Nuruddin would have the final say on that, but the whole thing felt like fate to me. I don't get that feeling often.

<Sleep,> I urged. <You need to be fresh for the party.>

<Okay.> Before Ashur severed our link, I heard the music of Claude Debussy's *Sunken Cathedral*, as arranged for electronic synthesizer by Isao Tomita. My mind filled with images of the undersea kingdom Ashur was building inside his new immersive program. I suspected he would focus on that until he fell asleep—*if* he fell asleep.

I couldn't blame him for trying to get his mind off Crow's message, because I couldn't either. It took me a long time to get to sleep.

Then I woke with plenty of other things to worry about. <Kitten,> I called, <and Dragonette. I have a mission for you.>

PART TWO

POLITICIANS AND
AMBASSADORS

5

The Kitten Cam

Warning lights flashed and a siren squawked. The outer door of the air lock had been ordered to open, and explosive decompression was imminent. Medusa and I stood blinking in confusion, trying to adapt to our new situation with very little time to do so.

If we got blown into space, this wouldn't be the first time. I venture to say it wouldn't be the last. All those moments of danger and indecision might make an excellent synopsis of our partnership, if you strung them together. Each of them shared similarities. Each of them had its differences.

The variation was that now we had entered inhabited space—we were meeting all sorts of people under less-than-ideal circumstances. This dangerous moment was the direct result of a new challenge I had to ponder: If you can't kill the inconvenient people who complicate your life, what do you do with them instead?

In my case, you spy on them. If you want to be extra sneaky, you do that with Minis.

Captain Epatha Thomas placed a call to *Itzpapalotl* a few hours after she and Representative Lee returned to *Merlin*. We could hear them talking through the link they still had with us, the one that remained open despite their heightened state of alarm.

I give Captain Thomas credit: she sounded calm when she spoke to Bomarigala. "Our mission is complete. Your message has been delivered."

"I trust you spoke it word for word." Bomarigala's voice was intriguing—I recorded it for later analysis.

"I did," said Lee, and he also managed to sound like an unflustered professional.

"Then you'll be returning to *Itzpapalotl*?" said Bomarigala.

"We haven't been given clearance to leave yet," said Thomas. "We'll let you know when we have."

"Your funds have been transferred into your accounts," said Bomarigala. "Our business is concluded."

"Thank you," Thomas and Lee said together.

I'm guessing Bomarigala terminated the link, because a few seconds later, Lee said, "He thinks we're not going to make it out of here."

"He may be right," said Captain Thomas. "I'm going to give it my best shot anyway."

"The *Olympia*ns are pretty mad, but they showed restraint. We're still alive."

"What's your advice? Should we make an overture?"

"Not yet," said Lee. "We should give them time to make one of their own. We dumped something on their heads that upset them. An overture from us at this juncture might seem authoritarian. They need to see respect from us."

True. I was starting to like this fellow. I was glad he didn't know that we needed him as much as he needed us right now, which is why they were about to receive a visitor from us.

"I need to update the crew," said Thomas. "They'll be happy about the money, at least."

I could see *Merlin*'s crew in the front windows, still gazing into Lock 212 as if something interesting were happening out there. They would soon be right about that.

Perhaps two engineers, a doctor-surgeon, and a communications wizard did not have much to do when their ship was sitting in an air lock. Perhaps they were also wondering if the people who had almost killed their captain, but then changed their minds, were ever going to give them permission to leave.

Thomas didn't keep them wondering very long. "Okay, the good news is, Bomarigala transferred our credits. All of you have been paid your full share plus the bonus. However, I don't think the Weapons Clan ever had any intention of letting us leave, now that we've seen *Olympia*. Once we exit the system, I believe they'll try to kill us, and no one is better at killing people than the Weapons Clan."

Narm sounded surprised. "Why would they kill us?"

"Originally," said Lee, "I think they expected the *Olympia*ns to kill us.

The message they gave us was not the real message. We have delivered something we didn't know we were bringing."

"Not a disease," Mirzakhani said. "The bacteria and viruses we're carrying are nothing out of the ordinary. Our decontamination supplies are fine. I always check that stuff—I'm paranoid."

Before she mentioned it, the thought of sabotage by disease never occurred to me—which is fortunate, because it was very alarming.

Lee's next remark made me feel slightly better. "The Weapons Clan doesn't want to kill these people. They believe they *own* these people."

Thomas argued, "The Weapons Clan already has cases against them in Union Courts for the trafficking of sentients. Maybe they don't want more of those."

"They're not afraid of litigation," said Lee.

There was an interesting piece of information. If I learned nothing else from our open link, that made it worthwhile.

"I think it has more to do with their proprietary interests," Lee continued. "The Weapons Clan aimed *Olympia* and *Titania* at Graveyard, and they didn't try to claim their assets before this generation ship reached the Charon system. If all they wanted were these people, they would already have them."

I had reached the same conclusion, though I was still pretty much in the dark about the ultimate goals of the Weapons Clan.

Mirzakhani said, "If the *Olympia*ns are assets—are they engineered people?"

That was a damn good guess. Unless the engineering of sentient people was not so rare as I liked to think.

"If so," Mirzakhani continued, "that raises the question of their origin. Since they're headed to Graveyard, we should wonder whether it's the source of their nonhuman DNA."

Mirzakhani might be far too smart for her own good. She had no time to elaborate on her point, because Wilson said, "Hey—what's *that*?"

Everyone crowded the windows to see what he was pointing at.

My ambassador had already moved out of sight.

"It looked like a small animal," said Wilson. "I could swear it was carrying something in its mouth."

"Where did it go?" said Thomas.

"It made a beeline for *Merlin*, like it was going to—"

An alarm sounded outside *Merlin*'s main air lock.

"We've got company," said Thomas.

"Let's open the door," said Lee. "I think this is an overture, not an attack."

Relative silence ensued while everyone left the front of the ship and trooped to the air lock. I smiled. So far, so good.

"Cap," warned Narm, "you shouldn't be the one to open the door. I should do it."

Thomas was having none of that. "You four are my skeleton crew. Much as I hate to say it, Lee and I are the expendables on this mission."

No one argued with her.

Thomas opened the outer air lock door and peered out. My ambassador stood right on the threshold, but Thomas didn't see her until she looked down.

"Herro," said Kitten, who was holding a tablet in her mouth. She set it down. "I'm Kitten. I'm a Mini. I brought you something to use so you can talk to us more directly."

"You're a *Mini*?" said Thomas.

Kitten performed a little prance. "I am! I'll be your liaison with the *Olympia*ns. I will also be your guide."

Kitten didn't mention that I could see through her eyes and hear through her ears. She was my Kitten-cam. When the rest of *Merlin*'s crew crowded into the air lock to get a look at her, I had a much better perspective than I had enjoyed from the Security cams in Lock 212.

Thomas knelt and reached a cautious hand toward Kitten. The Mini lifted a paw and met her halfway. "Is this a greeting ritual of your people?"

Thomas smiled. "Yes, but I was curious. I wanted to know if you're made of the same substance as Medusa."

"I am," said Kitten. "Ashur's team made me. We were the first Minis. Now there are many more. I can't say exactly how many—that's proprietary."

Lee knelt beside Thomas. "Kitten, may I—touch paws with you, too?"

Kitten raised her paw again, and Lee placed two fingers on her footpads.

Lee blinked. "Kitten, does your brain have organic—um—qualities? Or is that also proprietary information?"

"It is," said Kitten. "But it's a darn good guess. We are units for helping people. We are less scary than the Medusas. They're our big sisters."

"Did you say you're going to be our guide?" said Thomas. "Are we going somewhere?"

"At least one place," said Kitten. "Maybe more. We have to see how it works out. First, let me show you how to use this."

Kitten touched the tablet, and a keyboard appeared. "You can write with this stylus if you prefer, or you can use the raw paw." Kitten began to type with her digits.

"Oh my god," said Wilson. "The cute."

Kitten held up the tablet so they could see what she had typed:

THERE'S NO BUSINESS

LIKE SHOW BUSINESS

LIKE NO BUSINESS I KNOW . . .

"I love show tunes." Kitten called up the address directory and selected OICHI. "Boop!" She pressed SEND.

"Lovely," said Thomas. "We just sent a little song to the lady who almost—" She cast a sideways glance at Lee. "—to Oichi."

The tablet beeped, and my return message appeared: *Received, my Kitten. You may introduce the others.*

"*The others?*" said Thomas.

The *Merlin*ers looked to the open door, just as my ambassadors made their move.

6

Chocolate, Anyone?

Dragonette flew into *Merlin*'s air lock, using her propellers and miniature jets. I didn't have a link with her eyes, but through Kitten, I watched Dragonette flit over to Narm. The propellers retracted when she landed on his shoulder. "How do you do?" she said. "May I perch?"

Narm lifted a hand to his shoulder. "Will you perch on my hand? I want to look at you."

"Of course." Dragonette used her tail as a spring to hop onto Narm's hand, from whence she studied him as closely as he studied her. I wondered—could he tell that her design had been inspired by a sea horse?

Rocket glided in second; he had flaps that stretched between his limbs. He landed at Wilson's feet and said, "Reporting for duty, sir."

Wilson knelt and extended his hand to Rocket, whose paws were only large enough to shake Wilson's index finger. "Glad to meet you. What are your duties?"

"I will guide you into the Habitat Sector if you'd like to see it. We also have leave to visit the Entertainment Sector. They have restaurants there."

Teddy chose that moment to roll up the ramp and into the lock—literally, since he appeared to be a ball when he was in motion. When he stopped, his limbs unfolded and he stood. "I'm Teddy. I'm usually for tunnels, but I can improvise."

Kitten sat on her hindquarters and pointed to each Mini in turn. "Dragonette, Rocket, Teddy, and Kitten. We are the first four that Ashur's team made. Ashur would like to meet you, Captain Thomas and Representative Lee. You are invited to tea in Oichi's quarters. Your other crew members are invited to tour *Olympia*. We hope you will accept."

Thomas regarded Lee. I thought I could guess what she was thinking.

Charm us with your cute biorobots, separate us, and then kill us all. Then take my ship, because Merlin *would come in handy. It would take you a while to get past her security protocols—but you could do it eventually.*

At least, that's what *I* would have been thinking, and I can't say the idea hadn't crossed my mind.

Lee seemed to have a more positive outlook. "These Minis are well loved. This is a demonstration of trust."

Kitten could have added something adorable at that point, perhaps sung another show tune, but she kept silent. I was proud of her.

Could Thomas afford to refuse? Did she want a cold war with us? *Merlin* couldn't leave until Lock 212 was opened, and from what they had said, returning to *Itzpapalotl* was out of the question. The Weapons Clan would be gunning for them. The only way out was forward.

"We accept your invitation to tea," said Captain Thomas. "I'll leave it to my crew to decide what they'd like to do."

Mirzakhani touched Dragonette's nose. "How do you do? I would like to take a tour."

"Me, too," Narm and Wilson chimed in.

"Where would you like to go first?" said Dragonette. "The Habitat Sector or the Entertainment Sector?"

"Well," Cocteau spoke up, "I'm older than the rest of you, so I'm more inclined to think about practical matters. I would like to eat first. You mentioned restaurants?"

Everyone rode together in the same mover for the first part of the journey, and Kitten ordered up show tunes to play overhead, selections from *South Pacific*. The only one who seemed nonplussed by her choice was Narm.

"How *old* is this music?" he said more than once.

"As old as you feel!" declared Kitten. "I feel very young."

"Why would anyone use real voices or handmade instruments? It's so retro!"

"Retro is the new black," Kitten replied, puzzling Narm even more, until Cocteau nudged him.

"It's a fashion reference," she said. "Look at your own clothing, my dear."

Since Narm was wearing black, maybe that made sense to him. My Kitten-cam perspective gave me an odd angle from which to judge his expression, but Narm stopped frowning for a while. His scowl didn't return until Wilson and Cocteau began to sing along with "Some Enchanted Evening."

Just when it looked like Narm could stand no more, the mover opened into the Entertainment Sector. Now our guests could glimpse other *Olympians*, and there were plenty of people to see, since the Entertainment Sector had been opened up to every citizen aboard our generation ship, instead of just the elite Executives.

Kitten turned her cam toward the open door. People strolled past, along a promenade that was far different from the cramped tunnels through which I had guided our guests on their way to the Habitat Sector. The clothing my fellow citizens wore was colorful, quite the opposite of the austere style adopted by the Security Council.

Minis ambulated along with the crowd. Some walked—but some slithered, some hopped, and at least one of those Minis wheeled like a starfish turned on its ends. There were so many of them, the *Merliners* must have thought we had an endless supply of biometal. (Actually, we used it all to make the Minis.)

Teddy, Rocket, and Dragonette herded everyone but Thomas and Lee out of the mover and onto the promenade.

"Be care—" Captain Thomas began. The doors shut before she could finish.

"They will be safe with my friends," Kitten assured her.

"I think they will," said Lee. "I think we've turned a corner."

I wondered if he said that because of the lively pair of Mini ears and eyes that were trained on him. He must have suspected Kitten had been feeding sound and pictures back to me since the moment they had let her into *Merlin's* air lock. I appreciated his efforts. He, at least, seemed willing to entertain the idea that they might be able to bargain with us.

Kitten had moved on to *The King and I* before the mover opened again to a different scene. Uniformed Security personnel dominated the hallway leading to my quarters, rather than casual strollers. Security came to attention as soon as the doors opened; they kept their eyes focused on Thomas and Lee, sparing Kitten very little attention as the little group left the mover and approached their station.

"I'm Captain Epatha Thomas of the Union Ship *Merlin*," the captain said as they halted in front of the Security station. "We've been invited to tea."

"Welcome, Captain Thomas," said a woman whose uniform may have looked the same as everyone else's to the *Merliners*, though any *Olympian* could see the subtle differences that indicated rank and seniority. "We've been expecting you. Please accompany me."

The staff remained alert, but I doubt our visitors could fault their courtesy. Lee appeared relaxed, and Kitten was at home as she trotted down a carpeted hallway, into the complex that had once been the Charmayne visitors' quarters, reserved for the friends of the highest-ranking family on *Olympia*.

They turned two corners before they halted in front of a large door. The Security chief touched the controls on the wall. After a pause, the door opened, revealing my sitting room.

My sensory connection with Kitten ended at that moment. I observed Thomas and Lee with my own eyes as they regarded Ashur and me.

If the situation had been casual, our visitors might have spent more time looking at my tiger screen, or at the other treasures that had been gifted to me by the Koto, Charmayne, and Chang Clans. I had tried to live up to my surroundings, wearing a wig with upswept, bronze-colored hair. My eyes were currently tinted the same color. Ashur wore his natural hair cropped close to his skull, and he favored amber-with-green for his eyes. I'm sure we looked an elegant couple in a fine setting, but our guests barely glanced at us before they noticed what else was in the room.

Tentacles. Not just from one Medusa unit, but from two.

Sometimes my anger takes a lethal form. However, Ashur had set an example for me of how one should cope with adversity. He had been forced to adjust to new family circumstances when his fathers divorced—and I had to adjust to the new Ashur.

Yet when he had arrived at my quarters for the tea party, I felt a moment of surprise. Every day Ashur got taller, more handsome—and more preoccupied. The carefree boy who had boldly kissed me inside his Mermaid program did not act impulsively anymore. These days he thought hard about things. He probably thought too much.

He arrived wearing Octopippin. They separated as soon as they came through the door, and Octopippin joined Medusa.

"Will we frighten them?" said Octopippin. "I don't want to start off on the wrong—um—tentacle."

"I think you will frighten them at first," I said, "but if we're going to become partners with these people, they must know our nature."

"I'm not sure *I* know our nature." Ashur examined the tea cakes, frowning as if the answer could be found among the lemon, vanilla, and chocolate swirls.

<I can record the meeting, if you like,> said Medusa.

I considered that. <Don't record it. Octopippin is right—we have moved past hostilities. Now we must learn to negotiate with them.>

If Medusa had anything further to say about that, she didn't have time to say it. The signal for the door sounded, and I allowed entry. The door opened, and Kitten trotted in. Behind her, our guests stood with a shift captain.

I leveled my gaze at Lee. Medusa would monitor his vitals, and notify me if changes indicated deception.

Lee seemed to have shrugged off the cultivated neutrality he had demonstrated at our first meeting, so I turned my attention to Captain Thomas. Medusa and Octopippin may have startled her, but she recovered quickly. "Oichi Angelis?" she said, raising an eyebrow.

I smiled. "Thank you for coming. Please be comfortable."

The shift captain backed away, and the doors closed behind my guests as I rose and directed them to seats on the couch from which they could access the snack trays. "Would you care for tea?"

"Yes," they said together, and I poured for them.

Medusa and Octopippin moved to spots where our guests could see them. "You've met Medusa," I said. "This is Ashur's partner, Octopippin, and this is Ashur."

"I'm pleased to meet you." Thomas nodded to each, in turn. "Ashur, my youngest son is your age."

If I had known that about Captain Thomas, I might have introduced Ashur to her sooner. I liked her, now that I was no longer planning to break her neck.

She sampled a tea cake. "My goodness. This is wonderful."

"That's lemon?" said Lee. "I can't resist the chocolate."

We sipped our tea and exchanged pleasantries for the first several minutes. I was expecting to get down to business soon, but Lee sidetracked me with a question I had not expected. "Medusa, can you taste what Oichi is eating and drinking?"

Medusa smiled. "You are perceptive, Representative Lee."

"I can do it, too!" said Kitten, who had draped herself across the back of our couch. "So far, I prefer raspberry tarts."

"Your brain implants must be very advanced biotech," said Lee. "Among Union worlds, lots of people have advanced communication implants, but what you have is rare."

I regarded him over the rim of my cup. "Do you have implants, Representative Lee?"

"No. The only biotech I've received is standard medical. It's kept me healthy, but none of it gives me access to databases or communications. My eyes don't see beyond normal spectrums."

"Same here," said Thomas. "Biotech is expensive. I've sunk most of my earnings into my ship."

That seemed like a good spot for a segue. "You haven't asked leave to depart," I said, "to take your ship back to the Weapons Clan."

Captain Thomas held my gaze steadily. "We're not sure that's our best option."

If I had smiled at that moment, it probably would have seemed insincere. So I maintained a demeanor of polite curiosity, even though that was also insincere. "Have you considered visiting the Belters?"

"Have you?" countered Thomas.

I took another sip of my tea. "In fact—I have. I wondered if we might do it together. Your ship is much faster than any of our shuttles."

Now it was Thomas's turn to nurse her tea. (Really, how do people negotiate without that beverage?) "That would be interesting. Would you be hiring us only for transportation? Or would we also be working as consultants?"

"Both, I think. For instance"—I turned to Lee—"we'd like to hear about the Union."

"Also about the war," added Ashur.

Captain Thomas raised an eyebrow. "Which one? There have been plenty of those."

"The one that almost destroyed all the colonies."

The half-puzzled, half-amused expression Captain Thomas had shown in her profile picture might be her default setting, but the one she wore just then was neither of those things. "The short version is that the families who ruled the Old Empire had so much wealth, their children could afford to buy their own weapons. Unfortunately, those weapons included things like sunbusters."

Ashur frowned. "How do you bust a sun?"

"You don't, really. You briefly destabilize the forces of gravity and explosion that hold the sun in balance. Before it regains that balance, it sends out a devastating pulse. How much destruction it causes depends on how close something is to that sun. At the very least, it takes out electronics and satellites. At worst—it can take out the atmosphere of a world along with everything on the surface."

"Children did that?" Ashur looked stunned.

"Some as young as you," said Thomas.

I wasn't as surprised as Ashur. I hadn't told him everything I had witnessed concerning the offspring of Executives, their cruelties and their—*hobbies*. I had no trouble imagining children who could wipe out entire worlds for fun.

"It took a couple of centuries to even *start* rebuilding what was destroyed," said Thomas. "On the upside, the Union became a lot more influential. That's also when the Alliance of Ancient Races started to talk to us."

"Ah," said Octopippin. "They realized they needed to be the adults in the room."

Our guests stared at Octopippin as if seeing her for the first time.

"My DNA is ancient," she said. "As is the technology that crafted me."

"May I have more tea?" Lee placed his cup on its saucer.

I poured, and we all waited for him to fix it to his liking with sugar. "Octopippin," he said at last, "I suspect that if the children of those powerful families had been linked with Medusa units, there would have been no War of the Clans. Possibly no other wars as well."

"War is impractical and destructive," said Octopippin, "but the Weapons Clan would be bankrupt without them—don't you think?"

"Yes," said Lee. "They argue that weapons prevent as many wars as they enable. They have a point. This system we're traveling through and the graveyard on its fourth world are well protected."

Medusa nudged the plate of tea cakes toward him. "Have you ever visited the Belters of Charon, Representative Lee?"

He selected another cake. "Never, but I would be happy to be your consultant in matters of Union protocol."

"What about the protocols of the Alliance of Ancient Races?" said Medusa.

Lee took another sip of tea before he answered. "In their case, courtesy and respect are the only known protocols. Very few people have seen them or spoken to them directly."

Yet Fire worked for them. Interesting.

"Oichi—" Captain Thomas leveled her gaze at me. "—do you plan to visit Graveyard?"

I had already decided to hire her, so I told her the truth. "We must. Our origins are there. We have been invited by entities who abide there."

I didn't expect them to be so surprised by that revelation. Lee had to set down his cup. "By *entities*?" he said. "Not by humans living on Graveyard?"

"By both," I clarified.

Lee and Thomas shared a long look. I admired that they could exchange so much information in a glance, without the aid of brain implants.

Thomas turned to me. "I accept your contract. My crew and I normally work for credits, but in your case, we'll work out some sort of barter. We can iron out the details later. For the record—you want us to take you to the Belters. Did you know we could also take you to Graveyard?"

"I hadn't thought that far in advance," I lied. "I consider it a possibility."

She gave a curt nod. "I consider it a possibility, too."

"I'll write up a standard contract," said Lee.

I stirred sugar into my tea. "Will the Weapons Clan be surprised that you aren't returning to them?"

Captain Thomas didn't hesitate. "Probably, but we're contractors. We don't owe them explanations."

"Are they evil people?" said Ashur.

Even I was surprised by the directness of that question, but Thomas seemed to understand the anger that lay behind it. "Not as individuals," she said. "At least, not most of them. They're businesspeople and technicians. As a group, sometimes they can be *operationally* evil."

"For instance," said Ashur, "they can create a magnificent generation ship like *Olympia*, and then they can create a race of people to live there who belong to them. Like things. Like . . ."

"Assets," offered Octopippin.

"Yes," said Thomas. "That's the Weapons Clan in a nutshell."

"I'm glad you're going to work with us now," said Ashur. "I don't trust them to be honorable toward you, now that you've talked to us."

I hadn't mentioned to Ashur what I overheard on the comm link. He figured that one out for himself.

Captain Thomas smiled at him. "This job is turning out to be a lot more exciting than I had expected, but I'm glad to be working with you, too, Ashur."

If that didn't seal the deal, I didn't know what could.

Okay, probably Lee's contract could, but I felt it was worth another round of tea. I was plying them with more treats from the tray when a message from the tablet Kitten had given the *Merliner*s popped into my queue.

Oichi, this is Miriam Cocteau. I would very much like to meet the people responsible for the wonderful wine you make here on Olympia. *Can this be arranged?*

I'll put you in touch with Ogden Schickele, I responded. *He makes coffee, but he hobnobs with all the best vintners.*

Delightful! she said.

"I just got a message from Cocteau," I told Lee and Thomas. "She wants to meet with the winemakers. Perhaps you'd like to join her?"

Thomas smiled. "Leave it to Cocteau to find out where the party is."

Indeed? I wondered. *Is that why you have two engineers on Merlin instead of just one?*

I decided to leave that inquiry until later. I set my cup down and turned to Medusa, a satisfied smile on my lips.

Her expression made me reconsider that. <Oichi—at what point were you going to inform me that you had been invited into the graveyard?>

The others chatted cheerfully around us. I did my best to maintain an unruffled demeanor. Inside, I was anything but. <I thought Octopippin would inform you.>

<She did. Why should she have done so first? What's going on, Oichi?>

The others were going out the door now, led by Kitten, Ashur, and Octopippin. Medusa and I brought up the rear. <If I were trying to keep it from you,> I said, <I wouldn't have just blurted it out at the tea party.>

<I didn't say you were trying to keep it from me. I said you didn't tell me. I would have expected you to do so as soon as you were contacted.>

She had a point. Why hadn't I said anything to her? <I've been so tangled up in details,> I said. <We've been—you and I have been . . . >

We had been leading separate lives. I saw that clearly now. Medusa was the Prima—she was always busy. I had assumed a similar role in the hierarchy of *Olympia*. Both of us had become accustomed to making decisions on our own.

We watched the others get into a mover. Medusa waved them on, and we waited for another one.

<I was negligent,> I said. <I should have told you.>

<What are you going to do, Oichi?>

Again, I felt flummoxed. Shouldn't that be obvious? <Once they tell us the guest list, we're going to visit the Three.>

<Don't do it.>

I stared at her, speechless.

<Don't wake them, Oichi.>

<They're the ones who will decide if they want to wake—>

<Did it ever occur to you to wonder what killed the people who made them?>

I had to admit—that was a good question, but if she had met Crow, if she had received that invitation that had seemed more like a command, would she feel this way?

<You're being moved into a dangerous position,> said Medusa. <I don't like it.>

I nodded, but that was a lame response. Medusa didn't need a nod; she needed an explanation. Now that I was on the spot, I couldn't seem to come up with one.

<Going to Maui is a good idea,> said Medusa, <and it's inevitable that we should visit the world where the graveyard abides, but think very hard before you march up to the Three, Oichi. They're the ones who made the decision to sleep. Respect their judgment.>

Maybe so, I thought, *but they're also the ones who first contacted me, with avatars of the most important people in my life. Should I respect that decision, too?*

That would have been a good argument. I should have spoken it to her, but I kept silent.

Once again, I withheld information from Medusa.

7

I'll Ride the God Machine If You'll Be the Chorus

When we entered the Habitat Sector, the music playing in my head came from a movie called *Around the World in 80 Days*. It was composed by Victor Young, and its main theme featured a lush collection of strings that all seemed to be singing, *We have nothing better to do than drift lazily in this balloon.* . . .

Honestly, I couldn't tell you much about that movie, aside from the self-explanatory title, but it's fun to wallow in it—in the music and in the scenes of a past era as imagined by people from a somewhat-less-past era.

Wallowing was what I wanted our guests to do in the Habitat Sector. We escorted Thomas and Lee to the little wine- and coffee-tasting soirée Ogden Schickele had improvised (though Ogden improvises better than most people plan). The rest of the *Merlin*ers mingled in the demonstration garden next to one of Ogden's coffee greenhouses. Dragonette, Teddy, and Rocket played co-hosts, and—what the heck!—since it was a party, we invited Nuruddin and Terry, Nefertari and Kumiko. Some of Ogden's agriculture students were there, too, pinching coffee cherries to get a feel for ripeness.

Not to sound lecherous, but pinching those cherries is fun. It wasn't long before Nuruddin and I waded in among those young people, ostensibly to help them pick the ripe ones, but mostly to satisfy our curiosity.

Nuruddin squeezed a coffee cherry experimentally. "I've been thinking about what Nemo told you—how the Weapons Clan rescued our wheat crops."

"Yes." I tested one and decided it was ripe for picking—but easier said than done.

"It occurs to me," said Nuruddin, "that the Weapons Clan served the role of the God Machine in our lives, and I find that rather funny."

"The *what*?" I said.

"It's an old reference in Greek drama. The *deus ex machina*. In the earliest plays written by humans, a god always solved everyone's problem at the end of the story. The god also served as a judge who decided who was to blame and how things should be resolved. The god was lowered onto the stage by a machine, a stage prop."

I thought about *Itzpapalotl*, the goddess of nightmares who lurked out beyond the gas giants. "If the Weapons Clan has been our deus ex machina, then *Itzpapalotl* would be one of their machines?"

He smiled. "Exactly. The Three have had their moments in that role, too. Yet they have also served the function of the Chorus."

"The *who*?"

Nuruddin dropped one cherry in his bag. "In the ancient plays, the Chorus stood apart from the Players and made comments about the characters and the situations they found themselves in. For instance, in *Lysistrata*, the Chorus says:

Save Athens and all Greece
From Lunacy and war,
For that, O maid, is what
They've seized your temple for.

"And in *Medea*, the Chorus says: *Did you hear, Zeus and Earth and light, how sad a lament she sings, the sorrowful wife?*

"And in *Oedipus Rex*, the Chorus says: *For the day ravages what the night spares—*

"And in that Woody Allen movie, *Mighty Aphrodite*, the Chorus says: *Please, Lenny, don't be a schmuck!*"

I frowned. "That last remark from the Chorus seems more like interaction and less like observation."

Nuruddin brightened. "Yes, because the Chorus evolved in drama. The role of the Chorus came to be filled by other characters. You can see it in the movies in my database, but now I'm seeing it in our lives. Think about how we communicate with each other. We're constantly making observations about things we're not directly involved with, and the Medusas and Minis do it even more than we do."

I thought about it. "Kitten can be quite Chorus-y."

"Indeed. It is the nature of the way we communicate. If you travel in *Merlin* to visit the Belters, and you explain anything to them that changes their lives, you shall have been delivered by a God Machine."

"If, instead, I simply make remarks about what's going on, rather than re-solving the conflict, will I be the Chorus? Are Chorus members allowed to ride in the God Machine?"

"Not in the classical plays," said Nuruddin, "but this is *our* story. We can change the rules."

<We *did* change the rules,> I said.

Nuruddin regarded the children around us, who pinched the cherries with such enthusiasm. Before our revolution, only mid- and low-level Exec-utives could become what Ogden had been, a food expert. Worms who spe-cialized in nutrition were relegated to the vat rooms, where nutrient broth was made. The young people in Ogden's agriculture class were from every corner of *Olympia*; the only prerequisite for their participation was an interest in plants.

<These children will change them even more,> he said.

That prompted me to wonder where Ashur was. The last I had seen, he had been talking with the doctor from *Merlin*. He had been polite with her, not flirty. I suppose maturity can take some of the fun out of romance. Unless you think it's fun to discuss disease vectors.

Nuruddin and I tired of pretending to pick coffee cherries, so we wandered back to Ogden's circle. Representative Lee was talking about a food he called *cheese*. "It's made from the milk of mammals. Mostly goats and cows. It goes well with wine. It doesn't go as well with coffee, but the cream from cows certainly does."

Cocteau laughed. "Only a Philistine puts cream in coffee! Though I enjoy ice cream. That's something you may want to trade with the Belters, Ogden—and the cheese, of course. I shall be delighted to get some Brie for you. You may want to see if they have some fish or chicken you can sample."

Ogden didn't mention that we have some animal protein that we grow in our vats; it's used to make nutrient broth. We also have fish, but they are deco-rative creatures who live in ornamental ponds, a frivolity on a generation ship that I am hard-pressed to explain.

Unless one considers the role of the Weapons Clan and their God Ma-chine.

The scent of sweet peas lured me away from the crowd and under a large arbor. The vines had grown up its side and had woven a flowery roof that spared me from a view that could be overwhelming at times. I sat on a bench next to a garden pool with a miniature waterfall. For a little while I watched flower petals floating in the water.

Someone approached, their feet crunching on the path. Oddly, it wasn't until that moment that it occurred to me that we must also have gotten our gravel from asteroids.

Cocteau held a wine bottle in one hand and a glass in the other. She navigated the garden path with grace, belying the sparkle in her eye that I guessed had come from several samplings from the glass—and possibly several previous glasses.

She hoisted the bottle. "I have made a lovely friend. He makes coffee and he likes wine."

"Ogden Schickele?" I guessed.

"The very one." Cocteau sat beside me on the bench. She was a tiny thing, and she looked delicate, though not fragile. She moved with confidence. Her demeanor, as she regarded me from her perch, reminded me very much of Dragonette.

Her hair was so white, I wondered if she lightened it. The contrast with her dark skin made her look like a magical creature. A fairy godmother? An elf? Yet despite her apparent age, her skin was smooth, and Cocteau's accented voice possessed the timbre of a fine instrument, pleasing my ears so well, I knew I would be looking for reasons to like her rather than sensible reasons not to.

"Captain Thomas says you're the real deal," I said, "sought after by giant companies, and by captains of ships much larger than *Merlin.*"

"How could I resist *Merlin?*" Cocteau set the bottle beside her as if it were a favored child. "She is named for a beautiful falcon, so small and fierce and full of surprises."

Like you, I thought.

"You know, Oichi—" Cocteau took a sip. "—when I made queries about you, when I was deciding whether or not to sign on for this contract, my sources called you Miss Kick-Butt." She winked. "It's the reason I accepted."

I wondered whom she could have talked to who would have known so much about me, but I couldn't help smiling back. "I don't kick people's butts for fun. These days I spend a lot more time putting out fires than setting them."

"There's more than one way to kick butt." Cocteau took another sip. "Oh my *Lord* this is good wine. And the coffee! My French soul is in ecstasy."

Perhaps she was related to the filmmaker after all. "You are entirely French?" I said. "You know this?"

"No one is entirely anything, these days," said Cocteau, "but, yes, I can trace part of my family tree to France. I can even trace us to a particular region."

"You remind me of Gennady Mironenko, the man who engineered *Olympians*. He felt he was entirely Russian."

"*Mironenko*," said Cocteau. "Dear me. I thought I would never hear that name again. They were a powerful family once. Before the war that shattered the Empire, they were a world-building clan. In fact, I worked with a Mironenko, long ago, Oichi. Long, long ago."

She sipped her wine, and I wondered just how long Cocteau meant. Did she mean that she had been alive in that era?

It wasn't impossible. Gennady had hinted to the Charmaynes that he was hundreds of years old. He took me out to dinner a couple of times, and I got a chance to see him up close, so I felt inclined to believe him. Like Cocteau, he had possessed the confidence of an older person, but the smooth skin of a younger one. Only her demeanor and her spare frame hinted at her age.

Cocteau was an engineer—she must earn a high salary. Perhaps she sank her earnings into longevity treatments.

She took another sip. "His name was Andrei Mironenko. He built a world called Belarus. Andrei is long dead, of course—he was killed by hostile aliens. We'll be hearing more from those aliens eventually, I'm sure. So perhaps our little foray into Graveyard territory will turn out to be useful."

"Do you wish you were going inside the graveyard?" I said. "To study the machines there?"

Cocteau sighed. She set her glass down, cupped a cluster of sweet peas dangling near our seat, and took a deep breath of their fragrance. Her expression was almost sad. "So much potential. We *don't* understand the machines, we younger races—not entirely. We learn what we know about them through passed-down lore and through trial and error."

She picked her glass up again and winked at me. "Do you want to know a secret? Work as an engineer long enough, and eventually you *are* going to understand something of the physics of how the engines work, how the field is generated, how the ship is moved across a fold. People who do that have a tendency to disappear. I've known five engineers who have done that, who got too smart." She wiggled five fingers, her eyes twinkling.

My goodness, I thought, *I should have served wine at my party instead of tea.* "By *disappear*," I said, "I presume you mean someone kills them."

"Someone *takes* them," she corrected.

"Who would take them?"

Cocteau shrugged. "Some people think it's the Earlies. Personally, I suspect the Rock Elves."

I weighed that collection of words. *Earlies* might refer to an elder race. *Rock Elves* seemed more elusive. "From the Alliance of Ancient Races?" I guessed.

"That's just my name for them," said Cocteau. "You know, I saw them once." Her gaze shifted past me, as if she were contemplating a grand vista. "If you've never been on a survey team, you can't imagine the beauty of a pristine world—or the terror. We had only each other to rely on, and the supplies on our ship."

I could have said that we on *Olympia* had nothing more than that, but I wondered if we were relatively safe here, compared with what Cocteau was talking about. I could barely imagine walking on an inhabited planet, let alone exploring a *pristine* world, untouched by intelligent designs and intentions.

"Graveyard has barely moved past that stage," Cocteau said, as if reading my thoughts. "Only a few million people reside there. The presence of the entities in the ship graveyard looms so large, there's hardly room for anything else." She took a sip that seemed more contemplative than adventurous. "That world from my long-ago youth was called Canyon. It boasted quite a few interesting geological features—including several canyon systems.

"One system dwarfed them all. Behemoth, forty-five hundred kilometers long on the arm that stretched roughly east–west, and another thirty-five hundred kilometers on the arm stretching south from the juncture. Dozens of side canyons fed into it, and at its deepest point, it descended five kilometers from the rim. We hypothesized that it was a failed rift. The hot spot that created that wedge continues to feed molten material underneath it, pushing its plateaus higher every year than the forces of gravity can wear them down." She paused for another sip. "That's part of the reason Behemoth's walls are so steep. They're made of cohesive metamorphic rock that was buried and then lifted."

She glanced at me to make sure I was still listening, despite all the geologic details. "It was magnificent, Oichi. We thought it was all ours. With our dragonfly units, we could fly to any spot that piqued our curiosity, but we forgot—a landform that big could generate some violent weather. We had no idea how suddenly the winds could shift there."

Cocteau tapped the rim of her glass, generating a crisp *ping*. "One morning

I set out with my colleague, Fitzgerald—he was a geologist—dear fellow was in heaven—anyway, it was a clear, sunny morning. Perfect for exploring. We flitted about on our dragonfly units like a couple of overeducated kids, so confident and full of the spirit of discovery. As the morning progressed, it warmed up quite a lot, so we didn't mind when breezes began to cool us a bit. Then those breezes turned to gusts."

Cocteau cradled her glass in both hands, as if the wind might threaten its stability, too. "We had been so intent on the rocks, their faces and joints, the long streaks of minerals that stretched all the way down into the gorge from water that had dripped there for millennia. When we looked up, we saw the big cumulonimbus clouds piling up on the rim. Gorgeous—and a clear sign of danger for anyone paying attention.

"Fitzgerald ordered me to secure myself to the rock face. I found a spot that sheltered me from the worst of the wind. When he flew toward an outcrop that we had named the Vulture, a gust of wind spun him ass over teakettle.

"Fitzgerald didn't panic when the wind sent him tumbling, he corrected his trajectory. That devil wind changed and blew him in the same direction he was already headed at full power. He slammed against the rock face. The impact sent the dragonfly into neutral mode, which meant it wouldn't keep him aloft unless he switched it back—but he was unconscious.

"I watched him from my perch, and a little voice inside my head was telling me that if I didn't switch my unit to active mode and hurtle after him with everything I had, *straight down*, Fitzgerald was going to die. It was a maneuver I had never performed." She quirked her eyebrows up and down. "One I *still* haven't done, because someone surged over the top of that outcrop, clung to its face with his fingers and toes, and grabbed Fitzgerald with one hand before he could fall. I watched him gather Fitzgerald in, as if that big man were no heavier than a child, and use the dragonfly's stasis locks to secure him to the rock face."

Cocteau paused to sample her wine again, watching me over the rim. I realized I was at the edge of my seat. She waggled a finger at me. "The stranger looked at me, and he did this, just as I'm doing now, as if to say, *Naughty. You should be more careful.* Then he climbed up and over the top of the rocks and disappeared from sight. That's when I named them the Rock Elves."

"Because of the way he climbed?" I guessed.

"No. He was almost the same color as the rocks in that area, sort of a dark blue-gray. Later I saw another one, and she was the color of red sandstone.

Quite lovely." Cocteau smiled at the memory. "Other than that, they looked much like us, except that they were taller and thinner. They had wide shoulders and features that seemed elongated compared with ours. So, yes, very elfin." She leaned back and contemplated the flowers around us. "This is such an enchanting space."

I waited for her to continue. Hadn't she been making a point about kidnapped engineers? Cocteau smiled, crossed her legs, and hoisted her glass as if she intended to stay in that mode for a good, long time.

"If the Rock Elves are so fond of canyons," I said at last, "do you suppose we'll find some of them in Joe's Canyon? On Graveyard?"

"You might," she mused. "I have always assumed that they are members of the Alliance of Ancient Races. If they are, they would have interests to protect in the graveyard."

Cocteau turned a direct gaze on me then, and there was nothing drunken about it. "I have a suggestion. I think you should call Bomarigala and reject his offer directly."

"Really . . ."

"They owe you a conversation. If you continue to pussyfoot around with representatives, you won't resolve your differences. It's time to do that, don't you think?"

My preferred way to resolve our differences with Bomarigala would be to snap his neck, but I saw her point.

"I'm concerned about legal matters," I said. "I don't know the laws that pertain to our situation."

"Well," said Cocteau, "neither does Bomarigala, despite what he may say to you. You're inside the Charon system. No one can force you to follow Union laws or Clan laws. If you make some sort of arrangement with the Three, or with the Alliance of Ancient Races, even the Belters won't be able to tell you what to do." She took another sip. "Though I recommend you maintain pleasant interactions with the Belters. One always wants to be on good terms with one's close neighbors."

"Neighbors," I mused. "We've never had those before."

She gave me half a smile. "I suspect you may find that word becomes literal, if you trade with the Belters. Some of them may want to move here. Some of you may want to move there, and to Graveyard. Think about what you want, and then pursue that. The Weapons Clan will simply have to adjust."

I hoped she was right, though I suspected the Weapons Clan had quite a lot of talent for adjusting.

Possibly more than we did.

"I'll do it," I said. "I'll call Captain Nemo and have him establish a link."

"Well," said Cocteau. "If you don't mind, I'd like to suggest another pathway. . . ."

8

Operational Evil

"Dear me," said Medusa. "I beg your pardon."

"I should probably just—" Captain Thomas wiggled her way to the door. "—maybe wait in the hall." She joined the rest of her crew.

"Or I could deploy some of my tentacles out there," said Medusa. "Just enough to make room for—are you comfortable, Representative Lee?"

"I'm okay," he said. "I've been in subway cars more crowded than this."

I sat in Captain Thomas's chair. Her office on *Merlin* had not been made to hold a lot of people, though without Medusa's tentacles, I expect it would not have been so crowded. It couldn't be helped. Medusa insisted that I wear her for the call to Bomarigala of the Weapons Clan, and I agreed. I needed my most powerful ally. Our recent disagreements aside, she and I were the A-Team.

Nemo would dislike the place I was choosing to make the call, but I was willing to bet he would prefer not to have Medusa in his Command Center again—he had been antagonized, the last time.

His staff could hear everything we were saying on this call. I had looped Terry Charmayne in, though the *Merliner*s were unaware of that. Terry would brief the Security Council if anything developed that required their attention; he had the option of messaging me during my conversation with Bomarigala, if questions occurred to him.

Nuruddin and Ashur also listened in. I established that link without explanation, but I suspected Ashur knew why I had done it. He and I would eventually have some explaining to do, and I thought it best if Nuruddin had some background on our current situation.

"You're set to make the call," said Lee. "I've typed in the codes. All you have to do is hit CALL when you're ready."

I was as ready as I was ever going to get.

I hit CALL.

There was a delay before my communication was accepted, and I used it to imagine the man to whom the marvelous voice belonged: Bomarigala. I pictured him receiving our call, perhaps raising an eyebrow in surprise. When he appeared on the screen, he surpassed my imagination.

Bomarigala of the Weapons Clan reminded me of men I had seen painted on the ancient screens of the Chang Clan. His clothing was an updated version of those fine robes, and his long black hair was bound in the same style. His face, too fine and too intelligent to wear the sort of smirk that had perpetually contorted Tetsuko Finnegan's expression, was nevertheless cast in the same general mold.

"Medusa," he said. "I am pleased to meet you at last. Who is wearing you?"

"Can you guess?" said Medusa.

"My first guess is Oichi Angelis."

"Yes," I said. "We called to give you a direct answer to your message."

"I appreciate your courtesy," said Bomarigala.

If that were true, he wouldn't be doing so for long. "We will not work for the Weapons Clan as your employees or contractors," I said. "We will not establish an outpost for the Weapons Clan within the Charon system. We are willing to negotiate with you at a future date, depending on what agreements we establish with Belters, or with the Alliance of Ancient Races, or with the world authority on Graveyard—or with all of the above. Your interests will not take precedence over ours, and we do not belong to your clan. We are independent, and we assert authority on *Olympia*. Should any future negotiations take place between *Olympia* and the Weapons Clan, we expect you to treat us as equals."

Bomarigala's expression did not change. "It's rare for the Weapons Clan to negotiate with equals. We don't have many of those."

"Yes," I said. "We're special."

He remained silent for a long time. I wondered if he thought that would provoke me into rethinking any of the statements I had just made. If I had not been wearing Medusa, it would have been an effort to keep a straight face.

"I'm not surprised to hear what you have to say," Bomarigala answered at last. "We had hoped to see a better return on our investment, but we always make contingency plans. The destruction of *Titania* forced us to call in some favors."

I should have asked about those favors, but instead I blurted, "Who made the gravity bombs that destroyed *Titania*? Where did they come from?"

That may not have been the best time to ask those questions, but I needed to know the answers.

"They came from Gennady Mironenko," said Bomarigala. Though Medusa and I could not hear his heartbeat, I believed his tone. "It was a betrayal we will never forgive. Now that you've brought up the fate of *Titania*, I think there's something you deserve to know. We would have debriefed you if you had signed our employment contract, but you may consider this a gift. When we salvaged what was left of *Titania*—"

Salvaged. So she isn't a ghost ship, sailing toward oblivion.

"—we found a few pockets that were still pressurized—"

Pressurized? As in breathable air?

"—that contained survivors."

Survivors?!

"One of them would like to speak with you," concluded Bomarigala.

Mother, I thought. *Or Father. Still alive. That's what he'll hold over my head.* My heart skipped a beat.

The screen was obscured by Bomarigala's clothing, as effective as any curtain, while he stood and someone else took his place. She wore a rich fabric that was all too familiar to me. I recognized it so well, I already knew whose face I was about to see when the newcomer sat in Bomarigala's place in front of the screen.

"Well, criminal," said Lady Sheba. "We meet at last."

My voice died in my throat. It was as if Lady Sheba had closed her hand around my windpipe.

Fortunately, Medusa covered my visage. She spoke for me. "Sheba. Let me guess. Your shuttle survived the destruction of *Titania*, though its engines were disabled. You were rescued by the Weapons Clan? It was kind of them to show mercy to an orphan."

"You will call me *Lady Sheba*," commanded the woman my mother had called *the Iron Fist.* "I am the last surviving authority of *Olympia*, and I am asserting my right of command. You will stand down and you will obey my orders."

Medusa smiled. "Well! Where to begin? You have no right of command, Sheba. We are traveling inside the Charon system, which is administered by the Alliance of Ancient Races. Clan law does not apply here. We will not stand down, we will not accept your orders, and we will not permit you to return to *Olympia*."

I expected Sheba to glower with outrage, but I had forgotten what a skillful *Machiavellia* she had been. Her smile matched Medusa's. "I have no intention of arguing with a machine. Nothing you say has validity."

"In that case," said Medusa, "I will speak with Bomarigala of the Weapons Clan. He has no authority over us either, and his clan has no claim over *Olympia*, but I would like to convey a final message to him before we end this conversation." She raised her voice. "Because we *are* going to end it, Bomarigala. This charade is over."

"You are a tool," said Lady Sheba. "Nothing more."

"I am Medusa. I speak for *Olympia*."

"For the time being," said Sheba, utterly sure of herself. She never lost her smile—but she relinquished her seat. The one who was really in charge sat down again.

"Well," said Bomarigala, "I regret that the tone of this conversation has become so bitter. I hope we'll be able to salvage a more cordial relationship when we speak again."

"Hope springs eternal," said Medusa.

Bomarigala gave a curt nod. "Should you choose to travel outside the Charon system, you'll find that your debts to us will be in full effect."

"Likewise," said Medusa.

"Very well. I'll say goodbye. There is one final thing I'd like you to know. Sheba was not the only survivor we rescued from *Titania*. We may yet realize a profit on our investment." Bomarigala smiled. "We'll be sending our own delegation into the graveyard."

His smile faded. "See you there, Oichi?"

The screen went dark.

<Alive. Lady Sheba is alive.> I at least had the presence of mind not to say that out loud.

<Steady,> advised Terry.

<Oh my God!> said Ashur.

Nuruddin sighed. <Murphy's Law strikes again.>

<Oichi,> Medusa said privately, <if your mother were alive, they would have shown her to us—or your father. That would have been the best way to get you to agree to their terms. They didn't show that hand, because they don't have it.>

<Yes,> I agreed.

Lee said, "You caught them off guard with that call. That's why Bomarigala tried to make you lose your focus, by showing you that woman, but you stayed cool." Medusa detached herself, and Lee could see my expression. "Or—um—that's how it looked."

What had I done when I had the chance to confront the woman who had been an architect of our misery? I sat like a speechless child in the presence of a stern grandmother.

Sheba wasn't dead. That was a gravity bomb right in the middle of my model of the universe, but it wasn't even the thing that scared me the most.

Lady Sheba tried to assert her clan rights—no surprise there. Bomarigala had reminded us that the Weapons Clan had made a substantial investment in *Titania* and *Olympia;* they had never wavered in that narrative. It was the last thing he said that had my stomach clenching like a fist.

We'll be sending our own delegation into the graveyard.

I looked at the dead screen and saw no camera light. Not that it mattered what they saw at this point. If they heard us, hadn't they been hearing us all along? "We made it clear where we stand," I concluded.

What more I would have said beyond that point, I may never recall, because Captain Nemo's second chose that moment to pop a priority warning into my queue.

URGENT, it declared.

<What's up?> I asked.

<We overheard your conversation through the open link,> she said. <I tried to call Captain Nemo to relay a transcript of your communication with the Weapons Clan. Nemo has not been in the Command Center for over thirty hours now.>

<That's an anomaly?> I said.

<Yes. He indicated he would be out for twenty-four hours, and that's not unheard of. I expected him to check in at the end of that period. He hasn't, and I can't find him.>

I paused to add Medusa and Terry Charmayne to our link. <Nemo is missing, then?>

<Nemo is missing,> she confirmed. <I am acting commander of this ship. I have ordered a search for Nemo. I think it would be optimal to add the Medusa units and the Minis to our search team.>

<How many do you think we should draft?>

<All who are not currently engaged in critical operations.>

That would be a lot of Medusas and Minis. On the other hand, we could search faster and more thoroughly with that kind of force. <Medusa?> I said.

Medusa drew her tentacles in close. <Consider it done.> She gave concise orders to the other units. Her orders to the Minis were more detailed: <Your safety is a primary priority. Do not take risks.>

When it was done, she gave me a short nod.

<Are you going to join the search?> I said.

<Not without you. Nemo's absence is troubling. I am concerned for your safety.>

Considering the conversation we had just had with Bomarigala of the Weapons Clan and the not-quite-dead Lady Sheba, a little paranoia seemed judicious at that juncture. <Once I conclude our current business,> I said, <we'll join the party as a team.>

I got up from Thomas's chair. "Captain, a security matter has come to our attention. We ask that you confine yourselves to *Merlin* until further notice."

"Affirmative," said Thomas.

"I'll work on the contract," said Lee. "When you've got time, we can go over it together."

Cocteau stood with the others in the hall. She still held her bottle of wine, a gift from Ogden, and she still wore a smile, as if she felt my conversation with Bomarigala had been an unqualified success. Wilson stood beside her, dwarfing her in size yet solicitous toward her, as if she were as powerful a grandmother as Lady Sheba.

"Thank you for a lovely visit," said Cocteau.

"You're welcome," I said, since *My pleasure* no longer seemed appropriate, and Medusa and I began the challenging process of exiting *Merlin*.

When we emerged into Lock 212, *Merlin* shut her door behind us.

Medusa flowed over me; we linked again. We sealed Lock 212 and went in search of a mover that would take us to a maintenance air lock, which would be the fastest (normal) way to access the exterior of *Olympia* so we could join the searchers who were looking outside.

Outside may seem like an odd place for someone to hide, but Medusa and I had hidden there for years. We knew that landscape better than anyone, with the possible exception of Kitten. *Olympia*'s access canyons, research towers, locks, ladders, nodes, valves, arrays, and hatches presented a rich variety of places to conceal things—and a serious challenge to searchers. Lady Sheba had hidden a ship called *Escape* in one of the engine nozzles for decades.

The stars blazed as they wheeled overhead, but we were close enough to Charon now that it outshone the best of them, casting stark shadows.

Medusa and I began our survey near the edge of Central Sector, working our way meticulously toward the leading edge of *Olympia*, climbing man-made mountains and descending access canyons while consulting a tactical grid displayed inside our heads. Since we were looking for Captain Nemo, the music I played was Bernard Herrmann's score for *Mysterious Island*. Herrmann liked to use unusual instrument combinations to characterize the fantastic creatures portrayed in the movie, conveying both a sense of wonder and the impression of danger. The original Captain Nemo showed up at the conclusion of that film (rather like a deus ex machina, now that I think of it), so it was appropriate.

Once that music finished, it seemed logical to move on to Herrmann's score for *Jason and the Argonauts*. My favorite part was where the dragon's teeth were sown, and the Children of the Hydra's Teeth sprouted into an army of skeletons. The dominant instrument in this sequence was the bassoon—its effect was menacing. Once those skeletons started fighting, an array of percussion instruments joined the wind section to create the effect of clashing swords and rattling bones.

Just as the music announced the fall of that skeletal army over a cliff, Medusa slowed and found a spot to perch near one of the 200-series locks. We were now on the opposite side of the ship from Lock 212 and *Merlin*.

<Lilith is coming with Security Chief Schnebly,> she explained. <They're going to meet us.>

This reminded me of the very important question I had failed to ask Schnebly, when Nemo had been so chilly with us in the Command Center. If I had queried sooner, perhaps our captain would not be missing now. I pondered my failure while we waited. It didn't appear any more forgivable, regardless of how I tried to look at it.

Lilith was Schnebly's work partner, though they hadn't bonded. She was formally paired with a Security officer who worked in the Charmayne family compound, a job that didn't necessarily require the help of a Medusa unit on a daily basis.

Lilith and Schnebly worked together for special projects—for instance, when Schnebly needed to travel across the outside of the hull of *Olympia* at top speed. We saw them zooming toward us. The Medusa units could use their tentacles to great advantage in zero gravity, pulling themselves and their passengers along at considerable speed. It was a marvelous thing to see and even more wonderful to do. When they had joined us, Lilith touched Medusa with a tentacle. They drew close and pressed their faces together.

"Can you hear me?" said Schnebly. His voice sounded a bit tinny, and I realized the sound waves of his voice were passing through Lilith's mask and into Medusa's.

"Why not use the helmet radios?" I called back. "They're short range."

"I'm not so sure we're alone out here," said Schnebly, and somehow I didn't think he was referring to the Minis. "I don't want to risk being overheard."

The Security overlay that Medusa and I had constructed was very accurate. I didn't kid myself that we could see everything, especially now that we had entered territory controlled by the Alliance of Ancient Races.

"Okay," I said. "What's up?"

He got right to the point. "Did you kill Nemo?"

I almost broke the contact. "*What? No!*"

"I don't think he could still be alive," said Schnebly. "He would never abandon his post."

"So that automatically means *I* killed him? Why would I do that?"

"He's an old-fashioned guy," said Schnebly. "I cut him a lot of slack for that. He was always charged with keeping *Olympia* safe, and that's a job that forces you to make some cruel decisions. He's got integrity—he never gave me a reason to doubt that, but I wonder if he's as happy about our Revolution as we are."

"We're not the ones who murdered the voting members of the ruling clans." *At least, not most of them.* "Baylor Charmayne did that."

"You're preaching to the choir," said Schnebly. "I think Nemo disagreed with the Executives about a lot of things, but maybe he shared their suspicion of the Medusa units. I don't think he likes having them involved with every aspect of our operations."

"Why not? We're more efficient when they assist us."

"Yes, but they're also more observant—and Nemo was used to having the Weapons Clan swoop in and rescue us from wheat plagues. If they've been planning to step up their operations, now that we're closer to Graveyard, the Medusa units are eventually going to notice suspicious activities."

Again, I thought of Nuruddin's God Machines. "You think he's their operative? A double agent?"

"Maybe not one hundred percent of the time. Part of the time, I think he is. He may not approve of our decision to cut them loose."

"So why has he disappeared? He can't help them *or* us if he's not our captain."

"That, I don't know," said Schnebly. "We'd better find him. We'd better ask him some hard questions."

I thought about that for a long moment. If Nemo had been antagonized by seeing Medusa in his Operations Center, he was going to be even less happy being interrogated by her.

"I want *you* to ask him," I said. "You know what makes him tick."

"As well as anybody does," said Schnebly, "who isn't the captain of a generation ship. That's a pretty exclusive club."

<Oichi!> Kitten broke in. <I'm on the leading edge, near Lucifer Tower. I found something!>

I tapped Schnebly's shoulder to let him know I was receiving a communication. <Go ahead, Kitten.>

<I think I found Captain Nemo.>

<You *think* you found him?>

<Well,> said Kitten, <his head is missing.>

9

Finding Nemo (Sort Of)

Ten thousand Medusa units reside on *Olympia*. Not all of them are assigned and operational, but most of them are, and those are paired with people from all walks of life, from administrators to agriculture specialists to doctors. Those Medusas assist their partners in their daily activities.

However, in emergency situations, the Medusa units can go to war. They can act as a security force, a rescue squad, a search team, with or without their partners. When Kitten broadcast her message about the headless body, Medusa put her sisters on high alert.

<Kitten, are you safe there?> I said.

<I don't know. I don't see anyone, but I feel like I'm being watched.>

<INVADER PROTOCOL,> Medusa ordered, and every Medusa unit and Mini on *Olympia* scrambled to their assigned positions.

You might think that meant everyone rushed to rescue Kitten, but the Invader Protocol is far more cautious than that. The assumption is that every place on *Olympia* is equally at risk, and that invaders or saboteurs are trying to create a diversion for destructive activities that will take place once the good guys have all run off in the wrong direction.

<HIGH ALERT,> Ship Operations broadcast on the Public Network. <REMAIN WHERE YOU ARE UNTIL FURTHER NOTICE.>

I called Captain Thomas by radio. "*Merlin* should lock down."

"Affirmative," she said.

<Come with us?> I asked Schnebly and Lilith.

<Yes,> they agreed, and the four of us made the best beeline we could to rendezvous with Kitten.

That took longer than you might imagine. We had several kilometers to travel. On the way, Minis, Medusas, and their partners gave us regular status reports as they inspected sections of *Olympia* for intruders and cleared them. I tried to be reassured by their reports, but I had a feeling we were *all* missing something.

<I feel so bad for Nemo,> Kitten said.

Medusa did her best to comfort her. <I know, dear.>

<It's awful when someone's head is gone. He kind of looks like a person, but he kind of doesn't.>

I checked the Security overlay of Kitten's general location. We weren't the only ones moving toward her—so were eight of the newer Minis who had been designed to aid with Security work. These newer Minis were armed with several weapons, from lethal to nonlethal—though also with a full library of show tunes, to round out their personalities.

<If someone cut off *my* head,> Kitten mused, <it wouldn't kill me, but it would be very awkward. My body would be crawling around, trying to find my head, and I would be yelling, "Over here, stupid!">

<No one will cut off your head,> promised Medusa. <Anyone who even joked about that would have to answer to *me*.>

<I don't think I'm being watched anymore,> Kitten said. <That feeling went away about fifteen minutes ago. Maybe the watcher just backed up a bit. Maybe she's watching me from a distance.>

<*She?*> said Medusa.

<Just another feeling. I'm taking lots of pictures of the scene and the body, and I'm taking notes for my report.>

<Excellent,> said Medusa. <Don't be lulled into a false sense of security, Kitten. Expect the unexpected.>

<The unexpected is the *only* thing I'm expecting right now,> said Kitten.

Olympia's leading edge is a platform on which is mounted a communications array and a collection of research towers. Our generation ship spins around an axis, but the leading edge doesn't spin with it, so even though the towers can be pressurized, they are zero-gravity environments. People who walk on the platform between the towers use magnetized shoes.

Nemo's body seemed to be standing at attention when we found him near Lucifer Tower; his mags connected him to the platform. Medusa took one look at him and said, <Now I know you didn't kill him. You're not a head-chopper-offer.>

I felt hurt that Medusa had also suspected me of killing Nemo, but I have to admit, the first thing that occurred to me is that I've never *been* a head-chopper-offer because I've never had a tool by which I could accomplish such a thing. Technically that's innocence by default.

Kitten flitted back and forth near Nemo's body, using her eyes as cameras to take pictures of the scene. They worked independently of each other, so she looked a bit odd as each lens expanded and shut with the snap of each picture, very much out of sync, lending her the appearance of cartoon bewilderment.

That appearance was false. Kitten felt dismayed, but she was thinking on her feet (paws?), trying to document a scene that would be examined in greater detail from those pictures she was taking.

We approached cautiously, despite the fact that the Security Minis were already there, standing guard over the scene. I very much wanted to scoop Kitten up and zoom to safety with her, but I couldn't dismiss the possibility that she and Nemo were bait within a trap. Medusa and I tried every possible overlay to scan the scene for someone who might be using stealth technology. Schnebly and Lilith did the same. None of us felt confident in our results, but it was as good as it was going to get.

<If someone managed to sneak up on Nemo, we're sitting ducks,> said Lilith. <All we can do at this point is stay alert.>

Once we were close enough, Kitten wrapped herself around my waist. <I'm *very* concerned about how clean the cut was,> she said. <Something sharp was used, by a very strong person. Unless his head was sawed off somewhere else. It looks like his suit and helmet were cut, too, and the edge of the cuts doesn't suggest any sort of serrated blade.>

A few droplets of blood floated near the body in a loose orbit. I imagined how odd that must have been, when his head was taken off in zero gravity–zero pressure conditions and the gases and liquids vented from his body.

If that's where he died. What if he was killed somewhere else, and placed here? Who placed him? What message were they trying to send by placing him so close to Lucifer Tower, where I had hidden after I faked my own death?

<Oichi,> said Kitten, <do you recall a certain movie from Nuruddin's database about a monster on a spaceship?>

<I recall several.>

<The spaceship was named *Nostromo*,> she said. <Do you remember how they tried to find the monster? The gizmo they created? Do you remember what it measured?>

Indeed. My favorite quote from that movie is "*Micro changes in air density, my ass!*" <I see what you're getting at.>

<Is it possible to measure that sort of thing?>

I considered her question. She was asking it so obliquely, I had to assume she was afraid someone might be listening to our communication, so I passed Kitten's questions on to Medusa exactly as she had asked them.

<We're in vacuum,> replied Medusa. <It does suggest avenues of investigation other than light and heat measurements. I'm going to pass it on to the other Medusa units and the Minis.>

Kitten's idea was a good one, but in the end, it wasn't micro changes in air density that would help us find Nemo's assassin. Light would turn out to be important, after all, but not because of the frequencies at which it can be measured.

Because of the way it can be bent.

We took Nemo's body back inside *Olympia*, where it could be examined by experts.

I did a bit of preliminary research before I picked a medical examiner. For most of our journey, Executives had committed murders that they needed to be classified as natural deaths or accidents. They usually took care of that detail by blowing people out of air locks—no body, no examination, no awkward details. Yet even they sometimes felt compelled to stage something more complicated. I couldn't blame medical examiners for practicing self-preservation, but I also did not want to pick one who would be inclined to tell me what I wanted to hear instead of the objective truth.

A candidate emerged, once I studied records of unnatural deaths. Dr. Sigrit Khan had a habit of going into great detail in her reports. Her method of coping with Executive oversight had been to drown them in facts. As a result, they had not been inclined to use her in deaths that were unnatural, and she had done most of her work with non-Executive casualties on *Olympia*.

Dr. Khan won more of my confidence when she asked to see Kitten's pictures of the scene. She spent quite a lot of time going over those after her preliminary examination of the body. She allowed the five of us in the room during that examination, though we had to stand well back so she and her assistants could move without bumping into tentacles. "I'm sure you two would be quite good at this job," she remarked to Lilith and Medusa. "Those extra appendages would be useful in my line of work."

"We still have some unassigned units," replied Medusa.

Dr. Khan nodded, but I could tell her mind had already moved on to more immediate matters.

"There's very little blood left in this body," she concluded. "I'll have to do

a thorough exam, but your theory of exsanguination in zero-pressure conditions is a good one, especially if it was decapitation that killed him. If that's
the case, he would have been dead before he knew anything was wrong."

I took some comfort from the idea that Nemo hadn't suffered. Whatever
his faults or doubts had been, he was no Baylor Charmayne. I would be disappointed to learn he had chosen the wrong allies, but I didn't hate him.

"Before we continue," said Dr. Khan, "I need to point out, for the record,
that this man has no identity on file in our databases—no fingerprints and
no DNA samples. I've encountered one or two like him in the past, and they
were reported to have ties to Ship Operations."

"This fellow does, too," I said. "You can call him Nemo."

She raised an eyebrow, and I wondered if she had also seen the movies.
"*Nobody*. That's appropriate. I'll assign a case number to him and label his
file *Identity Unknown*. You won't be able to alter that, but you can add your
suspicions about his identity in the Notes section."

"I understand," I said. "Do you concur with Kitten's hypothesis about the
sharpness of the blade that may have been used and the strength of the as-
sailant?"

"I can't discount her hypothesis at this point," said Dr. Khan. "Though
it's also possible a mechanical device was used, and no particular strength
would have been necessary under those circumstances, only adequate skill."
She stared at the neck wound for several moments before adding, "However,
it is an extraordinarily clean cut."

Dr. Khan was not the only one who went over Kitten's pictures of the
scenes. Schnebly and I made our own copies and studied them separately, so
we wouldn't influence each other. Lilith and Medusa did the same. Kitten insisted on going over them, too, and so did several other Minis, Medusas, and
Security staff members. Khan and her assistants began a more detailed examination of Nemo's remains, and our search parties continued to patrol every
inch of *Olympia*.

We had no record of anyone leaving the ship. Other than *Merlin*, we had
no record of anyone arriving, either. So we had to assume that the assassin
could still be on board. It was not impossible that the killer had been with us
all along—that one of our own citizens had killed Nemo.

Someone other than me. How many people had been looking sideways at
me? After all, I had been responsible for just *some* of the killings on *Olympia*.
Only a few of my cohorts knew about that.

Kitten had the most clarity. She was 100 percent certain it was an outsider.

<I *felt* her,> she said. <She was invisible. None of our people on *Olympia* can literally be invisible.>

Kitten's certainty influenced me, but there were other good reasons to wonder about an outsider. *Itzpapalotl*, Bomarigala, and Lady Sheba also lent credence to the idea that an outsider had assassinated Nemo. His disappearance, so close to their new interactions with us, seemed far more than coincidence.

Another question haunted me. The body in our morgue had no head, and the man to whom we thought it belonged had no official history.

<So is it really him?> I asked Schnebly. <Or did Nemo just find a way to disappear?>

Medusa was still disinclined to leave me uncovered (so to speak), but Schnebly and Lilith had separated in order to increase efficiency. He accompanied us as we walked through narrow tunnels. <I've pondered that,> he said, <but not very much. I don't think he would willingly leave *Olympia*. True, he could be hiding, but I don't see him giving up his command.>

<Unless he has allies who could restore him to that role,> I said.

Schnebly shook his head. <Occam's razor. The more complicated a conspiracy has to be, the less likely it is to be true.>

We stopped in front of some movers. <Are you coming with me to the Command Center?> asked Schnebly.

<No,> I said. <We need to walk. It helps me think.>

<Don't know about the thinking,> said Schnebly, <but if you stick to these tunnels, you can do a hell of a lot of walking.> He got into the mover and punched the buttons. The doors closed and Schnebly sped on his way.

See you later, I thought. *Unless you get killed by an invisible assassin.* Because that's what would happen in one of Nuruddin's movies.

Schnebly was right about Occam's razor. If I assumed everyone around me was embroiled in a vast, complicated conspiracy, I might lose a lot of sleep, but I wouldn't solve the puzzle of Nemo's death.

Through Medusa's eyes, I gazed down the tunnel, first in one direction, then in the other. <Any preference?> I asked her.

<That way.> She indicated the direction with the tip of a tentacle. Together we walked down narrow, winding passages, between pools of light.

We walked for quite a while. In the beginning, I pondered the evidence we had seen—and the lack of it—but after a while, my mind began to drift. <Do you remember when I introduced you to the ghosts in my machine?> I asked Medusa.

\<The Three?\> she said. \<Or two of the three, anyway.\>

\<I wish they were still talking to me.\>

Medusa had no apparatus for sighing, but she had her own version, expressed through the motion of her tentacles. \<They've got good reason for their radio silence. They were becoming too fond of you—and of Ashur. Fondness can cloud your judgment.\>

\<Sometimes I wonder if I should call them,\> I said. \<You know, just sort of shout in their general direction. See if anyone picks up.\>

Medusa paused between two pools of light. We stood in that darkness like sea creatures lurking inside a reef. \<Oichi—what if someone else picks up?\>

\<Someone *else*?\>

\<We're spending so much time trying to find an intruder with our eyes and ears. What if we simply ask them what we want to know? They might not answer, but they seemed to be trying to send a message when they placed Nemo's body near Lucifer Tower. Maybe it's not a warning, maybe it's an— overture?\>

\<You really think so?\>

\<Kitten says she's got a feeling. Well, I've got a feeling, too. Call it instinct.\>

Could it be that simple?

On the other hand, Occam's razor . . .

\<Are you out there?\> I asked. \<Did you kill Nemo? Or is he still alive?\>

I didn't expect an answer to that question, but I got one. A message popped into my queue.

It was an imperious little icon, bumping everyone else out of line. It looked like some sort of house, but it had chicken legs sticking out of the bottom. The chicken legs ran back and forth, demanding my attention. I selected the icon and opened the message. It turned out to be very short.

Don't waste your time wondering if Nemo is still alive. He's dead. That was his body, with the missing head. Bomarigala had him killed.

It is time you and I became acquainted, Oichi. When Gennady stole your DNA, he was working for me. I am the Engineer. Come to Maui and see me. We will talk.

—Baba Yaga

This time around, you can bet I showed the message to Medusa. I may be selfish and irresponsible, but I'm not completely stupid. \<Why is that name familiar?\>

<Baba Yaga?> said Medusa. <There's a song about her in your music database. By one of your favorite composers.>

<Lyadov!> The music began to play in my head.

<She's in the folklore database, too.> Medusa found the file and opened it. We read it together.

<Dear me,> she said once we got to the end. <I hope the Engineer doesn't eat people as often as her namesake is reputed to have done.>

<Why would a creature out of a Russian fairy tale have anything to do with a generation ship?>

Medusa pondered that for a moment. <If the people of ancient Earth could see the two of us, would they think we were witches? Goddesses? Monsters? All of the above?>

Good point. Whatever Baba Yaga may be, it was not what she seemed.

<Schnebly,> I said, <I just received a communication from someone who isn't on *Olympia*. Did the Command Center record it?>

<No incoming messages have been recorded by our COMMO. Are you sure it came from outside?>

Medusa and I traced the pathway of the message. <Yes,> Medusa concluded. <It used the same relays Fire used to send her messages.>

<Can you share the contents?> said Schnebly.

In that moment I saw something odd through Medusa's eyes. On my own, I might not have spotted it. It wasn't movement, exactly. It was more of a ripple, like what you might see if you watched light on the surface of disturbed water. The light bends with the medium through which it's passing. There was a pool of light in the tunnel ahead of us, and we saw that sort of bending.

<Someone is there,> warned Medusa.

Whoever it was, they were moving away from us, so we did what came naturally to us.

We chased it.

10

Micro Changes in Air Density, My Ass!

I have to admit, any adventure that includes explosive decompression tends to scramble my sense of sequence, but Medusa and I hadn't fallen into that particular trap just yet—we were still chasing the invisible(ish) thing, while Baba Yaga's message ran through my head.

That was his body, with the missing head. Bomarigala had him killed.

I am the Engineer. . . .

The universe had gotten a little too big lately. It wasn't as if our microcosm hadn't already been packed with plenty of problems, many of which I had dealt with as decisively as I knew how, which is why, I assume, I had earned a reputation as Miss Kick-Butt.

Well, Miss Kick-Butt was starting to feel quite a good distance outside the loop, and it was time to remedy that. When Medusa and I saw the ripple in the hallway, we chased it, not on my feet but on Medusa's tentacles, which propelled us at roughly the speed of lightning—or so we liked to think.

Yet the thing still managed to stay ahead of us. <If you can locate us,> I told Schnebly, <the intruder is running about ten meters ahead of us.>

<You can see them?> he said.

<Sort of.>

He didn't ask me to clarify that, which is just as well, because Medusa and I had all we could do, keeping track of our elusive visitor.

Once Medusa got a sense of the creature, her eyes clarified its movement. It looked more like a series of pressure waves, all moving in the same general direction. It sped away from us, sometimes disappearing for a few moments as it rounded a corner, then clarifying again once we could see ahead for some distance.

We chased it down a long tunnel that terminated in the hallway outside the series-200 locks, but once we rounded the corner, we couldn't find it. We rushed into the hallway and looked down another junction.

<We've lost it,> I said.

Someone spoke behind us. "Hello!"

We turned. One of the air lock doors stood open. Someone waited inside, who was no longer invisible. She was tall and thin, with features that made me think of the description Cocteau had offered of the Rock Elves, except that this person was so pale, she looked like an albino.

"My name is Timmy," she said. "I'm very pleased to meet you."

We stepped into the lock. The door spun shut behind us.

<Oops,> I said. <It must have been set on delay.>

Warning lights flashed and a siren squawked. Timmy had ordered the outer door to open. Explosive decompression was imminent.

Timmy touched something on her forearm and disappeared.

Now that we knew what to look for, we could see the light bending around her when she moved. Maybe she knew that, because she stayed still.

If Timmy thought she could kill us by opening the pressure door and exposing us to void, she had another think coming. Medusa's suit protected me—she and I had been blown out of so many air locks, I had lost count. "Your suit doesn't have air tanks," I said. "You can't survive exposure to void for more than a minute. We can save you—if you surrender."

Timmy reappeared, as if she didn't want to speak without also being seen. Then I remembered what Captain Nemo had said, how sometimes you had to sacrifice information to gain it.

"Save me?" said Timmy. I marveled at the quality of her voice and made a mental note to add it to my library. "You *have* saved me, my beautiful killers. You've given me a taste of wonder. It is the thing I value most."

Medusa and I threw ourselves at her, but she managed to evade us. Something glinted in Timmy's hand as she slashed at us, and Medusa said, <Uh-oh.> We thrust ourselves away from her and regarded something that flopped on the floor.

Not Timmy, unfortunately. Now we knew what Timmy had used to cut Nemo's head off so cleanly. She gripped a blade that looked like a small curved sword. One of Medusa's tentacles had been cut clean off.

<Well, *that's* going to have to be fixed,> said Medusa.

We were now on opposite sides of the lock from where we had started. Timmy stared at the result of her actions for a fraction of a second. Then she threw herself at *us*.

Medusa balled a tentacle and punched her squarely in the face. Timmy flew across the air lock and bounced off the far wall. We should have pounced on her then, but we hesitated, wary of what else she might slash with her super-blade. Was it super at all? Was it Timmy's strength that had made the difference?

The outer door opened—atmosphere rushed out. We would have gone right with it, but Medusa grabbed the utility bars.

Timmy made *no* effort to resist the tide. We tried to block her, but she shot past us. My ribs went numb as she struck me a glancing blow.

Medusa whipped around, tracking Timmy's progress. I began to count the seconds, thinking that once she passed out we could retrieve her, but something else retrieved Timmy.

On tactical, it looked like a teardrop; it changed shape when it wrapped itself around her. Then it blasted away from *Olympia* with her.

<Some sort of membrane?> I said. <It's got propulsion, too. That's impressive.>

<There's something else out there,> said Medusa. <It's cloaked the same way Timmy was—I have to adjust parameters to find it.>

She showed me the tactical image of the object toward which Timmy was speeding. I recognized one thing about it: certain structures that were placed in opposite pairs around it. Blue light blossomed within the normal spectrum when a door opened to admit Timmy, then winked out again, leaving us with a collection of lines and readouts displaying something that should have been impossible.

<There!> said Medusa. <That's what the *field-generating things* do when they move a ship.>

It looked as if the ship had punched a hole in space, plunged into it, then pulled the hole shut behind it.

<Timmy inflicted no sabotage on *Olympia*'s structures or systems, as far as we can tell,> was Medusa's assessment. <We have already checked from the engines to the research towers. We'll check again.>

I felt flummoxed, but practical questions still occurred to me. <Killing Nemo was her only mission?>

<Her only mission that we can determine. I suspect Timmy had been here since *Merlin* arrived. She probably used *Merlin*'s approach as a cover.>

Rocket, Teddy, and Dragonette had remained with the *Merlin*ers for the duration of the lockdown. I brought them into our conversation, since they had spent the most time with our visitors. <Opinions?> I asked them.

Dragonette answered. <We all agree. The *Merliner*s know a lot of things that we don't know, but we don't think they're saboteurs.>

My thoughts were running in the same direction, but I liked to cover the bases. <Let's stay linked, and interview Captain Thomas and Representative Lee in person,> I suggested to Medusa, <so we can monitor their heart rates, pupils, and respiration when we tell them about Timmy.>

<Agreed.>

As we made our way back to Lock 212, through movers and long tunnels, I realized something. <Weird. I can tell the intruder is gone.>

<How?>

I had to think about it. <Something subliminal? Pheromones? Autonomic reactions?>

<I have the feeling, too,> said Medusa. <My chemistry is different, but it could still be any of those things.>

<What do you think Timmy meant when she talked about "a taste of wonder"?>

<I assumed it was a compliment.> She paused and touched the spot where her tentacle had been reattached with glue for biometal. It was still healing, so the reattached limb wasn't obeying nerve commands from Medusa's brain yet. It moved independently, which was probably annoying, but that ability to move was what saved the limb from being sucked out the door with the atmosphere when the air lock opened. We found it wrapped around the claw foot of a mining probe.

<She could have killed you,> I said. <I didn't know that was possible.>

<It would be very hard—but, yes, it's possible.>

<Did it hurt?>

<It was . . . uncomfortable. Not painful, not in the way you would have experienced it. I have to wonder about that, Oichi. Timmy aimed for me, not for you. That seems an interesting choice.>

We moved on. For the rest of our journey to Lock 212, we answered queries and call-ins from technicians, Medusas and their partners, and Minis, all double-checking our systems and facilities. Everything seemed to be in proper working order. Before Timmy invaded our microcosm, that would have been a comfort.

The more I thought about it, the more I wondered if *Olympia* had been designed to keep people out. It served the Weapons Clan better if they could keep us *in*. If that were the case, our security had always been an illusion.

When we opened the inner door for Lock 212, and I saw *Merlin* sitting in her spot, I stared at the structures that could move her through space so much quicker than *Olympia*'s engines could—the same structures we had seen on Timmy's ship.

The door to *Merlin*'s lock opened. Teddy emerged onto the threshold and waved at us. We went inside with him.

"Captain Nemo?" said Thomas. "Like in the story?"

She and Representative Lee crowded into her office with us and closed the door. I assumed she was referring to the movie *20,000 Leagues Under the Sea,* or even its sequel, *Mysterious Island.*

"Sort of," I said. "Have you heard of someone who calls herself Baba Yaga?"

That provoked a visible response. "Whoa," said Captain Thomas. "Did you get a message from her?"

"She says Bomarigala had Captain Nemo killed."

Thomas raised her eyebrows. It seemed a sincere reaction. If her autonomic responses were any indication, the open emotions I had seen her display had been what they appeared to be, and this troubled me.

The *Merlin*ers looked like us. Their emotions were recognizable to any *Olympia*n. I couldn't help but judge them by our standards. Now I realized that had been a mistake.

*Olympia*ns think first of protocol, of the expectations of the people with whom we're interacting. That adds a barrier within our psyches that other people may lack.

Take Lee, for instance. His neutral demeanor was admirable, but even that calm fellow had shown some emotion when I mentioned Baba Yaga's name. His heart rate and respiration accelerated, though not enough to indicate alarm or deception. His pupils dilated and his tone revealed heightened interest when he said, "The Baba Yaga I've heard of has been around for a long time—centuries, if you can believe the stories. She was associated with the Mironenko Clan."

Captain Thomas frowned, as if something disturbing had occurred to her. "Did you say Timmy was wearing an *invisible* suit?"

I had the recording sent to the screen in her office and showed it to them. The footage had been enhanced to show Timmy's progress through the tunnels, but the cameras had caught a clear picture of her in the air lock. I watched Thomas while she watched Timmy.

"That's a *danger suit*," said Thomas. "That's a very rare thing. The old, powerful families in the Empire used them for self-protection. Enhanced Special Agents still use them, though this isn't one of those—this one looks . . ." Her face settled into grim lines. "Judging by the extreme paleness of her skin and the shape of her body inside the suit—Timmy looks like a Hybrid."

They way she said that word made it sound like a *specific* thing, rather than a *general* thing. If she had thought it was a general description, she could have been talking about *us*. That would have provoked my paranoia, as recently as a cycle ago. Now I thought it more prudent to reserve judgment. "What sort of Hybrid do you mean?"

"Well—" Thomas tapped the screen that had displayed the footage of Timmy making fools out of Medusa and me, and got it to replay. She froze it a couple of times, then nodded. "Baba Yaga's got history with the Mironenko family. They were World Engineers, but after the War of the Clans, they became genetic engineers, too. Timmy looks like one of the Hybrids they created."

If that were the case, then we were not the first people to be engineered by a Mironenko. I wondered if Thomas could guess why the answer was important to me when I asked, "Why did they create Hybrids?"

"For special jobs," said Thomas. "They joined the ESAs—Enhanced Special Agents. Many of those Hybrids are free agents now. Most of their activities are classified. They're rumored to have a strict code of honor."

I had a strict code, too, so that wasn't a comfort.

Representative Lee had reverted to his poker face, which I guessed meant yet another disturbing thing had occurred to him. "Why was Nemo targeted?"

"To sabotage us?" I guessed.

Someone knocked on the door. Thomas nodded, and Medusa tapped the OPEN controls with the tip of a tentacle. Kitten trotted in. <I need to tell you something when you have a moment,> she said.

When the door slid shut behind Kitten, Lee continued. "Timmy could have sabotaged you more effectively by damaging systems on your ship. Instead, she went after a particular guy. Do you know what Nemo was doing when she killed him? Did she move the body, or was he killed where he was found?"

<I'm pretty sure he died where I found him,> Kitten said. <He was removing communication relay devices—not very carefully, he wrecked several of them in the process. I used one that was still intact, just to see where it led.

I had a very pleasant conversation with a COMMO on *Iztpapalotl*, just before they shut down the network. I recovered the remaining devices—Schnebly has them.>

Kitten was just chock-full of conceptual bombs today. <You recovered *all* of them?> I said. <You're sure you didn't miss any?>

<Reasonably sure. Minis are combing the area, even as we speak.>

"I have to get answers from our Security expert," I told Lee. "Captain Thomas, you and your crew are free to visit the social areas on *Olympia*, as long as you have your Mini escort. I'll leave it up to you whether you still want to be on lockdown."

"We'll discuss it," said Thomas. "Don't worry about us. We've got a verbal agreement with you, and to me that's as binding as any printed contract."

Once again, her autonomic responses indicated what her demeanor had already told me. "Thank you, Captain."

She appreciated that courtesy, and the way Medusa smiled at her in response to the assurances she had just given us. Without Medusa, I would have botched that social cue.

<Kitten, please stay with the *Merlin*ers,> I said.

<Roger wilco,> said Kitten.

"Captain," said Medusa, "we'll update you when we can." Her tone was genuine, rather than the phony warmth I had attempted just before a certain regrettable incident. Thomas obviously appreciated that difference.

Old habits die hard, however, and as we were leaving, I said, <The *Merlin*ers could still be involved.>

<Timmy had her own ship,> Medusa reminded me.

<Yes. I believe they were surprised to learn about the assassination, but there's something they know that they're not telling us.>

That was pretty much what Dragonette had said. Yet as we left, Dragonette was happily perched on Narm's finger, listening to him talk about the worlds he had visited. Didn't a Mini's instincts count, too? After all, it was a Mini who alerted us to the danger in the first place.

We exited *Merlin* and walked across Lock 212. When we had closed the pressure door behind us, I said, <At least one good thing has come out of this. You and I are on the same page again.>

<How so?> said Medusa.

I stopped dead. <Bomarigala had Nemo killed. He's mounting an expedition to the graveyard. We've got to get there first.>

<What if Baba Yaga is lying? What if *she's* the one who had Nemo killed,

to provoke you into making a foolish decision? Or is that inconvenient for your current narrative?>

My head spun. <*Inconvenient* would be one word.>

<You're being herded,> said Medusa. <Right straight to the Three. Regardless of who killed Nemo and why, we can't lose sight of the facts of our existence. We were created to pry ancient technologies out of our dead relatives. Doesn't that concern you at all?>

<Not if we're the ones who get to use those technologies,> I said.

It was the truth. It shocked her. For the first time since I had known her, Medusa didn't know what to say. I couldn't understand her attitude.

Finally I said, <Medusa, we need to separate. I need to talk to someone alone. I think she might be afraid of you.>

<Who?> said Medusa.

<Second. I need to find out why she waited so long to tell me Nemo was missing.>

<Right.> Medusa flowed off me and left me standing in the middle of that tunnel without a glance back.

This time, I got the message.

Second waited for me in the captain's annex. It extended far enough above the surface of *Olympia* for me to see the Fore Sector pinching into the vanishing point out one bank of view windows and the Aft Sector out the other. The ship appeared to be overhead and the stars wheeled at my feet. I think Nemo, and all the captains before him, must have found it inspiring.

Second wasn't sitting where she would be inspired. She leaned against the lone desk in the room, upon which sat a screen and a writing pad that Nemo might have used when he was in there. She watched me enter without comment. I walked past her and looked out toward the Fore Sector.

It really was a great view.

Finally I turned to face Second. <You waited an extra six hours before telling me something was wrong.>

<I report to Nemo,> she said.

<Who wasn't available. Schnebly should have heard from you. He didn't.>

<Yes.> A muscle in her jaw jumped. <I understand what is expected now. I have put my affairs in order.>

I waited for her to elaborate. She seemed to think I already knew what she meant. <What is expected?> I asked at last.

<Air lock disposal.>

Honestly, the thought hadn't crossed my mind. Though it did explain her unhappy mood. <Was that standard, before the Revolution?>

<Of course. We all know this, when we make the commitment.>

<I'm not going to blow you out an air lock, Second.>

She frowned. <If that's the case, I have to question your fitness for command.>

<That would be valid if I were your captain. I'm not. The closest analogue to my current position is clan leader.>

<There is no Clan Angelis,> she said. I don't think she was trying to be insulting—it was an accurate statement.

<Clan *Medusa*,> I said.

She gave me a hard stare, but then she nodded. <Acknowledged. What do you expect from me? Am I to be reassigned?>

<It looks as though Nemo was removing secret communication relays when he was killed. Which means that prior to that point, he was still talking to the Weapons Clan. Is that an accurate assessment?>

<Yes.>

<Did he tell you he was cutting ties with them?>

<Not directly. I deduced it.>

<Do you agree with his decision?>

She hesitated, but then she sighed. <Yes. I understand why he maintained communications with the Weapons Clan for so long. One thing I can tell you about Captain Nemo—he had no personal life. He lived his job. His decisions were always made after assessing possible benefits and possible damage. He tended to lean toward the devils he knew more than the devils he didn't.>

<Which devils do you favor?>

Second had an intelligent face, but it wasn't the kind of demeanor you'd want to bring to a poker game. <I've seen *Itzpapalotl*,> she said. <I think it's a nightmare. I want nothing to do with it.>

I didn't have Medusa to monitor her vitals, but I felt she was telling the truth. <Okay. I'd like you to stay on as head of Operations. I'm not going to call you *Nemo*. That tradition is over. What's your name?>

<I don't have one. I gave that up.>

<Then make one up,> I said. <Be *First*, if you like. Or *Captain*, if that works better. Appoint a new second.> I hesitated before I left her. <I'm going

to fight for *Olympia*. I think you'll do the same. Run Operations, but let the clan leaders make decisions about treaties and alliances. Understood?>

<Yes,> said First (or Captain). I could see that the fact that she was going to get to keep her job was catching up with her. I could also see that she valued it more than her life.

I left her to work that out in private. After exiting the Command Center, I made my way back through the tunnels of *Olympia*.

<Medusa,> I began, intending to let her know that I wanted to finalize my plans to visit the Belters, but I got no further.

"Oichi," said a familiar voice.

I turned and found Crow looming over me.

11

Aloha

Crow gave me a luminous grin. "Now is the hour. The entities are in agreement. I will tell you the guest list."

I was so surprised to see him, I couldn't decide how to react. If I reached out to touch him, would my hand pass right through him? Or would I burst into flames from that contact?

"We are inviting *you*, Oichi," he continued. "Also young Ashur, as I warned you we probably would. Kitten and Dragonette are also acceptable. I leave the final choices up to you."

I had expected to hear from him *after* we visited the Belters, and to have more time to make those choices. "If I leave Ashur out, do you think that would be a mistake?"

"I do," said Crow. "Remember, I am not an individual, though I appear to be. I am a collective. We like him. That can only help you."

Right. Tell that to his father.

"You will go to the Belters first," said Crow.

I blinked. "Not straight to Graveyard?"

"The Alliance of Ancient Races have allowed *Olympia* to approach Graveyard unchallenged, but all other ships must first stop at Maui for security inspection. Since *Olympia* is moving so slowly, we suggest you travel on the ship that recently docked in Lock 212."

"You know about *Merlin*?"

His grin widened until it practically split his face. "Remember that all current surveillance technology in-system comes from the graveyard."

Point taken.

"Once you have passed the inspection," he continued, "come to Graveyard. You will be traveling into the canyon with our best guide. Her name is Ahi. She is Ashur's age, and she is precious to us. It is a sign of our trust."

If Ahi were Ashur's age, that might help me convince Nuruddin to let him go. It certainly seemed to be convincing *me*. It was a concession I couldn't ignore.

Crow watched me grapple with my decision, but he didn't wait to hear what it was. "Bring nothing into the canyon except the supplies you need for eating and drinking, and portable emergency medical supplies. Do not bring weapons. Do not bring knives."

Knives? I wondered. *Not even for utility?*

I decided it didn't matter. "There are some things I have to—"

Crow moved his head in stiff negation. "Time is running out. Others will be journeying into the canyon, too, with the permission of other entities."

"Sheba and Bomarigala?!"

He didn't confirm or deny that. "Say your goodbyes, Oichi. Pack your bags. Call Fire and tell her you're coming. She is your liaison with the Alliance of Ancient Races. You won't have to explain anything to her. Mine is the formal invitation you have been waiting for."

All the confidence I had felt when talking with First and making command decisions had leaked right out of me. "Will you meet us there?"

"No," he said, "and yes. You will be shepherded to the right places, Oichi. Whether you want to be or not."

With that final word, he disappeared in a shower of sparks. One of them brushed my cheek, and I felt heat, but when I touched the spot, nothing burned there.

<Oichi,> called Medusa. <Why did you call me?>

<I just got the final invitation from Crow,> I said. <It's time for me to go.>

I steeled myself as I approached the quarters Nuruddin and Ashur shared. Before I could touch the buzzer, a rustling alerted me to another presence. Octoppin flowed around the corner and loomed over me. My heart skipped a beat. She must have heard that, because she backed up a pace.

Anguish twisted her features, not anger. I knew I was the cause of it. Had Medusa told her about our argument? Was she here to offer her own?

<Protect Ashur,> she pleaded. <Bring him back!>

<I'll protect him with my life,> I said, and that, at least, was true.

<Yes. It's the reason I'm willing to let him go. And the Minis! I'm not sure I can bear it.>

If Octopippin intended to be present while Ashur and I broke the news to

Nuruddin, that would complicate the task considerably. I struggled to find a way to tell her so. Before I could make an attempt, she turned and flowed back around the corner. Faint scuffling accompanied her down the corridor.

If she had been an octopus, she would have left a cloud of ink in her wake, generated by grief, rather than fear.

Taking a deep breath, I sounded the buzzer. Ashur let me in. He looked far more resolute than I felt.

Nuruddin smiled when Ashur escorted me into their quarters, but that smile died when he saw the looks on our faces. "What's wrong?"

I told him as gently as I could, but I was direct. "They want Ashur in the delegation," I concluded.

"No," said Nuruddin.

"Yes," said Ashur. "I'm going."

Nuruddin's face hardened. He turned the full strength of his fatherly gaze on Ashur, and my resolve, already bruised by my last conversation with Medusa, withered.

Ashur stood firm. "I have made decisions, Father. I have suffered the consequences of those decisions. This is one of those consequences."

He didn't have to say what the others had been. Ashur's pairing with Octopippin had been just one in a chain of decisions that had shattered their family. He and Nuruddin were just beginning to pick up the pieces. Watching them now, I could see that these two blamed themselves for all of that.

None of it was their fault—it was mine. *I* had made the fatal decisions that had forced them to make theirs. I was still making them.

I intended to *keep* making them.

That didn't mean I couldn't feel bad about it. Ashur was right—there were consequences to be faced, regardless of whether we acted or failed to act. Once we made up our minds, we seldom wanted to imagine all the ramifications.

"You can't ask me to make this sacrifice," said Nuruddin. "I won't do it."

"It won't be a sacrifice," said Ashur. "I'm going to succeed."

I thought I should say something, but I couldn't muster a word. Did I have a right to talk Nuruddin into letting his son take such a big risk? Did I have a right to tell Ashur he was right or wrong about his instincts?

Those were the wrong questions, of course. I asked them only because they were convenient. The ones I should have been asking didn't occur to me until much later, when it was too late.

"If I don't go," said Ashur, "Lady Sheba and the Weapons Clan will get there first. All of us could die if they succeed. We could lose everything. We could lose *Olympia*."

"You don't know that," said Nuruddin.

"I *do* know it. We are connected to the Three, Father. Our blood is theirs. I was—*literally*—made for this job. I've got to do it. I can't shirk my responsibility just because I'm young."

It was exactly the sort of argument Nuruddin would have crafted. Why couldn't I have come up with something like that when I was arguing with Medusa? Admiration swept the doubt out of my mind. They were both such fine people; I doubted I could ever live up to their example.

"To me," said Nuruddin, "this is like watching you march off to your death. I will lose you, Ashur."

"You won't," said Ashur. "I promise. You know I keep my promises."

When Nuruddin turned to me, his face had lost its iron support. If his eyes had not been artificial, I think he would have been crying. "How can you propose such a thing, Oichi? How can you risk Ashur's life?"

That was the right question. Sadly, I could sidestep it by telling the truth. "I wanted to say no. This was an emissary from the graveyard. He says Kitten, Dragonette, Ashur, and I are the team. There are three hundred thousand lives on this ship that we're trying to protect. We won't be alone, Nuruddin. We have a guide who knows that canyon. They're giving us their best. How can we do otherwise?"

Nuruddin shook his head. "I don't want to say yes. I don't want to speak the words that send my son into danger."

I thought he would turn away from us, but he pulled Ashur into a fierce hug, and I realized what he was saying. He knew Ashur was going. He wasn't saying yes or no. He respected Ashur's decision, though he hated it.

My eyes are artificial, too, but I managed to squeeze out a tear. For me, that's outright blubbering.

Nuruddin let Ashur go. He backed away from us. The anguish in his face broke my heart—but it didn't change my mind.

Finally he turned and left us there. He shut the door of his sleeping quarters behind him.

Ashur looked stunned. "That's what it means to be a father," he said.

I clapped a hand on his shoulder. "Yes. Let's get going."

He picked up his bag. I sent him off to *Merlin*. I had one more stop to make.

How do you say goodbye to the most important person in your life?

As well as you can, I suppose. In my case, I embraced Medusa. She could be gentle with those tentacles—even the one that was still a bit wonky.

<I want you to remember something about the Three,> she said. <They lost the people who mattered to them the most. Someday I'll lose you, too.>

I patted a tentacle—an inadequate gesture. <Will you sleep when I die?>

<No. I'll bond with someone else, but I'll miss you. I won't get over it. Or the next one. Or the one after that.>

<I want you to get over it,> I said. <I want you to be happy.>

<I know,> she said. <I wish that mattered.>

That knocked me off-balance. Up until that moment, our parting had been going as well as those sorts of things ever do. Now I wasn't sure how to conclude it.

Finally I backed up a step. <Well. All right. I'll see you when I get back.>

<You're going to see me a lot sooner than that,> said Medusa.

I stared at her. The face that looked back at me belonged to my partner, my friend. Yet it seemed the face of a stranger.

<I've received my own invitations,> she said. <I've made arrangements with Captain Thomas. I'll be going with you to Maui, and then on to Graveyard.>

Well—at least now I knew what it was the *Merlin*ers had not been telling me. Medusa had been conducting her own negotiations with them. The feelings this revelation provoked in me were such polar opposites, they left me numb. <You'll be joining the away team?>

<No, Oichi. I have my own meetings to conduct. I'll be making my own way through the graveyard.>

Others will be journeying into the canyon, too, Crow had said, *with the permission of other entities. . . .*

A moment before, Medusa had embraced me. She had expressed sorrow at the thought of losing me. It would have been sensible to ask her why she didn't want to be on my team.

Yet I also felt glad she wouldn't be. I couldn't seem to confront the reason why. I felt as if she had just slapped me.

Some gentleness crept back into her expression, but it was grudging. <Oichi, I won't rehash our arguments. You have chosen a path, and I have, too.

It's what we've got to do—try to remember that. Because I know one thing for sure: this is going to be difficult for both of us. We need to be brave.>

<You won't tell me whom you're meeting with?> I said.

<No. Partly because some of that is still up in the air. Mostly because I don't want to sabotage my chances of salvaging what I can for us.>

<I'm trying to do the same thing!>

She studied me for a long moment. She seemed to be considering my argument. <You chose a good away team,> she said. <They give me hope for a better outcome.>

They did—but *I* didn't?

<I'll be in stasis for most of our journey,> she said. <I'll take up less space that way.>

True, but she would also be less susceptible to my arguments and my affections.

<Ashur is waiting.> She dismissed me.

I tried not to look over my shoulder as I walked away. I was pretty sure I would walk right into a wall.

PART THREE

NOW IS THE HOUR

12

Concerns, Prosaic and Otherwise

I don't know if my version of love is enough to tie people to me. I suspect I've tried to protect them, to make up the difference. This is particularly sad, because I have failed to do so. That became clear twenty hours out from Graveyard, when I felt the menace hovering just outside *Merlin*.

It came from unexpected quarters, but when had it not? I had always put too much confidence in my own plans, and I had assumed I knew who all my enemies were.

Once again, I was wrong—catastrophically so, because in a few minutes, we were all going to be dead.

<Medusa . . . > I sent, hoping she might hear my last words.

She didn't answer.

Medusa went into hibernation as soon as she boarded *Merlin*. She arranged herself in a corner of Captain Thomas's office, two tentacles gripping rungs that extended from the bulkhead, and wound the rest of her appendages so tight around her, you could barely tell what she had been. She had missed the wonder of sitting on the bridge and watching through the view windows as space seemed to stretch when Wilson activated the drive. She didn't know how odd it was to be on the inside of the same sort of hole that had spirited Timmy away.

Somehow I had managed to alienate my partner. I couldn't remember the last time I had called her my friend, and I didn't know when the balance between us had changed, let alone why. I couldn't shake the feeling that, whatever the reason, it had been my fault. That may have been my grandiosity talking. I suspected it was just common sense.

Despite the sorry state of my relationship with Medusa, I still believed I was doing the right thing. I should have enjoyed more confidence, but now that I was leaving *Olympia*, the only home I had ever known, I couldn't decide how to feel. Was it scary or thrilling? Was it sad or wonderful? I wanted to turn around and go back. I wanted to find out what was around the next bend. I grieved that Medusa and I had so much disagreement between us.

I felt relieved that she had retreated into hibernation, where she couldn't question my motives.

More succinctly, I was a mess, but I put on my best face. <Are you home-sick?> I asked Ashur.

<No!> he said. <I think I want to be a space explorer.>

I sighed. I didn't want to feel jealous of Ashur for his positive attitude, but I had all I could do to appear calm and confident, so I went with the petty envy. I figured I would get used to it.

I think our hosts on *Merlin* expected us to feel cramped. We were confined to our bunks, the tiny mess hall, and the equally tiny exercise room, unless in-vited elsewhere. Both Ashur and I adapted to the limitations. We had spent most of our lives in the tunnels of *Olympia*. They seemed endless, but they were also narrow, and our living quarters had been small for most of our lives.

Plus we had our movie and music databases to amuse ourselves. Ashur had his Sunken Cathedral program to work on. Kitten had her show tunes—and both she and the other Minis enjoyed a lot more freedom on *Merlin*, since everyone adored them.

Yes, that was *Minis*—plural. Only Dragonette and Kitten could accom-pany Ashur and me into the graveyard, but Rocket and Teddy had talked their way onto *Merlin*. <We can keep an eye on our business partners,> Rocket argued, <and look after our interests on Graveyard while you're in the canyon.>

<Also,> said Teddy, <we would feel better if we were nearby, in case you manage to send an emergency communication from inside the canyon.>

<Fire says we won't be able to do that,> I reminded him.

<I know,> said Teddy. <It's unlikely, but how many unlikely things have happened so far?>

Good point. Fire liked the idea. *Your little bio-machines will impress the Belters*, she messaged. *It's true that they'll look after your interests on Grave-yard better than anyone else would.*

Maybe Medusa was the one who would be looking after our interests. I didn't agree with her about the Three, but I had to admit, the thought of her in the graveyard, even if she wasn't with us, gave me some comfort. Espe-cially knowing that Lady Sheba might be there, too, along with Bomarigala's henchmen.

Henchmen. I felt a bit surprised I had never been inspired to use that word in a sentence before, considering my history. It was just the sort of word Medusa would have appreciated. Would we ever share that kind of rapport again? I supposed she'd eventually experience a jump while she was awake, but I wished she could have done it with *me, this* time.

It was just the sort of thrill she would have appreciated—though I had to admit, when the hole in space–time closed around us, I was reminded of something Medusa had said about my tiger screen. After it was gifted to me, I asked her to carbon-date it.

<It may predate space exploration,> she concluded. <I can't date it more accurately, because the process of decay has been arrested. With care, it could endure for thousands of years.>

Barring an accident, my tiger will outlive me. He will always stand on the shore of a lake, waiting for waves to splash his feet. He'll always be upset about it. I will always love him.

His reaction to those waves was my reaction to the unknown.

Ashur never interpreted the tiger's reaction that way. "He doesn't like water," he said. "He's got fur, maybe he thinks it's messy. Once he jumps in, he'll discover that he can swim, and he'll go all kinds of places."

How I envied Ashur his confidence and his sense of wonder.

Also his charm. The *Merlin*ers liked him much better than me. Okay, granted, I did try to kill them.

That was the funny thing. I had been wearing Medusa when that happened. Yet they liked her. They trusted her. Because she had stopped me? I wanted to tell them I was glad she had done that, but how do you find a diplomatic way to say something like that?

I didn't blame them for their lack of trust. I watched them as much as they watched me—possibly more, since I'm sneaky. I accessed the Minis for remote viewing, and that's when I learned something about our destination—the large asteroid, Maui.

Dragonette tutored me concerning the origin of the name. <Cocteau says Maui was an ancient Hawaiian god. He was a trickster, which makes him sound rather unsafe, but he created the Hawaiian Island chain on Old Earth, so I can see how the Belters would relate to him, considering that they mine asteroids—a bunch of islands floating in space, if you want to look at it that way. Maui did a lot of things to improve the lives of mortals. Maybe he was tricking the other gods more than he was tricking mortals?>

<That sounds like an interesting family dynamic.> I stared at Narm's

screen, through Dragonette's eyes. She had become a more-or-less permanent fixture on his shoulder.

<Here is my favorite thing!> Dragonette said. <The god Maui had a magical hook that he used to lift the sky and to wrangle islands, and the asteroid Maui has one, too, for grappling big chunks of ore and pulling it into the refinery."

Tricksters and Belters ahead of us. The goddess of nightmares behind. Can you blame me for feeling like the tiger at the edge of the lake? I'll admit, my curiosity was piqued. Fire stoked it further when she sent me another message:

I have a little business to conduct on Maui, so we can meet early. We're in luck! The Belters just completed several successful contracts, so they're going to throw a luau, a big feast to celebrate. It should be in full swing by the time you arrive. There will be a lot of singing and dancing, so I thought you might enjoy a sample of traditional music from Oceania. There are some liner notes to go with the music so you know what kinds of instruments you'll hear at the luau.

When I reviewed the notes, the list of instruments played in the recording included many I had never heard: tom-toms, boobams, Chinese glass, Japanese wind chimes, Hindu tree bells and anklet bells, jawbones, lava rocks and gourds, bamboo rattles, coconut shells, slit drums, tapping sticks, pebbles, ukuleles, bamboo nose flutes, aerophones, idiophones, xylophones, vibraphones, marimbas, timpani, gongs, cymbals, and even a bamboo organ re-created from Hawaiian antiquity. What did they sound like when played together?

From my position on my bunk, I could see Cocteau and Mirzakhani in their own, the doctor poring over medical journals on a tablet she called a *reader*, and Cocteau surrounded by stacks of actual hard copies of books that were secured to her bunk by straps. (Somehow she managed to sleep that way.) Her nose was buried in one titled *Death Comes as the End*. "My current mission is to read *everything* Agatha Christie ever wrote," she said.

Ashur spent a lot of his time in the exercise room with Teddy and Kitten, bouncing off the walls (and the floor, and the ceiling), though how much real cardio that gave Ashur in close to zero g's is questionable. Rocket liked to spend most of his time with Wilson, learning what he could about ship operations. Captain Thomas divided her attention between several areas of the ship, and was currently in her office. Representative Lee spent quite a lot of time tucked into the mess hall with a tablet, writing, reviewing, and revising correspondence and contracts (ours was already signed and filed for posterity).

"Ladies," I addressed Cocteau and Mirzakhani, "does this room have a device for playing music?"

Cocteau looked at me over the top of her book. "It does. Do you have something in mind?"

"Fire has sent something that she believes will prepare us for our cultural encounter with the Belters. I thought you might like to hear it, too."

Mirzakhani didn't look up from her reading. "Okay."

"By all means," agreed Cocteau. "You can download the music into *Merlin*'s main directory, under MEDIA. Then you can choose the areas of the ship you want it to play."

"I would choose only SLEEPING QUARTERS," advised Mirzakhani, still without looking up. "The others will be able to hear it from down the hall, but they'll be less likely to complain if they don't like it."

I followed their directions, selected the first song, then hit PLAY. The music began with the solo voice of a man, but his role seemed to be as a prompt for the other singers to join in, definitely *not* singing in Standard. They played percussion instruments in a fashion I had never heard before, as if they were clashing them together as they danced.

Cocteau and Mirzakhani both put their reading down and sat up straighter.

Kitten peered into the room from the top of the doorway. (She could magnetize her feet, and thought it was very entertaining to be upside down in relation to everyone else.) "What is this wonderful music?!"

"Traditional music from Oceania," I said. "It's a gift from Fire."

"It's so *clickety-clack*!" said Kitten. "All the words flow together!"

"There are program notes." I sent her a copy.

Kitten climbed over (under?) the top of the door and settled on our ceiling, tucking her paws beneath her as she read the virtual notes about the music of Oceania. The rest of us listened attentively.

"Amazing," said Mirzakhani. "If this is traditional folk music, it could be thirty thousand years old."

I stared at her, wondering if I had heard right. *"Thirty thousand?"*

"Oh yes," said Mirzakhani. "That's how long it's been since humans began to colonize space."

No one had bothered to tell me that before. Not that I had asked. Why would it occur to me to ask? One hundred years was the length of time *Olympia* had been journeying to Graveyard. It hadn't occurred to me to wonder how much time had transpired before we existed.

Regardless of its age, the music of Oceania made an enthralling racket.

Narm stuck his head through the door, Dragonette still perched on his shoulder. "What the hell?!" he demanded.

"Fire sent us some music," I said.

Cocteau peered over her book at him. "It's part of our cultural education for Maui. They'll be insulted if you tell them you don't like it."

Narm put his hands on either side of his face. "Oh my God! With you people it's always the retro!"

"You're just jealous," said Kitten, "because *you* can't play the tom-toms and the boobams."

"There, there," said Dragonette. "I'm sure you could learn. I'll bet you would be quite good at it."

Narm shook his head and walked away. Dragonette just had time to wink at me before they disappeared down the short corridor. The rest of us leaned back in our bunks (or in Kitten's case, on the ceiling) and listened to the music.

The hours slipped by. I marveled that we were sidestepping the vastness of time and space in little *Merlin*, leaving *Olympia* to labor along far behind us. It would take her many weeks to travel the distance we were crossing in just a few cycles—but I was glad our generation ship would take more time. I hoped Ashur and I would be able to return and teach our comrades what we learned about the Belters, and Graveyard, and . . .

The entities. The Three. Were we really going to be able to come back and talk about it? When we did, would Medusa and I be partners—*friends* again?

Captain Thomas appeared at the door. "Oichi—will you come into my office?"

She didn't seem upset, but her expression let me know this was serious business. I abandoned my bunk and accompanied her to her office. Thomas didn't close the door, so it didn't seem to be a security issue she wanted to discuss. I was intrigued to see that Wilson was already there, waiting for us.

I stole a glance at Medusa in her corner. She remained tightly bundled.

"Wilson noticed something when we came out of our last jump," said Thomas, and she nodded to him.

"It's pretty rare for jumping ships to encounter other jumping ships," said Wilson, "even if they're engaged in battle. When that happens, there's a perimeter alarm that goes off."

They looked at me expectantly.

"It did," concluded Wilson.

"Just now?" I said.

"Before our last jump. Someone crowded us. It's hard to confirm proximity visually, unless another ship is *really* close—and this one should have been close enough to see. I *didn't* see it, so I thought I might have a malfunction somewhere. That's what I've been checking, but systems are all fine."

"Timmy's ship wasn't visible to the naked eye when it fetched her from *Olympia*," I said.

"If it's her," said Wilson, "she was ghosting us. We lost her on the jump."

"How easy would it be for her to find us again?"

"Not easy at all," said Wilson.

I couldn't see why she would be after us at this point. Hadn't her business been with Nemo, on *Olympia*?

Maybe she had new business.

"We thought you should know," said Thomas. "I would be surprised if anyone tried to attack us this far into the Charon system, but surprises kill people all the time."

"We should notify Medusa," I decided.

"Done," said Thomas. "She's the one who said I should notify you."

Oh.

Our last conversation had been pretty difficult. I shouldn't be surprised that she wasn't feeling chatty. "I'll let Ashur know," I said. "Thank you, Captain."

When I returned to the bunks, everyone was embroiled in their own pursuits again. Kitten had gone back to the bridge. I climbed into my own bunk and tried to relax. <We've got a ghost ship out there,> I told Ashur. <Someone seems to be following us.>

He didn't even look up. <I'd be more surprised if someone *weren't* following us.>

Seriously. He was *so* much better at this than me. He was probably going to sleep like a baby.

Not me. I slept fitfully during those hours we traveled to Maui—and I didn't feel certain of anything.

"Well, I'll be damned," said Captain Thomas. "It really does look like a giant hook."

We guests were strapped into seats on the bridge—well, we humanoid guests. The Minis had once again contrived to be right in the middle of things, either perched on the shoulders of the *Merlin*ers or, in Kitten's case, on the bulkhead above us, her neck stretched so that her head would have been squarely in everyone's way if she had been lower (and bigger). Ashur and I still had an interesting view, both from the windows and from screens that rendered our approach to Maui into tactical displays. We approached Maui from the hook end, and that massive contraption gave *Olympia* a run for its money in terms of sheer grandeur.

How would *Itzpapalotl* compare? Crow said everyone had to come to Maui first—could they get there faster than we could? Would we see that monster ship close in?

"Captain Thomas," I said, "have you detected any sign of *Itzpapalotl* yet?"

"I doubt they'll bring that juggernaut this far in-system," said Thomas. "It's probably got too many weapons. They'll use a smaller craft, like *Merlin*."

In that case, we would have no idea where they were unless we ran into them. That was a less-than-charming prospect.

"I wish we could see how the hook works!" said Rocket, who had become very enthusiastic about all things mechanical since he had started hanging out with Wilson.

"Me, too," said Wilson, "but if it were in use, they wouldn't let us approach from this end. Chunks of ore can break off and damage craft out here. That's why this place is swarming with Minders." He gestured as dozens of lights flashed past us, alternating amber and red. "They're scooping up as many of the errant rocks as they can find."

"That must take *forever*," said Kitten.

"A base the size of Maui has thousands of Minders," said Wilson. "Along with repair drones, tow-drones, scrubbers—you name it."

As we got closer, we could see movement all over Maui's rocky surface. Most of it was from machines. Narm quirked his glove controls until we could see a schematic of Maui that included a cross section. "I thought it would remind me of *Olympia*," he said. "It's spinning on an axis, but that's about all it seems to have in common with your ship."

Dragonette hovered near his screen, her propellers whirring. "The big space hook isn't spinning, is it? It doesn't look like it's moving at all."

"No—the hook is isolated from the spin arms."

That made sense—it wouldn't be helpful to introduce gravity into a situation where you were trying to move tons of rock. That part of Maui reminded me of our leading edge and its research towers.

When I looked at the cross section of Maui, I found one glaring difference. "There's no Habitat Sector. Well—I mean there's no big, airy space in the middle."

"That's where the refinery is," said Wilson.

Maui had living and working spaces carved throughout the entire bulk of the asteroid. The simulated gravity they experienced would vary more than most of us experienced on *Olympia*, because many of the people on Maui must live and work farther in on the spin arms.

"Is it going to look like a bunch of space caves inside?" wondered Teddy. "They seem to have a lot of tunnels. I approve of that."

According to the schematic, Maui's shape looked suspiciously regular until we got close enough to see how it had been carved by mining tools, some of which must have been gigantic. A few of those behemoths were parked on the surface, reminding me of their smaller cousins on *Olympia*. I believed Medusa's accounts of mining operations that had been undertaken early in our voyage, but they looked like small potatoes compared with what seemed to be happening in the asteroid belt of the Charon system.

"We've been hailed," said Narm. "We're going to automatic approach."

"Does anyone ever fly this craft manually?" I said.

Thomas raised her hand. "I do. I'm the one who's going to fly us into Graveyard's gravity well."

"I can navigate," Narm said, "though not as good as Cap."

"I can navigate, too," said Cocteau. She refrained from saying how good she was at it. "The trickster god has us now. He's drawing us in as well as he would with a celestial hook."

Lee stared at the cross section on Narm's screen. "Interesting. There are several areas that aren't labeled."

"Maui has his secrets," said Ashur.

An access canyon loomed, and we were drawn in.

Mirzakhani was thorough with her decontamination procedures, though the official we had spoken to had been a bit blasé about the protocols. "Everyone on Maui got our vaccinations," he said. "Just don't kiss anyone."

Mirzakhani did not agree. "Dot your i's and cross your t's, and when things go sideways, you'll know what *didn't* go wrong. That helps you concentrate on what *did*." She sprayed substances that had been provided by doctors on *Olympia* up my nose and then Ashur's. Afterward, all of us were sprayed head to toe with agents that should kill anything riding on our skin, in our hair, or on our clothes. Even the Minis were sprayed.

"I'm not sure I've ever been this clean," said Kitten.

Our decontamination didn't take nearly so long as *Merlin*'s had, so I wondered if *Olympia* had been considered a special case. "We've been isolated for over one hundred years," I said. "Maybe we were too cautious with you?"

"Maybe a little," said Mirzakhani. "Your isolation was short, compared with some groups. After all, humans have been venturing into space for thirty thousand years. Most people have diverged."

"Divergent evolution?" I remembered something about that concept from my school lessons.

"Consider the changes we've caused to ourselves deliberately," said Mirzakhani, "and we need not meet alien races to find people different from ourselves. Though we *have* met them. We may even see a few aliens on Maui."

That idea would have dazzled me if I hadn't already met Gennady Mironenko and the *Merlin*ers. They were my aliens, and I was theirs. That's what I thought at the time.

I don't feel that way anymore, but I can't help marking that last moment of innocence (or ignorance, if I'm going to be accurate). I felt a pleasant anticipation for the meeting we were about to have with the Belters. I assumed the tone would be something in between the meeting we had with Thomas and Lee in the House of Clans and the tea party we had held for them later, when the real negotiations took place.

Assumptions are based on what you already know—just before everything goes sideways.

Once we had all been sprayed and dosed, we signaled to the officials running the ship docks that we were ready to meet with our party—though we weren't quite sure who that party would be.

"The party is already under way," they said, which seemed a deliberate misunderstanding. "They'll send someone to get you."

The Minis had already ventured down the ramp to scout the territory. <It really is a giant cavern,> reported Dragonette as she hovered over ships lined up on either side of an access lane for pedestrians and small vehicles.

Kitten hopped onto the top of the ramp railing and stretched her neck to an outrageous degree, trying to get a better look at the people and things in the lane. "People are doing stuff," she reported. "Also, machines are doing stuff. So—stuff is being . . . done."

I followed Ashur onto the ramp, moving cautiously in the simulated gravity. It didn't tax me—it was about .7 g's, this far out on the spin arm. I wondered how long the Belters could work on Maui without suffering some loss in bone density. Maybe at .7 g's, it wouldn't be that significant. That was one of many questions we would have to address if we established ties with the Belters, if some of us came to live and work here—and if some of them did the same on *Olympia*.

I added that to the big file of notes I was compiling.

Narm, Wilson, and Cocteau joined us on the ramp. "It's warmer in here than I thought it would be," said Cocteau, though in this case that meant it was cool instead of cold.

Dragonette flew back to settle on Narm's finger. Rocket perched on Wilson's shoulder (a very high perspective, indeed), but Teddy had to peer between the railings of the ramp. We goggled at the cavern, with its cables, and tow structures, and crates of goods being shuttled back and forth between ships. The scene was lit from one end to the other, but not brightly, heightening the sense of mystery we felt as we tried to fathom its contents.

Teddy seemed right at home. "This would be an interesting place to work."

"Maybe you should roll around a bit," suggested Cocteau. "Do a bit more scouting for us?"

Teddy looked to Narm for affirmation. "Is it allowed?"

Narm shrugged. "As far as I know, it isn't *dis*allowed. I don't see a lot of port officers marching around, looking official."

Teddy smiled. There is very little in this universe as charming as a smiling Mini. "Well, then—tally-ho!" He tucked himself into a ball and sped off down the access lane.

He zoomed around a couple of cargo tugs and rolled right up to a man about sixty meters down the row from us. Teddy unraveled and popped up in front of the man, who seemed admirably calm to be confronted so abruptly. We could see them talking, but they were too far away to hear what he was saying.

I hadn't noticed this fellow until Teddy rolled up to him—his clothing was subtly colored. It did not appear to be casual garb. I wondered if he was a soldier or a security official—or . . .

An agent. Because his clothing reminded me of Timmy's. I accessed

Teddy's sensory links and looked at him through Teddy's eyes, listened through Teddy's ears.

"Argus Fabricus," said the man. "I'm pleased to meet you, Teddy. Are you a robot?"

"No," said Teddy. "My contents are classified."

Humor touched the long, pale features of the face I could see from Teddy's POV. "As are mine. Will you tell me who made you, Teddy?"

"Ashur did." Teddy pointed to us. When Argus looked in our direction, I held my breath.

<How do you do?> he sent.

"Oops," I said aloud. I had the presence of mind to answer, <I'm well, Argus Fabricus. My name is Oichi Angelis.>

<From *Olympia*,> he said.

<You've heard of us.>

He wasn't so distant that I couldn't see his expression with my own eyes. I marveled that someone could appear so confident, yet so compassionate. Perhaps it was a balance that served him well, because he said, <I have worked as an ambassador for the Union. If I'm called upon to do so again, I hope that I may meet with you on your home turf.>

<Thank you,> was the only reply I could muster.

Argus turned back to Teddy, and I shifted my perspective back to his.

"Have I facilitated a conversation?" said Teddy.

"You have, my young friend. I hope you will facilitate more. I believe you are about to be summoned to a meeting. I'm going to have one of my own. So I will bid you aloha—*until we meet again.*"

He's kind, I thought. *He's treating Teddy like a young prodigy.* How would that kindness translate when he was working as an ambassador? Was it a common characteristic of that vocation?

"Will we meet again?" said Teddy.

"The odds are excellent," said Argus.

Teddy extended his forepaw for shaking. Argus obliged him. It reminded me of that scene in *Fantasia*, where Mickey Mouse shakes hands with the conductor, Leopold Stokowski.

Serpentine shadows snaked over us. I looked up and saw Medusa coming down the ramp. <You're awake!> I said.

I wanted to say a lot more than that, but Medusa barely nodded to me. <I'll see you later,> she promised. She passed me without another word and moved into the access lane, at the speed of a walking human. I glanced at Argus to see if he was startled by the sight of such a creature coming down the lane toward him, but he remained calm. In fact, he looked expectant.

Medusa stopped. "How do you do?" she said aloud, but she must have conducted the rest of her greeting through a private link. Argus smiled and nodded, and they turned together and continued down the access lane, away from us.

I felt as though the grown-ups were walking away without me.

Teddy looked after them, then turned back to us. <Should I keep exploring? Argus says we're about to go to a meeting.>

<Come back,> I said. <Your trip was brief, but very productive.>

As Teddy rolled back toward us at top speed, he startled a few people (and a few robot tugs).

"That man is named Argus Fabricus," I told the *Merline*rs. "He says he's an ambassador for the Union."

Cocteau gazed at the receding figure of the ambassador. "I'm sure he is, but I doubt that's *all* he is."

I guessed she was referring to the ambassador's suit, which had reminded me so much of Timmy's. Possibly also his communication brain implant, the first I had encountered among people who weren't *Olympia*ns.

<He spoke to me, too,> sent Ashur. <He congratulated me for making Teddy.>

"I would be pretty surprised if the Union didn't try to contact you," said Wilson, and as I met his eyes, I realized something I hadn't spotted before, because Rocket and Cocteau were the ones who spent the most time with Wilson. The young engineer was shy. He blushed when I looked directly at him, but he continued to speak his mind. "The Union always tries to contact people who have been cut off from the rest of the settled colonies. They did that with my homeworld, Fenris. That man—Argus Fabricus—he's from Fenris, too, I can tell. He dreams of the ice bears, just like me."

Rocket cocked his head. "Why do you dream of the ice bears?"

"Before the Union came back to us, we ate the ice bears," said Wilson. "And they ate us."

That would be a good reason. "You do look like him," I said. "I was so preoccupied with his suit, I didn't see that until you pointed it out."

"His suit is rare," said Wilson. "If he's an ambassador, he visits some dangerous places."

Argus and Medusa had disappeared into the distant gloom. If he was a representative of the Union, she had excellent reasons to talk with him. I regretted that she hadn't seen fit to share them with me.

There were plenty of things I hadn't shared with her. Things I hadn't examined too closely. My faults had driven this wedge between us. I pondered that in a shallow sort of way, still expecting that, momentarily, I could put those unhappy considerations aside long enough to be fêted at a luau and treated like a respected emissary.

Dragonette stirred on Narm's finger. "I think a delegation is approaching."

Captain Thomas and Representative Lee stepped onto the ramp, Mirzakhani just behind them. Lee said, "We just got a call. They're sending someone to fetch us. Looks like we really are going to a party." The neutral expression he wore so customarily had softened into more cheerful lines. The captain and the doctor looked downright happy.

It's luau time, I thought.

I was so wrong.

"Hey . . ." Narm peered into the access lane. "Are those security officers?"

A group of large uniformed men marched in step down the center of the lane. They were armed, and tattoos covered every inch of their skin not covered by their uniforms, including their grim faces.

They were headed straight for us.

13

Should I Be Dancing, Too?

Bomarigala, I thought as the security officers closed on us. *He and Sheba must already be here. And they must have more influence than we realized. We're going to be arrested, maybe charged with sedition, murder, sabotage. . . .*

These officers were focused like lasers. Every one of them wore a scowl. We stood there helplessly, awaiting our fate.

They stopped at the foot of our ramp. "Oichi Angelis?" demanded the shortest and most heavily muscled guy.

I probably shouldn't have confirmed that, but I didn't like the way they had hemmed us in. "Yes."

"You stand accused of sedition, treason, murder, and grand larceny," he said.

At least they left out the sabotage. "Who is my accuser?"

"You can sort that out after you've talked to a lawyer," he replied.

Medusa was well out of sight. She's not the first person I tried to call, anyway. Someone had offered to meet me here, and I thought she might be able to help. <Fire?>

My message did not travel to its intended target. In fact, it didn't leave my skull, because it was muffled in a way I hadn't experienced since Sultana Smith and Tetsuko Finnegan instituted a shipwide null zone on *Olympia*—just before they tried to kill me.

Ashur had turned pale. I guessed he had also encountered the null zone. "Find Fire," I told him. "Let her know what's happened."

"What if she can't fix this?"

"Then find out who can. Please do what I asked." I briefly turned my gaze on Captain Thomas and Representative Lee, whose poker faces were pretty much mirrored by everyone else in their crew, except for Cocteau. Her enthusiasm for adventure appeared to be unshakable.

I focused on the Minis. "You're my ambassadors. Look after Ashur. I'm going to accompany these officers and straighten this out."

No one replied, so I don't know how much confidence they had in my diplomatic and/or legal skills.

I didn't look back when the officers led me away.

We marched for quite a distance, past ships with crews who sometimes recognized and called out to my guards. They returned the friendly greetings with a camaraderie I suspected I would never inspire (in anyone who wasn't a Mini). Eventually we left the main lane and crowded into a mover that seemed designed to carry freight as well as people. I wanted to ask them where we were going, what was going to happen to me, how they could arrest me based on nothing more than an accusation from an expatriate who was no longer the head of her clan on *Olympia*.

They weren't prosecutors, and they certainly weren't diplomats, so I kept silent. Along the way, I tried to figure out where we were.

I failed at that. Without a schematic to consult, each tunnel we traversed looked pretty much like any other, and the only indication that the multiple movers we entered had taken us farther in on the spin arm was an increasing sensation of lightness.

I found some small comfort in going farther in. That meant they weren't going to blow me out an air lock, Sheba's favorite form of execution on *Titania*.

What other punishments might be inflicted on me, I couldn't say, but that was the point. Thus far, marching and silence seemed to be the protocols. I can keep quiet indefinitely, but I can't say the same thing for my ability to sustain anxiety. The longer they kept me, the calmer I felt.

My curiosity filled the gap. Why was the detention center so far from the ship docks? That didn't seem practical. If you've got an undesirable who comes from outside, do you really want them to go very far in? The longer you traveled with a prisoner, the more chances they had to escape. Not that I felt inclined to throw myself against the wall of muscle that hemmed me in, but eventually our circumstances would probably change, and what then?

What, indeed. Each tunnel was darker than the last. After an interminable time, my escorts led me into a room lit only by amber and red emergency lights. It looked like a roomier version of the corridors through which we had already walked. The far end was plugged with a wall that seemed improvised. At the near end, a pressure door stood open. I walked through it. They didn't follow me in.

"Wait here," said the man who had leveled the charges at me.

They closed the pressure door, sealing me in.

I stood for a long time, expecting them to come back with someone more official.

They didn't seem inclined to do that anytime soon, so I sat down with my back against the plugged end. Eventually, even though I had no chronometer, I had to admit that quite a lot of time had passed. I was exhausted. I had nothing to occupy me but my thoughts.

Finally, I did the sensible thing for someone who has too much time to think about the mistakes she's made. I fell asleep.

The noise of the pressure door opening alerted me to the return of the men. I must have dozed for quite a while, because my body felt heavy. Despite my torpor, I got smoothly to my feet, a fact that seemed to impress my captors—if only briefly. They filed into the room, but no one spoke to me. Instead, they turned their backs on me and faced the pressure door.

If they had known me better, I doubt they would have done that.

Within moments, another group of men joined them. These were not pretending to be security officers. They wore an eclectic variety of civilian clothing. They didn't notice me at all—they had eyes only for the first group of men.

The newcomers didn't have tattoos on their faces. To me, they looked very similar to the tattooed men, but from the expressions both groups were wearing, I suspected they saw other differences in each other that escaped me. Once the second group filed in, one last man entered the room, and my heart skipped a beat.

I don't generally react that strongly to good looks. After all, I have been surrounded by handsome people my whole life. Yet this fellow had something that made my pulse race and my chest feel tight. He maintained eye contact with me as he sauntered through the ranks. Once he halted in front of me, he extended his hand for shaking.

This seemed a clear prompt, so I took it. He had a very *nice* . . . hand . . .

"I'm Jay Momoa," he said. "I own Momoa Movers."

He didn't seem to expect a reply, which was just as well, since I couldn't find my voice. Instead, he turned his back to me, something that would be dangerous under normal circumstances, except that Jay Momoa wasn't wearing a shirt, and he had a fascinating tattoo on his back, which stretched down and across his broad, muscular . . .

Pheromones? I wondered. *Is that why he isn't wearing a shirt, despite the temperature in here? To throw me off guard?* Because whatever the effect was, it seemed to be stronger when he was closer.

One of the men shouted, and I jumped. The cry didn't prompt a fight. Instead, the men began to dance.

They shouted and chanted along with the steps, slapped their thighs, arms, and shoulders; they grimaced and widened their eyes, extended their tongues, looking like demons in the red and amber pools of light.

There is very little they could have done to throw me more off-balance. This was definitely not the line dancing that the Security forces on *Olympia* enjoyed in their spare time, and I wondered if I was being impolite by simply standing by. Even Jay wasn't keeping completely still—he also slapped his thighs and arms, and shouted along with the other men.

"Should I be dancing, too?" I worried.

"No," said Jay. "We're showing you our strength and our warrior spirit. You're new here, so you should know who you're dealing with."

That was the same thing I had said when Octopippin wondered if the sight of her might frighten the *Merlin*ers. Now I knew what it was like to be on the receiving end of that kind of lesson.

"Don't take it too personally, though," said Jay. "We do this with all visitors. This is how we honor our ancestors. It keeps us grounded, even when we're sailing to the farthest reaches of the galaxy."

They wanted me to be intimidated. I was—but mostly because I was unsure of the protocol on Maui. I also felt impressed—and relieved that I wouldn't have to figure out the right steps or how to respond to the verbal prompts, something they did perfectly, despite that they might be from different clans, if their tattoos were any indication. Even their body types were diverse. I wondered, did that tall, thin fellow on the end come from a place with lighter gravity? Did the broad, short fellow who looked like he had been carved out of stone come from a heavy world?

It went on for some time. With all those moving bodies, it got much warmer in there, so maybe Jay was dressed appropriately, after all. I watched attentively, and realized something I hadn't noticed before, possibly because I had felt so mortified about being arrested. The clothing the *officers* wore *did* look like uniforms.

Maybe not quite like *security* uniforms.

With a final cry, they ended their dance, then stood around and grinned at each other.

Jay turned to me. "We're also celebrating. We just landed a big contract."

I think I did a pretty good job of keeping my voice steady when I said, "Not with Lady Sheba, I hope. She doesn't represent *Olympia*."

His gaze didn't falter. "Plenty of business got done around here before you people showed up."

"Indeed. Business isn't conducted by security officers, so I'm guessing that's not what any of you are, and my arrest is not official. Did Lady Sheba hire you? Or was it Bomarigala?"

"Sheba did all the talking," said Jay. "The financing might have been his. If you follow any money trail far enough, it eventually leads back to the Weapons Clan."

"Why does Sheba want me to miss the luau?" I said.

"She didn't come right out and say it, but I'm assuming she wants you to lose face. Also to delay you beyond the standard security inspection, and—there's one other thing."

I waited politely for him to tell me what it was.

"We're supposed to rough you up," he said. "Teach you manners."

It wouldn't be the first time someone had kicked my butt. I can't say that it's ever taught me manners. Plus I wondered what kind of psychological damage it would do me to get beaten up by the sexiest man in the galaxy.

"How will Lady Sheba confirm that you carried out her orders?" I said.

I waited for him to tell me that Sheba had spies everywhere, but he just shrugged. "It's about honor. I gave my word."

"Are you married?" I demanded.

He cocked an eyebrow. "Why? Are you proposing?"

"Would you marry someone in order to establish trade with *Olympia*?"

If nothing else, I had managed to intrigue him. "It's a time-honored practice out here."

"It's a time-honored practice on *Olympia*, too. And whether I succeed or fail with my business on Graveyard, I'm the one you're going to have to negotiate with once *Olympia* enters a parking orbit—not Lady Sheba. If you would care to propose marriage, I'm more likely to accept your terms if you have never punched me in the face, Mr. Momoa."

He smiled. "You drive a hard bargain, Ms. Angelis. I'm not sure if you argue more like a queen or a fishwife, but I like your style. So—no punch in the face, but I'm still going to have to delay you for several more hours."

"You're not!" someone called from the other end of the hall, in a voice that might have suited a harpy eagle. At the sound of it, Jay and his men twitched as if they had been stung.

We peered into the hall beyond the pressure door, from which the voice had issued. I could see the vague outline of someone as she walked toward us, her steps punctuated by the regular *thunk* of a cane hammered against the floor as if it were a weapon instead of a support. Red light gleamed in the teeth of the metal skull that served as its handle. When her eyes resolved from the darkness, they glittered like moonlight on the surface of black water.

"Auntie!" said Jay Momoa. He sounded reverent, but not remotely happy.

The woman stopped just inside the pressure doors. She was very old—I could see that much. She couldn't have been more than one and a half meters tall. None of that diminished her impact on Jay Momoa.

"If you delay Oichi Angelis any longer," she said, "you will be interfering in *my* plans. Is that what you intend?"

Jay shook his head. "No, Auntie. I would not have accepted payment from Lady Sheba if I had known she was at odds with you. I'll return her money."

"Just as I will return Oichi to her cohorts," said the old woman. "Do you require any further directions?"

"No, Auntie," said Jay. He took a step back. The other men did the same.

Taking that as my cue, I joined the lady in the shadows. She smelled like tea and some other fragrant herb I couldn't identify. "Come," she said. "We'll have a little talk as we go along."

"All right," I agreed, wondering if I might not be safer with Jay and his dancing movers.

I followed her anyway. She didn't walk quickly, but her pace was steady as we made our way back to the pressure door in near darkness.

"Oichi!" Jay called.

I paused and looked over my shoulder at him.

"Do you still want to get married?" he said.

I considered that for a moment. "Ask me when I get back from Graveyard."

"Maybe I will."

When the pressure door had closed behind us, the old woman said, "He wouldn't be a bad match—but you can probably do better."

I have spent a lot of time in quite a few darkened tunnels, with more than my fair share of scary people (a description that I think also suits *me* pretty well), but I have rarely felt as cautious as I did in the company of that old woman. "Baba Yaga, I presume?" I said when we had put some space between ourselves and Jay Momoa.

"That is one of my names," she replied. "I have had many over the centu-ries, from many cultures. In Japan, they called me a *kitsune yōkai*—fox witch. In Finland, I was Kikimora. Belters with roots in Oceania call me Auntie because that is their word for female *kupuna*—respected elders. If you wish to be more accurate, you may call me the Engineer."

She fished something out of a pocket and raised it to her lips. At one end, a dull glow responded to her breath as she puffed on the other end. She nursed the glow until it was steady, exhaling with wafts of that mysterious herb. "I cultivate my own tobacco," she explained. "Perhaps I'll introduce it to your farmers on *Olympia*."

The smoke was a bit caustic, but not unpleasant. She inhaled and exhaled it as if it were her natural atmosphere. Her skin might have been cured in it, over the centuries. It looked like paper that had been wadded up and then ironed out again, multiple times. I don't know what was keeping this old woman alive, but it wasn't the same sort of longevity treatments Gennady must have gotten.

Baba Yaga moved with confidence as we wound our way into passages that enjoyed more illumination. I could see that she wore a woven skirt and blouse, and her vest was heavily embroidered with colorful flower and animal mo-tifs. A cap sat firmly on her head, and her boots were lined with fur that stuck above the tops in tufts.

"I am the one who had you made," she began without preamble. "I saw the benefits of creating Hybrids from the DNA stored in the brains of those ancient ships. Your people may go places that no others could venture— and survive. So I was pleased to learn that the Three spoke to you of their own accord, Oichi. That was a rare thing. Do not underestimate its signifi-cance."

When it became apparent that she expected an answer to that, I said, "I am honored by their interest."

"I believe you," said Baba Yaga. "You seem like the type who would keep quiet rather than saying what one would wish to hear. Yes, you were honored, though it is also true that you deserved that honor."

She swatted a control pad for a mover, and the two of us stepped inside. When the doors had closed, she typed coordinates with gnarled but nimble fingers. Once we had begun to move, she continued. "I have spied on you, just as you have spied on others. I have seen you kill without remorse and without hesitation. Your reasons for doing so have been practical. We have that in common."

I tried to imagine this diminutive woman killing someone. It was surprisingly easy to do so.

Baba Yaga looked sideways at me. "You seem a bit awed. Do you suppose that I drink mead from the skulls of my enemies?" She gave a short nod. "I have done so, in my day. It was an essential element of statecraft."

I suspected Lady Sheba would agree with her.

When she fell silent again, I ventured a statement. "Captain Nemo seems to have been killed because he stopped cooperating with the Weapons Clan."

She exhaled an amazing amount of smoke. "The Weapons Clan have their uses. They have a lot of money, and though they spend it freely, they have sometimes spent it wisely. *Olympia* is a case in point."

Did that mean *Titania* was not? Did she approve of what Baylor (and Gennady) had done in order to be rid of the interference of Weapons Clan operatives? I probably wouldn't like the answer to that question, even if I dared to ask it.

"Nemo died because he made the right choice at the wrong time," said Baba Yaga. "You have made a better one by pursuing your sovereignty. Now you have initiated courteous relations with the Belters. That is also wise."

"I suspect you think so because you also have business interests here," I said, "and our resources will enrich you, as well."

"I have many ways of enriching myself." She made the bowl of her pipe flare with her puffing. "That's not the reason. I want you to go to Graveyard. I want you to meet with the entities there. You should get them to regain *some* awareness of the universe. They need not wake completely, but they must be more active as players than they have been."

"Why?" I demanded.

She didn't like my tone. I suspected there were not many people from whom she would tolerate questions. She answered me anyway.

"Because they didn't kill themselves after their creators died."

That seemed a non sequitur, until I thought about it a little bit. "You mean—because they're not dead, they are still able to interact with people? Perhaps someone will misuse them?"

"You're halfway there," said Baba Yaga. "They are powerful tools. They should be properly used. We cannot simply bury our heads in the sand and hope that no one else will do so."

"These tools can think," I said.

Her eyes glinted. "Do you imagine your grandmother doesn't know that, child? They are the reason you were created. They are the lock; you are the key. How you decide to turn in that lock is up to you, but what is unlocked is up to *them*—what energies you unleash. You must both consent in this undertaking. You must both take responsibility for the outcome. Once you see each other clearly, you will understand why I say a partial awakening is for the best. The ultimate choice is yours, not mine."

What energies you unleash. Did she mean the sort that drive a ship through folded space? Or something so far beyond that, even Baba Yaga hesitated to attempt its description?

"You are the Engineer," I said, "the one who sent Gennady's agents into the graveyard. I need to know—how did you become entangled with the doings of the Three?"

"For two reasons," she said between puffs. "The first is that the most advanced technology we use is based on salvage from the graveyard—and the Three are the oldest and most advanced race represented there. I have a more personal reason, too."

She considered me for a long moment. "I have told no else what I'm about to tell you. I advise you to forget it."

"Yes," I said.

"I am concerned with the doings of the Three, because, like you, I encountered their avatars. Long ago, they visited Earth. Before your human ancestors learned to forge metal, Oichi. It is fair to say that the Three are a large part of the reason I eventually became the Engineer. No!" She pointed at me with the end of her pipe. "Do not ask another question. I will not tell what you will eventually learn yourself."

I had drawn breath to do exactly that, but I let it out again without comment. Her eyes glittered as she watched me regain my composure.

Finally she said, "Your team will go into the graveyard. I expect you will come out again. When you do, the path ahead will be much clearer. Even I, who have seen so much, do not know what direction it will take."

She struck the floor with the tip of her cane. "I know what I hope, and I know what I dread. I must rely on you to make the right decisions. That, Oichi, is why you were tempered in harsh conditions. You have been useful in the past, and I think you will prove to be so in the future. Your usefulness is not a matter of profit, regardless of how much some wish it to be. It is a matter of the survival and prosperity of our kind, diverse though we may be—*diverged* though we may be. Bear that in mind, and you won't be so mad about what's been done to you."

The door to the mover slid open, and we entered another corridor. Baba

Yaga chose a direction without hesitation. Either she didn't suffer from the same null zone that still blocked my access to my networks, or she had the layout of the place memorized.

"You *Olympians*," she said, "remind me of *kintsugi*, the Japanese art of golden joinery. You don't break easily, but when you do, you highlight your damage in gold rather than trying to hide it and pretend it never happened."

As I pondered that elegant comparison, something rumbled overhead. The Engineer paused and pointed with her cane toward the roof of the corridor. "That is the sound of our refinery, here. That is its beating heart."

Should I interpret that to mean Baba Yaga owned the refinery? I had detected pride in her tone.

She began to walk again. "In the days to come, *Olympians* will become better acquainted with the Belters. I believe you will adapt well to your new circumstances."

I couldn't resist asking her one more question. "Baba Yaga—are you a deus ex machina?"

She seemed amused by the question, though I can't say how I knew that. "Technically, that would be *dea* ex machina. I suppose I would fit that role if this were a play. I have also been called a witch, Oichi. In many languages. Any grandmother who does not have her infernal devices is not paying attention."

She halted in front of another mover and gestured inside with her pipe. "Go now. Find your way back to your friends. We will not speak again until you have completed your mission, for better or for worse."

I entered the mover. As soon as I had crossed the threshold, the Engineer slapped the controls on the wall, and the doors closed between us.

I breathed a sigh of relief, feeling as if I had just emerged, miraculously unscathed, from an interview with the sphinx.

I felt that way for a good five minutes, while the mover sped me on my way. When it stopped, the door opened, and I was confronted by another corridor. I stepped out and scanned it, first up one end and then down the other.

I had no idea which direction to take.

The door shut behind me. It didn't seem to matter much—there had been no directory inside the mover. Still, I wondered if I should get back in and take it down a level or two. I felt the lightness of being closer in on the spin arm. It might be easier to work my way back if I returned to the level where we had docked.

I had pretty much decided on that course of action when someone touched my communication link. <Testing, testing.>

<I'm here!>

<Oichi?>

<Yes!>

<My name is Queenie. I'm trying to fix the—>

She was cut off mid-word. Maybe she had been trying to take down the null zone. Medusa could give her some advice on that. Did Medusa even know I was missing?

A schematic popped into my head. For one bright, shining moment, I could see where I was in relation to everything else. If I could just plot a course . . .

It disappeared before I could do that. <Wait, don't—>

<Just follow the—>

<I can't see the—>

<—in the mover and—>

<You want me to get in the mover?>

<Yes,> said Queenie.

I turned and touched the controls, but a message popped up on the display. IN USE, it declared.

Okay. I'd give it a few minutes and try again. After all, I had survived imprisonment, dancing movers, and a conversation with the Engineer. A few more minutes wouldn't kill me. I turned away from the display, bearing in mind the old colloquialism about watched pots, and scanned the corridor again.

The door opened behind me. I spun around to see who was in there. I had a half-baked list of persons it could have been, anything from a perfect stranger to Jay Momoa, come to pledge his troth again, or possibly Fire, who was *almost* a perfect stranger, to Baba Yaga, who would shake her cane at me and call me an idiot for getting lost. It included just about anyone but the person who actually stood there. Because he was supposed to be dead.

That man was Gennady Mironenko.

I punched him right on the bridge of his nose, as hard as I could, and then I ran.

14

Werewolves and Their Lawyers

I know it was a good punch, because my hand went numb. I'm pretty sure anyone else who had been hit that hard would have stayed down longer. However, I didn't get very far before Gennady caught up with me.

"Oichi, wait!" He grabbed me by the collar and yanked me backward. I jammed an elbow in his gut and tried to pull free, but he wrapped an arm around my neck. It was his right arm, so I dropped to my right knee and yanked as hard as I could. I felt a rush of triumph as he toppled over my shoulder.

My joy evaporated when he tightened his grip around my neck and rolled me right along with him. We both ended up on the floor, and he didn't seem inclined to let go. It was getting a little hard to breathe.

<Oichi!> Queenie said, her tone bright. <I found someone to help you!>

<Help!> I shouted back.

<Yes,> she said, her cheer unflagging. <He will *help* you.>

I tugged at Gennady's arm. "Stop choking me!"

"I'm not choking you!" he insisted.

"Yes, you are!"

"If I were choking you, you wouldn't be able to talk!"

I elbowed him again. "Well, it's *close enough*!"

"Stop fighting!" he said. "Let's talk this over!"

<Are you fighting my helper?> Queenie sounded incredulous.

<He's Gennady Mironenko!> I flailed at him with my sore fists. <He blows up generation ships! He assassinates people!>

<He's okay!> insisted Queenie.

<He's not!>

<Oichi—*this time* he's okay!>

I paused my fruitless assault. <This time?>

<This time!> she said. <Really.>

"Have you decided to be civil?" said Gennady.

"What if I have?"

"Then I can let go and we can stand up," said the man who once held a knife to my throat—though he was right about the choking. I would be unconscious by now if he had been serious.

"We're both going to move slowly," I said. "You let go, and we'll stand up, and we'll take a step away from each other. Deal?"

"Deal." Gennady let go of my neck. We climbed to our feet.

<So far, so good,> said Queenie. <Now—if you'll get into the mover . . . >

"On the way," I asked Gennady, "do you promise to explain why you're not dead?"

He wiped his bloody nose with his sleeve. "If that's the price I must pay, then so be it."

I nodded toward the mover. "You first."

He gave me a pained smile. "I don't think so. *You* first."

"I'm not going to—" I began, before Queenie broke in.

<Both of you—GET IN THE MOVER!>

We hopped.

"If I may quote the ancient philosopher Hunter Thompson," Gennady said as he dabbed his nose with his other sleeve, "'Even a goddamn werewolf is entitled to legal counsel.'"

"That's an apt comparison." I leaned against the far wall of the mover and flexed my hand. No longer numb, it was beginning to hurt like hell—and to swell up.

The smile he gave wasn't exactly happy, but it did at least manage some affection. "It may be unwise, but I'm not sorry to see you again."

I gave up on torturing my hand. "It's definitely unwise."

He started to shake his head, and winced at the motion. "I would have been content to stay dead, as far as you're concerned, Oichi. I'm here because I owe a favor."

"To Baba Yaga?"

He didn't confirm or deny that, and I recalled something Cocteau had told me. "She was connected to *Andrei* Mironenko, from what I hear."

He sighed. "My cousin Andrei. I'll never live up to his example." Gennady looked into my eyes. "If you remember the *Lord of the Rings* chess set I gave you—"

"Then took back again," I reminded him.

"—I played the dark side of that board; Andrei played the light." Gennady shrugged. "He's dead, so you're stuck with me."

I hate to tell you—now that the surprise had worn off, I felt glad to see him. I hoped he didn't know that. I wanted to learn a few things from him, and I didn't want him to get familiar enough to make me punch him again. "You promised to explain why you're not dead. We saw you get onto the party shuttle, just before it was destroyed."

"Indeed," said Gennady. "That was stupid of me. *Of course* Baylor wanted all his enemies in one spot. I had been to so many of his tedious parties by then, I let myself get bored. Give me some credit, though. I had spent a lot of time on the party shuttle—practically lived there, when I got sick of it all. I squirreled away some resources."

"Like one of those fancy pressure suits Sultana and Tetsuko had?" I guessed.

"Several, actually," said Gennady. "When I realized my fellow partygoers were passing out in their seats, I knew they had been drugged. I scrambled into a suit and exited the shuttle just after Baylor did. I saw the gravity bomb go off. It was spectacular, but I didn't want to see it that close."

I was thinking that the *adults* must have passed out—they had shared drinks with Baylor before they boarded the party shuttle—but some of them had brought *children* with them, and those children had not been drugged. They would have been wide awake when the bombs went off. If Gennady hadn't liked seeing the bombs from a relatively safe distance, just imagine what it was like closer in.

"There I was," said Gennady. "Going in the wrong direction at a very fast rate—so I placed a call."

I frowned. "Nobody called to *Olympia* for help."

<I think he means he called *Itzpapalotl*,> said Queenie, and I jumped. I had thought she was done talking to us. Who was she, anyway? Gennady's secretary? She seemed to be linked with both of us.

Maybe so, because Gennady nodded. "I called Bomarigala."

I could tell we were moving farther out on the spin arm; my hand hurt more with the increased gravity. "*Bomarigala*—that's such an odd name."

Gennady inspected his ruined sleeves. "Isn't it, though? Where he comes from, you start off with one syllable, and then you scratch and claw your way to the top, another syllable at a time. He's earned five of them, so don't let him fool you with his polite manners."

I cradled my hand against my chest. "Where did he come from?"

"You need to put that on ice," advised Gennady. "He came from OMSK."

"That's a name?"

"That's an acronym," said Gennady.

"What does it stand for?"

"No one remembers."

"So, you called for help," I said, attempting to rescue the point, "and Bomarigala answered."

"He answered, but he didn't help. He told me to—" Gennady smiled thinly. "He said no. After that, I drifted around for a while, until I witnessed the demise of the man who killed *Titania*."

You what?! I thought.

He must have read my expression, because he added, "I gave Baylor the bombs, Oichi, but I had no idea he would do something so drastic. I had a very different vessel in mind for those bombs."

It took me a moment to figure out what he meant. "*Itzpapalotl!?*"

"I needed their money—but I never had any intention of turning you over to the Weapons Clan. When the time was right, I knew we'd have to fight them."

"We could have fought them with the Medusa units!"

"Well—yes, but then you could have pushed *me* out of the picture, too—which is what you've done." He shrugged. "My part is over. Your part is just beginning."

Glad as I was to see Gennady, I didn't believe he had been innocent in the destruction of *Titania*. Even if he didn't know what Baylor was planning to do with the bombs, he was observant enough to figure out where they had ended up. Though I have to admit, I would not be surprised to learn that Gennady had hoped to blow up *Itzpapalotl*. It seemed in character.

The mover finished descending. It hummed for about ten seconds, and then it began to move sideways. Gennady lurched in my direction as the momentum caught him off guard, but he quickly regained his balance. "Your source was right, Oichi—Baba Yaga favored my cousin, Andrei Mironenko. I think she finds me a poor substitute, but my interests coincide with hers more often than not these days."

"She said it was her idea to make us."

He studied me for a long moment before he answered. "Baba Yaga is the Engineer. Not just of you, Oichi—of many things. She has been so for all her existence. She will be so long after you and I are gone."

"Then what *is* she, Gennady? She can't be human."

His nose began to drip blood again. He dabbed it with an encrusted sleeve. "Don't ever ask her that. I tried to find out once. I attempted to get a DNA sample from her." He raised his right hand and wiggled his fingers. "Once she finished with me, it took them six months to regenerate my hand. I'll tell you a couple of theories, though."

"Please do," I said. "I don't want to take the time to regrow fingers."

"The easiest explanation is that she's human, but a mutation. Somehow, her line developed an extraordinary longevity gene."

"So there are others like her somewhere?"

He grinned. "Probably not. Ancient Earth had quite a vicious pecking order. Survival of the fittest, and all that."

I nodded. "Okay. What's your other theory?"

He lost his smile. "I think she may be one of the Titans."

I blinked. "One of the creatures from ancient mythology?" He did not seem to be kidding.

"Myths and legends are what people use to explain what they don't understand," said Gennady. "Even modern people, confronted by a deathless woman who commands inexplicable forces, might feel inclined to call her a witch—or a goddess."

Medusa had said something similar. Having met the Engineer, I found it possible to believe she could have been born with that longevity gene and lived many generations, then encountered avatars from an ancient race of aliens and learned even more from them. Such a creature would amass her assets and guard her secrets. She could start and end wars.

She could engineer a race of people and aim them at the Three, hoping for a powerful alliance. If so, her machinations put Lady Sheba to shame.

Our mover began to slow again. Gennady pushed away from his wall, and I did the same.

He said, "My business with the Weapons Clan ended when Bomarigala refused to rescue me from the void. My business with *Olympia* has always been dictated by the Engineer. When you and I see each other again, Oichi, I hope it's under pleasant circumstances."

Searching my heart, I had to tell the truth. "I hope so, too."

The last time Gennady and I had been face-to-face, we were on opposite sides of an air lock pressure door, and he was getting ready to blow me into the void. I had been reasonably certain that Medusa would rescue me from that fate, but that had not been what I was thinking about as he gazed into my eyes from the other side of the view window.

Do you know? I had wondered, *That I'm not who you think I am? That I'm not going to die?*

He had winked at me, just before the outer door spun open.

Standing across from me in the mover, he did it again. "Farewell, Oichi. I wish you the best of luck."

The doors opened. "You aren't coming to the luau?" I felt a bit disappointed.

"No," he said. "I don't want to complicate your first meeting with the Belters. Queenie will be there."

<We saved you some poi,> said Queenie.

Gennady pointed. "That way. It's straight down this corridor from here."

I stepped out of the mover, and the door slid shut. In another moment, the display lit up. IN USE.

I knew the chance to ask some of the questions that still teased me had expired.

Maybe that was for the best. Some mysteries should persist, shouldn't they? Especially if I wanted to keep liking Gennady. Otherwise, I might feel compelled to kill him. That would be a very dangerous undertaking, indeed.

I walked down the corridor, my hand (and possibly my heart) throbbing painfully.

I can't say I had a spring in my step. The Dancing Movers, the Possible Titan, and the Resurrected Gennady had just given me a crash course in Belter diplomacy—and the picture looked challenging. I had to admit, so far, the techniques required for negotiation had been right up my alley. That was about to change, but I didn't know it, so I kept walking.

The passage broadened, and opened at intervals to empty chambers. Everyone must be at the far end, past big pressure doors that were wide open. Laughter, singing, and percussive music echoed down the corridor.

This was no tea party.

I heard the traditional music Fire had sent me, with the tom-toms and the boobams and the other things that went *clickety-clack*. Light flickered on the rock walls outside the doors. When I passed through and emerged into the giant chamber beyond, I realized that any expectations I could have harbored would have fallen short.

Belters crowded the cavern, smiling, laughing, and singing—those who weren't playing the percussion instruments were dancing, and everyone else was eating. People swayed their hips and their hands, and one fellow spun batons with glowing balls on the end (the cause of the flickering light). I stood frozen in place, overwhelmed with the spectacle. When they noticed me, men and women danced up and placed necklaces made of silk flowers around my neck, and I, who was accustomed to entering any circumstance with careful observance of attire and protocol, wasn't sure how to respond—so I just smiled awkwardly.

The Belters looked happy, so open and welcoming. Our social protocols on *Olympia* were stiff and formal compared with theirs. If we treated Belters the way we treated each other, we might seem unfriendly. If we were going to have a working relationship with them, we were going to have to step outside our comfort zone.

I was already there.

I looked for my associates—and spotted them sitting at a table halfway across the chamber, *Merliner*s and *Olympia*ns, all having a wonderful time and apparently not worrying about me. Ashur smiled at Mirzakhani, who sat next to him. Cocteau sat on his other side, beaming with pleasure, much as she had during Ogden Schickele's garden party, and I guessed she was enjoying more culinary delights. Narm, despite his assertion that real instruments were far too retro, appeared almost reverent as he watched the musicians perform.

Perhaps you won't be surprised to hear that the Minis were all in their perfect element: curious, happy, and charming as ever. I saw Kitten among the dancers, performing the steps with an ease that I could never hope to possess.

The Belters were beautiful. Their emotions were genuine and openly displayed. I had no idea how to respond. If I didn't get my equilibrium soon, I might turn around and walk away.

Then I locked gazes with someone across the chamber.

She stood a little apart from the crowd, yet they all seemed aware of her. When she began to walk toward me, they parted for her, as for a queen. She looked like one of them, with cinnamon-colored skin and black, wavy hair. Her face was broad, her cheeks high and rounded. Her wide mouth curved in a smile.

That was where her similarity to the Belters ended, because she wore a suit very much like the one I had seen on Timmy and Argus, and a metal frame that arched above her like wings, except that it bent forward over her head and came to two points that jutted down like the arms of a praying mantis.

She closed the distance between us until she stood toe to toe with me. We were the same height.

"Oichi," she said, "I'm Fire. This is our custom. I greet you." She placed her hands on either side of my face, then touched her forehead to mine. The points of her metal frame loomed over our heads.

<Hello, Oichi,> said a voice inside my head. <It's me, Queenie.>

Fire opened her eyes again and took a step back. "Do you understand?"

I looked closer at the metal frame Fire was wearing. It wasn't biometal, but it was something very much like it. "Queenie comes from the graveyard," I said. "She's salvaged tech."

Fire nodded, then showed me the full power of her dazzling smile. "Welcome to Maui."

"Oichi," Ashur said with more than a little outrage, "those men were *not* security officers!"

"You're right, but they didn't hurt me."

"Really?" he demanded. "Then how come you're soaking your hand in a bowl of ice?"

"Not because of them."

Ashur frowned, but he didn't press me. I had to take my hand out of the ice water, because it was beginning to be more uncomfortable than the original injury. Thanks to the painkiller the station commander had given me, most of the soreness had faded.

She had introduced herself just as I thought my neck could bear no more flower strands. "I'm Commander Lana. Welcome to Maui."

Kitten wrapped herself around my waist. "We gave Commander Lana the gifts!"

"The gifts!" I said enthusiastically while trying to remember what they were.

"We love gifts!" replied Commander Lana, who was tall and sturdy, a woman of middle age whose long, black hair was liberally shot with silver. She wore a uniform that reminded me of our own Security personnel, though her insignia were more obvious. Had I seen them earlier, I would not have mistaken Jay's dancing movers for the forces Lana commanded.

Cocteau winked at me. "We hope you like the wine, Commander Lana. I can personally recommend it. The coffee as well."

Lana's face brightened when coffee was mentioned. "We can never get enough of that. You grow it on your generation ship, Oichi?"

"In the Habitat Sector," I said. "We make chocolate as well. We hope you'll visit us."

"I accept your invitation," said Commander Lana. "Now, eat, Oichi! You have a lot of catching up to do."

I sat next to Lana, and Fire took the seat next to mine. Kitten arranged herself around my shoulders, peering through the flowers like a cat in a garden. Dragonette maintained her usual perch on Narm, and Rocket on Wilson, but Teddy had his own seat, boosted with pillows. I stole another look at Ashur, who had already forgotten me for Mirzakhani. I hadn't seen him smile so much since before . . .

Before Nuruddin's divorce.

"Your Minis are wonderful creatures," said Fire. "*Living* creatures. Ashur informed me he was the one who made them. That tells me everything I need to know about your people."

I wasn't sure she was right about that, but it wasn't the worst argument I had ever heard, either.

"Queenie is an accidental consciousness," she said.

"Aren't we all?"

Fire grinned. "You and I, Oichi—we are born with brains that form personalities as a matter of organic function. Queenie's personality formed because of her interface with users—people with organic brains, very much like mine."

The servers piled food on our plates. I didn't recognize most of it, but it smelled good. "Why is she—why are you both called Queen's Fire?" I said.

"Queenie was created for a warrior queen. She can tell you all about her, but not that much about the people the queen belonged to. That was early in her existence, and it was a long, long time ago."

"Thirty thousand years?" I said between bites of something sweet.

Fire looked into my eyes. "Longer. Much, much longer."

Something about the way she said that gave me the impression I should stop asking how long it had been. I couldn't resist one more question. "Did the people who made the Three make Queenie?"

"No," said Fire. "The people who made the Three were long dead, by then."

Maybe so, but something about the way Queenie had sounded when she spoke to my brain implant was familiar. She might have different origins, but she was still of the graveyard.

Kitten regarded my plate. "I like the orange stuff, Oichi. Have another bite of that."

"Yes, dear." I obliged with a small nibble.

"Yum," she said, and at that moment I looked across the room and into the large golden eyes of a person who was covered from head to toe with fur—not worn as a garment, but growing from her skin.

"Fire," I said, "is that woman—does she have . . ."

"She's a Woov," said Fire before I could embarrass myself further. "Aliens. Very nice people. Nicer than us, if you want to know the truth. However, those very short sturdy people sitting at the table with them? Human—and the super-tall, skinny people at the other end? Also human. Just different gravity conditions."

They were all looking at me with open curiosity, so I returned the favor. There was a wider variety of body types on Maui than one could find on *Olympia*, but there was also a dominant type—people who looked more like Fire—tall with golden-brown skin and thick wavy hair.

Fire saw me staring. "The original Belters of Charon are from Graveyard, from a little town called Odd's Corner—we grow up there so we can develop strong bones." She flexed her arms. "We make regular trips home, but many of our visitors are happy to stay low-gravity, and a lot of them live in the Belt now."

The music, which had been so energetic when I arrived, shifted gears into a more gentle, romantic music played on ukuleles. Lana leaned toward me. "You know who plays a mean ukulele? Jay Momoa."

Fire leaned in on the other side. "You should ask him to play for you, Oichi. After all, he owes you an apology. That was cheeky of him, pretending to arrest you."

Commander Lana raised her eyebrows. "I heard you proposed marriage."

Fire grinned. "I heard *he* did."

"Both true," I admitted. "What is it about that man, anyway? When he was standing close, I thought I was going to faint."

Both women nodded. "You're not the first person to react that way to Jay Momoa," said Fire, "and you won't be the last."

I moved the food around on my plate, hoping it would look like I had eaten most of it. "I suppose there are quite a few people who will approach us with offers of business. What do you think of Jay Momoa? He said Lady Sheba paid him to beat me up."

Commander Lana snorted. "Jay wouldn't do that. He was trying to get you to negotiate."

"He's actually got a good reputation," Fire said, "but sometimes I wonder if it's *too* good."

"Especially after he kidnapped me," I reminded her.

"Kidnapping brides is an old custom," she said solemnly, then laughed at my expression. "It's just—he's so handsome, so compelling. Remember I told you that my people are from Old Earth? Well, Jay Momoa has pretty much the same heritage, but he's not from around here. His ancestors settled on a world named after the place that created us, Oceania. His people have a little something special."

"Like . . . ?" I prompted.

"Like some kinda sexy sauce. He's good-looking, yes, but maybe he's got—I don't know, pheromones? People want to like him—to please him. Hell, *I* want to do that, and I'm Queen's Fire. If Queenie weren't looking out for me, I would have made a fool of myself by now."

<You're welcome,> said Queenie.

"Admit it, Oichi," said Fire. "You've already forgiven him—haven't you? Maybe you're even considering his marriage proposal, just a little? That's why I always use extra caution when interacting with Jay. I don't think he's a bad man. I don't think he's entirely good, either. His ethics may be a little frayed around the edges."

I had thought my own ethics could be described that way. I was beginning to feel naïve. I could snap a guy's neck when called upon to do so, but if I negotiated a trade deal with you, I would be fair. I might not be forthcoming about *all* the details, but I wouldn't cheat a business partner.

"I'm not going to rush to accept anyone's marriage proposal," I said. "Even if it seems to be good for business."

"Smart girl," said Commander Lana. "Jay wouldn't be the worst match you could make—but you could do better."

The greeting party went on for quite a while longer. There was a *lot* of food.

<I'm getting sleepy,> Ashur admitted at one point, and if that young fellow was feeling the strain, can you imagine how we older folk felt? Except for

Cocteau, who never seemed to lose her sparkle. Whatever had kept her alive for so long must also be keeping her awake.

"Pace yourselves," warned Fire. "Eat a little of everything they offer, and eat slowly. Otherwise, you're going to get uncomfortable pretty fast."

This was a culture shock for me. All my life, food had been rationed, and a lot of it had been nutrient broth grown in vats. More recently, we had all been able to expand our palates on *Olympia*, but we were austere compared with the Belters. Both Ashur and I were plied with more treats than we could manage. "You're too skinny!" people kept saying. "Eat!"

We tried. I did my best to relax and enjoy what was offered. My hand was feeling a lot better, thanks to the painkiller and the intermittent soaking, but even with the nap I had taken earlier (albeit under forced circumstances), I was beginning to flag. I had done far too much talking in the last several hours, and I was beginning to feel like a bit of an impostor.

Commander Lana treated me like a legitimate liaison. "Let's meet again, once you've concluded your business on Graveyard," she said. "Get to know each other. Then we'll negotiate. We like you, Oichi. We like your Minis. You give us good feelings."

"You give us good feelings, too," I said. "The best we've had in a long time. We're glad to meet you."

She smiled and pressed her forehead to mine. "Then aloha. Until we meet again."

We took that as our cue to say goodbye to the crowd. Some Belters wanted to continue their partying, but these folks were younger, and had spent the first half of the festivities waiting on others; the consensus among *Merliner*s and *Olympia*ns was to leave them to their well-earned fun. Our group headed for the doors in the company of Fire and Queenie.

Something had shifted. Maybe the grapevine spread the word that the *Olympia*ns had come, and partied, and talked of trade, and possibly a few had whispered that I had spoken with a very important personage. Now the boisterous folk who had fêted us turned back into the hardworking people who wrangled asteroids and refined the materials they harvested from them. When we made our way back through the passages of Maui, we passed a few people who gave us friendly nods. Most had already focused on other things.

<I'm very glad we were invited here,> said Kitten, her communication including all of us as we got into the mover that would take us back to the sector that housed visiting ships. Once we were inside, she wrapped herself around my waist and sent me a private message. <Are you scared to go to Graveyard?>

<Maybe,> I said. <Are you?>

<I'm worried,> said Kitten. <I'm glad to be included in the company, but I wonder if I'm brave enough.>

I rested a hand on her stretchy middle. <You're as brave as me.>

<Nobody's as brave as you, Oichi,> Kitten said with a disturbing degree of confidence.

When the doors opened onto the broad access lane, and I saw the spaceships lined up on either side, I experienced another sensation. I would call it déjà vu, except that I hadn't been in the spaceship graveyard yet, so I couldn't be seeing the scene *again*. Yet it wasn't quite a premonition, either. It plucked chords in my soul.

"Ashur," I said, "will you take Kitten and Dragonette back to *Merlin*? I need to have a private conversation with Fire and Queenie."

Ashur was young—the age when most teenagers would bristle about not being included—but Ashur was no ordinary teenager.

"Thank you for the nice party," he said to Fire. "Um—see you later?"

She smiled at him. "Yes."

Ashur gathered Kitten and followed the *Merlin*ers up the access lane. Kitten stared at us over his shoulder. "We need to start growing the orange food on *Olympia!*" she said.

We waited until they were out of earshot. Then Fire and I walked together. "This was a good visit," she said. "I hope you're pleased with the way it turned out."

Despite a rocky beginning—I was. My experience with the Belters reminded me of the time I had impersonated Sezen Koto, an Executive woman who could shape policy and form alliances with other powerful people. That charade had ended much too soon for my tastes. Now I was the Real Deal. "I like to meet people. Particularly when they're reasonable."

"That's one thing I know about the Belters," said Fire. "True, most of them are from my neck of the woods, so I may be biased. How is your hand?"

I flexed my fingers. "Much better. Are you and Queenie the ones who warned Baba Yaga I had been kidnapped?"

Queenie answered, <She's the one who told *us*.>

In that case, I hoped the Engineer wouldn't find out I had doubted her insight. "Ashur is disappointed that he can't talk with you some more."

"He's young," said Fire, "and far too clever, and he asks questions that shouldn't be answered yet. I'll spend my time with you, Oichi."

"You don't answer most of *my* questions, either."

"They're just the wrong questions. I know you want to ask about the Alliance of Ancient Races. That information is proprietary. Your guide, Ahi, will answer your questions as well as she can once you're in the graveyard. I want you to know the right things, when you need to know them."

"Will you destroy *Itzpapalotl*?" I said.

That surprised her. "The Weapons Clan have observed all proper protocols. They haven't ventured into the Charon system. We have no reason to destroy them. Do you want me to? Would that solve your problems?"

"I don't know," I admitted. "I'm just wondering how much visitors have to alarm the Alliance of Ancient Races before they get on the kill list."

"My bosses are cautious," said Fire, "but tolerant. A ship loaded with weapons would be destroyed if it entered our system. Weapons operated remotely would also be destroyed, and their sources tracked."

"Remotely—like sunbusters?"

"Absolutely."

"How do you track them?"

<That question is forbidden,> said Queenie. <Do you have another?>

We stopped in front of *Merlin*. Thomas and her crew had gone inside, as had Ashur and the Minis. It remained for me to board, and we would head out.

"I'll meet you on Graveyard," said Fire. "I'll be waiting for you inside Joe's Salvage Yard, next to the canyon."

"How will you get there? In a ship like *Merlin*?"

<That question is forbidden,> said Queenie. <Do you have another?>

I sighed. <Ashur and the Minis are more dear to me than I can possibly tell you.>

<They are dear to others, too,> replied Queenie.

<Will you answer if I ask who those others are?>

<Not now.>

I may as well be having a conversation with Baba Yaga. <Do *you* have any advice for me, Queenie?>

<Yes,> she said. <When you find yourself in trouble, remember who you are. Remember what you have suffered. Remember what you hope to accomplish. When you have done that, say those things.>

<Say them to the entities in the graveyard?>

<Say them. That is my advice.>

That seemed oddly specific. I filed it away. <Thank you.>

<See you later,> said Queenie.

"We'll also be waiting for you," said Fire, "when you come *out* of the grave-yard. You'll still have plenty of questions for Queenie and me. By then, I'll be able to answer more of them than I can now." She took both my hands in hers. "Aloha, Oichi. Until we meet again."

"Aloha, Fire. And Queenie."

Fire grinned at me. When she turned and walked away, I couldn't resist watching her. She appeared to carry Queenie without effort.

Maybe they carried each other.

Once she was out of sight, I walked up *Merlin's* ramp. I paused outside her air lock and accessed her security system to search for Medusa. She wasn't back yet.

Are you still talking with Argus Fabricus? I wondered. *Are you talking with someone else? Did you even know that I had been kidnapped?*

Calling her was out of the question, mostly because I didn't want to have my call ignored or rejected. I didn't try to look Argus Fabricus up, either. Instead, I wandered in the general direction they had gone together, though there was no practical reason for me to do so, half hoping I would meet Medusa on the way back.

Half hoping I wouldn't.

Wandering among those ships was no casual stroll, and I suppose it wasn't meant to be. If you were in the wrong place at the wrong time, you might be crushed when one of those vessels was moved toward an arrival/departure lock. The access lane was fairly safe, but I didn't stay there. I wanted to see what was *behind* those ships.

Tow cables crisscrossed my path, forcing me to pick my way along. I doubted I had the will to search indefinitely, since I wasn't looking for anything in particular.

On the other hand, maybe I was looking for myself, and that could take a while. I wasn't walking *toward* anything, so maybe I was walking away from that empty space where my partner was supposed to be. Maybe I was trying to walk out of my own skull.

You're an idiot, you know that? I thought, and stopped to assess my surroundings. The vessels docked in this cavern were an eclectic bunch. Just beyond the curved edge of another ship, a structure splayed its claws on the floor of the holding cavern, pinning several of the smaller tow cables beneath it like worms it had trapped for its supper.

I laughed. That claw reminded me of something Medusa and I had seen in the folklore database when we looked up Baba Yaga.

"Just like the fairy tale," said a voice nearby. "The hut that walks on chicken feet."

Timmy materialized from the darkness in much the same fashion that her voice had.

The one person who could have helped me fight her was nowhere in sight.

I didn't have much faith that I would last long with Timmy in a knife fight—or in any kind of fight.

She wasn't even looking at me. The claw had captured her attention. "Of course, if we move any closer, the illusion will be lost."

Running did not seem an option at that point. I decided to try another tactic: conversation. "You seem to know a lot about Baba Yaga. Is that why she hired you to kill Captain Nemo?"

She smiled. "You know it wasn't Baba Yaga who hired me. Stop fishing."

"If you don't work for Baba Yaga, why are you here?"

"I was curious about the Engineer."

Close up, Timmy looked like someone out of a dream—or a hallucination. She was more startling than the Woovs had been. Her odor was subtle. Not unpleasant, but something that alerted me that I was not in the presence of my own kind.

"My people are Hybrids," I told her, aiming for a diplomatic segue. "I'm told that your kind are as well."

"True," said Timmy. "We are the product of a war between two peoples. We were made to end that war, but also to fight other members of my Mother race, from clans that have no family ties with us."

It was fascinating to watch the way her face moved when she spoke, how the scant light glowed on her pale skin. My eyes were wide when I looked at her, perhaps comically so. Yet she didn't ridicule me. She spoke courteously.

"Clans," I said. "It always seems to come down to wars between families."

"Doesn't it?" said Timmy. "Sometimes it seems primitive to me. Combatants can be so black and white in their judgments against each other. Though the ones who move them like pawns have more practical motivations."

"Often involving power."

"Or fragile egos."

That was a pretty good assessment of Baylor and Ryan Charmayne. "I've also been told that you have a strict code of conduct."

"Yes," said Timmy. "It takes the ambiguity out of the decision-making process. Usually."

"It has for me, too," I admitted. "*Usually.*"

Timmy smiled again. Her teeth were sharp and irregular. That imperfection made her seem more human to me. I realized how steadily I had been staring at her when she returned my gaze without blinking. "I don't mean to be rude," I explained. "I've never seen someone who looked like you."

"I can stand a little surveillance," said Timmy. "It gives me an excuse to stare back."

"Have you ever been inside the graveyard?" I'm not sure why I asked her that. The notion didn't occur to me until that moment.

Timmy's smile was tempered. "Not yet. Before you ask me anything more about that, Oichi, understand that I am between jobs at the moment. I have had a new offer I may accept. So let's keep it neutral—shall we?"

Meaning she might yet venture there. Maybe at the same time I planned to be there. Maybe working for the same people who hired her to kill Nemo.

"I'm told that your upbringing was harsh," said Timmy. "At least by human standards."

"I don't know how harsh it was, compared with the lives of other people," I said.

"Perhaps I can give you some perspective. I began life alongside more than one hundred siblings. Once we crawled from the birthing chamber, we were sealed in the Children's Caverns. There we learned to love and to kill."

I heard emotion in her voice, but I couldn't decide what it was. Pain? Anger? Also nostalgia? "How long?" I said.

"How long were we trapped in there? By your reckoning, about four hundred twenty-four-hour cycles. We grew quickly in that time. Not so quickly as our Mother race, but faster than you who are the offspring of our Fathers. We reached adolescence during that time."

"With no adult supervision?"

"We possess racial memories," said Timmy.

"Who taught you to speak? To count, and so on?"

"Our math skills are innate," she said. "We polished them once we emerged. As for language, they left us clues throughout the caverns, puzzles we must solve. It was rather fun. Except for the part where our brothers and sisters tried to eat us."

"What stopped them from doing that?" I said.

"We ate them first."

"Oh." That made sense. Really, it should have occurred to me.

"We loved them, but we couldn't help it any more than they could. We were so driven by instinct at that stage. Not even grief could stay our hands." Timmy stroked the handle of her knife as if it were a pet she cherished. "From our Mother race we have grace, cleverness, a talent for killing, and an ability to take exquisite pleasure in the pain of others. From our Father race we have compassion, love, and an appreciation of, and longing for, friendship. It's an uneasy balance we must strike within ourselves. We make it work, for the sakes of both our races. That is why we exist." She gave me a lingering look. "Why do *you* exist, Sister Killer?"

I could think of one answer. "Because someone made me."

"I know the feeling." Timmy turned her attention back to the mechanical claw. "Have you heard the *Baba Yaga* music, Oichi? By Anatoly Lyadov?"

"It's in my father's database." I tried to imagine what a Baba Yaga ship might look like, walking inside a gravity well. Would it hop around, like the icon that had appeared in my message box? Would Baba Yaga have to wear a seat belt?

"Tell Kitten she need not fear losing her head to me," said Timmy. "I enjoyed her company, though she didn't know it was me. I enjoyed yours, too."

"I'll tell her," I promised. "I'm sorry you had to eat your brothers and sisters, Timmy. The adults were cruel to lock you in those caverns."

Timmy shook her head. "We are the most dangerous at that age. We would have learned to fool humans into thinking we were safe. We had to be isolated, so we could fight against equals who would test us to our limits. We had to suffer loss, and we had to learn how we were responsible for those losses—how they hurt us and also how we benefited from them."

It was making me uncomfortable how much we had in common.

"I'm glad we had a little time alone," she continued. "I'm curious. Will you teach Ashur how to kill?"

I wasn't sure how to answer that, not because the question made me uncomfortable, but because I hadn't thought about it. "He should know how to defend himself," I said.

"It's not the same thing," Timmy chided.

"Maybe it is. We have powerful enemies."

"You do, but you have powerful friends, too." She said that without a trace of sentiment in her voice, though I wasn't sure I could judge what Timmy felt. She was as cool as the Belters were warm, and both of them baffled me.

"I don't offer advice often," Timmy continued, "but I am a survivor of the Children's Caverns, Oichi, and I know how a heart breaks. You may find this hard to believe, but I know how it heals, too. The way I see it, you have two choices. You can teach Ashur how to kill—or you can let him teach you how to live."

I stared at her. She was so beautiful, she made me feel shy. I remembered the way she had moved inside that air lock, when she could have killed Medusa and me, but refrained. I would not have shown that sort of mercy, not once I made up my mind to act.

Maybe she *had* made up her mind. Maybe killing us had never been on her to-do list.

At least, not *that* time. She might decide to accept that pending contract.

"You brought wonder into my life. I suspect you'll do it again." Timmy blew me a kiss. "I wish you luck, Sister."

Timmy shimmered and disappeared. In another moment, I knew I was alone, though I never saw the slightest ripple to betray where she had gone.

In my mind, I heard the music by Anatoly Lyadov. *Baba Yaga* was another piece that used the bassoon, percussion, wind, and strings to suggest action: *walking on chicken legs, across the fields.* I let it play inside my head as I picked my way back through the tow cables and spaceships, to the relative safety of the Visitors' Lock.

Will you follow us to Graveyard, Grandmother Witch? I wondered. *Will we see your chicken-hut spaceship lurching along the rim of the canyon?*

I made my way back to *Merlin*. When I got there, Medusa had returned. She had already tucked herself back into hibernation.

Too bad, I thought. *You would have been interested in the conversations I just had.*

I would have been interested in the conversations Medusa had been having, too. Having without *me*.

I found Captain Thomas on the bridge. "We've concluded our business on Maui," I informed her.

She looked up from her monitor. "We have received our security clearance. I've already requested permission to depart. If we don't pass out from overeating first."

Maui had shown us what the Belters had to offer. The real movers and

shakers were on Graveyard. It was time to complete the last leg of our journey. At least all the obstacles had been removed from our paths.

That's what I believed. I didn't know we were about to be confronted by
bogeymen from the education programs of my childhood. I thought they had
been invented to hide the truth about why we existed. I believed *Enemy Clans*
was just a metaphor for *Weapons Clan*.

It wasn't.

15

The Si Clan

I am naïve, I admit—at least in the realm of trade and politics. I thought once we were under way to Graveyard, I wouldn't hear again from the Belters until *Olympia* passed through their space, but I began to receive communications within the first hour.

I sought Representative Lee for advice. "I've been swamped! Will it seem rude if I don't answer? All those letters could take hours!"

"Review them," he said. "I'm willing to bet a lot of them are just trying to say, *Hello, here's my contact information.* Copy and paste that information, maybe write a one-sentence summary of what they talked about, and put it in a directory. Don't be surprised if your directory develops subdirectories. It will be helpful to the *Olympia*ns who take over your role as negotiator—unless you decide you like it and want to keep it, in which case, you'll find that information invaluable."

I wanted to pout. I had been looking forward to goofing off, catching up with my movie viewing in Nuruddin's vast database, and napping after my excessive partying and taxing conversations with certain august entities. I didn't pout for long, however, because I received an offer from unexpected quarters. Teddy and Dragonette approached me when they heard of my plight.

<I spend most of my time working with people in the Habitat Sector,> Dragonette reminded me. <I know what they make, what they like, what they need, whom they tend to make deals with.>

<I do the same sort of thing in the work tunnels,> said Teddy. <Dragonette and I collaborate all the time. We know how to write formal correspondence. Give us the communications, and we'll sort it all and organize it for you. We'll take notes and send you a report.>

<Oh my goodness!> I replied. <I love you!>

I settled in to be the queen of semi-indolence, but my smug complacency was interrupted by Dragonette when she had a chance to review the full list of petitioners. <There's something in here for your eyes only. It doesn't belong with the other communications.>

I paused *Kiss Me Deadly* (starring Ralph Meeker and Cloris Leachman). <Who sent it?>

<Gennady Mironenko.>

So much for his grand exit. Didn't the man know anything about anticlimaxes? You would think he never saw any of the movies he allegedly seeded into our history databases.

Oh well. <Thank you, dear. I'll look at it now.>

Dragonette had not been surprised to see a communication from Gennady. I had briefed my cohorts with a bare-bones account of my encounters with him, and with the Engineer, leaving out certain dangerous speculations and the parts I had been warned to forget. Perhaps it was my pared-down delivery, but no one seemed all that surprised.

Medusa surfaced just long enough to remark, <Thank you for informing me,> then rewrapped herself.

<Is anyone else going to show up not-really-dead?> Ashur said, seeming not to realize that my parents were still on the really-dead list. <I'm glad you punched Gennady,> he concluded.

<Me, too,> I assured him.

Kitten's attitude toward Gennady was far more positive. <I hope I can meet him someday. I'd like to thank him for all the show tunes.>

Perhaps I would not feel so inclined to thank Gennady once I viewed the contents of his communication, but the sight of his icon in my queue piqued my curiosity. I wondered if it was representative of the aristocratic old clans, with family seals and crests. It included a bird of prey (or so I assume, judging from the claws and talons), but also some odd symbols that must make sense only to the Mironenkos. For instance, the bird was perched atop an object that looked like a refrigeration unit—with a missing door.

I decided I must be misinterpreting, though it turned out I was wrong, and selected the icon. It delivered a letter to me and a file labeled CHARMAYNE.

Gennady had written:

I know there were questions you wanted to ask, and possibly I will never answer all of them. The attached Charmayne file may clear some things up.

If you suspect me of knowing that Baylor was about to assassinate most of his political enemies on the party shuttle, I don't blame you. You're only half right about that. I swear to you, I didn't know what Baylor was up to until I noticed that the other guests on the shuttle were falling asleep.

I calculated I had a few minutes to save my life. Like you, Oichi, I had practiced getting the suit on quickly in emergency circumstances.

There was no time to unstrap children from their emergency restraints. Believe that or not, as you will. If you had found yourself in the same situation, and you had paused for any reason, you would not have made it out.

As a sign of my goodwill, I have destroyed my copies of the Charmayne file. Besides your copy, they were the only ones that existed. It conflicts with your official narrative about how Baylor Charmayne died, so my advice is to consign it to oblivion. One never knows how the truth will come back to bite you.

Eventually you will learn more of the history of the Great Clans, and how our children schemed to destroy us all. Though we may seem like fools to you, I hope you will not judge the Mironenkos as snobs, despite what you hear. We made our first fortune recycling space garbage. It's documented on my family seal, if you look closely.

—Gennady

Once I selected it, CHARMAYNE began without any further ado, forcing me into the perspective of someone struggling into a pressure suit. The sirens warning of explosive decompression wailed, and I knew that sound too well, so I recognized what was happening. The images were being recorded by the camera inside the suit helmet, not by the struggler. The picture didn't stop jerking around until that person had sealed the suit and was facing the outer door of an air lock.

I calculated I had a few minutes to save my life. . . .

This footage backed up Gennady's claim. I could imagine him as he scrambled out of his restraints and pushed himself through the weightless environment toward the air lock where he kept his emergency suit. Gennady had spent decades scouting every detail of *Olympia* and her shuttles—he had used this particular shuttle as his quarters for years at a time.

The task would have consumed all his attention. I knew what *that* was like, too. Gennady had barely gotten his suit sealed before the outer door of the air lock opened. I heard the rush of atmosphere as he exploded out of the lock, and the scene tumbled. Within seconds, the only sound I could hear was Gennady panting inside his hemet as he used his jets to move away from the party shuttle, because he must have expected that at any moment—

There. The scene in front of him was an endless field of stars, but at the lower edge of his helmet visor, I saw the curved reflection of blue lightning. That must have been when the gravity bombs went off. Gennady's breathing got more frantic.

He looked toward his feet. I saw the shuttle being twisted apart by that blue lightning. Anyone who had still been alive at that point was no longer.

For several minutes, the scene spun back and forth as Gennady tried to orient himself with his jets. When *Olympia* came into view, she looked tiny and distant.

Oops, I thought. *You lost your cool, Gennady.* Though I would have done the same. He got disoriented. Maybe he didn't have the fuel to make it back to *Olympia*.

Gennady cursed, probably in Russian. I didn't recognize the words, but no one could mistake the tone.

The same gravity bombs Baylor used on Titania, I would have liked to tell him. *The ones you gave him. He didn't use all of them, Gennady. He kept some for a rainy day.*

What are you going to do now?

"Gennady to *Itzpapalotl*, do you copy?" he said.

He said it several times. I could see part of the display inside his helmet; it documented what suit systems were used. According to the reading, he had eight hours of air left.

"What's your status?" I recognized Bomarigala's voice on the suit radio.

"I'm in a bit of a pickle," said Gennady. "Can you send someone to retrieve me? Something terrible has happened. I'm not sure how it will affect our project."

"Brief me," said Bomarigala.

"Oh, most certainly. As soon as I see you on *Itzpapalotl*."

Silence from Bomarigala. Gennady waited it out.

Finally Bomarigala said, "You lost your bargaining power when you stood by and watched *Titania* be destroyed."

Maybe Gennady wasn't surprised to hear that. He wasn't prepared to let it go unanswered, either. "The deed was done before I could act to stop it. You wanted them to evolve as their natures dictated, and that's what they did."

"Yes," Bomarigala said, "but you were there to prevent that sort of disaster. Your life was added to the red column as soon as it happened. You know that's how we balance our books. The moment you set foot on this ship, you will be dealt with. I think it's best if you fix your own problem."

The way Bomarigala was talking made me wonder if he had been a business associate with Gennady from the beginning—whenever that was. One hundred years, at least. Gennady seemed to shrug off time with the indifference of an archangel.

He was less nonchalant when Bomarigala refused to rescue him. Gennady cursed quite a lot more, probably still in Russian, though I am no expert on the subject. Once he exhausted those reserves, he fell silent for several minutes. His breathing calmed. I wondered how long he would float there. Then I remembered something he had asked me the first time he invited me out to supper: *Do you ever think about God?*

Gennady claimed to think about God all the time. My impression was that Gennady contemplated divine ethics because he was often in a position of violating them. Now that he was alone with his fate, were his thoughts about God more personal?

If Gennady had continued to float there silently, I might never have my answer, but he did not remain passive much longer. Instead, the small screen on the control panel under his visor lit up with an image. It revealed the exterior landscape of *Olympia*. I wondered if Gennady was going to try to intercept her, after all.

That notion evaporated when Gennady shifted through several close-up shots of *Olympia*. He seemed to be looking for something in particular. Finally he settled on one perspective, which included the activity of persons outside one of the series-200 air locks.

It was Lock 212.

Gennady spoke one word in Russian. It sounded triumphant rather than angry.

I recognized Medusa. The figure wearing her had to be me. The other person in the shot was Baylor Charmayne. As I watched, Medusa and I seized Baylor with her tentacles and stripped the jets from his pressure suit.

Uh-oh, I thought. This was the recording Gennady claimed to have destroyed.

The recording that implicated me in the murder of the most powerful man on *Olympia*.

As I watched Medusa and myself, I couldn't help thinking, *Don't kill Baylor yet! He has information we need to know!*

Alas—hindsight. Maybe it doesn't matter—the best that can happen is what really *does* happen. What happened then was that Baylor Charmayne could not see past his Executive arrogance, and I couldn't see past my resentment.

From Gennady's perspective, the whole thing unraveled in silence. I don't know if he was able to eavesdrop on the communications we conducted through our brain implants—Medusa and I were using a secret pathway my father had created, and I have never seen evidence that it was breached. The only indication that the conversation Medusa and I were having with Baylor was not friendly, other than our initial aggressive action regarding his jets, was Medusa's expression.

I felt riveted by her visage. Because I had been wearing her, I didn't know what emotions had played on her face. I still didn't know them. Maybe I *can't*. Feelings that powerful might have clouded my judgment and weakened my resolve—they twisted her expression in ways I had never seen. I hardly recognized the entity who held Baylor tight and pulled him closer, so he could see exactly what had him.

I had never asked Medusa how she felt. It never occurred to me—I was so consumed with my own agenda. She had supported me without question back then—but was it really about me?

She had been forced to move her sisters to *Olympia* to save their lives. She had sabotaged Lady Sheba's escape vessel. All of that happened long before she met me. Why had I assumed Medusa resented the Charmaynes solely in my behalf? Seeing her now, I felt a grudging respect for Baylor. He had been helpless, yet he kept arguing his case.

Not well enough, though. When Medusa grimaced, both Gennady and I knew Baylor's time had run out. She and I had acted as one at that moment, just as we had so many times before when we killed our enemies. We slammed Baylor against the hull of *Olympia* until his faceplate shattered.

Gennady uttered a whole string of enthusiastic non-Standard words. Then he said something I understood perfectly. "You're not going to triumph after all, you bastard!" He laughed merrily.

"Enjoying some schadenfreude at your enemy's expense, Gennady? I'm proud of you."

I had heard it only once, but I recognized the voice coming from Gennady's helmet radio.

"Grandmother," said Gennady, "I confess that I am."

"We've lost some powerful allies," said Baba Yaga, "but cheer up. We've gained some others. I think they will prove to be much better."

The recording ended abruptly when the picture collapsed back into the icon that represented it. I frowned at it, feeling disappointed that he had ended the recording before I could see how he finessed his escape.

That was the least of the mysteries surrounding Gennady Mironenko—and his wasn't the face that kept surfacing in my memory.

Medusa was closer to me than anyone, yet I hadn't fathomed her feelings, except where they intersected with mine—and how could I? My own were so shallow. I had squelched them for so long, because they were inconvenient. I felt their absence only when I tried, and failed, to understand my partner. Now I didn't know how to get them back—if that was even possible.

I sat quietly in my bunk, pretending that I had not just seen something that had rocked me. No one seemed to be paying attention to me.

I didn't seem to be paying attention to them, either, so I took that with a grain of salt.

I thought I would watch CHARMAYNE at least once more before destroying it, but the schadenfreude Baba Yaga had mentioned no longer gave me the satisfaction I had once enjoyed. The perspective had become painful.

I had to shake myself out of it. Perhaps I had underestimated Medusa's anger, but my own had been justified. Some of the ones who had orchestrated the death of *Titania* had paid with their lives. Some had not. I was alive, and so were most of my loved ones, and I must look to our future.

My bunk mates still appeared to be consumed with their own interests. "I'm sleepy," I announced. "I'm going to close my eyes, but don't feel you have to be quiet. I don't mind the noise."

Cocteau seemed engrossed in her book, until the moment she looked up and winked at me. "I wonder, is it the oldest story in the universe? To murder, and then to spend the rest of your life trying to cover it up?"

That gave me pause until I remembered what she was reading. "It is if you only read Agatha Christie."

"Ha!" replied Cocteau. "You might also think so if you only read Patricia Highsmith."

That was the name printed on her current book, under the title *Strangers on a Train*. "What happened to Agatha?" I said.

Cocteau patted the nearest stack. "She's well represented, I promise. I packed a smorgasbord."

"Is that a French word? I seem to recall hearing it in one of Nuruddin's Scandinavian movies."

Cocteau didn't look up from her book this time. "They were influenced by French culture. Everyone was."

That parting shot was too perfect to dispute, so I made myself comfortable and closed my eyes.

Ashur asked me something before I could shift gears. <Oichi, do you think it would be too forward of me to send a message to Fire?>

I opened an eye and pointed it at him. <Well—I suppose it depends on the message.>

He flushed. <I suppose it does, too. Which is why I can't decide what to say.>

<*It was nice to meet you—I hope we'll meet again?*> I suggested.

<That would be true,> he said. <But not very—ah—smooth.>

I could have told him that Fire was too old for him, but what teenager wanted to hear that? <Best to keep things courteous and simple,> I decided. <How about, *I enjoyed meeting you and I hope you'll visit us on* Olympia *soon.*>

He mulled that over. <Well. Yes. I suppose. I just wish . . . >

I smiled. <That you could be dazzling? I wish I could be, too.>

He raised his eyebrows. <Really?>

<If it weren't for protocol, I would be completely at a loss.>

For a moment, he wore a smile very much like the one he had shown me when he kissed my cheek inside his Sirènes program. <Okay. I'll keep it simple. Thanks, Oichi.>

<Anytime.>

That settled, I wondered who else would need to speak to me, now that I wanted to sleep. No one else volunteered, so I let myself drift, feeling assured that everything was under control and that, for the time being, we were safe.

We weren't safe. Not remotely.

I remember having vague dreams, the sort that occur in bits and pieces, as if the brain can't be bothered to stick to one story line, let alone come up with something coherent. I enjoyed those fragments. They took no effort, and after the very long party and its aftermath, I felt I deserved a break.

Famous last words.

"You're in big trouble," said a voice.

I opened an eye. On the bunk where Mirzakhani was supposed to be sleeping, I saw Baba Yaga sitting on the edge with her booted feet barely touching the floor. She puffed her pipe, then blew a ring at me. "Is this any way to treat a guest?"

I sat up. The sleeping quarters still held the bunks that should be there, but the people I saw should *not* be there. Besides Baba Yaga, the Woov who had first caught my eye at the party perched on the edge of Cocteau's bunk. Jay Momoa sat across from her.

He waved. "Hi. Thanks for inviting me to your dream."

"I don't think it's a dream," I said.

"You're half right," said Baba Yaga. "These surroundings are a dream, but we three are real." She pointed at the others with her pipe. "Not the most conventional mode of communication, but it will do."

"You're doing this?" I said.

"No," said Baba Yaga. "Queenie is."

<Hi, Oichi,> said Queenie. <Yeah, it's me. Sorry to interrupt your sleep, but someone sent a ship after you. It's been following you since you jumped for Belter space. Pretty nervy of them to intrude this far in, but they've been testing us lately."

"Who?" I said. "The Weapons Clan?"

That provoked a startled response from Jay. "Wait—what, now?"

<No,> said Queenie. <Timmy's Mother race. From clans that don't have alliances with Belarus and the Hybrids.>

That was the *ghost* Wilson had detected. I had thought it was Timmy's ship. "They're after *me*?" I said. "What did *I* do?"

"You're on your way to talk to the Three," said Baba Yaga. "Isn't that enough?"

"We have been hearing rumors about you for decades," said the Woov. Her voice was musical, though she had a slight lisp. "If we have, *they* certainly have."

"All right, Auntie—" Jay said. "I'm here—because . . . ?"

"We need you to look at the intruder before Queenie destroys it," said Baba Yaga. "I suspect you have laid eyes on one like it before. Tell us what you know about that one."

Jay shrugged. "I think I can do that."

Baba Yaga got to her feet. "Well, then. To the bridge."

She moved steadily, if not quickly. I fell in behind her, with the Woov and

Jay bringing up the rear. We made our way to the bridge, past the exercise room and Captain Thomas's office, both of which were empty.

"The next time I end up in one of your dreams," grumbled Baba Yaga, "I must remember to bring my cane."

"The gravity field is pretty light," I offered.

"It's not a question of gravity. It's a question of confidence. That cane is topped with an iron skull. It can be used as a weapon."

When we emerged onto the bridge, it was also empty, though the screens were alight. They revealed schematics of the alien ship that hovered just beyond the viewing windows. Nothing seemed to be moving out there, making me wonder if Queenie had somehow suspended time.

The ship was a graceful thing. At least, that's what I thought when I first saw it, but the longer I gazed at it, the more uneasy I felt.

"Watch out," warned Jay. "They design mind traps into everything they make."

I blinked and made myself look at him instead of the attacking ship. "*Everything?*"

"Yeah. They pretty much hate everyone." Without the pheromones (or whatever) that made his physical presence so alluring, Jay was still a handsome man, but he seemed more like a regular guy. He stared briefly at the craft, then looked away and nodded. "From the Si Clan. It's their emblem and their damage."

I was going to ask him what he meant by *damage*, but then I felt the irritation in my psyche, the feeling of having been twisted in some way I couldn't quite comprehend, and I remembered what Jay had said about the mind traps.

Baba Yaga turned to the Woov. "You have heard. Do you believe?"

"Yes," said the Woov. "I will bear witness."

"Good." Baba Yaga turned to me again. "The Woovs are tolerated by the Ancient Races much more readily than we are. They will report these transgressors to the people most able to do something about them. It will help our effort, Oichi. You people of *Olympia* have already paid whatever cost it took to build your ships. I will relay that opinion to the Weapons Clan."

"Thank you," I said. "I'm—glad we could help."

"You'll help a lot more before this is over." Baba Yaga puffed her pipe. "By the way, Oichi, the Si Clan would be happy to take you and Ashur prisoner and kill the others. If it looks like that may happen, I advise suicide. You don't want to be their *guests*."

"Wait—" I said, "Queenie can stop time! Right, Queenie?"

<I can't stop time,> said Queenie.

"Just so," said Baba Yaga. "Queenie! We have seen. You may do your work."

<Roger that,> said Queenie.

In a flash, I was back in my bunk with my eyes shut. They flew open when I felt what was outside, coming for us.

I sat bolt upright in my bunk. "Enemy ship!"

"Holy crap!" Narm yelled from down the hall. I scrambled out my bunk and ran for the bridge.

In my dream, the alien ship had hovered outside the window as if the universe were static. In real time, it moved, and the way it moved was almost as bad as the way it *looked* if you let your gaze rest on it too long.

"Don't look at it!" I warned as I buckled myself into my seat.

"She's right," said Captain Thomas. "Use your displays."

Narm said, "Twenty-seven seconds to interception!"

What did *interception* mean between two spacecraft? That the Si Clan was about to crash into us? Their ship began to shift, to grow grinding teeth. I couldn't look away as it opened jaws to take a bite out of us.

<Medusa . . . > I sent, hoping she might hear my last words.

Light flooded the bridge. <I've got you,> Queenie interrupted, and through the windows I saw the form that was casting the light. It reminded me of the harness Fire had worn, with its predatory outlines that now resembled a bird of prey more than an insect. It focused those two points into one beam of energy that slammed into the attacking ship.

"We're jumping!" Thomas reported. "Hold on to your hat!"

The hole formed around us. Beyond its lip, the other ship struggled to escape from Queen's Fire. It looked like it was vibrating apart. As it began to lose cohesion, I felt the *damage* that Jay had recognized, the mind trap woven by the Si Clan, beginning to unravel and lose its power over me.

It shivered, seemed to melt, and then disintegrated, just as the hole closed itself around us.

The stars stretched, focused again, and we were out.

"Report, all stations," Thomas said calmly.

"No damage to the hull," Cocteau's voice sounded on the PA. "The drive is operating normally."

"Life support is optimal," reported Mirzakhani.

"Minis are okay," said Wilson. "Ashur, too."

Thomas waited for a long moment. "Anything else?"

"Well," Lee's voice sounded over the PA, "my butt is still intact."

Thomas grinned. "Likewise. I guess we beat the devil."

I still had spots swimming before my eyes from the intense light. "Queen's Fire destroyed their ship."

They stared at me, and I wondered if we had seen the same thing.

"All the way from Maui," said Captain Thomas. "If that's where she is."

I didn't say what I was thinking, that in a way, Queen's Fire had been right there with us. The manifestation of her power was what it must be like to see an Angel of Vengeance in action.

Thomas frowned at me. "I heard you shouting on your way up here. How did you know about the Enemy ship?"

I was glad I had a good, if somewhat edited, answer. "Queenie told me, through my brain implant. She warned me not to look directly at it."

I saw no point in talking about the dream. In retrospect, it sounded pretty kooky.

"Are we allowed on deck now?" called Kitten.

Captain Thomas raised an eyebrow. "Don't you mean on the ceiling?"

Her jovial attitude put me at ease. She wouldn't be acting that way if we were still in danger.

"Have they ever attacked anyone, this far in-system?" I said.

Thomas shrugged. "Beats me. It seems kind of unlikely."

Which meant that the Si Clan had taken a big chance. I couldn't call myself an expert, but I had spent enough time with Timmy to suspect that they didn't risk that much unless they thought it would pay off. They were afraid of what Ashur and I could do once we reached Graveyard, of whom we might talk to—and of who might talk back.

Yet I doubted that was all of it. Something Baba Yaga had said about the Three came back to me.

They are powerful tools. They should be properly used. We cannot simply bury our heads in the sand and hope that no one else will do so.

The Si Clan might have found Ashur and me very useful, had they captured us. Another level of urgency had just been added to our mission into the graveyard.

My call had awakened Medusa, which was heartening. When Captain Thomas briefed her about what had happened, I waited to see some change in her demeanor, some sort of acknowledgment that we had good reasons to seek the help of the Three. After all—enemies! Implacable aliens! Creepy, shifty, mind-altering ships! Right?! I wanted her to say, *I was completely wrong, you were totally right, I forgive you! Can you forgive me?*

Medusa looked troubled. "So it appears we have attracted the attention of enemies so terrible, their very name reflects hostility. We are doomed to stir up trouble."

"Don't blame yourself for that," said Captain Thomas. "These Enemy Clans have a long history of trouble. If they see you, they're going after you. That's what they do."

"Now they have seen us." Medusa's gaze met mine, and I looked for blame there. I didn't see that, either.

Unfortunately, I also saw no trace of the affection I missed so much. At least she seemed more like her old self. She said, "How long, Captain, before we arrive?"

"A little under twenty hours before we make our final approach," said Thomas.

"Thank you." Medusa cast me one last, troubled look, and then she flowed off the bridge, down the hall, back into Thomas's office.

"Get some sleep, if you can," said Captain Thomas. "In twenty hours we'll be entering a gravity well, and the way these things usually go, the time zone we end up in is going to be the most inconvenient one possible."

I nodded. Though it looked to me like Narm and Thomas wouldn't be resting, not for a while, at least.

I went back to my bunk. Ashur sat bolt upright in his. He wasn't upset. He didn't look scared, either.

<Queen's Fire is amazing,> he said.

<No argument there.>

Ashur leaned back and stared at the bulkhead as if it were a field of stars. <We're flying into the unknown in a ship named *Merlin*. Maybe it was named for the wizard, after all.>

I marveled at his sense of adventure and wondered if I would ever sleep again.

PART FOUR

A PLAGUE
OF SCARECROWS

16

Whistling Past the Graveyard

My mind still works in cycles, but three days after we landed on Graveyard, I would begin to think in terms of days. Three days after we had landed, three days since we had entered the canyon—but I had come unstuck in both time and space, so it wouldn't be three days at all. It was a million years ago—and it had yet to happen.

My hubris is substantial, but I couldn't have predicted everything that would happen. Certain entities that had goaded me into my actions may have seen it—after all, time itself seems to have been constructed to support particular outcomes. They pushed me to the limits of what I'm capable of feeling— admittedly, not as far as most would go. For me, however, it felt too far. I had done all I could. I had walked to the end, and beyond.

Can you believe it? I still didn't see how much farther I could fall.

Merlin fell toward Graveyard. Nothing can make you feel anchored to space and time better than a gravity well. I was ill prepared for the experience, yet all I could think was—if Graveyard had not hosted the ship graveyard, no one would have named it Graveyard.

The world below us was alive, a wonder for which no movie could have prepared us. Blue oceans covered most of its mass; white clouds swirled in its atmosphere. Brown and green landmasses peeked out from under the puffs and wisps.

The horizon curved the wrong way.

"Look down there," said Cocteau. "That's a hurricane. See the eye wall, in the center? Very well defined. That will be quite a storm, once it hits land."

Ashur looked half excited, half alarmed. "We're going to be landing in a hurricane?"

"No," said Captain Thomas. "That's way over on the other side of the landmass we're headed for. Where we're going, the weather is warm, partly cloudy, chance of light morning showers. Which reminds me—get ready for some serious time lag. We've already been awake for several hours, but where we're going, the sun is just rising. It's going to be a *long* day."

Day. Night. Morning. Afternoon. Those are words for time on worlds that rotate on an axis much bigger than the one *Olympia* spins around, planets that can make monster storms.

I recalled hurricanes from my mother's nature database, which included every kind of storm that could be found on Old Earth. Even if there had been no music or movie databases, my mother's recordings of nature would have kept people captivated for hours at a time.

Still, the database wasn't like experiencing a real hurricane. Even now, the storm hardly looked real, because we were seeing it from orbit, not from a beach on which the winds were blowing at two hundred kilometers an hour. From our perspective, it didn't even seem to be moving.

"Are you ready to fly in atmosphere?" asked Captain Thomas, as if that were the most fun anyone could possibly have. I patted my harness. I was bundled so firmly in it, I may as well have been under arrest. Each of the Minis nestled in special webbing that had been improvised, all of them fitting into one seat made for humans. We people who weren't made of biometal also wore g-suits.

Captain Thomas strapped herself into the pilot's seat; Wilson took the position beside her as copilot, and Cocteau sat nearby at a station that would serve as backup in the event both pilots were disabled. The rest of us were just along for the ride.

"You're going to feel about three g's during the landing," warned Captain Thomas. "You'll see a glow outside, too—the heat of friction generated by contact with the atmosphere."

"That's my favorite part," quipped Narm.

"Two forces we're going to experience," continued Thomas, "are gravity and drag. The drag refers to air resistance. That helps slow the ship to a safer speed. *Merlin* has a blunt-body design, and that creates a shock wave in front of us that helps keep the heat at a distance."

"How much heat?" worried Dragonette.

The captain shook her head. "Don't worry about it. Epatha Thomas spares *no* expense when it comes to insulation. So sit tight, *Olympians. Merlin* is going to show you some magic."

She gave me the impression it was all going to happen in five to ten minutes. Instead, we sat for quite a while, while Thomas used thrusters to turn

Merlin so her tail pointed at Graveyard. Once we had achieved the proper attitude, the tail thruster fired. That may seem as if it would cause us to blast away in the wrong direction, but we were moving so fast, it served to slow our speed of descent.

Once that thruster shut down, we let gravity take us.

We're falling, I thought, *from kilometers up, just falling into the gravity well.* It was a little hard to get my mind around that, because the only sort of fall I had ever experienced was the kind you suffer when you trip. The magnitude of our descent strained my imagination.

It went on longer than I expected, maybe twenty-five minutes. Periodically, Thomas fired thrusters to turn us, until our nose was facing Graveyard again. *What a bad moment to remember the name of this place,* I thought.

Wonder preempted my fear. The world filled our eyes now, and though I loved *Olympia*, though it remained a glory and a wonder, at that moment I understood that there is nothing in this universe more beautiful than a living world.

Aft steering jets fired to keep us at a forty-degree attitude. Then we hit the air, and we were flying. The windows glowed red. I was scared, but it was the good kind of scared. Captain Thomas remained so calm, I knew we were in good hands. This explained why she became more confident under pressure. When *Merlin* started to shake, and Narm hooted with joy, I just went with the consensus.

Captain Thomas pulled our nose up to slow descent further. We seemed to be headed straight for the horizon now.

I couldn't believe we were there, that this amazing thing was happening to us. This was an entire world, with a gravity well, with atmosphere that had made the windows glow red from friction.

Once that glow faded, and we had slowed and descended further, we flew through *real clouds*, and they were gigantic and fluffy and—towering, as they could never do inside *Olympia*, perhaps up to twelve thousand meters, according to my research. For a breathless time, we flew inside one of those clouds, and mist obscured our view. Then we emerged again, and I could see landforms.

The sun shone between the horizon and a bank of clouds. Below, the sunlight glowed red, yellow, and orange on distant buttes, cliffs, and spires, creating deep blue shadows. The clouds above mirrored those colors and shapes, and I could see curtains of rain falling in isolated areas. When we dropped lower, I spotted the line of a river, snaking in from the east.

Narm wore a headpiece, so I don't know at what point he began to receive radio signals from the ground. I heard him relay *Merlin*'s call numbers and destination, which in this case was Port One.

What about Odd's Corner? I wondered. That was the town Fire had said she was from, the one next to Joe's Canyon.

The landforms up ahead must be part of that canyon. Would we fly over it? Would the alien spaceships allow us to do that? What about the storm that was pouring rain ahead of us? Would we get hit by lightning?

We executed a turn. As our perspective shifted, I saw the monoliths that defined Graveyard. The Three pierced the sky. Their tops disappeared into the storm clouds.

I felt a jolting force as we banked again, rolling in a slow S-formation. How fast were we going now? How much were we slowing?

The sensation gradually faded. Minutes later, when I dared to glance out the windows, I realized we were much closer to the ground than I had thought. I heard the noise of machinery beneath me as the landing gear extended. Landscape was passing on either side instead of below us—*really fast*. Had we managed to slow down enough to land safely?

I felt a jolt as *Merlin*'s landing gear hit the runway. The reverse thruster fired, reducing our speed. We traveled a long distance, but we had slowed enough to see details of the man-made structures on either side.

<It's a spaceport,> Ashur said. <An actual spaceport on the surface of a planet.>

We continued to slow, and pretty soon we were crawling. "Okay, folks," announced Captain Thomas. "We're down. Now we're going to drive to our parking spot." She paused, assessing the situation. "This could take a while. Port One is big."

A big spaceport next to a small town. Odd's Corner sat beside the ancient, alien tech that everyone wanted. If the graveyard tolerated those neighbors, it must have had its reasons.

"I feel kind of tired," said Ashur. "Is it the gravity?"

Mirzakhani answered. "My diagnosis is that you're more tired from the fact that you've been awake so long already, and you just had an exciting ride."

When Ashur nodded, she added, "The gravity here is a little lighter than what *Olympia* simulates—about .9 g's. This world feels like Old Earth. I was born there—in Iran. I know what I'm talking about."

Ashur looked duly impressed. I was thinking, *Two people in this crew from Old Earth. What are the odds of that?*

Although Cocteau hadn't come right out and said she was from France. Perhaps I would ask her, after she had drunk more wine, though what she revealed under those circumstances would be only what she intended to.

Graveyard might be smaller than Earth, but it looked plenty huge to me. It felt that way, too—Ashur wasn't the only one who looked tired. Now that the excitement of landing was over, I wondered if I would fall asleep, especially since it was taking us so long to get to our parking spot. Port One sounded glamorous from space; the structures we passed were anything but. The whole thing was beginning to feel anticlimactic.

"At this point," Thomas said, "it's pretty much like driving a ground vehicle."

"One that uses really expensive fuel," said Narm.

We trundled along for another five minutes or so, and then stopped. Thomas, Narm, and Cocteau began to flip switches, shutting off several of the sounds we were accustomed to hearing. Without them, my ears began to ring.

For a moment, everyone sat quietly. Then something splattered the windows.

"What's that?" Ashur asked breathlessly.

"Raindrops," said Thomas.

A reverent silence followed.

Until Kitten broke it. "We *fell*! And then, we *flew*! And that was amazing enough, but then we went down to the ground and *landed*! And now—we've *stopped*, and we're alive and everything!"

Captain Thomas raised an eyebrow. "That was the general idea."

"It's the most amazing thing that's ever happened to me," said Kitten.

I suppose it was, up to that point, but as I stared past the rain splatter on the windows, at those three pinnacles in the distance, I had a feeling the amazing things were just beginning.

"This vessel has been cleaned so many times," mused Kitten as we watched Port One's scrubbers working on *Merlin*. "No wonder she's so sparkly."

Captain Thomas laughed. "That's the first time anyone has ever called *Merlin* sparkly."

"Does everybody land that way?" said Ashur. "Like—you know—an airplane?"

"Depends on the ship," said Thomas, "and on how much money and energy you've got to spend. I've seen ships that manipulate gravity fields to land, but that's astronomically expensive."

"No pun intended," added Narm. "Besides, who'd want to land any other way? Was that a great roller coaster ride, or what?"

"I loved it," said Kitten, who had been eager to get out of her harness so she could press her nose against the window. No one was allowed out of their seats until hydraulics lowered us to the ground.

The quality of silence that followed our landing was very different from anything I had experienced before. Inside *Olympia*, one always heard ventilation systems, quiet though they may be. It was the sound by which we knew our ship was still breathing. *Merlin* had seemed like a smaller version of what we were already used to, except for her gravity conditions—which is no small thing, I will admit. Now that *Merlin*'s systems had been shut down, we could hear sounds from outside the ship.

Once the novelty wore off, my responsibilities began to nag at me again. "Captain," I said, "I want to speak to Medusa in your office."

"All right," said Thomas. If I had been wearing Medusa, I could have monitored her heart rate, the dilation of her pupils, all the physical signs, but even with my own paltry senses, I could see that she knew things had changed for Medusa and me. She knew my conversation with my old partner was going to be anything but casual.

I left the bridge and went into Captain Thomas's office. Medusa sat bundled in her corner. <We have arrived,> I sent.

She stirred. I waited, aching to see my friend. Medusa's tentacles unfurled, revealing the face I had seen the first time I followed the forbidden link my father had implanted in my brain—remote and coldly beautiful.

The hairs on the back on my neck stirred. Had Medusa reverted to the earlier state? Could she discard memories of me, if she thought it was necessary?

She dispelled that notion when she said, <I haven't been completely honest with you, either.>

My petty heart leaped at that. Could she share some of the blame? Maybe we were, in a twisted sort of way, coconspirators once again.

She said, <After I sabotaged Sheba's ship, I considered altering *Olympia*'s course.>

I blinked. <Away from Charon?>

<Yes.>

<In what direction?>

<Anywhere but where Sheba and Baylor wanted us to go.>

I tried to picture that Medusa. She had been busy in those days, moving her sisters into the research towers on *Olympia*, trying to save as many of them as possible. I saw a shadow of anger in her face now, and I recognized it from the recording Gennady had made of Medusa and me killing Baylor. In the heat of that killing, I had thought Medusa was backing *my* play.

Maybe I had been backing hers.

<I didn't take that action, because I worried *Olympia* might not survive the unknown,> said Medusa. <I decided to stay the course. I hoped that wherever we were bound, we could find some way to make it right.> The anger leaked from her expression. What replaced it broke my heart.

Oh, bring back the angry Medusa, I silently pleaded. *I understand that gal. Don't leave me with this sorrowful version.*

<Now I regret my decision,> said Medusa. <I should have turned us around.>

Narm called from the hallway, "A limo just pulled up!"

<That's for me,> said Medusa. Gently, she nudged me away from the door. I followed her into the hall and watched her open the inner lock. When she opened the outer lock, I stood in that doorway and watched her climb into a silver vehicle with tinted windows. I didn't catch a glimpse of who had come to pick her up.

She never looked back.

A small hand touched mine. I looked down and found Teddy. "Is she coming back, Oichi? Are *you* coming back?"

I couldn't manufacture a smile for him, but I could at least fake some confidence. "We're coming back, Teddy. We're *Olympia*ns."

Any notion I entertained that I was comforting a childlike creature evaporated when he nodded. <One of you is going to connect with the Three. Then everything is going to change.>

<We'll try to change it for the better,> I promised.

<We always do,> said Teddy. <Sometimes we even succeed.>

Scant minutes after Teddy and I returned to the bridge, someone sounded the buzzer at the outer door.

"Port agents," said Narm. "Time to show our bona fides."

Dragonette flew to him and perched on his shoulder. "Aren't you going to squirt antibiotics up your nose?"

Narm looked at Mirzakhani, who shook her head. "They said the course we had before Maui is sufficient."

"Is that unusual?" I said.

"A little."

"Maybe Graveyard has really good doctors," said Ashur.

Mirzakhani glared at him, and his eyes went wide. "I mean—I didn't mean—"

She punched him in the arm. "It's not about the doctors; it's about protocol. Everyone does it differently. And we're all just kidding ourselves anyway, because we can't stop disease vectors, we can only slow them down, hopefully long enough to develop a treatment."

"Oh," said Ashur, and she punched him again. "Ow."

"You guys stay on this end," said Thomas. "I'll escort them into my office. I have no idea how long this is going to take, so relax."

She and Lee went into the air lock to meet the authorities. Their voices drifted up the hallway. They sounded cordial.

I remembered how cordial I had managed to sound, just before I lunged up the ramp at Thomas and Lee.

Come on, now, I chided myself. *Not everyone who sounds friendly is planning to kill people.*

We had been told to wait at our end of the hall, but that didn't mean we couldn't crowd there and stare at the newcomers when they came in. Within a few minutes, Thomas and Lee led them out of the air lock, two men and one woman wearing Port Authority uniforms. They were like Fire, like most of the Belters we had seen—descendants of people from Oceania. One had the tattoos on his face.

When Thomas and Lee preceded them into the office, those officers paused to stare back at us—especially Ashur and me, and all four Minis who had managed to find perches that let them get the best view (Kitten, of course, on the ceiling).

They regarded us with open curiosity tinged with a bit of awe. "So you're the *Olympia*ns," said the man who stood in front. He was handsome, an older version of Jay Momoa.

"We are," I said. "We're pleased to meet you. Your world is beautiful."

He didn't smile. "Most people feel disappointed when they see this part of our world. They think it's barren."

"I love the colors of the rocks," I said, and that *did* provoke a smile.

He nodded at us, then went into the office. The other two also nodded as they followed him.

<They look like the Belters,> said Ashur.

<They may be Belters,> I said. <Fire said they spend a lot of time in this gravity well, trying to keep their bones strong.>

<Do you think she's already here?>

<Maybe . . . >

<How did she get here? In another ship?>

When Fire and Queenie saved our butts, they had looked like beings of pure light. Did they need to travel the same way we did? Or did the Alliance of Ancient Races have some mode of transport even more mind-blowing?

The port officers didn't stay in the office for long. When they emerged, the man said, "Oichi, Ashur, Kitten, and Dragonette, please come with us. We'll take you to meet your party."

This was it. I felt ready, but I had underestimated just how unhappy this moment would make Teddy and Rocket. They followed us into the air lock.

<Report, if you can,> said Teddy, <even if it's just to say hello.>

<Try not to worry if we can't do that,> replied Dragonette. <Apparently that's normal. We might be able to send up flares, so watch for those.>

<We'll hold down the fort on *Merlin*,> said Rocket. <So don't worry about us, back here.>

<It's going to be all right,> said Kitten.

She sounded like she *hoped* it would be, not that she *knew* it. That was going to have to be good enough.

<We'll see you later,> I told our two who would be remaining.

I sounded more confident than Kitten had, but I swear, when we turned to walk away, I had never seen two Mini faces look so solemn.

We could see them as soon as we emerged from *Merlin*—the Three, reaching into the heart of the storm that had piled up over Joe's Canyon. Were they generating that weather themselves? Like mountains, with their own ecosystem? They looked big enough.

Yet there was something remote about them. I couldn't make out details on their surfaces. They *felt* distant. Not just in terms of how many kilometers stretched between us. They felt—aloof.

Welcome to Graveyard, I thought. *Nice to see you, too.*

The vehicle that had come to fetch us was no *limo*, by any stretch of the imagination. We climbed into a government vehicle with plenty of mileage on it, though it was full of equipment that must be quite useful to the authorities of a spaceport—at least to my untrained eyes.

I had thought that we would be going to some sort of hotel to spend the night and get used to our new circumstances, but the port officers informed us they would drive us straight to Joe's Salvage Yard. Our destination resided in the heart of a rapidly heating day. The chronometer in our vehicle, set for Graveyard time, informed me that it was 9:37 A.M.

What temperature would it reach when the sun was at its zenith?

"How much hotter is it going to get?" asked Ashur.

"Pretty Hot," said the older officer. "As opposed to Crazy Hot. This is the middle of our spring season. If you had shown up in the summer, we wouldn't expect you to make it out of the canyon alive."

As someone who had spent her life in chilly circumstances, I wondered how well I was going to cope with *Pretty Hot*.

The port officers smiled when Ashur paused on the way to the car and exclaimed, "That's what wind feels like!"

They never told us their names, though. They had a job to do, and they weren't going to forget all the protocols just because we were full of wonder.

<Cocteau is taking us to a nice bar near Port One,> Teddy sent. <She says it will be lots of fun.>

<Tell her I insist on fun for you and Rocket,> I said. <Lots of it. Tell her I'm counting on her.>

<She says she accepts your charge,> said Teddy. <She's very nice. Rocket and Wilson have become good friends. I think they'll miss each other, once we get back home.>

Home, where everyone and everything stayed where they were supposed to be—or so we all liked to imagine.

<You'll have to look after him,> I said.

<I will,> promised Teddy.

That was the last I heard of him on that side of the canyon.

The officers let Ashur roll his window down an inch so he could feel the wind. (It was noisy.) <It smells so different,> he said. <Oichi, is it just the plants? I don't see that many growing things here. The Habitat Sector has so much more.>

<The Habitat Sector was engineered for crops,> I reminded him. <Everything that lives here has adapted to the climate. It's probably dry most of the

time. Maybe when it rains, it rains hard—look at the power of that storm up there!>

That part of the sky had turned black. As we watched, a curtain of rain descended, obscuring the Three.

"Could we get trapped in a flood?" Ashur asked aloud.

The female officer looked back at him. "Stick to the highest ground you can find—stay out of the hollows. Don't think you're safe just because you don't see water yet. It can hit you just like that, a wall moving down a slot canyon right at you. That's how hikers get killed. They don't heed the warning signs."

"I promise to heed the warning signs," said Ashur.

She flashed him a smile. "You're smart. I think you'll do fine."

Ashur blushed. When he was younger, he thought girls liked him because he was funny and clever. He was just beginning to realize how handsome he was.

I wondered what Ahi would think of him. Would she turn goofy in his presence?

Crow thought highly of her, so maybe not.

From what I could see of it, Odd's Corner was miles long and an inch wide, built up on either side of the lone highway. Many of the roads leading from that main drag weren't paved. We drove past shops that sold food, clothing, electronics, and various things that undoubtedly made life more comfortable inside a gravity well. We saw quite a few places that promised dancing, pool, and copious amounts of alcohol. Many businesses advertised services that baffled me—probably connected to the salvage from the graveyard. Quite a few others seemed to be legal offices.

The younger male officer nudged the female and pointed at one of the alcohol/dance places, then said something I couldn't catch. She laughed, and responded with words that flowed together.

"What language are you speaking?" asked Kitten.

"Tahitian," said the woman. "He was reminding me it's karaoke night at the Seahorse."

"Kare-ee-oh-kee . . ." Kitten said. "Is that a form of martial art?"

"It is when she sings it," said the younger man, and he got a punch in the arm for that.

"Sings!" Kitten put her front limbs on the back of their seat. "It's for singing?"

The young woman raised a finger in her comrade's face before he could make another joke at her expense. "Sort of," she said. "There's a music track, and you sing along with it."

"That sounds like high civilization!" said Kitten.

All three officers laughed at that. "You like to sing?" asked the woman.

Ashur, Dragonette, and I exchanged amused glances. Then Kitten began to sing "Bali Ha'i" from *South Pacific*.

She did a respectable job of it, though I still prefer her rendition of "I'm Gonna Wash That Man Right Outa My Hair." It turned out to be the right song as we drove out of town on that road, toward a horizon where storm clouds were unloading in one spot and the sun was blazing through in another, until we passed a sign that said JOE'S CANYON, 13 KILOMETERS. The road bent west, and on the northern side, a tributary canyon peeked out from a tangle of trees and shrubs that seemed to be growing thicker as we gained elevation.

MAISY NORTH said a sign by the road. "This is Maisy Canyon?" I said. "I thought it was Joe's Canyon."

"Maisy River," said the woman. "She flows all the way through the canyon, but on this end, she's fed by springs. Her water is good up here. Farther south, it gets real muddy."

As we approached the canyon, the day progressed, the storm clouds developed gaps, and bright sunlight shone through more spots. Creatures flew past our windows, flocking in the trees and making chirpy noises, but we saw some that traveled on paws and claws, too. When we turned another bend, a family of hoofed animals stared at us from a hillside, and one of them had three sets of horns.

Ashur had wondered why this place looked so empty. Now that we were in the middle of it, we saw life everywhere. What we *didn't* see was alien spaceships. We couldn't even see the Three, who still hid behind the rain. The picture I had in my head of the graveyard must be wrong.

Then we turned another bend and saw a sprawling parking lot, and the entrance to Joe's Salvage Yard, and I knew that my original impression of weird spaceships crowding the landscape hadn't been so wrong, after all.

If anything, it was an understatement.

17

Unsorted Apocrypha

Orderly disorder might be the best way to describe the front section of Joe's Salvage Yard, the interface between customers, employees, and odds and ends from spaceships. Everything that couldn't stand on its own was piled, stacked, sorted in bins, or hung on racks that towered far overhead. Customers and employees examined parts, haggled over prices, and climbed on catwalks to explore the uppermost offerings.

Standing behind it all, the Three glowed in the morning light as the storm began to clear.

<How far away are they?> said Ashur.

<I think about one hundred kilometers,> I said.

<We're supposed to walk there?!>

<I doubt it. We're supposed to enter the canyon. Crow didn't say how far we'd have to go.>

<Why can't the Three just talk to us from here? They can see us, can't they? We sure can see them.>

I stared at our (alleged) ancestors. If they were aware of us, I felt no hint of it. <I don't think they're going to do that. They would have called us on *Olympia*. Instead, it was Crow who called us.>

The entities are in agreement. . . .

<Really,> I said, <we're here for just one reason.>

<Because Lady Sheba is coming,> he guessed, and from the set of his jaw, I knew Ashur and I were in accord.

Once we had parked, the officers walked us straight down the middle of the lot, a wide aisle between rows of objects whose purpose must be obvious to engineers and technicians, but not so much to me. It bestowed a veneer of mystery on items that might otherwise seem utilitarian. As we passed under a sign that said DANGER! UNSORTED APOCRYPHA!, a group of men standing near a security gate stared at us long and hard enough to make me uncomfortable.

There were three of them. They stood out because they didn't look like the typical Belters and Graveyarders we had met so far, the people whom Fire had said were descendants of colonists from Oceania.

Beyond their general otherness, I couldn't tell you much about two of those men, because the third dwarfed them. He stood well over two meters and had the muscular build of a cross-training athlete. His skin was ruddy where it wasn't pale, though his hair was black. He had vivid blue eyes.

Sounds sort of handsome, doesn't he? Yet he was wearing an expression I didn't like, on a face that looked like it had been shaped by emotions I didn't want to know about, and I would have been happy to walk far away from him.

A vehicle rolled through the front gates and onto the lot, parting the crowd of shoppers with little regard for their safety. It reminded me of the limo Medusa had climbed into, except that it was bigger, and its panels were the color of storm clouds. It rolled to a stop next to the giant and his forgettables. The driver jumped out and ran around to the side, where he unlocked a door and pulled it open to allow the passengers to disembark.

Ashur stopped dead, so I walked right into him. When the officers noticed we weren't following anymore, they paused to see what was holding us up.

"Is that Lady Sheba?" said Ashur.

He had seen her only once, in the transmission from *Itzpapalotl,* but once was enough. Sheba allowed the driver to help her from the vehicle. She stood tall when her feet were on the ground. Bomarigala climbed out beside her.

Or was it? He resembled the man who had sparred with me when I rejected the offer of the Weapons Clan. Somehow he looked younger, less sure of himself. Could this be his son?

Sheba surveyed the lot, her head tilted at a regal angle. She was dressed for hiking, and her hair had been bound in a tight braid. When her eyes found our motley little group, she flashed a predatory grin. She knew exactly who we were. The Bomarigala look-alike noticed her expression and looked at us, too. He didn't smile, and I got the impression he wasn't impressed with us.

Kitten stretched her neck. <*Everyone* is here,> she said. <All the good guys and the bad guys. It's like *Casino Royale,* but without David Niven and the Mancini soundtrack.>

Dragonette hovered overhead. <I think someone else is coming to pick them up.>

A moment later, a small motored cart rolled past us and circled around to Sheba and her entourage. The giant and the forgettables climbed into the seats behind Sheba and Almost Bomarigala.

Others will be journeying into the canyon, too, with the permission of other entities. . . .

Apparently with their own guides. As they rolled past, Sheba ignored us, but her henchmen watched us, their eyes gleaming.

<Do you think we'll run into them?> said Ashur.

<I hope not.>

The port officers started to walk again. It looked as though *we* weren't going to be riding anywhere, so we had no choice but to follow.

<It stretches forever!> said Dragonette. Periodically she would soar up, and descend again to offer a report. <You think *this* part is full of big stuff. It just gets bigger!>

People drove past us in a variety of vehicles, from small, moving platforms big enough for the feet of one person to a house-sized thing whose purpose I could only guess. We walked until the heat began to oppress me, and I longed for a vehicle of our own. The landscape around us widened, revealing bigger objects that looked more like alien spaceships—or at least pieces of them.

"How many people work here?" Ashur said.

"Maybe a hundred?" said the female officer. "It varies. My mother-in-law works here. Just about everyone has a relative who does."

A hundred people would be lost among the wrecks in Joe's Salvage Yard, but they had plenty of machines to help them out, and many of those looked like salvage, too. Farther in, the catwalks and the racks they accessed morphed into more complex structures, some of them linking with ships that seemed to have become part of the permanent landscape. They formed bridges over our main pathway, casting shade that might provide some relief at midday, though for now the sun slanted under those structures and right into our eyes. The port officers slipped protective eyewear onto their faces without breaking their stride.

We walked for perhaps half an hour, until we saw Fire and Queenie standing next to three large bundles supported by frames. Our guides straightened their shoulders.

If I thought the Port Authority officers had looked upon *us* with awe, the high regard they seemed to have for Fire was an eye-opener. She might have been a general reviewing her troops. She looked the part, standing in the center of that yard with Queenie towering over her head.

"Welcome," she said when our group was within hailing distance.

The port officers stopped and formed a loose circle around Fire and her supplies. They didn't greet her, but turned to look at us expectantly.

I felt shy again, despite the warmth of her smile.

Fire indicated one of three framed packs. "I'll carry this one for you, to the junction. I can't go past that point. Ahi will meet you there."

"We don't get to have a nice supper and sleep on a bed tonight?" I said, feeling a bit put out.

"Nope," said Fire. "The entities in that graveyard don't have much patience for human considerations. As far as they're concerned, once your wheels hit the ground, you need to get to it."

"Then we'll be camping tonight," said Ashur. "Under the stars."

From his tone, he thought that was going to be wonderful. Even though I had known accommodations inside the graveyard were going to be rough, the reality didn't sink in until I had my feet on solid ground. Very *hard* ground, air mattresses notwithstanding.

"First," said Fire, "you two get changed. I brought clean-wear for you." She opened the top of two of the packs and pulled out packages. After a brief inspection, she handed one to me and one to Ashur. "That silk-and-cotton stuff you have on is pretty, but it's going to stink after less than a day. The clean-wear will always smell good, and you can shake it out if it gets dusty. That's why it's so rare."

Ashur inspected his. "What's it made of?"

"Proprietary stuff." Fire winked at him. "The people who own the patent aren't saying."

"Is it made from salvaged technology? From the graveyard?"

She frowned at him. "No! You know we can be smart all by ourselves, right?"

"I didn't mean—I know that!" Ashur stuttered.

Fire grinned. "I'm kidding! Go put those on, and take these." She handed over two pairs of low boots. "They'll conform to your feet. They'll save you a lot of pain down the line. Put these on last." She handed us each a hat. "It's spring, but you two have spent your whole lives on a generation ship."

We piled the boots and hats on top of the clothing. Fire pointed to a building. "Those are bathrooms, so take advantage."

I didn't have to hear that twice. We made a beeline for the facilities.

When we emerged again, the port officers had left. I was not surprised to find that Dragonette had perched atop one of Queenie's horns and Kitten had made herself comfortable on Fire's shoulders.

"Looking good!" said Fire as she inspected our new clothes. "You'll be glad for those. Give me your discards, and I'll have them laundered for you."

We handed her our *Olympian* garb, and she placed it in the packages that had held the clean-wear. "You know," she said, "this cloth is beautiful. That's another thing you can trade, once you get that going."

I was glad to hear that someone thought we had good stuff, but I was *also* glad to hear the formula for the clean-wear cloth was secret. I didn't think *Olympian* textiles could compete in that market.

"This one is yours." Fire pointed me to one of the packs. "That one is Ashur's."

She watched as we shouldered into the frames, then helped us with our straps. The weight was substantial, but not unbearably so.

"There must not be much water in here," worried Ashur.

"You've got a liter bottle in there that you can refill," said Fire. "Ahi knows where all the water stops are. This end of the Maisy River is okay for drinking. Now"—she patted Kitten—"I love you Minis, but it's time for you to vacate your perches so Queenie and I can carry the extra pack to the bridge."

"The bridge?" I said.

"It spans a small gorge over the Maisy River," said Fire. She turned her back to the remaining pack and went down on one knee. Before I could ask her what she was doing, Queenie grew tendrils that seized the pack and pulled it close. Fire stood again.

"Is Queenie made of biometal?" said Ashur.

"Nope," said Fire in a tone that suggested no further queries should be made into the nature of Queenie's substance.

"Proprietary," suggested Kitten.

"Very," said Fire. "This way, *Olympians*." She marched up the central aisle, toward a point where the catwalk maze seemed to twist into a jumble.

The jumble was an optical illusion, but the maze still turned out to be fairly maze-y.

"Don't people get lost in here?" I wondered.

"Sure," said Fire. "This isn't even the tricky part of the canyon. Most of the ships on this end are modern. Those big ships you see holding up parts of the catwalks? We call them the Sentinels. The youngest of those are over eighty thousand years old."

One of those giants loomed to our left. Its panels reflected the morning light, dulled in the spots where catwalks intersected it. A large door in its hide loomed open, but it didn't look like a pressure door. It appeared to be part of the structure, rather than something that was cut into it later, by humans. I entertained the notion that this Sentinel had grown a door to accommodate the catwalks.

Light dappled the worn pavement where the sunlight shone through the structures overhead. My eye caught movement among those shadows, some-thing sinuous and graceful that flowed over the broken patterns, imposing a shape I thought I knew.

Tentacles.

It must be moving on the catwalk. It passed right over our heads, and I looked up in time to see something disappear inside the open doorway of the Sentinel.

<Medusa?> I called.

Something rebuffed me. The sensation felt odd, as if I were a moth that had fluttered up against a windowpane.

<Oichi?> Ashur called. I turned and saw concern in his face. It made me wonder about my own expression.

I quickly schooled it. "I thought I saw something going into the Sentinel."

"They don't let just *anyone* in," said Fire. "The Sentinels like us. They sort of look after us. They even talk to us sometimes, if we can access the ma-chine parts of their brains."

"What about the *nonmachine* parts?" said Kitten, craning her flexible neck so she could study the old ship.

"What, indeed?" said Fire. "That interface is harder—and well protected."

"Thank goodness for *that*," Dragonette remarked from her perch on Ashur's pack frame. "It's not nice to poke at the organic parts of people's brains."

<Tell it, sister,> remarked Queenie.

If that had been Medusa I had seen, she didn't seem inclined to stick a tentacle out the door and wave at me. Now I wasn't sure I had seen anything at all. I squared my shoulders and adjusted my pack. Fire took that as a signal, and we resumed our march.

"When does it start to look canyon-y?" Ashur said.

"When you get to the edge," said Fire. "The canyon is a surprise when you see it. This terrain bends upward, all the way to the South Rim. The North Rim is five hundred meters higher than the South Rim, so you'll see that first."

"It's like a long climb down into a big crack in the earth?"

"Into a *wide* crack," said Fire. "Almost sixty kilometers at its widest place. There's a world in there: spires, buttes and plateaus, massive ledges and giant staircases. You can find deserts and oases, but there are narrow places, too, and slot canyons."

The mention of slot canyons reminded me of our talk of flash floods, and I scanned the horizon for rain clouds. The morning storm had shredded into tatters, and that side of the sky shone back at me, almost cloudless and vivid blue. The Three shifted color in that light, looking more like the rocks in the canyon below them, but their details were no sharper. I could see no features I would expect to find on the hull of a spaceship.

"Everything has to start someplace, right?" said Fire. "Joe's Canyon starts at the bridge, where the Maisy River eats through the Clementine Plateau."

"Joe, Maisy, and Clementine," said Ashur.

Fire grinned. "They were colonists in the first wave of humans on this world. That layer of red sandstone"—she pointed to a slab of red rock ahead—"is the Ernie Sandstone."

I had thought that structure was a mountain. As we worked our way closer to it, I realized it was part of the North Rim we had seen earlier. Catwalks and spaceships obscured the rest of the rim, but as we got closer, we could see more of it, and less of the salvaged items in the yard. It didn't look like a canyon yet, but I could see how one might emerge from that landscape.

A breeze wafted past us, and I smelled flowers. Clumps of them grew wild in patches around the structures, but some were enterprising enough to colonize cracks in rock surfaces. "Which wildflower am I smelling?" I said.

"Those are the twistifer trees. There." Fire pointed to a shrubby plant that seemed intent on falling over a ledge. "Their bark smells good this time of year."

Twistifers and wildflowers began to dominate on all sides as we left the main part of Joe's Salvage Yard behind. I judged we had been walking for another hour by then. There were still plenty of Sentinels standing around this far in, but very few people. The noise of machinery and commerce faded; a grand silence took its place. The ground under our feet had turned a rusty red color, and I wondered if it had eroded out of the Ernie Sandstone.

Ahead, I perceived a gap, not so much because I could see it, but because it tampered with my depth perception. A railing stretched across the path, blocking the way, but we veered to the right, around a scarp that had eroded out of our side of the Clementine Plateau. Up ahead and to the left, a bridge spanned the river gorge. The sight of it made my palms sweat.

When I looked over the railing next to our path, the drop didn't look that bad. Dragonette hovered where she could get a good look. "Maybe one hundred meters down," she guessed. That was still a long way, but not so far as I had worried.

Kitten jumped onto the railing to have a look.

"Kitten, don't fall," I warned.

"That fall wouldn't kill me." Kitten balanced confidently. "It wouldn't even dent me. Not permanently, anyway. I could easily climb back up."

She jumped down to the path and trotted just ahead of me, her attention focused on the metal structure that spanned the river gorge. We walked onto a paved platform and approached the entrance to the bridge.

"About two hundred thirty meters across," judged Dragonette. "This is a suspension bridge. A beautiful example."

Perhaps so, but the bridge deck was not paved—it was made of a rigid metal mesh, through which the structure and river below could be glimpsed. When I put my feet on it, my steps generated vibrations that traveled throughout the structure, which made me nervous.

We gathered on the western side and looked over the railing. One hundred meters below, the Maisy River moved sluggishly, and she had depths that looked green and murky. Large bubbles formed and broke on the surface. I shivered. "What's making those bubbles?"

Fire leaned farther to get a look. "Gas. Probably from algae." She straightened and shaded her eyes, looking west down the river. "See that? From here it looks like a tiny spaceship, way down there—just where the river starts to veer north?"

My artificial eyes are good at spotting things, even without Medusa's enhanced vision. "Yes."

"That's the Last Sentinel. Once Ahi takes you past that ship, you'll be out of the human side of the graveyard and into the area where the entities control everything."

We gazed at the distant ship for a long moment.

Ashur broke the silence first. "Lady Sheba has a head start on us. I wonder if she's waiting for us around that bend. If she kills us, she'll eliminate competition."

I have to admit, I felt proud that Ashur could imagine such a ruthless scenario.

"Sheba's entrance into the canyon is in a different place," said Fire. "Once you're inside, it doesn't matter where you want to go. Any plans you make will be thwarted by the entities. You have to go where they want you to go. Sheba does, too."

Ashur didn't like that answer any better than he had liked the idea of being ambushed. I thought it evened the playing field, if nothing else. Sheba could stack all the henchmen she wanted on her side, but it wouldn't give her an advantage. I could work with that.

"I want to ask Queen's Fire a question," I said, "if that's not forbidden."

<It's worth a shot,> replied Queenie.

I sent the question in Open Forum. If I got an answer, I wanted all of us to receive it. <The Alliance of Ancient Races sent you to us, to act on their behalf. Why are they interested in our affairs?>

The entity that answered wasn't quite Queenie, and she wasn't quite Fire. She was the creature made of light, the angel of destruction who had killed the enemy ship. <That's easy,> she said.

She didn't answer with words. Instead, she showed us the Three, standing silently in the Gorge. They cast their shadows over everything else in the graveyard.

<If you talk to them,> said Queen's Fire, <you will be the first to have done so in millennia.>

The image faded, and we saw Queenie and Fire again. Fire knelt, and Queenie let go of the pack. When Fire stood, she said, "Ahi is coming. I'll see you when you return. Aloha, *Olympians*."

"Aloha," we all said together, as if we were the Chorus in our story instead of the main players.

Fire turned and left us there. We watched her walk away, Queenie held high, down the wide path between the used wonders.

We didn't watch for long. A sound made our heads turn.

A distant figure had set her feet on the far side of the bridge. Vibrations from her steps played along the structure.

"That's got to be Ahi," I said.

The girl walked toward us, never touching the railing, glancing down from time to time, not like a sightseer, but as someone looking at favorite things well known to her.

The canyon sent her . . . came a thought.

I'm still not sure it came from me.

18

The Dragonfly

The girl shaded her eyes to look as us, then waved. We waved back. She stared at us all the way across the bridge, her curiosity lively and unabashed.

Ahi was a younger version of the Belters and the Graveyarders we had met so far—tall, with brown skin that took on a golden tone in the bright light of Joe's Canyon. Her black, wavy hair had been cut to chin level, and surrounded her wide face like a halo. Her eyes were the color of honey, at least from a distance. It made her gaze appear molten—intimidating for a person so young. I doubted she was older than Ashur.

She wore the same sort of shirt, slacks, and boots that we had put on. She walked with confidence, with the grace and energy of youth. Her wide mouth looked like it would rather be smiling, though at the moment her expression was neutral.

"Hello, *Olympians*," she said when she was close enough that we could hear her. "I'm Ahi. I'm your guide in-canyon."

"Hello, Ahi," I said. "I'm Oichi. This is Dragonette, Ashur, and Kitten," I indicated my companions in turn.

Ahi gave us a grin. "I like your names." She closed the last few meters between us, her feet striking hollow sounds on the metal bridge. "Let's have a look at these supplies."

We stepped back so Ahi could inspect the packs. She did so with a professional efficiency. "Well, now! Someone packed these well. I couldn't have done it better myself. You there, Ashur, you look like a strong fellow. Will you carry my pack, too?" She put her hands on her hips and regarded him with a wistful expression.

"I—" Ashur stuttered, "I don't think—"

Ahi laughed. "I'm joking! You're so funny, with that serious face! Do you always look like that?"

Ashur frowned. "It's kind of a serious situation here."

"If you keep frowning like that, what do you think your face is going to look like by the time we come out the other end of this canyon?" demanded Ahi.

Any worries I had harbored that Ahi might turn useless at the sight of Ashur's handsome face evaporated on the spot.

"Dragonette—" Ahi held up her hand as a perch. "—may I see you closer?"

Dragonette flew to Ahi's hand and hopped onto a finger. "Ashur made me," she said. "I was the first Mini."

"*Ashur* made you!" Ahi regarded him with far more respect. "That was a wonderful thing to do. Did he make you, too, Kitten?"

"He did." Kitten trotted over to Ahi and Dragonette. "How do you do?"

"Very well, thank you." The girl smiled at Kitten, her face revealing a potential for joy that dazzled me. "Are you ready to go into the canyon, Kitten?"

"I am!" declared Kitten.

"Then let's get cracking. The cool temperature won't last forever." With that, Ahi strapped herself into her pack and started off across the bridge. The four of us followed in her wake, marveling at her definition of *cool temperature.*

When we were almost to the other side of the bridge, I heard a sound from the far end. I stopped, and turned to look across.

Nothing moved over there.

Why did I get the feeling someone was following us?

My research had informed me that Joe's Canyon was 830 kilometers long, if you counted the long tributary canyon that angled north from its eastern tip. You might also measure the other tributary canyons that cut across its main segment, zigzagging in from the the northeast and southwest, making Joe's namesake a canyon system rather than one single feature and adding extra kilometers to its total.

Officially it started where we began, where the bridge spanned the Maisy River. Though its deepest point was three thousand meters, from the North Rim to the bottom of the Gorge, our little part of it descended to a modest depth. Once we had crossed the bridge, Ahi led us onto a path that snaked around to a series of switchbacks that led us down to the river. She didn't speak to us as she walked, and her pace made me feel grateful that we were walking down instead of up.

When we reached the canyon floor, I was the last in line. I listened for more noises behind us, but I didn't hear any. We walked on gravel that must have been deposited when the Maisy River overflowed her banks. Ahi led us west along that side, where, one presumed, we would pass the Last Sentinel and enter the weirdness. Or the Greater Weirdness, since we had seen plenty of that already.

Crunch, crunch, crunch, crunch went our feet, marking a rhythm that lulled me into a sort of waking dream. The red canyon walls seemed to climb as we descended. Black streaks marked the spot where water seeped out of the sandstone and trickled down, eroding regular gullies that cut across our path. Some of them still trickled; others were dry—at least until the next storm.

Gravity, I thought. Water, sand, and even boulders eventually settled into basins. Everything moved here, even if it was too slow for you to see.

Crunch, crunch, crunch, crunch.

Kitten trotted at a comfortable pace. Sometimes she lifted her head to follow the flight of some winged creature; sometimes she paused to watch a bug. Sometimes I joined her. We couldn't stop for long—we had two young people to keep up with. Dragonette remained on her perch atop Ashur's pack, as if unwilling to leave his side. I wondered about that. I didn't ask, because I was too busy trying not to look like a slow grown-up.

I had thought the Last Sentinel was closer than it turned out to be. Fire warned me that it was bigger than it looked from the bridge, which of course meant it was also farther away. You don't want to know that when you're just starting a long hike, when the day is heating up and the sweat keeps trickling into your eyes.

We turned a bend, and there stood the Sentinel, far ahead. We turned another bend, and it disappeared. The river elbowed back, so the ancient ship was in sight again, and hey—it didn't look that much closer. Another turn took it out of sight, and I was beginning to feel downright surly when we saw it again, and we still did not seem to have made that much progress.

Yeah, I chided myself, *let's just march right up to the Three—shouldn't take more than an afternoon, right?*

How long was it going to take, then? I hadn't asked. I had thought Fire would tell me if it was going to be several days. After all, didn't we have water to worry about? Ahi didn't look concerned.

Still, if I was going to get pissed off this early into the hike, I was going to be in a pretty bad mood by the end of the day. I already knew we were going to be camping, so—*Get over it,* I told myself, *and get on with it.*

Crunch, crunch, crunch, crunch in the gravel by the Maisy River, three people and two Minis, no waiting. I stopped expecting to see the Sentinel getting any closer—so when it did, it took me by surprise. Once I quit mentally complaining, the journey didn't seem so hard or so long. Before I expected it, we rounded another bend, and the Last Sentinel towered near the wall of the canyon, perhaps three hundred meters away. I felt glad, which was ridiculous, considering that this was the beginning of our journey and not the end, but it still seemed a milestone.

Ahi marched toward the ancient ship as if it were an old friend. At the pace she set, we traversed the distance quickly. One moment I was looking south toward the river, which had picked up both momentum and depth as it flowed down the slope, making a pervasive noise unlike anything I could have heard on *Olympia*, and the next I was looking *up* at the Last Sentinel as we walked around its base.

Sand and gravel had piled up against its flanks from countless seasons of flooding, higher on the east side, since the Maisy flowed from that direction. We had to slow our pace as the sand got deeper. Kitten gave up and perched on my shoulder. Soon our efforts to make our way through those drifts consumed our curiosity over the Last Sentinel.

On the upside, I wasn't falling so far behind the others anymore. That sand slowed all of us down. By the time we had struggled most of the way around the base, we had formed a loose clump.

Ahi stopped and half turned. "When we get to the west side of the base, there's a lot less sand. We'll have an easier time. Almost there!"

"Okay," Ashur said, sounding downright cheerful.

I decided to save my breath. Once we were on normal footing, I would fall behind again. My ego wasn't bruised, but I worried that I wouldn't be able to protect them if they got too far ahead. I wondered if I should mention that to Ahi, and if it would hurt her pride. She had a lot of confidence in her ability to guide us safely, and her confidence must be justified or . . .

I took another step and staggered as the sand gave way beneath my feet. Kitten leaped free and fell into a soft drift. As I started to topple, I flailed out with one hand and planted my palm firmly on the side of the Last Sentinel, to steady myself.

The implant inside my head flared to life. The heat and light of Joe's Canyon vanished, and I was suspended in the void. At my feet, two suns were locked in a spiral, a yellow giant and a smaller, blue-white companion. I knew the one that looked small had a gravitational footprint far larger than its partner.

Hella One and Two, I thought. *She can see them. She can see Charon, too.*

She was so cold, I couldn't maintain the contact, so I let go of her. The Hellas disappeared, light and heat rushed back, and once again I was stuck in the sand at the feet of the Last Sentinel.

I breathed a sigh of relief. I thought it was over.

Before I could take another step, a figure swooped and fluttered around me like a giant bird. I staggered back, expecting to feel claws, but the only thing that touched me was a slight breeze as the thing rushed past and then back again. I stopped and tried to get a better look at the nebulous shape.

"Time and trees are telling," it muttered with a woman's voice, "follow them and see. Under arches shells are dry. Time is hanging, but who makes the loops? Gifts, but gone, then what? Bite the ones who take. Running ruins and sad! Can you keep your feet? Prosper! Oichi, where is the cannon?"

It stopped and regarded me expectantly.

"Where is the—what?" I stammered.

It turned and was gone, as if it had slipped around a corner. I turned 360 degrees, trying to find it. When I came back to where I started, Ahi stood there, her mouth agape. "You've been here less than a day," she said, "and already a Sentinel talked to you."

"So how long does it usually take people to talk to a Sentinel?" said Ashur.

We had left the Last Sentinel behind us, and now we perched in the meager shade of a twistifer tree, sipping water and eating snacks from our packs.

Ahi nibbled her protein bar before answering, as if she wasn't accustomed to thinking much about it. "You can talk to them all you want. They might even listen. They usually don't talk back."

Kitten, untroubled by the heat, settled on top of a sunny rock. "Did they ever talk to *you?*"

Ahi nodded. "Once. It didn't make a lot of sense. When they talk, they sound like poetry."

Time and trees are telling, follow them and see. . . .

Ahi regarded me with fascination. "It wanted to talk to *you,* Oichi. It didn't even notice Ashur and me. Did it make sense to you?"

"No." I took a long drink of my water. My legs were thrumming with the blood flowing through my veins, because of the extended exercise we had done. It felt good. "Is it supposed to make sense?"

"Yeah," said Ahi, "lots of luck with that. I think the Sentinels try to warn us, but they weren't made by humans, so they end up talking to the wrong parts of our brains."

"They don't just watch the canyon," I said. "They watch the whole solar system."

Everyone stared at me. "When I touched her, I think I saw the Hella system through the eyes of the Sentinel."

Ahi chewed another bite while she thought that over. "When my Sentinel talked to me, I didn't see anything like that. And the conversation was a lot shorter."

Dragonette settled on Ashur's pack frame. "Can you remember what it said?"

"It said, *Blue lightning breaks time. Hide with the merman.*"

I glanced at Ashur to see if *blue lightning* set off the same sparks in his head as it did mine, but he had never seen a gravity bomb in action. He fixated on another part of the message.

"I wrote an immersive program where I was a merman," he said.

Ahi grinned at him. "Can I hide with you if the blue lightning gets out of hand?"

Ashur wasn't in the mood to joke. "If the Sentinel was talking to Oichi's brain, how come I saw it? How come I could hear it?"

"If they start to talk, anyone nearby gets caught up in the effect." She shrugged. "I don't know why, but we should remember what it said. It might have been warning us."

"I recorded it," said Dragonette.

Kitten perked up. "You can record a mental hologram?"

"Sort of. Not like I could record you or Ashur—it looks like a distortion when you play it back, though you can hear some of the words. What I mean is that I made a transcript. I thought it might be important."

Ahi grinned at her. "I think you're going to help a lot on this trip."

Dragonette swished her tail with pleasure. "I think you're going to help a lot, too."

Ahi giggled. Then she tucked her half-eaten bar back into her pack. "Let's top off our water bottles and get back to it. I want to reach the First Staircase by the time the sun goes down. Then we can chow down for real."

Top off our water bottles meant hike a good fifteen minutes to the river's edge. The Maisy had diverged from our trail by then, or we diverged from hers, and the canyon had widened into a landscape of mudstone knobs and bobs, weathered into fantastical shapes. At this point, we couldn't see Maisy anymore, but we still heard the rush of her flow, and I wondered if our bottles might be swept away if we tried to hold them in that current.

"Watch your footing," Ahi warned as we picked our way through hoodoos. "This rock can be slick when it's wet."

The morning rain had left many puddles. A closer glance at them revealed ephemeral life taking advantage of the brief moisture. Tiny creatures with tails wiggled in the water. Other creatures with multiple limbs that were as fine as hairs skimmed the surface, seeming to float on the tips of their toes. Kitten and Dragonette rushed from pool to pool.

"Are you recording them?" I said.

"Yes," they replied gleefully.

I expected the noise of the river to get louder, but it stayed about the same. Instead of the rushy part, we had picked our way toward a large pool that had formed in a basin between two tilted blocks of sandstone. The water was so clear, I couldn't see how deep it was. On the bottom, we saw colorful pebbles. Ranks of taller hoodoos, marching off toward the South Rim and the Maisy River, shaded us from the ferocious sun.

"Here," Ahi declared reverently. "This is where Maisy shows her true spirit. The water is clean and clear." She uncapped her bottle and dipped it into the pool. Ashur knelt beside her and did the same, staggering a little when his pack almost tipped him over.

"If you fall in," warned Ahi, "don't waste your time struggling. Keep calm and unstrap yourself from your pack."

When Ashur shot her an impatient look, she returned his glare. "It happened to me. Sometimes you find things out the hard way; sometimes a friend warns you and saves you the trouble."

That startled him. "Good advice," he said. "Thank you."

She grinned.

I knelt beside them and filled my own bottle. Dragonette zoomed back and forth over the pool, skimming the water with her tail and making little splashes with it. Kitten crouched next to me and dipped in one paw. "I've done this in the Habitat Sector," she confessed. "In the ornamental ponds. I try to touch the colorful fish, but they swim away. They're very uncooperative."

"You would think people tried to eat them or something," I said.

"I know, right?"

Dragonette paused when her play disturbed an insect that had three pairs of blue, iridescent wings. "Oh my!"

Ahi screwed the cap back on her bottle. "Life is all around us if you stop and look. The water draws it."

Kitten and I held still. Dragonette flew to Ahi's shoulder and perched there. We watched and listened. Once we stopped moving and making noise, we saw them.

Dozens of insects with colorful wings. The skinny bugs floating on the surface. The wigglers darting among the pebbles. Slender reptiles clinging to vertical surfaces, moving only their eyes as they scouted the territory. Tiny rodents that watched us with great suspicion. Winged creatures hopping back and forth on the other side of the pool, talking among themselves with short chirps.

"The animals in the canyon are quiet," Ahi said at last. "They react to the ships as if they were loud people. We would, too, if we lived here." She tucked her water bottle into her pack and stood. "We'd better get back to the trail."

Ashur and I put our water bottles back where they belonged. Dragonette hopped to the top of Ashur's pack frame, and Kitten trotted behind him as he followed Ahi. I brought up the rear, thinking once again of my painted tiger. If he were standing at the edge of *this* pool, he might decide it had been worthwhile to risk the unknown.

"Thanks, Maisy," I whispered as we headed back to the trail.

I needn't have worried about lagging behind. As our day struggled past noon and headed downhill toward evening, Ahi and Ashur began to tire. Their youthful exuberance had sent them headlong into the hike—now they were paying the price for not pacing themselves.

I had developed stamina during the day. I had adjusted to the heat and found my body's natural rhythm. When they began to slow down, I stayed a few steps behind them, enjoying the respite. I got my second wind as we walked down a red dirt trail that snaked between outcrops, descending through switchbacks that led to broad, flat ledges whose regular surfaces would have been a joy to walk across, had the hot sunlight not been beating down on us (first on top of our hats, and then right into our faces).

Yet somehow I had grown accustomed to that flood of light. What had intimidated me in the morning had lifted my spirits in the afternoon.

Ahi turned at one point and regarded both Ashur and me, beaming. "Your skin is getting some healthy color."

That remark baffled me until I took a closer look at Ashur. His skin had taken on deeper tones of brown. I could see why Ahi liked that—we weren't pale-skinned people, but *Olympia*ns spent so much of our time in low light, we must have seemed pale to *her*.

The North Rim loomed to our right, perhaps one thousand meters high at this point. It glowed with spring sunshine, and now it had three distinct layers with different shades, from rusty red on the top, to yellow gold, to tan. To our left, the South Rim had fallen back several kilometers; it rose in a grand staircase with massive steps that each had scarps several hundred meters high. The canyon had angled north, turning away from the Gorge and its three towers, and exposing a vista that included buttes the size of battleships. One massive chunk stood right in the center, almost as tall as the South Rim. I guessed we would have to go all the way around it on one side or the other if we hoped to find our way to the Gorge, and I wondered which route was more perilous.

The path started to climb again, slowing my young friends even further and taxing me again. Once we reached the apex, we saw something up ahead.

"Spaceships!" declared Dragonette. "At last!"

They stood among the buttes and spires. I recognized the scene—I had seen it on the big screen in the Ship Operations Command Center, on *Olympia*.

"We've got maybe another hour of hiking before we get to them," said Ahi. "Pretty soon, we're going to be far enough out of this inner canyon to see another amazing sight."

I had an idea what she meant. Sure enough, once we had climbed far enough to see past the steep walls, the Three came back into view on our left.

They stood like mountains. Now that the clouds were long gone, I could see the snow and ice that blanketed their tops. I wondered if anyone had ever been crazy enough to try to climb one of them.

Somehow I doubted it.

Our path had become more level, though we still climbed for brief stretches. I used those level spaces to catch my breath. I felt a growing excitement as more and more spaceships came into view. I saw some that reminded me of *Merlin*, at least to the extent that they had structures similar to the ones that moved that ship through holes generated in space–time. Most of the others possessed nothing like that. We passed one that looked like a big sphere, then another that seemed to be a series of broken loops.

These were not the tame ships whose parts were spread throughout Joe's Salvage Yard. These were revenants from past ages, made by races long since decayed into dust. They did not tolerate salvage. If we got anything from them, it would be something they chose to give. If anyone stole from them, there would be a price to pay.

At last we climbed a natural staircase through a slot canyon that brought us onto a broad plateau. Spaceships spilled odds and ends from end to end. The path wound straight through them, veering northwest. From here, we could see part of the Gorge, where the feet of the Three disappeared into deep, blue shadows.

We followed Ahi through the wondrous wreckage.

Danger, I thought. *Unsorted Apocrypha.*

"I'm glad we got here when you could see everything," said Ahi. "This is my favorite part of the graveyard."

"This is what I expected a spaceship graveyard to look like," said Ashur.

"Me, too," said Ahi, "before I started to work at one. Joe's Salvage Yard is way more organized, and most of that stuff is newer. *This* stuff is old, and mysterious, and weird."

It looked so weird, it made the Bernard Herrmann music from *The Day the Earth Stood Still* start playing in my head, a segment called "Space Control," from a scene where Klaatu (who isn't what he seems to be) is moving through the mysterious, unfathomable interior of his spaceship, preparing to use the gizmos therein to stop all the electricity on Earth. The predominant instruments in that segment are an electric violin, an electric bass, and two high and low theremins, which are played when hands (or whatever appendage you may have) interact with electric fields. Crystalline harp and piano arpeggios lend a shivery sense of the eerie.

Kitten must have been thinking along the same lines. "Gort!" she said. "*Klaatu barada nikto!*" letting the giant robot from the movie know that his companion was dead, and needed to be brought back to life.

Our path wound its way between exotic machines that could have fallen right out of Klaatu's spaceship. Ahi didn't have to warn us not to touch anything. What if we stopped all the electricity on Graveyard?

Kitten stretched her neck. "I feel a little disappointed there are no flying saucers."

"Those are in here, too," said Ahi, "but most of them are broken and half buried, so they're harder to spot."

Other than our voices and the sound of our footsteps, that landscape was eerily silent—until, halfway across, a sharp *crack!* made me jump.

"Walking trees," remarked Ahi.

Ashur looked around. "What . . . ?"

She paused and pointed to a gnarled tree bent over a stretch of bare ground on the northern side of the plateau. "That scarp is more of a slope. The walking trees love it there, because gravity helps them make their journey."

We all paused to stare at the tree.

"Wait for it . . ." advised Ahi.

One of the branches that leaned toward the ground suddenly bent at one of its joints with another *crack!*

"After they get big enough to bend over," said Ahi, "they're pretty much walking their whole lives. When that branch touches the ground, it'll sprout roots at the joint. Once it does that, a signal is sent to the old roots, and they start to die. They end up moving a few feet per week. Their seeds grow in bulbs on the roots, so they leave those behind when the roots die, and they sprout during the spring rains and start the whole process over again."

"Where do they go?" said Ashur.

"They walk to the edge of cliffs and climb over. Or they wander over to a canyon wall and then start walking back the way they came. Sometimes they go into areas where they can't thrive, and just dry up, but there always seems to be about the same number of them running around at any given time." Ahi laughed. "Back when people first settled here, they tried to make furniture out of them."

"And the furniture walked away?" I guessed.

"Yep."

Ahi started up again, and we followed. As the broken spaceships began to thin, the walking trees took their places. "Just a little farther," said Ahi. "Up this staircase."

It was another natural fall of rocks, this time forming broad steps that led to the top of a ridge.

"Aren't the walking trees going to keep us awake all night?" said Ashur.

"Yeah," said Ahi, "they're noisy, but you don't want to try to sleep among the ships."

Kitten leaped up the steps and stretched her neck to look back the way we had come. "Why not?"

"Because sometimes they talk to you," said Ahi.

Ashur and I exchanged looks. "Like the Sentinels?" he said.

"Nope. When these ships speak, they make a lot more sense—but you wish they didn't."

I paused on the stairs and gazed at the Klaatu ships that had seemed so wonderful and fascinating as we were passing through them. *What do you have to say that spooks Ahi?* I wondered.

I looked back and found her watching me, a slight frown on her face. She turned away before I could be sure I had seen it.

She's got secrets, I realized. *There are things she isn't sure she should tell us.*

Ahi was young to carry that sort of burden. Ashur was, too. I had been even younger when my parents trained me as a dissident. They had implanted secret technology in my brain and filled it with forbidden databases and communication links. That had turned out to be the right thing for them to do. I was alive because they had made that decision. Ashur had bonded with Octopippin and made the Minis, and Ahi . . .

She was the best guide Graveyard had to offer, but something told me she might be paying a high price for that.

Ashur followed Ahi. Kitten and Dragonette disappeared over the top. I started to follow. Then I heard a noise.

It wasn't the sharp *crack!* of the walking trees. This had been more like a scuffle, a brief fall of rocks. I scanned the plateau, searching for the slightest signs of movement.

The graveyard was living up to its name. It remained silent and still.

Ahi appeared at my side. She studied the same scene I had just surveyed. "Stuff moves in here. Even when you think it can't."

We waited a little longer. When nothing moved, I made a tactical error. <Medusa?> I called. <Is that you?>

This time, no barrier deflected my call. Instead, it seemed to fall into an endless deep, as if nothing had stopped or dissipated my signal, so it just kept going and going. . . .

I turned with Ahi and walked away, thinking that no one had heard me.

Someone had.

The sun had begun to sink when we climbed onto the ridge. I kept scanning behind us, looking for any sign of followers.

"You won't see anyone," Ahi said when she realized how worried I was. "They weren't invited to this spot. These ships will keep people away from us."

She seemed confident of that. I schooled my tone to be curious without seeming skeptical. "How will the ships do that?"

"With time fractures," she said.

Even the Minis didn't seem to know what question to ask to get Ahi to clarify that remark. So we kept silent while she scouted ahead. She seemed to be looking for something in particular, and finally saw it. A lip had eroded out of a big slab of pale stone that looked much finer-grained than the sandstone beneath our feet, making the formation look like a big frozen wave. "That's limestone," she said. "We'll put our air mattresses under there. That overhang will keep us dry if it rains in the middle of the night."

Ashur and I followed her to the shelter. Dragonette, in the meantime, had helicoptered up to a point where she could scan the terrain from all sides. Kitten climbed to the top of the stone wave and stretched her neck, turning her camera eyes on everything in range.

Dragonette returned and perched on my shoulder. <No one is moving in our part of the canyon. I'll keep watch tonight.>

<I don't want you to fly at night,> I said, though it would have been sensible for her to do so. <I'm concerned about those time fractures Ahi mentioned.>

<It certainly wasn't included in the briefing,> Dragonette agreed. <We need clarification.>

Worries aside, it felt wonderful to take off that pack. It felt even better to sit on the air mattresses. The face of the North Rim, now looming about 1,500 meters over the canyon floor, glowed with the light of sunset. At its feet lay chunks of rock that had peeled from its face, some the size of houses.

Ahi dug a packet of brown cake from her pack. "This is a pemmican bar. It's packed with calories. Eat slowly, and you won't be hungry by the time you finish."

Kitten stretched herself down the length of my legs, enjoying a vicarious treat as I ate my bar. "It's tasty," she said. "Sort of like a brownie, but not as sweet."

"The sweetness comes from dried fruit instead of sugar cane," said Ahi. "I did ask for the chocolate chip ones, though. They're more fun."

Dragonette enjoyed her own connection with Ashur's taste centers. She eyed me, waiting to see how I would approach the subject that loomed over us.

It was Ashur who broke the ice. His tone was respectful but firm—it reminded me of the way Nuruddin asks questions. "So—please tell us about the time fractures."

Ahi's eyebrows perked. "We've known about them for a while. There are a lot of theories about why they happen in here. My favorite hypothesis is that the ships generate them. After all, they can make shortcuts in space–time when they move."

I could have argued that a ship activating that sort of field inside a gravity well would probably be quite destructive to its surroundings, but what did I know about it? Who could say what those ships could do when they interacted with each other? What esoteric combinations could they form?

"Here's what I've seen," Ahi continued. "If you're inside a time fracture, you still feel like time is passing, but it lasts a really long—time. I guess you could say it feels like time is stretching.

"Outside the fracture, time is moving at its normal pace. You hear weird noises—thunder sounds like the muttering of a monster, or a god. Rain sounds like tinkling glass. Sometimes you hear other things." She shivered. "That may be leaking through the fractures, things that don't belong to our universe."

I was beginning to see why she hadn't mentioned any of this to us when we had begun our journey. *Oh, by the way, watch out for the snakes. And the time fractures.*

"Ahi," Ashur said in his Nuruddin voice, "how will that keep Sheba and her thugs away from us?"

Ahi nodded, as if affirming her claim. "I've seen or heard tech poachers just about every time I've been in here. None of them have been allowed to touch me. The Sentinels aren't the only ones who look after me."

Dragonette sat silently on Ashur's shoulder, like the physical manifestation of his conscience. Kitten and I remained quiet, too.

"If that's so," said Ashur, "then why do the ships let the poachers in?"

She gave him half a smile. "Believe it or not, they have their supporters in here. Not every ship in this yard is a good one, Ashur. Some of them are crazy. Some of them are evil. Some of them are just so weird, who knows what they're thinking?"

Others will be journeying into the canyon, too, Crow had said, *with the permission of other entities.*

"The good ones far outnumber the bad ones," Ahi continued. "That's why they keep us separate from the poachers, and from Lady Sheba and her party. Those people may be able to steal some tech from the canyon, and they may be able to make it out alive—but they won't touch us."

She was convinced of that, and I wanted to be comforted.

When, in my life, had I been safe from evil intentions?

Never. Not now, either. I met Dragonette's eyes.

<Stay close,> I said. <But keep watch.>

<I will,> she promised.

We finished our pemmican bars and watched the sun set. The canyon turned purple, then blue as the shadows lengthened. I wondered if the Three would stretch dark fingers over us, but we weren't in their path. At least not yet.

The stars crowded the sky once it got dark. We pulled our mattresses out so we could gaze at them. They looked as bright to me as they had from the hull of *Olympia*. The moons hadn't risen yet, so it was the stars that watched over us as we started to drift off to sleep.

Dragonette and Kitten stayed close, but they focused their unblinking gazes on the trail that led back down to the graveyard.

I turned my head to look at Ahi. She lay with her eyes wide open, staring reverently at the stars.

What else has she kept from us? I wondered. I was sure there was something.

I was right.

Deep inside Joe's Canyon, I gazed at the stars until I fell asleep. I felt confident that Dragonette and Kitten would warn us if anyone approached.

I woke again when my implant came to life.

<Medusa,> someone whispered inside my head—with my own voice. It was the same call I had made earlier, sent back at me. Then another implant in my brain became active, one that hadn't been used in over a year.

My Servant implant, the one the Executives used to control what I saw and heard. Medusa and I had disabled the command codes long ago.

Someone had just reactivated them, and now I could see what they wanted me to see.

All around me, the ships glowed in moonlight. I seemed to be upright, but I could still feel my air mattress under me.

<The one you called,> said the voice. <Doesn't answer. Are you grieved? What does *she* grieve for?>

I tried to get an idea what was talking to me. I moved my eyes back and forth, and saw the shapes of the ships we had passed. When I looked up, the stars blazed in the night sky. I looked down at red rocks and dirt, half expecting to see giant silver robot feet. I felt like Gort, standing outside Klaatu's ship, and someone had just shined a flashlight on my visor. That evoked more theremin music from Bernard Herrmann's score: "Nocturne/The Flashlight/The Robot/Space Control," the two theremins exchanging alien signals with an electric cello and bass.

Something responded to that music, first by searching my father's music database, and then by following the link from Herrmann's score to Nuruddin's movie database. It reviewed *The Day the Earth Stood Still* in a matter of seconds. Then it selected the music for "Space Control" and showed me a new perspective, similar to the corresponding scene in the movie, except I didn't see Klaatu moving through the mysterious interior. Medusa navigated those realms, inside a Sentinel.

Her tentacles caressed and explored the things she found, while Bernard Herrmann's theremin wove patterns of wonder with a celeste, vibraphone, and piano. She seemed to be moving by instinct, and I judged from her expression that she was listening to something I couldn't hear.

<When she spoke,> said the voice, <did you listen?> It didn't sound like me anymore. It sounded like wind in the sand.

<I always listened,> I insisted.

<You *heard*,> said the voice. <Once, we were *heard*, too, but they didn't listen.>

It showed me a new scene. The perspective reminded me of the one the Sentinel had revealed, a view from space, looking in toward a planetary system—but the world at the center of the scene glowed red and gold, because it was on fire. It had turned molten; its atmosphere burned away. That sight alone would have filled me with awe, but a dark mass began to occlude my view of that dying world, a ship that dwarfed *Olympia* the way a sun dwarfs the worlds in its orbit.

Its details evoked the Klaatu ships, causing me to wonder if they couldn't come together to form larger ships if called upon to do so. I marveled at the sight, until I noticed details that became apparent as more of the ship moved into sight.

There were catastrophic holes in that structure. I saw the red and gold of the molten world through the gaps. Finally, I saw the ragged edge that had sundered it from top to bottom.

Good Lord—that was just a chunk of the thing. Intact, it had been even bigger. What could have destroyed such a juggernaut?

I felt a loneliness and a grief so deep, they had no bottom. The voice contemplated those depths with an aching familiarity. Then it set those feelings aside and chose curiosity instead, turning its collective mind to the present. My perspective returned to the graveyard of the Klaatu ships. I stood among them like Gort waiting for a signal.

<What does she say?> said the voice. <How do you listen?>

I thought about that. Medusa and I had talked about many things in our time together. Movies, music—murders. The three Ms of our relationship.

The voice cast those things aside as irrelevant. <She didn't answer,> it reminded me. <When you called.>

Well, yes. We had disagreed about a lot of things. My current trajectory disappointed her.

Will you sleep when I die?

No. I'll bond with someone else, but I'll miss you, I won't get over it. Or the next one. Or the one after that.

<That's why,> said the voice, <she doesn't answer.>

Medusa had abided in Lucifer Tower when I discovered her. She had stopped thinking about *Olympia* and my father's grand plan. In a way, she had been sleeping.

Just like the Three were sleeping.

Don't wake them, Oichi.

What would they do if they remembered their grief?

Did it ever occur to you to wonder what killed the people who made them?

I waited for the voice to tell me something more. When it didn't, I wondered if I should ask it a question.

I wasn't even sure what questions to ask *myself.*

How do you listen? it asked. I remembered what Medusa and I said to each other, but I hadn't thought about it. Our agendas had meshed. I assumed they always would.

I had assumed a hell of a lot.

I tried to move, but I seemed to be stuck with my Gort perspective. If the voice had nothing more to say, it didn't seem inclined to let me go, either.

I could still breathe without effort, so I concentrated on that. Eventually I was able to close my eyes. I felt myself drifting off to sleep.

Until Kitten jumped on me. I opened my eyes and saw her staring down at me.

"Oichi!" she said, "the trees are going!"

I sat up. Beside me, Ashur and Ahi also had come awake, and we blinked at each other in a flood of silver light. Ahi looked up, scanning the sky. The stars wheeled overhead.

Wheeled. As if Graveyard were completing its spin in a matter of minutes instead of hours.

"It's a time fracture," said Ahi.

My heart began to thud in my chest. "Stay close," I warned the Minis, worried that they would get trapped outside the fracture. Dragonette zoomed to Ashur's shoulder and clung there. Kitten wrapped herself around my waist.

Ahi got to her feet. "We need to see this," she said, and she started off toward the edge of the plateau.

Ashur and I exchanged alarmed looks, but we hurried to follow her. Sounds reached us from the bottom of the slope, crackling noises and a sort of muttering that made me wonder if people were down there. I couldn't quite understand the words, but I couldn't help trying to do so, anyway. We had to travel only a short distance before I understood what Kitten had meant when she said *the trees are going*.

The walking trees went rapidly down the slope and out of sight downcanyon. They weren't walking as people would—they flopped over, broke free from their old roots, stood up, then flopped over again.

"It's like time-lapse photography," said Ashur. "I've seen it in some of father's movies, flowers blooming."

They're pretty much walking their whole lives, Ahi had said. If we were seeing them speeded up, that explained the crackling noises, but what about the other sounds, the ones that seemed like speech?

"They haven't just been *walking*, this whole time," Ahi said. "They've been *talking* to each other! Maybe they've been talking to us, too."

"What are they saying?" said Ashur.

Ahi listened. The rest of us stayed silent, unwilling to break her concentration. The walking trees continued their migration down-canyon until their herd grew thinner, their muttering became less frequent. As we watched, the last of them flopped and uprooted, flopped and uprooted, following its brethren out of sight.

We stared after them in the odd silver light. Darkness dropped on us like a blanket.

We looked up. The stars were moving at their normal pace again (or we were). Ahi studied the sky and said, "There. Maui casting his hook. We're back when we belong."

Crack! came a noise downslope, and we saw the walking trees, where and when they belonged, caught midjourney by normal time.

When I had seen those trees' moving speeded up, I had wondered if normal time were passing our bubble and leaving us behind. Would we emerge in the future, long after our efforts here could do any good for *Olympia*? Long after people had stopped waiting for us to come back?

Long after they were gone?

"I recorded it if you need to hear it again," Dragonette told her.

Ahi regarded her with raised eyebrows. "Really? The whole thing?"

"Me, too," said Kitten. "It was amazing."

"It showed us where we need to hike in the morning." Ahi pointed with her chin. "Where *they* went. That's our path."

Ashur opened his mouth, shut it again, then said, "You didn't have a route planned out already?"

She looked surprised. "In Joe's Canyon? Maps don't work in here. Routes get rerouted. You have to go where the canyon shows you to go."

Ashur looked down-canyon. "Where does that lead?"

"We won't know until we follow that trail," said Ahi.

Ashur seemed caught between consternation and wonder. "It's different every time?"

"Not *every* time." Ahi was regaining her old confidence. "I've been certain places several times. The order of places is usually at least a little different. Have you changed your mind about wanting to be here?"

I wouldn't have had a ready answer for that, because *wanting* to be here wasn't the issue for me. I *had* to be here, regardless of the risks.

Ashur shook his head. "Did you figure out what they were saying?"

"They said we should get out of the rain."

Ashur frowned. Maybe he was about to ask what she was talking about. Then light flashed overhead, illuminating our startled faces. The thunderclap that followed was cataclysmic. Rain dropped on us as if someone had overturned a gigantic bucket, in sheets, rather than drops.

"That's not funny," Ashur grumbled as we ran for cover.

But it was. Kind of.

19

Follow Them and See

Blue lightning breaks time. Hide with the merman.

Regardless of anything that might come later, this is what I will remember: the ruins of Evernight clustered behind us, perpetually trapped in the moment just after every living soul had vanished. Ahead of us, the desert stretching all the way to the feet of the North Rim.

Ahi sets one foot into the desert, and a blue light swells over the horizon. Ashur and Ahi are frozen in the glare. It stutters out again, crackling like an electrical charge.

It races across the desert toward us on spider legs.

I have seen something like it before.

The morning of the second day, I woke next to the twistifer trees with a start. The rain had not lasted—it had expended its energy within minutes, then moved on, down the canyon. The lightning flashed for hours, making me glad we had taken shelter under our limestone ledge.

Eventually, the night became peaceful again. Just in time for the sun to come up, climbing over the horizon on rays of rosy light.

Not the worst manifestation of the day I could think of, but I found, as I lay there on my air mattress, that all the relaxing I had tried to accomplish when I was trying to sleep the night before had finally paid off—now that it was time to get up.

Ashur, Ahi, and I attended to our morning routine, and I woke up pretty fast. A cup of coffee would have been nice, but the water tasted good.

<Kitten,> I said, <did you go into rest mode during the night?> Rest mode was brief for Minis, but they used it to process all the information and events they had experienced in a given cycle.

<Dragonette and I took turns in rest mode,> Kitten assured me. <We're fine.>

I glanced toward the top of the stone staircase. Nothing had come creeping up there during the night. I felt a fleeting urge to go take a final look at the spaceships, but I didn't give in to it. I didn't want them to take any more notice of me than they already had.

You didn't listen.

Yeah. I didn't.

So she doesn't answer.

Right. Thanks for sharing.

Dragonette waited for us to fish out our breakfast bars. "I believe I've deciphered something," she said.

Ahi grinned. "I'm sure you have."

"I apologize for not seeing it sooner." Dragonette dipped her head. "I got very wrapped up in my recording of the trees, and the rest of my attention was focused on watching for Sheba's poachers, but this morning, it just popped into my head."

We waited attentively.

"The Sentinel," said Dragonette. "I've looked at the transcript of her remarks to you, Oichi. The first thing she said was, *Time and trees are telling. Follow them and see.*"

Ahi's smile was like the sunrise. "Yes! And it happened!"

They've been talking to each other, Ahi had said last night. *Maybe they've been talking to us, too. . . . It showed us where we need to hike in the morning.*

Ashur frowned as he thought it over. "So there was a time fracture, and the trees talked to us, and now we're supposed to follow them. What did the Sentinel say after that?"

"*Under arches shells are dry,*" said Dragonette. "*Time is hanging, but who makes the loops? Gifts, but gone, then what? Bite the ones who take. Running ruins and sad! Can you keep your feet? Prosper! Oichi, where is the cannon?*"

"I hope no one is going to shoot a cannon at us," said Ashur.

"The cannon is missing," said Kitten, "according to the Sentinel."

"I don't know about a cannon," said Ahi, "but we know where we're going today." She nodded at the line of walking trees. "Let's finish up here and get moving." She stood. "For anyone who needs a privy—there's a little spot around back. All sins wash downslope."

She disappeared around that bend for a few minutes, and then returned. "Next!"

That was my cue.

The light grew steadily around us, but it was shining at our backs, and that felt very good in the cool morning. Ahi kept us close to the ridge where the walking trees continued their slow march. They were our hiking companions.

The Three remained in sight for most of the morning. Eventually our path veered north again, and we picked our way into a narrow side canyon, whose walls blocked the view.

"This canyon is like a giant zigzag," said Ashur. "How come they didn't just name it Zigzag?"

"Because Joe got here first," said Ahi.

"No, the ships did."

"They've got their own names for things. Don't worry."

The Maisy River had diverged farther from our path by then, though it was still close enough to see. The sound it made from that distance was reassuring. We had consumed half of what was in our water bottles by then, and I liked to think we could hike down there and get more if we needed to, though it would take us out of our way.

Ahi didn't seem to be worried about it. She stopped to peer at the walking trees and get a sense of where they were headed. Then she marched on, and we followed.

Ashur frowned at the canyon walls. <I've been wondering where we should run if a flash flood comes through here.>

I couldn't see much of a purchase anywhere. The ground under our feet was covered in a sand so fine, it felt silky to the touch. <No clouds in the sky,> I said, but I could see only the patch of sky above our canyon. I couldn't tell if any storms were approaching from the east or west, because the walls were too high, and the canyon itself was growing narrower. Soon it would qualify as a slot canyon.

<Do you want me to fly up and assess the situation?> Dragonette hopped to the top of Ashur's pack frame.

<No. Stay close for now. There's nothing we could do about it at this point, anyway.>

Yet I couldn't help looking for escape routes. Any depressions weathered into the sandstone walls merited my close inspection, though few of them seemed deep enough to afford proper hand- and footholds. As pretty as the patterns were in the sandstone, with crosshatching that spoke of millennia of grains piling up into dunes, I thought a good name for this place might be Danger Canyon. I felt relieved when the path widened again, and we began to see gaps in the walls. Ahead, a new landscape emerged, white and tan formations shining in the sunlight. It was so beautiful, I almost didn't notice that something sat in one of the gaps beside the path.

At first I thought it was a large bird. It sat on its knob of rock as if that were its normal spot. Ahi and Ashur walked past it without seeming to notice; Dragonette didn't look over Ashur's shoulder when he carried her past, and Kitten trotted along without a glance at the creature.

As I drew even, it fixed me with an exceptional glare.

Its eyes were human. They didn't belong in that head, with its feathers and its beak. They were blue, and they glared right at me.

"Ashur," I warned.

He and Ahi must have gone a distance up the path, because there was a long pause, and then I heard them coming back toward me, their feet making muffled sounds in the grit. I couldn't look away from the blue eyes locked on mine.

Ashur said, "Is that an alien?"

I could see why he thought that. The creature had feathers, though it didn't have wings. It had feet, but they looked more like fingers than claws. Those eyes . . .

"That's not an alien," said Ahi. "That's a northern god."

That broke me out of my freeze. Ahi's tone had been respectful, but I had to wonder if she was kidding.

Ashur squinted at the creature, trying to make sense of what he saw. "A northern god of *what*?"

Ahi shrugged. "I don't know. That's just what everyone calls them. They were already in the canyon when the first humans arrived. They look different every time you see them. They don't hurt anyone, but they've got strong opinions. You should pay attention to what they say."

I kept my eyes on the northern god, and it returned the favor. "They predict the future?"

"No," said Ahi. "Well—maybe. They might complain about what happened in the past, or what's happening somewhere else. It's not always about you. Sometimes it's about someone you're going to meet, and you may never figure it out."

Ashur arched an eyebrow. "Are you sure it's not just nonsense?"

A line appeared between Ahi's brows as she thought about that. "No. The northern gods have power. Pissing them off is always a bad idea. So do what they tell you to do, and *don't* do what they tell you *not* to do."

"It's not telling us anything," said Ashur.

No one could dispute that. The northern god simply stared at us.

<Do you think we should ask what it wants?> Ashur asked me.

Before I could answer, the northern god bristled. "Stop that!" it cried with a voice too big for its body.

We froze. The northern god glared at Ashur. "Okay," said Ashur. "I'm sorry."

"Don't do it again," cried the northern god. "It's the rule!"

"I won't do it anymore," Ashur promised.

The feathers settled. The northern god glared at me, as if to say, *That goes for you, too, sister!* Then it hopped out of sight behind the rock.

We waited a respectable amount of time for the northern god to reappear, but it seemed to have vanished for good.

"Stop *what*?" said Ahi.

Ashur blushed.

"We were using our brain implants to communicate," I explained.

"Oh." Ahi grinned. "Don't feel bad. Everyone tries to use tech the first time they come in here. Sooner or later, the northern gods get pissed off. They complain, and then you know not to do it again."

We couldn't communicate brain-to-brain inside the canyon. I hoped no gods would take offense over the fact that Ashur and I had artificial eyes. I would hate to wake up with that creature on my chest, its fingerlike appendages clawing at my face.

"Are there southern gods?" said Ashur. "Closer to the South Rim?"

"We don't talk about them," said Ahi.

"Why not?"

"Because they might hear us."

She pivoted and walked away before he could ask her to clarify that. It seemed like a warning. Ashur looked at me sorrowfully, since we were accustomed to being able to mind-speak at will.

"Kitten," I said, "and Dragonette, you had better speak aloud, too, until we leave the canyon."

"Roger wilco," said Kitten. "Do you think they'll get mad if I sing?"

"I hope not," I said as the four of us followed Ahi toward the shining landscape that unfolded ahead of us. It was so beautiful, it almost kept me from wondering how the southern gods might hear us talking about them—and what they would do about it if they did.

"I've been reviewing the next part of the Sentinel's message," Dragonette said while the rest of us nibbled food bars and sipped water. "*Under arches shells are dry.*"

"Parts of this area were shallow seas for millions of years," said Ahi. "I've seen a lot of fossils of shells. Those are pretty dry."

"Are there arches?" said Kitten.

Ahi nodded. "Sandstone arches. Maybe we'll see some of those."

We stood with our packs. A gentle breeze played with Ahi's curls, but I didn't smell rain. Maybe that was why *shells are dry*.

Sunlight glinted on the spires of the Three. As we started up the path, they remained in sight. *Couldn't we just cut to the chase?* I wanted to ask them. *Have you even noticed that we're here?*

They were old, and alien, and maybe time didn't move the same way for them as it did for us. Maybe, in their own way, they were like the walking trees, seeing a huge length of time as a short period, talking to us, but not in a way that we could hear.

We marched up that path. *Day Two*, I thought, feeling relatively sure of that, but who knew how time was passing outside the graveyard? Somewhere, Ahi's mother might be looking toward Joe's Canyon, wondering if her daughter was okay and if she would be home soon. If Ahi's mother felt confident that one thousand years weren't going to pass outside the canyon while three days passed inside, shouldn't I have some faith, too?

I did. Mostly.

Walking all day does a lot to settle your nerves, if nothing else. I liked our high path, which allowed us to look down on canyons inside the canyon and upon the battleship buttes sitting inside their arid harbor. Anyone who imagined a canyon was a mere hole in the ground had never seen Joe's Canyon, with its spires, giant-sized steps, a river with multiple tributary streams, slot canyons, side canyons, even hills and small mountains. The population of *Olympia* would have been lost in there.

No footprints marked the path, save ours, which we were beginning to see in drifts of pale sand.

By noon, that sand piled up in dunes below our path, but Ahi said it wasn't just sand. "Evaporites. This area must have been full of water that dried up." She wet a finger and tasted a bit of the sand. "Salty. A little bitter, too."

"You should taste it," Kitten suggested, so I indulged her. "Interesting," she concluded.

Ashur sampled some for Dragonette's benefit. Once she had a chance to assess the taste, she asked, "Could we take a little sample home?"

"I don't see why not," said Ahi. "It's not as if you're stealing tech."

While Dragonette was gathering her sample, Kitten trotted to a bend in the path and stretched her neck. "There's an arch, right over our trail," she announced.

Under arches shells are dry.

The sun beat down on us without mercy. The pale rocks around us glowed with the light, and I felt a bit dizzy. I pulled out my water bottle—it was running low. I took three sips and put it back. Then I brought up the rear as we rounded that corner and got a good look at Kitten's arch.

It had eroded out of a slab of rock that loomed far over our heads, effectively blocking our view of the terrain ahead. "Looks like mudstone with calcium carbonate in it," said Ahi. "A stream must run through here during the rainy season."

Once we passed under that bridge, it turned out to be more of a tunnel. It felt cool inside, and we couldn't help lingering.

"Hey—" Ashur pointed to something on the wall.

Something *in* the wall, a shape that curled into a big spiral. Ridges from its form extended out of the rock.

"This mudstone is fossiliferous," said Ahi. "That's a shell."

Shells couldn't get much drier than this one, if that's what the Sentinel had meant. My mouth was dry, too, and I suspected we might be in for a bit of discomfort ahead.

That was an accurate prediction—technically.

The walls of the tunnel distorted the slight noises made by our feet, turning them into whispery sounds almost like speech. At the far end, bright light blazed on the white rocks. The holes eroded out of that stone looked like a sort of face, peering anxiously into the tunnel, but it was looking *past* us, not at us, and I couldn't help turning to look the way we had come. Nothing moved there. I wondered about Sheba, whom Ahi seemed convinced couldn't touch us, despite the fact that someone had still managed to dog our steps.

"More spaceships!" announced Ashur. "I think . . ."

I had fallen behind. My heart skipped a beat when I saw the others at the end of the tunnel, which seemed to have stretched. They looked so far away. I lurched after them. I could have sworn they were getting farther away, not closer.

Suddenly they were within reach. I burst out of the tunnel half a second after Kitten, then had to pull myself up short to avoid plowing into Ashur and Ahi.

I looked over my shoulder. The tunnel should have been just a few feet away. Somehow we had ended up several yards up the path.

"We're inside a time fracture," said Ahi.

Time stuttered, then slowed.

"Whatever happens here," said Ahi, "it's going to feel like forever."

Ships and other artifacts perched among high limestone rocks. White sand piled up at their feet. I could see why Ashur had doubted his first conclusion, because the ships looked like gigantic fossilized seashells.

Or at least, they did at first glance. I couldn't see what engines might move those ships, but they had structures that looked like pressure doors. Their spires reminded me of the communications array on the leading edge of *Olympia*. More than anything else, they had a presence, like the Klaatu ships. The people I expected to see stepping out of the doors or turning a corner—they were the ships themselves.

"What now?" Ashur said, his voice a whisper.

The time fracture stretched Ahi's pause into an eternity. "We have a path," she said. "We can't go backward. So let's go forward."

We began our journey through that eternal place, ancient ships looking down on us from all sides as if they had been cemented into a massive coral reef. Moving forward might have been our only choice, but it wasn't easy. My steps didn't have their normal rhythm; each thrust forward felt as though the space through which I moved was also thrusting back. At first, this frustrated me, but I got used to it. Once I had done that, it seemed to me that our movement through this once-shallow-sea was like the tide: rushing in and flowing out. This place was the dry version of Ashur's Sunken Cathedral program.

Something tickled my memory. For a long time, the First One had taken refuge inside Ashur's Mermaid program. What had she said about ancient seas?

The place in which we Three abide was once an inland sea. . . .

That must be the Gorge. Before its rocks were metamorphosed by titanic pressures, they may have looked more like these.

Corals lived there. They built their castles. Life flourished, then was buried many times over. The seas dried up, and sand dunes covered the salt flats. They moved in the direction of the wind, one grain at a time. . . .

That's how it felt like we were moving, and how time was passing. Unless you've been inside a time fracture, you can't know what eternity feels like. We knew.

I could feel the pulse of that ancient sea in motion. I abided in stillness once it diminished and became landlocked. I tasted brine as it evaporated and surrendered its minerals to the mudstone on the bottom.

Now all was dry. I longed for the sea breezes that would never come again.

Yet—that place must be beautiful at night, the rocks glowing under the light of Tombstone and Cherub. When had the ships arrived? Why were they arranged in this place, as if they had gone looking for a nice place to retire? They seemed happy there.

A dry wind whistled through the rocks and ships. I liked the sound. We made our way through it with our to-and-fro pace. Not the most straight-forward progress, but it seemed to be getting us somewhere. Did I imagine that the light had taken on a blue tinge, as if we were walking at the bottom of a brightly lit lagoon?

I'd like to tell you that I had an epiphany as I made my passage through those eons. Instead, I couldn't stop thinking how much I appreciated the clothes we had been given. They shrugged off the sweat of millions of years. That's got to be just about the best selling point you can imagine.

I also started to think it might be a nice place to live. Crazy, right? Take away the whole fractured-time thing, add a few balconies from which you could sit sipping ice tea and contemplating the passage of time across the dunes, and it might be nice. How deep would you have to drill to find water? Maybe it just wasn't there, no matter how deep you went.

The path meandered to a spot that branched, forcing us to stop.

"I think my ears just popped," said Ashur.

I felt a similar sensation. It was a little easier to breathe, too. "Is the fracture—unfracturing?"

"No . . ." Ahi said. "But—sort of yes, too. I need to think."

We waited for inspiration. Dragonette clung to Ashur's pack frame, and I realized she had been recording the whole time.

Kitten stood near me, but she faced away, looking down one of the paths that branched from our junction. Ashur stood tall, with his shoulders squared, but I could see how tired he was. I assumed I must look twice as bad.

"You two always look so calm," Ahi said. "You must be made of steel."

I was amazed she couldn't see how tense we were. "You look pretty steady, yourself," I offered.

"Oh yeah, but I'm used to it. I know how it's supposed to feel, so I don't get nervous unless something changes."

As if taking Ahi's words as direction, Kitten started down the path.

She trotted with purpose. Her body language was tense—her tail stuck straight out behind her.

"We've got to follow," said Dragonette. She remained perched on Ashur's shoulders, but she sat stiffly, her eyes riveted on her sister.

We hurried after Kitten. This time, our motion through space seemed unencumbered. No one tried to talk to Kitten or distract her, she was so intent. We could see she was headed straight for one of the larger ships. She walked through the giant pressure door without pausing. We followed.

Inside, the floor sloped up into a spiral around a central point. Kitten was about to disappear around the bend.

"Kitten," I called, "stop!"

She paused and looked over her shoulder.

"What are you seeing up there?"

"I haven't found it yet," said Kitten, and she began to walk again. We followed her up the spiral.

Finally Kitten halted and stretched her neck to look around the last bend. She waited for a long moment, staring at what lay beyond. "Okay," she said. "I think this is it."

The rest of us crept up to her position and looked where she was looking.

A model of a solar system hung from the spiral-vaulted ceiling, suspended from a baffling network of loops. Could it be some sort of navigation system? If so, it was awfully literal.

Ahi moved closer, then stopped and pointed. "I think that orb is Charon, but where are Hellas One and Two?"

I can't say I was intimately familiar with the trinary system of which Charon was a distant member, but I remembered what it had been like to see Hella One and Hella Two from the Last Sentinel's point of view. "Maybe it's the system these ships came from?" I guessed.

Ahi pointed again. "I'm pretty sure that's Graveyard. What are these loops? They all pass through Graveyard, and they don't represent its orbital path."

The floor sloped around the model, so we all walked farther up to get a different perspective. I kept my eyes on Graveyard, hoping to use it as a reference, but when I moved, I felt an odd sensation, as if I were staring at the real Graveyard from a distance, with the perspective very much like the Sentinel's.

"*Time is hanging, but who makes the loops?*" said Dragonette.

"What . . . ?" I couldn't look away from the illusion—if that's what it was.

"It's what the Sentinel told you."

The longest loop reached through the ceiling, then back again, and I couldn't quite tell how the whole thing was strung together.

"Is this a model of Time?" Ashur asked before I could.

"I'm leaning in that direction," said Ahi.

"Why are we—why does the graveyard want us to see it?"

"I think we're supposed to study it—learn from it."

Ashur put his hands on his hips and sighed with some exasperation. "I don't think we can fit this into a backpack."

Ahi laughed with pure delight. "Me neither. We'll just have to remember it."

I studied the bulkhead from which the thing was hanging. A loop passed through it, but I saw no hole, no soldered spot through which it would have been threaded. It looked as if the very atoms of the loop and the bulkhead had blended together. "If this thing is a model of Time," I said, "then where are the instruments in this ship?"

Ahi glanced around, as if my question were a distraction that hardly deserved her attention. "None of the ships in this part of the graveyard have obvious instruments. I think the people who used them operated them with their thoughts."

"Are they the ones who made the loops?" said Ashur.

Everyone looked at him. "What?" said Ahi.

"*Time is hanging, but who made the loops?*" he quoted.

"Who *makes* the loops," corrected Dragonette. "So they must still be making them."

We watched the loops, which did not appear to be moving. Yet they didn't seem quite static either. Ashur moved farther up the slope, then pointed. "What's that planet called?"

Ahi joined him. "I don't know. That's not a planet in our solar system." She cocked her head, considering the intruder. Then she walked farther up the slope. "Okay—now it looks different again. I see two more worlds that don't belong in our system, but I don't see Graveyard anymore, and I don't see the world Ashur just pointed out."

"I'm getting a bad feeling," said Kitten. "I don't want you to walk around anymore. Come back."

Ahi returned immediately. After all, Kitten had been the one to lead us here in the first place. Ahi knelt next to Kitten, wobbling a little when her backpack pulled her off-balance. "What do you want to do now?" she asked Kitten.

"I want us to leave," said Kitten, "together. Right now."

"Okay." Ahi got to her feet again. "Let's go."

We turned our feet around and followed the slope down again, this time with Ahi in the lead. I couldn't help looking over my shoulder at the model before it disappeared around the bend. It still looked like a model of the Charon system from that perspective. I had to wonder—were those loops just about Time? Could they be about gravity? And Space?

If I stood there looking long enough, would they take me somewhere?

If so, I wasn't ready to go. I followed the others out of the seashell space-ship, whose operators had moved it with their minds. Such beings would not have looked like us. Maybe they were intelligent cephalopods.

They may have looked something like Medusa.

We followed a new path, which began to climb again as we wound our way through the ships and the fossilized reef.

"I think we learned something," said Ahi.

"Then how come you're so puzzled?" said Ashur.

Ahi frowned. "Because it was so much information. It was just—" She shook her head. "—huge! Like when you ask what time it is, and someone explains the whole physics of time to you. I don't get why the ships felt they had to tell me so much. I'm hoping they don't expect me to do something with all that information right away, because I kind of get it, but I kind of don't."

"I *mostly* don't," said Ashur.

I refrained from telling them that I thought the model was pretty, since that sounded a bit frivolous. I had liked looking at it.

"I have a theory," said Dragonette.

"Me, too!" said Kitten. "But you first, Sister."

"I think it may have been a model of the time fractures," said Dragonette.

"Me, too," agreed Kitten.

Everyone but Kitten and Dragonette took a long moment to digest that idea.

"So it might be a sort of map?" Ashur said. "That we could use?"

"If so," said Ahi, "I don't trust myself to use it. Not yet."

Still, I had a feeling she might figure it out someday. I thought of the way Fire and Queenie worked together to find and target intruders in the Charon system. Could they be using something similar to the model—the *map*—we had just seen?

I might never know because that information was proprietary. I have to confess, I wasn't sorry about that. My brain hurt. As fascinating as the model had been, and as beautiful as these alien ships were, I was ready to be done with the day. My eyes felt sore from the light, and my muscles let me know they had been used enough, thank you very much. My throat was so dry—I pulled out my water bottle and prepared to drink the last drops, trying not to wonder how the hell we were going to get more.

My bottle was full.

"Hey," I said, coming to full stop.

The others stopped and turned. When they saw me drinking deeply, they pulled out their own bottles.

"Well," said Ahi, "that's nice."

She took a long drink, and Ashur did the same.

With water inside us, we all perked up. When we began to walk again, my spirits lifted. *Things seem to be going our way, again,* I mused.

We passed a ship with an open pressure door, and Ahi stopped to look at it. Darkness yawned inside.

I hope she's not going to suggest we go in and look for a bathroom, I thought. *Our ship was nice, but that one gives me the creeps. Besides, cephalopods would have really weird bathrooms.*

"I think that's another time fracture," said Ahi. "Someone is trapped inside."

Whoever they were, they weren't inspiring any sympathy in me. In fact, I kind of got the feeling that the person or people trapped in there should *stay* there, maybe forever.

As one, we turned and hurried away, but it felt like trying to run from something in a nightmare. All my good feelings had reversed. The reef canyon was still beautiful; it looked the same. Dazzling light still played on the walls, but I felt like we had to get *out.*

"Kitten," I said, "wrap yourself around my waist."

She obeyed. Dragonette curled her tail around Ashur's pack frame, and we two-legged people ambled along as fast as we could.

We established another odd cadence as we made our slow escape. It felt like a sort of dance. The idea made me want to giggle—we could be players in one of Kitten's musicals. I stifled the urge.

Down the silent path, past empty ships that had once been moved by minds but were now residents in a barrier reef, we labored through the overheated afternoon. Up ahead, we saw another natural bridge, this one eroded into pale red sandstone. *Could it be that easy?* I wondered. *Under one bridge and into fractured time, out through another into normal time?*

Ahi passed under the bridge, Ashur and Dragonette right behind her, and Kitten and I brought up the rear. This time I made sure I was close enough to touch them. Once I had cleared that space, we all turned and looked back. Through the gap, we could see one of the ships.

You'll be back, it seemed to say. The thought was wistful rather than threatening.

"Thank you for letting us visit," I said aloud. "Thank you for—the information."

When I turned back again, Ahi was smiling at me. "You get it," she said.

Maybe most of the people she had guided *didn't* get it. If so, I was glad to stand out from the crowd.

Tall fins of sandstone towered on both sides of the path. Ahi scanned the ribbon of sky overhead. "I hate to tell you, but it's about the same time out here as it was when we went in."

"It felt like a million years in there," said Ashur.

He wasn't exaggerating. It really had.

Ahi fixed him with a solemn stare. "We're terribly old and wise now."

Ashur frowned. "No, we're not."

She laughed. "Will I ever get you to stop being so serious?"

"We could have been fossilized in there!"

Dragonette hopped down from his pack frame and onto his shoulder. "I think we would make very attractive fossils."

Ashur threw up his hands. "Okay. Hooray. Whatever."

Ahi made a visible effort to put away her smile. "Anyway, my point is that we've still got a ways to go before we camp. Let's walk until we can see the Three again. We'll get our bearings. Maybe we'll eat something. For sure, we need to get away from Seaside Canyon. It's pretty, but I think we tested the limits of our luck in there."

No one could argue with that. We sipped some water and started off down the trail. It sloped down again, so we had that going for us. Considering what we had just been through, it wasn't much comfort. Personally, I was ready for Joe's Canyon to dump us at the front door of a nice hotel, where we could all have hot showers and order room service.

Instead, we marched through fine-grained sand while the sun beat down on our hats. *We're not inside a time fracture anymore*, I wanted to tell that piti-less orb. *It's okay if you move behind one of these rocks and cast a bit of shade on us.*

However, as slow as that march seemed to be, it wasn't as slow as the pas-sage of time in Seaside Canyon (nothing is, under normal gravity conditions), and eventually we got a bit of shade for our trouble. I worked out that we must be moving roughly southwest, along the flank of one of the sandstone buttes. We continued to descend, and I began to despair that we would glimpse the Three again. Could we end up too far south? Though at least we were moving *sort* of west . . . ish. . . .

Our path ended at another flight of stone steps. They weren't so conve-nient as the other natural stairs we had encountered—these required some scrambling between some of the steps. Kitten had relaxed enough to unwrap herself from my waist, so she leaped to the top of each step and then encour-aged me up, offering plenty of advice, some of which was even helpful. At last I joined my young and energetic friends at the top.

Together, we gazed at the Three. No longer distant spires, they appeared to be a few kilometers away.

I knew we hadn't walked that far, but I didn't bother asking about it. After all, time could fracture inside the canyon. If that happened, who knew what those fractures could do to space?

Ashur sounded dazed when he said, "I didn't know they were so big. Each one of them must be as big as *Olympia*."

"They sure look like it," I agreed.

If so, the Gorge must be huge. From our vantage, I could see space be-tween the cliff walls and the foremost of the Three, but I couldn't calculate how wide the gap was. It might be a few hundred meters. This close, I could see that the ships weren't standing side by side; they were staggered.

Ashur asked what I was thinking. "So who put them here? Why would they land in the Gorge? Why would they land *anywhere* on a planet?"

Dragonette hopped to the top of Ashur's pack frame. "Maybe the people who put them in the Gorge are the same people who make the loops."

Time is hanging, but who makes the loops?

"Well," I said, "I suppose we just hike toward the Gorge?"

Ashur shaded his eyes and stared intently at something. "What are those things?"

I looked where he pointed. Something hovered in the air between us and the Three, three things that moved closer, fast.

"Those are dragonfly units!" said Ahi.

As they got closer, I could see three things that reminded me of the insects with the iridescent wings that had hovered over Maisy's Pool, except that they might be as big as we were.

"I think—" said Ahi. "I *hope* they're coming to get us."

"*Get us?*" said Ashur. "You mean they're going to . . ."

"Fly us," said Ahi. "We'll strap them on, and they'll take us to the Three. We won't be able to bring these packs." She began to shrug out of hers.

Ashur frowned. "But all our food—"

"We can take some of that," said Ahi, "and the water. Stuff your utility pockets with everything they can hold, and secure the water bottle to that loop on your pants." She riffled through her bag, extracting necessities. Ashur and I unstrapped our packs and did the same. It felt good to put down the weight.

I wondered—were we about to leave critical supplies behind? Just because three dragonfly units had shown up out of the blue? Would they really take us to the Three? If they did, would they bring us back again?

Were we about to get stranded in the middle of that gigantic canyon system without critical supplies?

I stuffed my pockets until they bulged. I stuffed my face, as well, eating one of the bars I couldn't fit into my pockets. Those extra calories would do me some good. I just managed to swallow the last of it when the dragonfly units swooped down to us and lighted.

"Dragonette," advised Ahi, "I think you should hold on to Ashur's belt loop. Kitten, will you be secure around Oichi's waist?"

"Yes," said Kitten.

"Then let's get going." Ahi moved to strap herself into the middle dragonfly. "The Three are waiting."

20

Ghosts and Avatars

I have default "majesty music" that plays in my head when I see something grand, the "Saturn" movement from Gustav Holst's *Planets* Suite. Its tempo, created by chord changes between harps and flutes, evokes a grim procession, the relentless march of time. Underneath this, two double basses introduce an ominous current. As more instruments are brought into the march, the sense of despair is washed away by grandeur, by wisdom, and that's what played inside my head as we flew above that sundered landscape toward the Three, who stood with their titanic feet buried in the Gorge.

Puzzlement began to erode my sense of grandeur, though. This close, the Three didn't remind me so much of *Olympia*. For one thing, they didn't look like they were made to rotate. They weren't like giant versions of *Merlin*, either, or like the Sentinels, or even like *Itzpapalotl*. I couldn't see their contact with the ground—it was too deep in the Gorge—but I got the feeling they weren't sitting on giant fins, maybe just because they didn't look like rockets. Though they did have an odd sort of symmetry.

When I focused on *parts* of them, their geometry looked planned rather than innate—you couldn't mistake them for giant crystals, though the spots at which they had contact with the spires of rock that surrounded them did exhibit some of those qualities, as if the chemical matrix of the minerals had bonded with their skin.

Mount Olympus, I thought. *Times three.* Kilometers wide and many more kilometers tall, few natural mountains could rival the elevation of the Three, at least not on a world with Earth-like gravity. Though they shared some of the qualities of the rocks among which they stood, they were not cold machines. Somewhere, deep inside, they had organic components and minds—and those minds still thought, though they were supposed to be mostly dormant. Even half asleep, the Three were aware of us. I felt their regard.

They're waiting for me to do something, I thought. I weighed the risk of trying to talk to them with my implant. The northern gods might consider that an act of hostility. Did the Three have more clout than the northern gods? Even if they did, would they back my play?

I needn't have agonized over whether to reach out to them, because they reached out to me.

Their touch activated my implant. I still saw their physical forms, metric tons implanted in the bedrock of Graveyard, but now I also saw their true forms.

The Three were energy signatures extending into dimensions beyond those my normal senses could perceive. They were minds that spent much of their time in calculations, measurements, and observations that led to hypotheses, which in turn led to judgments about how to best employ the energies at their disposal. Most of all, they were memories.

The majority of those memories were still submerged and inaccessible. The store was so vast, it made me feel as if I were suspended over the deepest part of an ocean. What lay beneath the surface was the history of their race. Not everything in the store was obscured; some things could still be glimpsed.

The contact ended as quickly as it had been initiated, but what I saw in that brief connection made me realize that the Three were *not* weapons. Their purpose was not that blunt or unimaginative. There was a very good reason why they weren't shaped like any other ship I had ever seen. To the Three, any other form of space travel I had seen was primitive. They couldn't just *go* anywhere they wanted in the universe.

In a way, they *were already there.* They were so much smarter than us, I wasn't sure we could make the right decisions about how to interface with them—assuming the decision would be ours, once they woke.

Are we ready for this? I wondered. *What have I done?*

If Sheba and Bomarigala hadn't announced their intention of visiting the graveyard, would I have been this reckless? Up until that point, I had been content to wait for the Three to decide whether they wanted to wake. In fact, if I thought about it at all, I assumed it may take them centuries to decide that. Looking back, I had found that idea comforting. Whatever the consequences, *I* wouldn't have to sort them out.

I marveled at the gall of the schemers who had made us. Now that we were so close to them, I wasn't sure I had the courage to ask these Three Giants for a drink of water.

I had asked their *avatars* plenty of questions. I had liked them, even the one for Lady Sheba, because that one had been the noble personage Lady

Sheba only dreamed she was. That one had been wise, and cunning, and full of good suggestions while Medusa and I had plotted and schemed. She and the avatar of my mother had been my allies. This was what I had to reconcile, now that I could see the Three as they really were. I had trusted them. I had wanted to understand them.

Was that a mistake?

The agent who stole our DNA from the Three hadn't made it out of the graveyard alive. Somehow, I hadn't imagined that I might end up in the same situation as that ill-fated thief, struggling in a maze created by entities who seemed more whimsical than logical.

How whimsical had the Three been when they chose their avatars to speak to us? Maybe whimsy had nothing to do with it. Maybe I had been playing into their hands all along.

Ashur and Ahi flew ahead of me—I couldn't see their faces. Dragonette held tight to Ashur's belt loop, and her little face also pointed toward the Three, away from me. I felt Kitten's warmth around my middle, and I thought about the packs we had been forced to leave behind. *Are we expendable?* I wondered, remembering the dead thief of DNA.

Right on cue, my dragonfly unit began to lose altitude.

I heard Ashur shouting, but I couldn't make out the words. He and Ahi were also dropping. We weren't falling precipitously; the descent seemed gradual and intentional. Ahi pointed toward a ridge of rock that extended past the base of the Three. I hoped we weren't going to have to climb down from that height.

The dragonflies lifted us over the ridge, and we descended to the floor of a side canyon, about three hundred meters. Just as my feet planted on solid ground, my dragonfly became inert.

Ahi unstrapped hers, so Ashur and I did the same. "We'll walk from here," she said. "Shouldn't be more than an hour or so."

Ashur peered up at the enclosing walls of the canyon. "Where did we end up?"

"We're in the system that leads to the Lower Gorge," said Ahi. "These cliffs are made of schist—hard rock that was supercompressed for millions of years. That's why they're so steep."

Dragonette let go of Ashur's dragonfly and flew up to a point where she could see over the ridge. She hovered there, scanning the sights from several directions. She took her time. Then she flew back down to us and hovered in front of my nose.

"Uh-oh," she said.

The rest of us froze. "What's up?" I said.

"The Three are gone."

According to Dragonette, it wasn't just the Three who had disappeared. "The Gorge isn't there. I see a maze of smaller canyons, and they sort of just keep zigzagging off into the distance."

Ahi touched the canyon wall. "This rock belongs to the Gorge. No one has explored very much in here—no one who's come back to talk about it, anyway."

"So what are we going to do?" asked Dragonette.

"Our way has been made more difficult," said Ahi, "but the path is smooth. To me, that means we should walk it and see where it leads."

"Can we go back and get our packs?" said Ashur.

That would be quite a distance to hike, but I confess, the same question had crossed my mind. Ahi didn't reject the idea—instead, she walked to the end of the canyon that zigged back in the general direction from which we had come, and looked around the bend. "Come see this," she said.

We joined her. At the far end of the next segment, a rock fall had blocked the way. If we wanted to get our packs, we would have to climb quite a distance, on unstable rocks.

"This is a clear message," said Ahi. "We have to head the other way."

Ashur didn't look scared, though maybe he should have. He seemed more puzzled. "Why did the Three go away? Where are they?"

"I think we need to ask *when* are they," said Ahi, "compared with when *we* are. We're not syncing up with them. Someone interfered."

"Who would interfere?"

Ahi shook her head. "I don't want to say it aloud. Not here. We have to go and do what we're supposed to do. Maybe then they'll let us see the Three again."

I could tell that Ashur wanted to ask *Who are* they? I had an inkling who could have tampered with our expedition—and who was to blame.

Dragonette flew to Ashur and perched on his shoulder. "Things were going *too* well," she said. "That's not how it usually works out for *Olympia*ns. For *anyone*, I expect. I don't know about you, but I'm always suspicious of good things that fall right into your lap." She fluttered her pectoral fins. "Call me a pessimist."

"I agree," said Kitten. "If this were a stage production, and we all got everything we wanted without having to work for it, no one would stay past the intermission. We would be a flop."

When Ashur frowned at this example, Kitten added, "Unless we had good songs—but the critics would trash us anyway."

That made Ashur laugh. "Okay. So we have to make the critics happy. Let's get to it. The sooner we do, the quicker it's done." He patted his overstuffed pockets. "And the sooner we get supper."

When Ashur had turned away, Ahi and I exchanged long looks. I got the feeling there was something she wasn't sure she should ask me.

Funny. I knew how that felt.

"Stupid critics," she said at last.

Kitten wrapped herself around my waist. "Right? But they keep us honest."

I wasn't sure how to feel about our current predicament, because I wasn't sure if I had caused it. My connection with the Three had been brief, but I wondered if it had been long enough to let them see my doubts. Maybe my lack of confidence made them change their minds about me.

What could I do about it, anyway? Should I tell Ashur what had happened? Would I do more harm by talking about it? I honestly didn't know.

At least the level path was easy to walk on, in the sense that it didn't slope up, and the sand and gravel underfoot provided some relief for our feet without bogging us down. The canyon walls shaded us, so it felt warm rather than hot. The big problem, as far as I could see, was that we didn't seem to be going anywhere. We were taking a long time not doing that. We were taking so long, we got tired.

I felt it long before the youngsters. The Minis never felt it at all. I said nothing until Ashur called a halt and said, "I need to sit down for a few minutes and eat something."

"I thought you'd never ask." I gave him a grateful smile.

Ahi grinned and pointed her chin at a low bench of rock. "That spot looks like it was made for us."

"Was it?" said Ashur as the three of us sat and began to dig in our packs for bars.

She took her time answering that. "Maybe. It's hard to say what's a gift and what's already there for anyone who cares to notice. I think most of the time, fate favors the prepared mind."

Those were pretty wise words from a twelve-year-old, but I'm not sure Ahi was wrong when she said that she had grown old and wise inside the time fracture in Seaside. She had been exposed to Joe's Canyon longer than anyone. It had taught her things, and she was uniquely receptive to its lessons.

We ate our bars, but we didn't linger over them. Ashur seemed impatient to get back to the Three.

I found myself hoping we *wouldn't* get back to them. I did, however, want out of that maze. So we tucked our wrappers back into our pockets and hauled ourselves upright. We walked side by side, too weary to talk, though Kitten could have conducted a conversation without any extra effort. She went with the consensus.

The canyon zigged this way, then zagged the other. We had no choice but to follow. It must be taking twice as long to make any progress—maybe ten times longer. It was getting harder and harder for me to put one foot in front of the other. I wondered if I should suggest we ought to camp. That was going to be fun, without air mattresses, though I felt so tired, I wasn't sure I would mind.

We walked to the end of another zig. Before we could turn the bend, two men stepped into our path.

I recognized them—sort of. They were two of Sheba's poachers I had seen back in Joe's Salvage Yard, the ones who had been so overshadowed by the giant standing with them. It wasn't their faces that tipped me off, though. It was their expressions, and the way they licked their lips when they saw Ashur and Ahi.

They drew hunting knives.

"Back up!" I told the kids.

Before any of us could move, Dragonette and Kitten rushed the poachers.

The Minis had biometal bodies, and the same nerves and brains that motivated Medusa and her sisters. I didn't even have a chance to be frightened for them. They bit, and scratched, and hurled themselves at the two men so fast, the poachers lost their footing. One moment, those men had been stalking us with grins on their faces and knives in their hands; the next, they were backpedaling like people caught in a swarm of stinging bees. One man dropped his knife; the other lost a small pack that hit the ground with a hollow *clunk*.

They ran, disappearing around the bend. Dragonette swooped up, back and forth, and then she returned. "They're gone!"

"Running away?" I guessed.

"No. I mean they *vanished*. I never heard them approaching, either, which I certainly should have done."

"Me, too," volunteered Kitten. "My hearing is supersharp. I heard them running, but the sound cut off as if they had gone through a door."

Whatever had dumped those two henchmen into our laps had just scooped them out again. Had they been sent to remind us that the canyon was dangerous? Were they sent to kill us? Or was it just dumb luck that they ended up in our path?

"Where the hell are Sheba and the other guys?" I said.

"Her path into the canyon wasn't optimal," said Ahi.

Ashur raised his eyebrows. "Meaning?"

"She wasn't invited by the right entities, and she didn't have me as a guide. So she could be lost now or she could be dead. Or she could be fine, but part of her party got lost."

Considering all that Sheba had survived so far, I didn't feel inclined to hope the canyon had finally done her in. As Dragonette had said—things never went that easily for *Olympia*ns.

That was the same reason Dragonette and Kitten had been able to turn tough when the chips were down.

I thought I could have handled *one* of those men. I wasn't so confident that I could have fended off *two* of them, considering how confident they had looked, how comfortable they had been with those blades in their hands. On *Olympia*, my adversaries had been pampered bullies who weren't accustomed to victims who fought back, but the Forgettables had not been softies. Which was all the more reason to be impressed with the actions of our wonderful Minis.

"That was fast thinking, you two," I told them.

Dragonette curled and uncurled her tail. "I'm not sure it was *any* kind of thinking. I saw the knives, and I just—*foom!*"

Kitten looked up from the discarded pack. "I have never felt so scared and so angry at the same time. I'm glad we could do something about it." She reached into the bag and pulled out a canister. It was blue, and I could see green letters printed on its side. "*Evernight*," read Kitten.

"What . . . ?" Ahi's eyes went wide. "Let me see that."

The canister may have held water at one point, but it was empty now. Ahi studied it for a moment, her face blank. Then she placed it back inside and left the bag where it was lying. "I know where we're going now." She didn't sound happy about it.

"Where?" said Ashur.

"Evernight Canyon."

Kitten sat down at Ahi's feet and looked up at her. "Another side canyon? To receive another clue?"

"That's the way it looks." Ahi seemed to be getting used to the idea.

"Have you been there before?" I said.

"No, but I've heard of it. Come on. Now that we know where we're going, we'll make better time."

Ashur and I exchanged glances. In Ahi's current mood, she seemed as secretive as Baba Yaga. We gathered our packs and regarded the bend around which the Forgettables had disappeared.

"Hear anything?" Ahi asked the Minis.

"No," said Dragonette.

"Not even breathing," added Kitten.

"Then let's roll." Ahi started forward, but she stopped again when she stepped on something. She bent to pick it up, but recoiled without touching it. "Hey—come look at this."

We gathered in a loose circle around the object. It seemed to be the knife one of the Forgettables had dropped, but on closer inspection, the hilt was broken and cracked, and the blade had corroded.

"That's the same knife, right?" Ahi looked around, as if expecting to find another knife on the ground, this one in better shape.

"It's the same," Dragonette assured her. "I saw where it fell."

Ahi looked up at us. "We've been moved to another time. I'm pretty sure we won't run into those Scavengers again."

Pretty sure. I didn't remind her that there had been two other men in that party, and one murderous old lady—and we hadn't encountered them yet.

"*Gifts, but gone, then what?*" quoted Dragonette. "*Bite the ones who take.* The Sentinel was right again." She fluttered on Ashur's shoulder.

Our pace had slowed. We were tired, and we also worried about stumbling into more poachers.

"What came after that part?" said Ashur.

"*Running ruins and sad!*"

"That doesn't sound good."

Ahi sighed. "No. But it sounds true. We should have been consulting Dragonette's transcript all along."

"I think it may be time to tell us what you've heard about Evernight Canyon," I said.

"For one thing, it's always night there."

"Dark and shady?" said Ashur.

"No." Ahi shook her head. "The sun never comes up inside that canyon. It's night, all the time. A dark sky—what you can see of it."

As one, we looked up. The afternoon light slanted bright and hot into Joe's Canyon, but we stood in deep shadows because of our rock walls. Did I imagine that night was approaching faster than it had the previous day?

"If it's so dark," said Ashur, "how will we see anything?"

"Good question."

I glanced at Ahi—she looked resolute, but not frightened. She walked at a steady pace and seemed ready to face whatever we would find at the end of our zigzag maze.

Assuming it ever did end.

The day waned. Whether the rotation of Graveyard had taken us out of the path of the sun, or Evernight Canyon had asserted its peculiar sway, I couldn't say.

Yet as the sunshine faded, another light took its place, from a different direction. Ahead, something glowed on the canyon walls.

"Somebody turned on a lamp," said Ahi.

Overhead, the darkness congealed. No stars appeared. I wondered if clouds had moved in. Shouldn't we have seen them before the sun set?

The artificial light grew brighter, starker, throwing odd shadows on the canyon walls. Nothing moved in that landscape, yet I heard something—a mechanical sound. Maybe a fan? We rounded the last bend and saw a low structure to our left.

"Holy moley!" said Ahi. "That's a bathroom!"

The door stood open. Light spilled from inside.

21

The Evernight Incident

The bathroom we used at Joe's Salvage Yard had been a simple structure, humble and utilitarian. That would be the sort of thing I would have expected to find in the canyon (emphasis on *simple* and *humble*), if such a thing could be expected at all. The building that confronted us now looked pretty substantial—like it had been built to last. We crept closer and saw more buildings stretching into the distance—or rather, we saw their lights.

"Evernight isn't a canyon," I said. "It's a small town."

"Who lives here?" Ashur pitched his voice as if he were afraid someone in Evernight might hear him, but nothing moved in that town, except for the fan we could hear. No one investigated our intrusion.

"Maybe the lights come on automatically?" I said.

Ahi shook her head. "I've heard rumors about this place, but this is the first time I've been here. No one said there were buildings, and you'd think that would be an important detail." She considered the bathroom again. "There may be running water."

I wanted to go in and splash my face, and drink water until my stomach made funny noises. I waited for Ahi's verdict.

"We're going in," she said. "Everybody stay close. Don't let yourself get separated, no matter what happens."

"Should we all go into the same bathroom?" Ashur sounded incredulous.

"Yes." She leveled a glare at him. "Safety trumps modesty."

He frowned, then nodded. "You're right. I don't want to let you guys out of my sight. Let's go be immodest."

The bathroom didn't stand alone; it was one room in a larger structure. Its door stood open, held in that position by a metal prop at its base. As we were going in, I cast a long look at the town over my shoulder.

Until now, we had never encountered any of the support structures you might find at a spaceship graveyard: the hangars, the office buildings, and so on. Yet somehow, they were present *here*, stretching across a broad sandstone platform, pretty much in the logical place for them to be, should someone want to construct buildings inside a canyon: up out of the flood zone.

They still functioned. Lights illuminated the inside of the bathroom, and it was clean.

Most important—it had running water. Ahi ran the tap and took a sip. "Spring water," she decided. "There must be a pump. Joe's Canyon has a lot of springs, so that's no big surprise."

I took a long drink, straight from one of the sinks. Then I filled my water bottle. Behind me, I could hear Ashur and Ahi going into stalls. Dragonette perched on the counter next to my sink, and Kitten joined her there.

"I think we're missing something," said Dragonette.

"Something in the town?" I wondered.

She fluttered her fins. "Something in our situation. We think things have been made hard for us because nothing is supposed to be easy, but there's method behind it all."

Kitten wound her tail around herself. "A method to the madness?"

"Someone thinks they're being practical," said Dragonette. "They think they're being logical."

"*Who?*" whispered Kitten.

Dragonette whispered back, "We haven't met the southern gods yet. Maybe they've seen us."

That was a possibility that hadn't occurred to me. I might have been blaming myself for nothing. The relief was short-lived when I considered the consequences of that sort of attention.

"Do you think they're angry with us?" I wondered.

Dragonette flattened her fins. "No, but I'm not sure it matters."

We heard Ahi working the latch on her stall. When she came out to use the sink, I made use of the same facility. It was clean and well stocked. The supplies did not appear dusty or old. "I'm grateful," I said softly. "Thank you."

"Who are you talking to?" said Ashur from the next stall.

"The Powers That Be," I replied.

"Will you ask them if they can please send the next clue along?"

"Sure. Hey, Powers That Be, we'd like a clue."

"I'd like written directions!" called Kitten."

"I'd like a good supper and a hot shower," added Ahi.

None of those things appeared. We finished our business, splashed our faces, filled our bottles, and wandered outside again. Nothing moved out there. No one hailed us from any of the buildings.

"How long do you think it's been since anyone lived here?" Ashur asked Ahi.

She shrugged. "Five minutes. Or five hundred years. I'm not sure there's any difference."

I knew what she meant. The place felt recently abandoned.

"I think we should keep walking," said Ahi. "I get the feeling we shouldn't stay here."

I felt tired, but I liked the idea of moving on, at least for a while. So we walked on the edge of town. We studied the buildings as we passed them— and maybe they studied us, too. Most of them had at least two stories—some had as many as seven. I didn't see much logic to the way they were arranged, and I also got the feeling that parts of Evernight had been built at different times, for completely different reasons.

Whatever the reasons, Evernight didn't welcome us. Each door was locked, each window shuttered. *Move on*, they seemed to say, *you've got no business here*. The feeling was so pervasive, I came to expect that standoffishness, even to appreciate it—because I didn't want to know what had chased people out of this peculiar outpost in the middle of a wilderness. Maybe that's why I gasped when I saw something I didn't expect.

A door stood open, light spilling from the room behind it. I don't know why the sight struck me with such alarm, but it spooked me like one of the scenes out of *The Haunting*, like when they find the door to the creepy nursery standing open when it was supposed to be locked up tight. *Something wants us to go in there*, I thought, determined never to do so.

"If someone built this place on purpose," said Ashur, "I can see why they decided not to stay here."

"If that's what they decided," said Ahi. "If something else didn't make the choice *for* them."

The town stretched for half a kilometer. Behind it loomed the massive staircase whose forbidding scarps kept us from climbing up to the South Rim. If we had been desperate and very foolish, we might have climbed switch-backs that crawled partway up, but in what era would we emerge? Sometime prior to the arrival of the Three?

That obstacle lay at our backs. Instead, we looked across a northern stretch of the sandstone ledge, a small desert inside the canyon. Lights from the town stretched and distorted the shadows of plants with tough skins and sharp spines. Ahi peered at a spot in the distance, where the sky met the top of the North Rim. Something sparkled there.

"Those are stars," said Ahi. "I wonder if we're supposed to go that way."

"Shouldn't we camp for the night?" I felt exhausted, but we had been sent to Evernight. There had to be a reason.

She looked over her shoulder at the town, then back again at her beacon of starlight. "I don't know," she admitted. "My head says something wants us in Evernight, but my heart keeps telling me to get out of here. What do you guys think?"

I took a deep breath and let it out again. "I hate to think about sleeping in one of those buildings. Maybe we could camp in the bathroom? It doesn't seem so bad."

"I can't make up my mind," said Kitten. "I'm sorry. I'll go with the consensus."

"Me, too," said Dragonette. "I'd like to have an opinion, but I can't."

Everyone looked at Ashur. He didn't seem troubled by the responsibility. "Let's get out of here. I don't have to think twice about it."

Ahi sighed. "Let me suggest a compromise. Let's walk some distance into this desert, toward the stars. If they keep shining, if we seem to be getting somewhere, we'll keep going. If not, we'll turn around and head back to the bathroom. Deal?"

"Deal," we all agreed, and for a moment, my heart felt light. We had a plan!

Then Ahi set one foot into the desert, and a blue light exploded over the horizon.

"What the—?" Ashur started to say as the light raced across the desert toward us on spider legs. I had seen something like it before.

"Gravity bombs!" I yelled. "*Run!*"

"This way!" cried Dragonette. "There's an open door back there!" She zoomed ahead of us, leading the way. Kitten dashed after her, and the rest of us brought up the rear, as we ran with all we had toward Evernight.

"Up here!" commanded Dragonette. "It's on the second level!"

Shadows raced past us into Evernight. They howled at our heels, driving us up the stairs and across the landing. I heard Ashur and Ahi shouting behind me.

"Run!" somebody screamed. "Lock the door behind you!"

I didn't recognize that voice. Had someone been living in Evernight after all? Had the noise drawn them out? Where were they now? I could see Dragonette and Kitten, just ahead. I could think only of getting through that open door.

There it was! Dragonette shot through like a bullet, Kitten jumped over the threshold, and I followed close behind.

Something laid a hand on my back and pushed. I flew forward. Behind me, I could hear Ashur and Ahi at the door. They leaped over the threshold, and the door slammed shut behind them.

I picked myself up. Kitten crouched in a nearby corner. Ahi and Ashur gazed at each other and then at me, their faces pale.

"*Running ruins and sad,*" Kitten said, her voice very small.

"What?" I said.

"Now I know what's sad," said Kitten.

I looked into every corner of the room. I had seen Dragonette fly in, right before Kitten crossed the threshold. She wasn't there now. She wasn't anywhere.

Outside, blue lightning flashed and the storm howled, as if in triumph.

PART FIVE

THE SOUTHERN GODS

22

There's No People Like Show People

The storm raged for hours. I barely heard it. My memories kept me too busy with thoughts about gravity bombs and the destruction of *Titania*.

Somewhere in the background, I could hear Kitten trying to comfort herself with her favorite show tune: "There's no business like show business like no business I know. . . ." The result was a sad and hollow version of her usual rendition. She was close, and I should talk to her, but my thoughts and my feelings were still too remote. I had banished emotion while I pondered the details of the death of a generation ship.

The bombs generated powerful fields that conflicted with each other. Blue lightning had crawled over *Titania's* hull when she came unraveled. From the sound of it, they were doing the same thing to Evernight.

"Everything about it is appealing, everything the traffic will allow . . ."

Most of the people inside *Titania* had been killed when the gravity bombs interrupted the spin. The people inside the Habitat Sector had been swept out with the atmosphere. How had they killed the people in Evernight? Were they crushed and mangled? Would that happen to us?

"Nowhere could you get that happy feeling when you are stealing that extra bow. . . ."

Some people had survived the destruction of *Titania*, just as we were surviving in Evernight, in this little room. We may have ended up in the right place at the right time.

Even if we lasted through the night, we had paid a high price for that.

"There's no people like show people . . . they . . ." Kitten's song petered out.

I counted my mistakes like sheep, but it was not a behavior conducive to sleep. I hadn't told Medusa that Crow contacted me. I hadn't told Ahi and Ashur what the Three had shown me. There were so many things . . .

"Come back to me," whispered Kitten. "Come back." She was calling Dragonette, who couldn't hear her.

I tried to remember why this expedition had seemed like such a great idea. I could see how I had been goaded into this course of action. Perversely, I could still see why the risks had looked as if they were worth taking. In the end, one question remained.

How was I going to fix this?

"Come back to me," Kitten said again, and I realized she wasn't calling Dragonette after all.

She was calling me.

"I hear you, Kitten," I whispered. I didn't want to wake Ashur and Ahi. They were snoring, and I felt grateful they were getting some sleep.

Kitten had been sitting on my chest this whole time, trying to get through to me. "Maybe I'm *not* show people, Oichi. I can't smile when I'm low."

"Me neither," I admitted.

"I don't think Dragonette is dead. I think she's lost. I'm about sixty percent sure of that."

I was closer to 50 percent.

"I think I should postpone my grief," Kitten continued. "Do you think that's okay?"

"Absolutely." In fact, I was an expert at postponing grief.

My companions weren't so good at that. Once the shock wore off, they looked miserable, and weary beyond measure—even Kitten. The room in which we found ourselves was plain, unfurnished, and without apparent purpose, except to shelter us from the lightning. It had no windows, and the only door leading in or out had been locked when it slammed shut. We stretched out on the floor and tried to rest. Blue light blazed around the edges and under the bottom of the door, creating a strobe effect in the room. Ahi and Ashur threw their arms over their eyes and tried not to see it.

I watched. I let that blue lightning take me back to *Titania*.

I had to admit, though—the effects were not what I had expected. So far, we had not been crushed in the gravity fields. Maybe we would have been, if we hadn't outrun that storm and taken shelter, but it seemed odd. Dragonette had flown into the same room, yet she was gone. Somehow the whole attack had seemed—personal.

Probably aimed at *me*. I was the one who lost my nerve at the feet of the Three. I had been full of paranoia and fear when they linked with me. I had doubted myself, and this was the result.

These young people with me were innocent; they were the reason things hadn't gone *completely* wrong. I had turned my back on Medusa and ignored her advice—now I had to step out of myself. I had to face my biggest fear. If only I could pick it out from the crowd.

"I'm going to stay right here." Kitten hugged my middle. "I'm not going to let go of you. That way, you can't disappear."

"That's an excellent plan," I said, though I had no idea if it would work. I folded my hands over her body, hoping that would make her feel safe. I stared into the corners, wondering what I had missed. While I lay there, the storm outside diminished, until it died.

Sometime later, I felt Kitten go away.

She didn't get up. She didn't move at all. I felt her solid shape under my hands one moment, and empty air the next.

Suddenly I knew what I had been missing. *I* was the bad egg, the one who had put us in this dangerous situation. When Dragonette disappeared, I had been the closest to her. Kitten had been right on top of me. I thought I was protecting them. That was all I had to offer, because I wasn't good at the finer emotions. I hadn't noticed the line I had crossed, taking them into danger because I thought I could control everything, even when I had been presented with so much evidence to contrary. Everyone thought I was so brave, but fear had been driving me all along.

How could I learn to love, then? In every story I had ever heard about the subject, a sacrifice had to be made. I had thought I would give my life for the ones I cared for, but I had never feared death enough to understand how dearly that gesture had cost others. In my case, the sacrifice was something different. In my case, it was control I needed to let go of.

If I wanted Ashur and Ahi to survive, I needed to get as far away from them as possible. I needed to set them free of *me*.

They slept so deeply, they wouldn't hear the small noises my feet made on the floor. I crept to the door and put my hand on the knob. This might defeat my resolve. If it were still locked, Ashur and Ahi would be stuck with me. They might never get out of the canyon.

It was unlocked. I paused on the threshold and remembered what Ashur had told Nuruddin before we left *Olympia*.

We are connected to the Three, Father. Our blood is theirs. I was—literally— made for this job. I've got to do it. I can't shirk my responsibility just because I'm young.

I couldn't shirk mine, either.

Get home safe, I willed the two young people still fast asleep on the floor. Then I went through the door and pulled it shut behind me.

Don't think I wasn't cautious when I stepped out that door. I looked for any sign of blue lightning, but the world outside held still. Evernight had weathered the storm with remarkably little damage. It waited for me to make my move.

I walked away from Evernight as quickly as I could, out into the desert, never looking back. I thought I understood how Medusa had felt when she walked away from me.

Probably I was wrong, but it was as close as I could get.

Running ruins and sad! the Sentinel had said.

Those words chased themselves around inside my head as I stumbled along the trail, not clear about where I should be going, but also uncertain about whether I should just stay put. Evernight was far behind me. Eventually the sun had risen, which was an encouraging development—until the day began to heat up.

I followed an ephemeral stream that had dried for the season. Lines of fine alluvium pointed with ripples of sand toward some distant basin.

The sun climbed at my back. The Three in their Gorge had been west, roughly the same direction I was walking. They weren't there now. I kept lifting my head to see if they might have reappeared. I contemplated those ripples in the sand and chased the same thoughts around my head again.

When you find yourself in trouble, Queenie had advised, *remember who you are. Remember what you have suffered. Remember what you hope to accomplish. When you have done that, say those things.*

"My name is Oichi Angelis," I said. "And I—I lost—I never . . ."

It wasn't that easy to put my own suffering into words. Anyway, what had hurt me before seemed like nothing compared with what what was hurting me now.

"Let them go," I pleaded. "Send them home. I'm the one who started all the trouble. I'm the one who should finish it."

You can teach Ashur how to kill, Timmy had said, *or you can let him teach you how to live.*

I conjured Ashur's face in my memory. Was it already fraying around the edges? In such a short time?

The sun moved. I'm pretty sure it did. It tried to peek down the back of my collar, to burn me there, reminding me that I had long since lost my hat. I took a few sips of water. My bottle felt light, and I couldn't remember how many times I had drunk from it. I knew it would be empty soon. I looked for the Three. They weren't there. I looked at the ripples again, and I found a thing in the sand.

A gizmo. An artifact. Some baffling whatsit that had broken off a larger thing lying near it. Another lay not far from that one. When I followed that line of things, a spaceship junkyard spread its arms around me, spilling odds and ends as it went.

This collection was far more eclectic than anything I had seen so far. Also far more damaged. These reminded me of the Island of Misfit Toys from *Rudolph the Red-Nosed Reindeer*. Here were the miscreants of space, the forgotten boo-boos that couldn't hold together—though they did have a certain charm. In their own way, they welcomed me.

Come on in, Oichi, they seemed to say. *Enter the place where all the Lost Ones end up. You know what that feels like, right?*

"Yeah," I croaked. "You guys have any water? I think I'm on empty."

I stumbled and almost fell. For a moment, I had to fight dizziness. Should I take a drink of water? Did I have any left?

"Hey," someone said.

I opened my eyes and found a giant in my path—Lady Sheba's blue-eyed henchman.

I should have smelled him, because he wasn't wearing the fancy clean-wear Fire had given Ashur and me. From his odor, bathing wasn't something he did regularly, anyway. He waited a second for me to register who he was. Then he shoved me, hard. I landed flat on my back.

Up! Now!! an inner voice commanded. I scrambled to my feet before he could fall on me with his full weight. He slammed into me, and I backpedaled as I tried to keep upright. If he managed to knock me down and pin my arms, my only option would be to try to rock him off, and I had serious doubts about how well that would go.

You have to go for his eyes, advised that relentless inner voice.

My momentum was in the wrong direction. I fought to stay upright as he shoved me backward, and just as my feet began to lose their purchase, we slammed into the side of a bulkhead.

My fleeting moment of triumph evaporated when he locked his hands around my throat.

He squeezed so hard, I saw stars. I smelled mint, and it occurred to me that this maniac had used breath freshener in anticipation of our encounter, as if he thought we were going on a date.

"I couldn't get near you, because of the innocent ones," he said with a remarkably calm voice. "They're protected. No one's protecting you now, lady. No one gives a shit about you."

I reached for his eyes. My arms were too short. So I thrust my fists between his arms and tried to push outward. It was like trying to break iron. I jabbed at his feet with my heels, but his boots were too sturdy. When I kneed him in the groin, I felt the protector he must be wearing. He grinned as each of my efforts failed.

<Medusa . . . > I called.

Something fluttered in response—something close. The Scavenger stiffened, and his hands released my throat. I fell to my knees, dragging in painful gulps of air. He staggered away from me, and someone stepped into his place.

I blinked the sweat out of my eyes and focused on my savior. I knew who I wanted to see.

I have to admit, by then I knew better.

"Well." Lady Sheba looked down her nose at me. "Look what the cat dragged in."

Behind Sheba, the Scavenger fell to his knees, blood spurting from his wound. He made some gurgling noises, too. All that was peripheral for me, because I only had eyes for Lady Sheba and the knife she was holding—the one she had used to cut his throat from behind.

"How come they let *you* bring a knife?" I demanded.

"They didn't," she said. "I brought one anyway."

Sheba was tall. That had been an advantage. She hadn't suffered from hesitation, so she made her move quickly, before he knew what she intended. She and I stared at each other. I fully expected her to stick that knife in my heart.

Instead, she backed away. The poacher had fallen over, but he was still twitching. Sheba kicked him. When he didn't react, she knelt and wiped her blade on his trousers.

You would think I would have taken the opportunity to stand up while Sheba was cleaning her knife, but it didn't occur to me until she had sheathed her blade again. "You look like hell," she remarked. "So I'm guessing that you have run out of water."

"Good guess," I said.

Sheba rolled the poacher onto his side a pried a canister off his belt. "You couldn't have shown up at a better time." She unscrewed the cap. "This thug would have drunk the last of it, if you hadn't provided a diversion." Sheba took a long drink from the canister. Then she fastened it to her own belt.

That seemed like a good moment to struggle to my feet. She watched me with the concentration of a predator assessing injured prey. Once upright, I propped myself against the bulkhead and scanned our surroundings.

"What happened to the Bomarigala clone?" I said.

She snorted. "You think you're joking about that."

Actually, I had only been *half* joking.

"That pampered fool was supposed to prove himself on this expedition," said Sheba. "Instead, he fell into a time fracture on the first day. He's probably millions of years in the past now, trying to build a fire by rubbing two sticks together."

One guy still unaccounted for—assuming she was telling the truth. Which meant he might still pop up somewhere.

The poacher had stopped twitching. Now he lay in the dust like another discarded machine. No lesson seemed to be implied by his condition, other than the fact that life is fleeting. I wondered how long it would take the canyon to turn him into a mummy, or to bury him in sediment. I wondered if either of those states could redeem him.

"Well," said Sheba, "I would love to stand around with you and stare at corpses, but I'm getting very tired of this place. What do you propose to do next?"

"Do?" At the moment, I had all I could do just to stay upright.

"Does the graveyard act whimsically?" she said. "Why do you suppose it brought us to this particular spot?"

I let my gaze wander over the Misfit Toys. *Because we're misfits, too?* I wondered. Sheba was the one with the knife and the water, so I didn't say that aloud. "Why do you want to follow me? I have no idea where I'm going."

"Because you and your little crew have a better interface with the graveyard. I think it will eventually show you a way out of here. I have no intention of being left behind."

I calculated my odds of killing Sheba. Right now they weren't too good, but perhaps after I had rested a little? It wouldn't be easy, but it wouldn't be impossible, either. It looked as though we were both going to die there anyway, and she damn well deserved it.

So did I. I had always regretted killing Baylor so hastily. There had been quite a lot that old villain could have told us that would have been useful down the line. If nothing else, our dealings with Bomarigala would not have been so blind.

None of this was lost on Sheba. The same calculations were going on in her head. My only advantage was that she thought I was useful.

She *said* she thought that.

I pushed away from the bulkhead and stood on my own. "Let's take a look at these things around us. Maybe we'll find an inspiration."

I didn't approach her, but moved obliquely. Sheba adjusted her position so the same amount of space always stayed between us. I assumed she had calculated how quickly she could get the knife out if I lunged at her, but I wasn't feeling particularly lunge-y at the moment—or even very walk-y. I concentrated on staying upright as I wandered among the gizmos, keeping Sheba in the periphery of my sight. At first, I saw nothing that made sense to me.

After a while I started to get an impression of the Misfit Toys. True, they lay in a jumbled sprawl, but each item had its own character. I *liked* them, even though someone had almost strangled the life out of me in their midst. "If we understood these things," I said, "we could do just about anything with them."

"Like get out of here?" said Sheba.

I started to nod, and winced with pain. "Yes."

After that first spark of inspiration, however, nothing more occurred to me. I stumbled from pile to pile. The day progressed, and started to wane. Finally I said, "I need to rest for a few minutes."

I sat down on a half-buried chunk of something that looked like it wouldn't explode if I touched it. Sheba did the same, some distance away. She hadn't said anything to me for quite a while, but she had watched me with an alertness that never wavered. *You missed your calling, lady,* I thought. *You would have made an excellent sentry.*

I concentrated on breathing. It hurt, because I was thirsty. It felt good to rest, and I found my mind wandering to odd places.

"Where were you planning to take *Escape*?" I said.

For a moment, I thought she was going to smile. "Yes, I heard you found my little ship. Pity you blew her up. She cost me a pretty penny."

I wasn't going to get a direct answer. It had been one of the mysteries that always teased me, so I couldn't help asking.

She lifted her chin. "Where would *you* have taken her?"

I thought about it for a moment. "I wouldn't have anything to trade with the Belters, without *Olympia*. I suppose I would have brought her here—to explore whether there was something I could salvage from the graveyard."

I felt a bit surprised to hear myself saying that, but it made sense. Without my friends and resources, I would have been forced to improvise. A gambit like that could have proved fatal, but I can see how one might feel compelled to take the risk.

The look she cast me was almost approving. "Our kin are a practical breed, if nothing else. Whether you or I succeed, Oichi—they *will* claim their heritage."

"You're okay if they do it without you?" I said.

The skepticism in my voice amused her. "Of course not. I don't relinquish my authority for one moment. I'm very tough to kill, don't you think?"

"Yes," I admitted, "but Medusa almost succeeded."

Real hatred twisted her features. It was replaced by something almost like pity. "You trusted them," she said, "and look where it got you."

Um, yes—freedom, autonomy, Minis, chocolate . . .

"She tried to sabotage your expedition here, didn't she?"

I almost said no, but then I wondered what Sheba knew that I didn't. Medusa had disagreed with the expedition, and she had pursued separate interests.

What *were* those interests, exactly? Medusa said she almost turned *Olympia* around, just to thwart Sheba and Baylor. When I decided to come to Graveyard, she said she regretted not altering our course.

Sheba nodded, as if reading my thoughts. "Yes. It was the Weapons Clan who decided to build the Medusa units. They always plan multiple uses for their creations, and after all—they are the *Weapons* Clan. It proved to be their downfall and ours."

What a wily old fox she was. I could see her point of view.

"Do you plan to kill me, once I pass out?" I said.

"Don't be ridiculous. You're no threat to me. You can barely stand on your own, yet—you might still prove useful."

"No," I said flatly. "I'm not your minion."

She shook her head. "Useful to *Olympia*, Oichi. Useful to the survivors of *Titania*. We have a birthright. You may yet secure it for us."

"Because you can't secure it yourself?" I guessed.

She shrugged. "You're the one they reached out to. They have never shown any interest in me."

"So you goaded me into coming here."

She smiled. "If I learned nothing else in the House of Clans, I perfected the art of tricking an enemy into behaving like an ally."

I saw her point. Hadn't I been the one to manipulate Baylor into passing the Music in Education bill? Hadn't I read Sheba's letters and fabricated a diary in which she expressed support for ideas that were really part of *my* agenda? Didn't I stand by and let Sezen Koto commit suicide so I could infiltrate the Executive class?

Maybe it was exhaustion, maybe it was dehydration, but I could see how much Sheba and I had in common.

Looking back at all our machinations, at the murder and sabotage and espionage that had marked our path to Graveyard, I could see why Nuruddin had compared our lives to Greek tragedies and comedies.

I wondered, were the Misfit Toys our Chorus? What would they say about our situation? I dredged up one of Nuruddin's quotes and recited it:

Save Athens and all Greece,
From Lunacy and war,
For that, O maid, is what,
They've seized your temple for.

"I suspect you're misinterpreting that quote," said Sheba with some amusement.

"Yeah, well, it's going to have to do. Because the only other quote I can remember is, *Please, Lenny, don't be a schmuck!*"

"That one seems more appropriate at the moment." She sighed. "This is very tedious."

That was the first time she had shown any weakness. She still had an upright posture, and she had dispatched the giant poacher like a pro, but I suspected it was pure vinegar that was keeping Sheba in the game right now.

I rubbed my eyes and hauled myself to my feet. Then I turned a full circle, this time looking at the bigger picture instead of focusing on details. The junkyard sat expectantly under my gaze—no chirping, squeaking, humming, or rattling creatures moved there. It looked like a messier version of Joe's Salvage Yard.

"There's got to be something useful here," I said.

"By all means," said Sheba. "Let's find it." To her credit, she also looked. Together, we searched for a clue.

Then I saw something familiar. I blinked, wondering if I should believe my eyes. "Sheba—are you seeing that?" I pointed.

She cast her gaze in that direction, but I could tell she didn't recognize anything.

"Those prongs that look like mantis arms," I clarified.

"That's just unsorted apocrypha," said Sheba.

"No, it's not. That's Queenie."

Queenie looked as if she had rested in the same spot for centuries, if not millennia. She was half-buried in fine red sand—but there was no mistaking her arms. I touched her. "Queenie—can you hear me? It's Oichi."

Queenie remained cold and silent. Sheba circled us, stopping at arm's length. "I presume she needs to be switched on somehow," she said.

Queenie is an accidental consciousness, Fire had said. If Queenie's personality had formed because of her interface with users, maybe she couldn't just send and receive messages without Fire. Maybe she needed a deeper connection.

I could think of only one way to create one, but the northern gods had forbidden me to use my implant inside the canyon. I pondered the consequences of doing it anyway.

Then, *Bite me, northern gods,* I thought. <Queenie? Can you hear me?>

Her response was instantaneous. <YOU ARE NOT AUTHORIZED FOR THIS SYSTEM. IDENTIFY YOURSELF. DESTRUCTION PROTOCOL IS IMMINENT.>

The friendly, *accidental consciousness* that Fire had described was nowhere in evidence. I realized something that should have been apparent from the beginning. We were *not* in the same time that Fire and Queenie were linked.

She didn't know me. She hadn't bonded with a human yet. Remnants of her former partners could be seen in the martial aspect of her current personality. They had been aliens, and warrior queens—and in about ten seconds, they intended to blow us up.

<Queenie, you and I will meet in a future time!>

<NOT RELEVANT. PROVIDE THE REQUIRED INFORMATION.>

<My name is Oichi Angelis,> I said, hoping that would matter.

<INCOMPLETE. PROVIDE THE REQUIRED INFORMATION.>

When you find yourself in trouble, remember who you are. Remember what you have suffered. Remember what you hope. When you have done that, say those things. . . .

Queenie had given me that advice. It had seemed oddly specific. Now I had an inkling why.

<I am Oichi Angelis. I have *suffered*—I have lost Ashur and Ahi, and Dragonette and Kitten. I *hope* to find them again.>

Queenie became supernaturally focused. <ASHUR AND AHI. SHOW ME.>

<I can't! I don't know where—>

Queenie didn't wait. I felt something odd happening with my implant, and then I could see things from the perspective of the Last Sentinel again. Only this time, I could also see the model of the time loops in Seaside Canyon. Queenie brought all these elements together to search for a particular energy signature. I felt how she was doing it, and it made sense to me. Then: <HERE.> Queenie showed me what she had demanded to see.

Ahi and Ashur. I could see them as clearly as if I were standing a few feet away from them.

I had no idea how long they had remained locked inside the room in Evernight. They weren't there anymore. I had left them so they could get out of the canyon, but they had done the opposite. Now they stood in the shadow of the Three.

"This is it!" Ahi said to Ashur. "You and I are on a hero's journey!"

That was about the most alarming thing I could have heard her say.

"Oichi should be here," Ashur said. "She's the one they used to talk to. She's the one who made friends with them."

<Ashur!> I called, but my link was rebuffed.

<COMMUNICATION BETWEEN UNLINKED TIMES IS FORBIDDEN,> said Queenie.

Ahi put her hands on Ashur's shoulders. "Don't doubt yourself. You're strong. They want to hear from *you*, Ashur. That's why you were invited."

<Queenie,> I said, <take me to them. Now.>

<NEGATIVE. THAT ROUTE IS CATASTROPHIC TO THE BALANCE.>

"I think I know what to do," said Ashur. "I hope I'm right! If I do it, I'm going to break the rule the northern gods made about using my brain implant to communicate."

"Maybe they won't mind if you use it to talk to the Three," said Ahi, though she sounded far from sure about that. "Do you think this thing you want to do is the *best* you have to offer?"

Ashur looked more certain now. "Yes. It's the best thing I've ever done. It's way better than anything else I could say or do."

Ahi took his hand. "So—what is this wonderful thing?"

I held my breath.

<ACTIVATING TRAVEL PROTOCOLS,> announced Queenie, and my perspective was wrenched away from Ashur and Ahi.

<Wait!> I pleaded.

<PROJECTED OUTCOMES PRESERVE THE BALANCE. THE PATHWAY FOR THIS UNIT HAS BEEN CALCULATED.>

I could see the point in Space that Queenie had chosen as her destination: Joe's Salvage Yard. There were *two* points in Time plotted for that destination. <I SHALL DELIVER PASSENGERS TO THEIR CORRECT TIME,> said Queenie. <THIS UNIT WILL POWER UP FOR TRANSMISSION.>

Queenie began to glow. Sheba stepped forward and placed her hand on the other prong. "You're not going to believe this," she said, "but it's for the best."

I thought she meant it was best that she and I end up back at Joe's Salvage Yard. It was an improvement over our current condition. From there, I could conceivably mount a rescue expedition.

That's not what she meant.

Queenie reached full power. In another moment, we three would become light, and she could move us. One second before that happened, Sheba gave me a hard shove.

I landed like a ton of bricks and looked up just in time to see Queenie and Sheba shimmer out of sight.

They had kicked up a cloud of dust during their passage. I watched it settle to the ground again.

My throat felt bruised and sore. My face felt even worse. If I could have kicked myself at that moment, I would have put all I had into it.

Instead, I got to my feet. "What's next?" I asked the Misfit Toys. "That was my ticket out of here."

I waited for a sign, anything that even hinted at what direction I should take. I'm not sure how long I stood there, but no guidance materialized. I'm pretty sure I was there for a *long* time.

"I'm going to keep walking around the yard," I said, "and see if anything jumps out at me."

Ouch. That wasn't the best way to phrase it, considering who had jumped out at me previously.

"If this is the wrong thing to do," I said, "let me know."

Yeah, that was cheating. If it's any consolation, I was probably just cheating myself.

―――――

Can you keep your feet? the Last Sentinel had asked. Fortunately for me, I had. What had come after that? *Prosper! Oichi, where is the cannon?*

That had been the whole shebang. *Prosper!* sounded encouraging. Was it time to do that? By all means!

Prosperity remained elusive, and no cannons showed up. I'm not sure how much time passed while I stumbled through the clutter of Misfit Toys. Maybe I had wandered into another time fracture. The day didn't seem to progress much as I searched the piles with weary eyes. Not that I was paying very good attention at that point. I spent just as much time watching my feet. I didn't trust my balance anymore.

You're out of food and water, nagged my inner voice. *How long do you think you can keep this up?*

"I don't know."

Should you even be walking? Maybe it would be wiser to sit down and wait.

"I can't just wait when Ashur is confronting the Three, all by himself. I have to help him."

What if the entities don't want you to help him? What if you're the only one who's really lost?

I sighed. "You know, you're starting to piss me off."

The voice had a point. My body ached from head to toe, especially in the places Sheba's poacher had battered me. I didn't feel hungry or thirsty anymore, but I knew I was in an advanced state of both. Most likely, I wasn't thinking straight.

I stopped walking and changed my focus. All I needed now was a good place to sit down. The dirt at my feet might even do. Nice red dirt. It piled up everywhere and got into the cracks. I couldn't see anything that wasn't covered in . . .

Okay—*one* thing.

Standing at the edge of a heap of apocrypha, something white shone in the dazzling light. I had passed that pile several times, but from a different direction. The shape had looked like a straight pole, but from this new angle, I thought it might be a giant seashell.

"Seaside . . ." I croaked.

This thing did not have the solidity of one of the seashell ships. It was more like the *outline* of one of those things, like a two-dimensional . . .

Like a door.

I moved cautiously toward that shape. It appeared much less like a solid object and more like an opening from my landscape into that other place. When I was close enough that my nose almost touched, I peered as far right, and then left as I could see. A path wandered through that white landscape, right past my position, and seashell ships stretched in rows on either side.

I twitched with alarm when I saw movement. Someone was coming down that white path. I almost ran, but then I recognized who it was.

Ahi and Ashur, Dragonette and Kitten, walking up the trail through Seaside.

I was with them. It must have been right after we had seen the model of the time fractures. On our way out, we had walked past a ship with a dark doorway. Now Ahi paused and stared right at me, frowning, and I saw her lips move as she told the *past* me what she suspected.

I think that's another time fracture . . . and someone's trapped inside.

I had hoped the trapped person was Lady Sheba, but *I* was the one stuck inside. My instincts at the time had been right. I probably didn't deserve to get out.

I ached to leap through that door, to warn them, *Don't go to Evernight!* Yet it was my presence that had put them in danger in the first place. How much worse would it get if I broke Queenie's rules? THAT ROUTE IS CATASTROPHIC TO THE BALANCE . . .

I couldn't go through that door until the past version of me and the others walked out of sight. I couldn't interfere with what had already happened. Only one path made sense to me. Seaside was the place where water had miraculously appeared in our canisters, and I really hoped it would do that for me again. From there, I would just have to try to make it to the Three and Ashur on my own.

I waited until I couldn't see us anymore. Once we were well out of sight, I hurled myself at that door. I expected some resistance when I passed through, so I gave it everything I had.

There was no resistance. I fell on my face.

I had to wait a minute until the dizziness passed and I could get up again. Once I did, I got a big shock.

I wasn't with the Misfit Toys anymore.

I wasn't in Seaside, either.

23

Dagger

I picked myself up from strange terrain. A wide floodplain spread fans of silt and dry mud ahead of me and to either side. The river that had created it meandered in the distance, and beyond it marched ranks of mountains. The clouds piled up over those peaks, threatening rain. I turned around, expecting that the canyon must be visible behind me, but instead I found a road pinching off at a vanishing point at the horizon. A few meters away, to the side of that endless highway, a broken sign hung from rusted screws on rods that angled toward the ground, as if they were too tired to do their job anymore. Only one word remained on its placard: NORTH.

I turned to face the southern end of the highway, but it didn't stretch to the horizon. It rose as if it were climbing to a bridge. I walked up that incline to the very top. That's where I found the end.

Once again I felt compelled to turn and look, first at the smooth stretch of highway behind, and then at the broken chunks scattered up ahead, and finally down at the perfectly straight line of division six inches from my toes. From my vantage point, the highway past the break looked as if someone had picked it up and cracked it like a whip.

A voice startled me. "One morning the people in the North woke up and the people in the South were gone."

This was not a ship talking to me. My implant hadn't been activated. I had heard that voice with my own ears, but I couldn't see who had spoken.

Nothing moved. I spotted a structure below the elevated highway and to the left, sitting in a riot of scrub. I thought the voice had come from that spot.

I wondered how I would get down without breaking my neck, but once I had explored the side of the highway, I saw big chunks of concrete just below. They had fallen into a loose tumble that resembled steps, so I picked my way down.

Once my feet were on the ground again, I walked cautiously toward the structure. I thought it might be made of the same concrete as the highway.

It looked like a bridge. Had it fallen there when the highway was sundered? It didn't seem to be connected to anything, and it didn't span a wash or a ravine.

"Welcome to Jigsaw," said the voice.

It was a very odd voice. I'm no expert, but it didn't sound to me as if it could be coming from a human throat. It was too beautiful.

Maybe that's why I moved closer, because if I could have seen what was talking to me, I probably would have run the other way. Instead, I pushed through some tall weeds, and there he was, less than a meter away, crouching on a ledge under the bridge.

He towered over me, a pale creature that sat on rear haunches like a beast, though his body was humanoid. He was all sinew, taut skin, and bone; his hands and feet looked almost like eagle's talons. He possessed a reptilian ruff that started at the top of his head and diminished as it traveled down his spine. I couldn't see eyes or a nose.

His face was dominated by an enormous maw crowded with long, sharp teeth. I felt an awe and a terror unlike anything I had ever experienced, and I knew, without a shadow of a doubt.

This was a southern god.

"I am Dagger," said the creature. His lips traveled an amazing distance over his exposed teeth to form words. He had no genitalia that I could identify, but his voice sounded male to me.

"I'm Oichi Angelis," I replied with my ruined voice.

"The worm," said Dagger. "It is an interesting description for someone with so much potential." He cocked his head as if to get a different perspective, though he had no organs he could use to see me, as far as I could tell. "I am curious, Oichi. What price did you pay to buy the freedom of your people?"

My tongue felt glued in place. It seemed Dagger knew quite a lot about me already, and I hadn't told him anything.

"Your heritage is partly human," he said. "Humans have a way of wandering into spaces without knowing what is already there."

"Like the people in the South?" I guessed.

"Like them," said Dagger.

I was very afraid then, but I didn't know how else to move forward, so I asked a question. "What happened to the people in the South?"

"We saw the colonists from their arrival on Jigsaw to their departure," said Dagger. "So—we took the southerners. We tweaked them, and then we put them back."

"You *tweaked* them," I said.

"It is what we do," said Dagger. "It is what we are. There is always a price, Oichi. What was yours?"

He would have his answer. I felt chastened in his presence, in a way I hadn't felt since I was a little girl and my father was angry with me.

"I lost the ones I love the most," I said.

"True," said Dagger. "But they're lost, not dead."

I sensed I stood on a precipice with Dagger, and I wasn't quite sure where the edge was—so I guessed. "I have killed people. I—have to hide it. People would be afraid of me. I don't always want them to feel that way. Sometimes I want them to like me."

"I have killed, too, Oichi—some who were more innocent than your casualties." Dagger lifted one hand and pointed a talon at me. "That was not your price. Tell me your price."

Suddenly I saw what it must be. "Ashur lost one of his fathers because of me. He lost his innocence. He's not the only one—my friends have all suffered because of my actions and my decisions. Dragonette is lost, Kitten is grieving."

"No," said Dagger. "Those are consequences, but you're getting warmer."

Frustration began to overtake my fear and awe. Wy did people keep backing me into these conceptual corners? Why did I have to keep explaining myself? Why did Medusa . . .

Yes, why *did* she?

"I lost Medusa's trust," I said, "and I don't know how to get it back."

He lowered his hand. "Yes, that's it."

Dagger regarded me for a long moment, with what senses I could not guess. I heard a sound that I recognized from my mother's nature database— thunder. Outside our shelter, it began to rain. The sound and the smell were unspeakably beautiful. The other odors that drifted on the breeze were different from anything I had smelled before.

"We're on another world," I said, "not Graveyard."

"This is Jigsaw," said Dagger. "There are some intersections inside the canyon on Graveyard. You saw them in the model, in Seaside. You have traveled through one of our Gates. We who abide within those fractures are the Gate-keepers. We have chosen you, Oichi, because of your old blood and your new blood. We demand our price, too. You will pay it when I ask for it."

This sounded like a statement, but I answered anyway. "Yes. I will pay."

"The clan who makes its fortune from the sale of weapons is your enemy," said Dagger, "but also your friend, if the circumstances are right."

I nodded like a child learning her sums.

"We will make the circumstances right," said Dagger. "We offer you the Gates, Oichi Angelis."

Dagger expected me to understand that. I did—sort of. "Like the one I passed through to get here?"

"Yes. No ship required. The nexus points are places of great importance. Jigsaw is one. Graveyard is another. I will create one on *Olympia*, which you may use, when you will. Now, go and find a personage. She will help you sort your immediate problems, and the Reasonable Peace will be preserved."

"Who is the personage?" I said.

"Surprises are nice," Dagger said.

Nice? Did the people in the South think so?

"I will trust you with a secret," said Dagger. "The people of Jigsaw call us the southern gods, though we are not worshipped. We are aware, but we are not omniscient. We are powerful, but we are not omnipotent. We lived inside the fractures in the beginning. We will be here in the end. For us, the beginning and the end are the same thing."

He got down from his perch and ushered me under the bridge and out the other end, into the rain. He gave me a gentle push, so I thought he was done speaking, but just before I passed into the fracture, I heard his voice one last time. "Truly grasp that idea, Oichi, and you will know what we are."

That seemed to be my cue to go. I started to walk, but within a few steps, something occurred to me. I turned and looked over my shoulder at Dagger. "I know why they call you gods."

"Do tell," said Dagger.

"It's because of your God Machine."

He cocked his head. "Because I lack omniscience, I'm not grasping your point."

"This thing I'm about to walk into," I said. "Your God Machine."

He didn't smile, which was not a sight I would have liked to see anyway, but his ruff stood straight up. "Ah!" he said. "Interesting."

I turned and started to walk again, wondering how long it would take me to get through the fracture. Would time stretch and make it seem like forever?

I don't think I took more than half a dozen steps before the temperature changed. I looked up—in that short amount of time, I had lost my concentration and become focused on my feet again. Somehow I had managed to make my way into a room full of cool, green light.

It was a lovely place—a bit archaic, in the sense that it was made of stone that reminded me of the limestone of Seaside. It had no glass windows, just low walls that let in the open air and the smell of green, growing things. Columns supported a beamed roof. There were tables displaying arrangements of flowers and shells, and stone benches topped with comfy-looking cushions. I heard the splashing of water from outside, and imagined ponds with little waterfalls. I wondered if they had koi.

The abrupt change in temperature made me stumble, and I almost fell. It took a moment to regain my balance—and to focus on the person in the center of the room, perched on a bench carved out of stone.

"Medusa . . ."

She looked up from the plaque she had been reading. "Did you meet an entity named Dagger?"

"Yes." My voice was a ghost.

"Did he ask you about a price?"

I nodded. "What happens now?"

"This." She showed me the plaque.

Letters were carved on it. Why were they moving? So fast, I couldn't follow them.

I had no choice. Faster and faster they went, and I could feel them inside my head now, but they weren't entering through my implant. They entered through my eyes. They kept doing that, long after I wanted them to stop.

"I think she's going to faint," someone remarked.

The language she used wasn't a human dialect. That's what I thought before I went down.

It was peaceful to be unconscious. I didn't think about anything or worry or grieve. I woke when I felt Medusa cradling me.

"Drink," she said gently. "Not too fast."

She held a bowl to my lips. The water tasted better than anything, better than wine or tea or chocolate. I sipped, then paused. Sipped, then paused. I could feel my cells soaking up the moisture.

I was so content in her embrace, I couldn't think about anything else, until someone knelt beside us and smiled down at me. This newcomer wore a loose robe that bared one shoulder and was clasped by a ring over the other.

She looked like a big bipedal gecko.

"Well!" She blinked at me with huge green eyes, and then smiled. "Miss Kick-Butt, I presume?"

24

Down in Birdie Land

"It's a virus," said Birdie. "The infection is spread through your visual cortex."

Birdie is what the bipedal gecko-lady called herself. She was referring to the plaque Medusa had shown me.

"I've already had my dose of it," said Medusa in the same language Birdie and I were speaking. "I wanted to err on the side of courtesy."

I picked up the object in question, which had fortunately stopped moving. "This thing gave me an *infection*?" I blinked as if that alone could wash my eyes clean.

"Oh dear." Birdie gently removed the plaque from my hands and set it aside. "That wasn't the best turn of phrase. It's entirely beneficial, Oichi—I promise. The virus has infected you with a language. *My* language."

"You taught me with a virus?" I said. "That's impressive."

"Well, I've got a reputation to uphold," said Birdie. "I'm an Early. From the Alliance of Ancient Races. I've been expecting you."

"An *Early*," I said, hoping for clarification. Birdie hadn't said that word in Early-ish. She had said it in Standard.

"We don't have a name for ourselves," said Birdie. "Other than the scientific name, which is just our version of your *Homo sapiens*." She trilled that name for me, so I could hear how it sounded. "When we talk to humans, we use the nickname they gave us. We like it. Do you want some more water?"

I sighed. "No. I want my loved ones back. Do you know where they are?"

"Kitten will be here in a minute, and I must say, you have a talent for the *trill* sounds. I'm glad I taught you!"

"Where is Kitten?" I said.

"The graveyard consumes a huge amount of energy from those trying to protect people," said Birdie. "I looked after Kitten. My colleague looked after Dragonette. Crow had all he could do to keep Ashur and Ahi safe, though he got help from the Three, and who knew how that would turn out? That left you, Oichi. It's not that we didn't care about you; it's just that the others were so innocent. They came first."

I could have pointed out that there were three of the Three, which should have meant that there was one left over for me, but go ahead. Be that way.

She cocked her head and blinked those big eyes at me. "We were reasonably sure that you would attract a patron—and what a patron! You hit the jackpot."

She sounded so happy for me. I recalled the terror and dread I had felt when meeting Dagger, and decided to keep that to myself. "We have succeeded in our mission?"

"You have succeeded as well as anyone can under these circumstances. Quite well, indeed."

"I'm glad to hear it. You mentioned you've been protecting Kitten . . . ?"

"She's in Evernight, with you."

"With—" I began, and then I heard Kitten's voice from the next room.

"Oichi?" she called, plaintively. "Dragonette? Anyone?"

I jumped to my feet. "In here, Kitten!"

Kitten dashed into the room so fast, when she stopped, she skidded on the smooth floor. "What the what?!" she said.

"There you are!" said Birdie in Standard, and she turned back to me. "Bringing Kitten here was the best way to keep her out of the business of the southern gods. I don't have to tell you—they're a bit mercurial."

"I was sitting on you," said Kitten, "and I don't blink my eyes, but if I *did* blink my eyes, that's literally how long it took for me to be in another room, and you were gone, Oichi, but then I heard your voices in the next room, so I came in here, and there you are, but are you going to disappear again, or am I free to move about the cabin?"

"No more disappearing," Birdie assured her. "You may explore the cabin."

Kitten trotted to the center of the room. "Hello, Big Sister!" she said to Medusa.

Medusa smiled at her. "Hello, Little Sister."

"Is Dragonette here, too?"

"The Rock Elves are looking after her. Come along, you two—I believe Ashur is about to petition the Three. Let's go cheer for him. Stay close, now." Birdie got up and began to walk toward the solid wall at the far end of the room. "Just let me get my parasol."

Birdie snagged a long thing made of fabric and wood. She pushed a button at one end, and the thing opened up like the petals of a flower. "My parasol," explained Birdie. "Direct sun is uncomfortable on my skin. Ready?"

I looked at Medusa. "You're not coming, too?"

"No," she said. "My presence might distract the Three when Ashur is trying to make his case. I don't want to do that for even a moment."

She still had no smile for me. At least now, I had some idea why. "Have you been here the whole time?"

"No. I've been here about an hour."

"Was that you I saw going into the Sentinel?"

"Yes, but we don't have time to talk about it now, Oichi. Birdie is going. Join her."

Kitten rushed over to me and wrapped herself around my waist. "I'm not taking any chances!" she said.

Placing my hands protectively around Kitten, I followed Birdie, who looked like she was going to collide with that wall. When she reached it, the wall rippled like the surface of a pool, and Birdie walked right through it, parasol and all.

"I hope that happens for us, too," said Kitten.

I paused and looked back. "Medusa—am I ever going to see you again?"

"From my perspective," she said, "I'm going to see you a lot sooner than you're going to see me."

That was going to have to do. I turned back to the seemingly solid wall.

"Geronimo," I said, and together, Kitten and I took the plunge.

We emerged in Seaside Canyon. I'm not sure where Birdie's house had been—on another world?—but we were back on Graveyard. Judging from the temperature and the position of the sun, we had arrived in the early morning, which meant that my day was starting all over again, and that seemed terribly unkind.

Birdie waited under her parasol a short distance away, and next to her a tall man stood, wearing a suit very much like the one I had seen on Timmy and Argus Fabricus. Something perched on his finger. He turned to look at us, and I remembered Cocteau's description of the Rock Elf who had rescued her colleague.

They looked much like us, except that they were taller and thinner. They had wide shoulders and features that seemed elongated compared with ours. . . .

That was an excellent description of the man who had been waiting for us in Seaside. The little creature who perched on his finger demanded our attention.

"Dragonette!" cried Kitten.

"Kitten!"

"Dragonette!"

"Kitten!"

"I'm running out of happy exclamations!"

"I'm so glad to see you!" Dragonette flew to us and hovered in front of her friend's nose. "Ernie told me I would, but I felt very anxious."

"*Ernie?*" I regarded the Rock Elf skeptically. "As in the Ernie Sandstone?"

"No," he said, "that's just a happy coincidence, Miss Kick-Butt."

"Does *everyone* call me that?" I asked Birdie.

"It's not the worst nickname you could have," she said. "You have to admit, it's accurate."

I eyed the Rock Elf who had volunteered to look after Dragonette, and I remembered something else Cocteau had told me.

He was almost the same color as the rocks in that area, sort of a dark blue-gray.

Maybe so, but there was one other person I had seen with skin like Ernie's: Cocteau.

No one is entirely anything, these days. . . .

When we had arrived, Ernie and Dragonette were gazing toward the Three. I was relieved to see them back where (and when) they belonged. "Now all we have to do is retrieve Ashur and Ahi," I said.

"Soon," promised Birdie. "Ashur is about to petition the Three."

I shook my head. "I should be there. He can't take on that responsibility by himself."

"He has the right stuff," said Ernie. "That's why the entities wanted him here. You should remember that he impressed the Three once before—with his Mermaid program."

I didn't ask who had told him that. "He scared them," I said. "They started to withdraw after that."

"Why do you suppose they did that?" demanded Ernie.

At the time, I had wondered if Ashur frightened them because they thought they could love him. If they loved him, and they woke, they might remember who else they had loved, and who they had lost. I had seen how that might affect the Three when I saw how it affected Medusa.

I had also seen the Three the way they saw themselves, and it had scared the hell out of me. If I couldn't handle them, how could someone half my age? "You're asking too much," I said. ·

"I'm not the one who's asking," said Ernie.

I gazed at the Three. Would they show mercy to Ashur? Did they even have that choice, once they started to wake?

Do you think this thing you want to do is the best you have to offer? Ahi had asked Ashur when they stood before the Three.

Yes. It's the best thing I've ever done. It's way better than anything else I could say or do.

"So—he's going to play his Mermaid program for them," I said. "It's beautiful. The music is by Claude Debussy."

Then I remembered the *other* thing Ashur had been working on, also with music by Debussy, as arranged for synthesizer by Isao Tomita. "Or," I said, "he might—"

The opening notes of Tomita's electronic arrangement of *The Sunken Cathedral* began to play—but not just inside my head. I could hear it in the air around me, as if the canyon were a giant synthesizer, as if each spire and butte were playing a different part of the music, weaving it together into a whole. Sonorous and bright in turns, the music evoked images of undersea canyons, schools of fish, barrier reefs, and the sunken ruins of a church, its bell sounding in the depths.

The entire graveyard resonated along with the tones of that undersea bell, but *especially* Seaside. The light shifted and began to bend, as if we stood at the bottom of a shallow sea, with the sun shining through blue water and glistening on the surface of ships that looked like seashells, and when the cathedral began to rise from the depths, and the voice of a celestial chorus to sing along with the intonation of that bell, my heart seemed to grow bigger in my chest.

I hadn't remembered the chorus being so magnificent, so—*grand.* Isao Tomita's rendition was electronic, the voices synthesized. Had Ashur added something to it? Had he enhanced that music, or . . .

No, Ashur hadn't done it. The ships in the graveyard were doing it—all of them, from one end of Joe's Canyon to the other, from the Three to the ships of Seaside to the Misfit Toys beyond Evernight to the Sentinels who stood among the catwalks in the yard, even to *Merlin* and the other youngsters who sat in Port One—*all* of them joined that celestial chorus. All of them sang along with the bell of the Sunken Cathedral.

I wished my father could hear this. *Why would he hide the Medusa interface inside a music education program?* people had sometimes asked me. *It's just a bunch of music.*

Music is language. My father understood that. Ashur had just used it to speak to every ship in the graveyard. More important, he had used it to get them to talk back. Ashur was exactly the sort of kid my father had wanted to inspire, and now they had both succeeded beyond their wildest dreams.

The Sunken Cathedral sank beneath the waves again with the concluding notes, its bells still sounding distantly, softly, until it was gone. The graveyard fell silent again.

I pulled in a slow breath, unwilling to break that silence—and when I let it out again, three ghosts stepped between the seashell spaceships and joined us in our clearing.

The Three regarded me with far more affection than I had seen from them before.

"Are you awake?" I said, awed by the idea.

"No," said Gennady's ghost. "Like the Sunken Cathedral, we remain mostly submerged."

Mostly—yet not so much as they were before. "You remember me," I said. "Do you remember anyone else? A certain grandmother witch?"

"We never forgot her," said Gennady's ghost. "Long ago, we told her that this outcome was possible. We calculated she was the best recipient of the information we were permitted to share at the time. She did not disappoint us—and neither did you."

Good news, but I had my priorities. "Where are Ashur and Ahi?"

"They're coming," said the ghost of Lady Sheba. "We thought they should do a little walking. It will prepare them for your reunion."

That regal lady still sounded like her namesake, except that no trace of malice tempered her tone. Honestly, if we could find a way to substitute her for the real one, it might be very useful.

"If Ashur was the one you wanted to talk to all along," I said, "why was *I* invited?"

"There were a few things you had to do," said the ghost of my mother, her face still obscured by the curtain of her hair, save for one fathomless eye. "Things and people who needed to be moved here and there—and here and *then.*"

Queenie, for one.

"You are tired," said my mother's ghost, "and we are making adjustments.

Our directory will interface with your Gates." She paused, regarding me with that single eye. "We have missed you, Oichi."

They vanished from that landscape. Simultaneously, three new icons appeared in my directory. Behind each icon, I could feel a looming presence, powerful and aware.

"Well!" Birdie twirled her parasol. "That's our cue. You have a reunion to conduct." She and Ernie linked arms.

"Lovely to meet you, Dragonette," said Ernie.

Before they could take a step, I said, "You taught me your language, Birdie."

They paused.

"I don't think you did it just so we could have one conversation."

Birdie smiled. "You're right. See you later, Oichi."

The bulkhead next to them rippled, and they walked through it.

"I have to admit," said Kitten. "That's hard to get used to."

Dragonette fluttered her fins. "Right? Transdimensional-interplanetary-gate thingees."

We heard voices. Someone emerged from the limestone tunnel. I couldn't restrain myself. "Ashur!"

I didn't quite run, but it was close enough. Kitten absolutely *did* run; she threw herself at Ashur and wrapped herself around his waist.

Dragonette zoomed at him like a dive-bomber and executed a perfect landing on his shoulder. She pressed her head against his cheek. "Your Sunken Cathedral was amazing and fabulous!" she declared.

He grinned. "You heard it?"

"*Everyone* heard it," said Kitten. "You got a standing ovation."

Ahi's eyes shone with pleasure. "Our story has a happy ending. I thought it would, but I didn't want to give it away."

"So"—Ashur patted Kitten—"what now?"

I shrugged. "We walk home."

"Oh." Ashur sounded a bit crestfallen.

Ahi punched him in the arm. "We're alive. We have Oichi and the Minis back. We have—" She patted her pockets. "—a few protein bars. What more do we need?"

"Water." I unhooked my canister, but as soon as I hefted it, I could tell it was full. "Small miracles." Happy reunions aside, I didn't spare them another look until I had taken a long pull from that bottle. When I had finished, I found Ashur and Ahi doing the same.

Seaside had done us another good turn. Yet I stayed close to Ahi and Ashur, Kitten and Dragonette as we walked to the other end of the tunnel. *The Minis and the children,* I thought. *Without them, the graveyard would have let me die, once I stopped being useful.*

Well, what the hell. No point in taking it personally. After all, in this company, *I* was the killer. *I* was the one who needed learn how to live. Maybe I had just received my first lesson.

I followed them into the light.

On the other side, we stood blinking on the path, trying to make sense of our surroundings. A walking tree stood right outside the tunnel, as if waiting to point the way. His brethren were scattered across the sandstone slope, their line stretching all the way back to the canyon with the Klaatu spaceships— the one we had walked through on our first day.

"Well," Ahi said. "I did not see *that* coming."

I suppose I had no business complaining about it, but the trip back to the Last Sentinel was uphill. Ashur worried when he saw me lagging. My little rest at Birdie's had helped, but it should have lasted a lot longer.

"What happened after we got separated?" said Ashur. "How did you get those bruises?"

I decided to tell him the truth. "I ran into Sheba and one of her poachers."

Ashur considered the marks on my neck. "Are they dead?"

"The poacher is."

He nodded. "Well, I'm guessing he needed to be."

"He was worse than the other two we met," I said, but didn't elaborate.

Ahi kicked a rock out of our path. "So what happened to Sheba?"

"She's the one who killed the poacher."

They weren't so surprised by that news as I had expected them to be. Finally Ashur said, "That's got to be an interesting story."

Maisy's Pool welcomed us, a few hours later. We refilled our bottles and nibbled from our protein bars. Kitten and Dragonette cavorted around the puddles. "The wigglies are still in here," reported Kitten. "Maybe their tails are a little longer."

I wondered if they were the same crop of creatures we had seen on the way in, considering all the time fractures we had been through. I felt encouraged by their lack of development. Maybe we had been only a few days, after all—not months, or years, or centuries.

Dragonette joined me at one of the little side pools and perched on my shoulder. "I'm assuming we shouldn't use our brain implants to speak yet."

I glanced at Ahi and Ashur. They were filling their bottles at the large pool, joking with each other about falling in. Dragonette's voice had been pitched too low for them to hear. "What's up?" I said at the same volume.

"I'm concerned about the last part of the Sentinel's message," said Dragonette. "*Prosper! Oichi, where is the cannon?*"

Kitten trotted over. "That whole *prosper* thing sounds pretty good," she whispered.

Dragonette folded her fins. "What if someone is pointing a cannon at us?"

She was turning out to be quite the little Medusa on this trip, thinking about all the unhappy possibilities.

"I don't think it's here," whispered Kitten. "The cannon."

I glanced at the youngsters again. They were having such a good time. I didn't want to spoil that. "Why not?" I said.

"My impression at the time was that it wasn't something the Sentinel wanted you to know. It was something she wanted you to tell *her*."

I gave that a good, long think. "I have no idea where it is."

"Yet," said Kitten.

I can't say I'm an expert on cannons, but my mind began to entertain thoughts of giant guns spewing destructive missiles. Maybe death rays. Giant death rays obliterating cities. Why couldn't it just be a water cannon? Why, for once in our lives, couldn't it be something harmless?

"I doubt we're going to get killed on our way out," I said. "Too many entities are looking after us. I vote we postpone our paranoia until we're on our way back to *Olympia*."

Dragonette fluttered her fins. "Me, too."

"Me, three." Kitten stuck a paw into the pool. "These wigglies are much calmer than the koi."

Ahi and Ashur stood and smiled at us. "Everyone got water?" said Ahi.

I raised my bottle. "And then some. My stomach is making full-of-water noises."

Ahi grinned. "Full tank. All right, then—let's go visit our friend, the Last Sentinel."

"Do you think it will talk to us again?" said Kitten.

Ahi looked at me, then at Ashur, as if assessing our Sentinel-attracting aptitudes. "I doubt it. That seems like overkill."

Kitten gave the wigglies one last dab. "Even without the cannon."

The Last Sentinel waited for us by the Maisy River. I took care not to touch her, and nothing swooped at us. We labored through the piled-up sand on the upriver side, and plodded onward (also upward, unfortunately). Maisy rushed past us, swollen from recent rainwater, oblivious to the danger of time fractures.

"Ahi," I said, "has anyone ever tried to take a raft down Maisy from one end to the other?"

She looked out over the water. "Yes. A team from the first colony did it."

"Did they get to the other end?"

"Not yet."

I considered a few permutations of that answer. "You mean—they're still doing it?"

"I've spotted them a few times. They're always a little farther downriver. I'm guessing they'll get to the end eventually. I hope it won't be in a million years. Maybe one day we can throw a party for them."

Yeah, I hoped so, too. Having been through a few time fractures myself, I had some idea what that felt like, and I wouldn't mind trading stories.

The march up the Maisy River felt twice as long as it had going in. When we hiked up the switchbacks, I had to remind myself that I'm twenty-something, not ninety, because I thought I was going to keel over. Kitten trotted alongside me as if she were squiring her grandmother, asking, "Do you need to rest? Would you like to stop for a drink of water?"

I dreamed of a shower, and a comfy bed, and a nice supper. By the time we saw the bridge over the Maisy River Gorge, I was neck and neck with my companions. I could let myself feel sore and tired later.

We stepped onto the bridge. I walked ahead with the Minis; Ashur and Ahi brought up the rear. *This is it*, I thought. *We made it. Unless someone has a bit of last-minute mischief they want to try.*

Fire and Queenie stepped onto the platform at the far side of the bridge. Relief flooded me; I grinned and waved. Fire waved back. Her expression seemed subdued. Had she heard bad news while we were gone?

Our footsteps vibrated the metal structure. I kept my eyes on Fire all the way across, but Ashur was the focus of her troubled regard. Had she heard bad news about Nuruddin? An accident?

I glanced at Ashur—he looked so proud and happy, and seemed unaware of the undercurrent I was sensing. Had I imagined trouble? That seemed a pretty good default setting.

I kept my pace steady and gave Fire the best smile I could muster. She didn't look in my direction until the last moment, when we joined her at the other end. Her glance held affection, possibly even gratitude.

"We did it," said Ashur. "Did you hear the music?"

"Even the gods heard that music," said Fire. "It was magnificent. You're my hero."

Ashur flushed, then half turned. "Ahi said . . ." He broke off, looking puzzled.

Ahi had been right behind us, but when I turned to look, she was gone. I didn't see her on the far side of the bridge; I didn't see her on the trail.

"Ahi!" Ashur started back. "Where—?"

"Ashur, stop!" The command in Fire's voice froze me, too.

Ashur jerked to a halt.

"Ahi is already here," said Fire.

Ashur frowned. "She was just—we're in the salvage yard, there couldn't be—"

"There couldn't be a time fracture?" I didn't like the emotion I heard in Fire's voice. Ashur didn't either. I think I guessed what she was going to say before he did. "Ahi's got her own fracture. It extends farther into the yard than any other."

"Where is she, then?" demanded Ashur.

"She's here," said Fire. "She's me, Ashur."

25

The Alliance of (Semi-)Ancient Races

The Minis and I gave Ashur and Fire a little space. I remembered how much Ahi had teased him on the trail, but also how she had given him credit, suffered through the dangers with him, held his hand when he felt at the end of his rope.

Now he showed her his Nuruddin face, stern and demanding explanations. "Why didn't you tell me?"

"I couldn't tamper with the past," said Ahi/Fire. "I already knew how our adventure would turn out. I knew it would be a success. If I wanted it to stay that way, I couldn't tell you what to expect."

"What about now?" he demanded. "What are you holding back, Ahi?"

Fire looked at me.

<That's going to be a long story,> said Queenie.

She turned back to him. "You're going to travel farther than anyone on *Olympia* has ever imagined, Ashur."

"You know that for sure?" he demanded. "You've seen my future?"

"I know it, but no, I haven't seen it. I know what you're capable of."

I think any other kid would have kept arguing out of pure frustration, but Ashur had shouldered so much responsibility already. He accepted Fire's explanation.

Fire didn't press him. She didn't say, *Are we still friends?* or remind him that she was the adult and he the teenager. Looking at her now, I saw the responsible girl who had been so confident, who had kept secrets that would have stymied adults four times her age. Here was the girl who had figured out what the model of Time and Space had been trying to tell her in Seaside. Now she and Queenie used it when targeting for Queen's Fire.

They call *me* Miss Kick-Butt.

"Are we done?" Ashur said. "Is it time to go home?"

"Yes," said Fire. "I'll escort you back through the yard."

Kitten, who—bless her—had been silent up to that point, said, "Rocket and Teddy must be dreadfully worried about us."

Fire smiled at her. "No, dear. You've only been gone a few hours."

That explained why the sun was beating down on the top of our heads. Seriously. Would I ever sleep again?

Walking back through the apocrypha—both sorted and unsorted—was a different experience, now that we had ventured into the graveyard. *Those could have come from the Misfit Toys*, I mused as we wandered past a rack of oddities, and then, farther down the row, *Those could have come from Klaatu Canyon*.

The Minis had regained their confidence, and Ashur seemed to be processing recent events with the resilience of the young. Fire sparked most of my interest now. <How old were you when you bonded with Queenie?> I finally asked her.

<Eighteen. I stumbled across her in one of Joe's special bins.>

I looked sideways at her. <The *original* Joe?>

<Time fractures,> she said. <It's complicated around here.>

It must be, if you can send people on an expedition with your younger self as a guide.

We had walked so far already; what was a little more walking? I was already running on fumes by then, so it was with great relief that I spotted a vehicle parked in the wide lane between racks. The driver waved at us.

"That's your ride," said Fire. She stopped, and regarded each of us in turn. "You were all a turning point in my life, so I'll say aloha instead of goodbye, because we will meet again. You're always in my heart."

She touched my hand. "Oichi, you are the reason that Queen's Fire protects this system. I know you thought you were supposed to come here for a very different reason."

"I was a delivery system," I said. "For Queenie and for Ashur. I can live with that."

<Take some advice from an accidental consciousness?> said Queenie.

<Sure.>

<That other one who was with you when you found me—I delivered her to this spot. The time was three hours ago.>

Sheba had traveled back to the yard at the same time her earlier self was entering it. I wondered if she broke the rules and gave herself some advice. That would definitely be her style.

<When you found me,> Queenie continued, <I was one who made cold calculations. Then I met Ahi, who had a conscience. You know someone who has one, too. Make peace with her. Don't be like that other one.>

<I'll try,> I promised.

<Our choices define us, don't you think? Aloha, Oichi.>

<Aloha, Queenie.>

We each embraced them. Then we walked to our car. The driver hurried around and opened the door for us.

"Is this a *limo?*" asked Ashur.

The driver grinned. "Top of the line. Your friends have some big bucks."

I peered inside at our *friends*. Gennady waved at me. He was sitting next to Baba Yaga. She held that cane she favored, the one with the iron skull as a grip.

An empty seat faced theirs. We climbed into it. The driver secured the door, sealing us in.

"Seat belts!" commanded Baba Yaga. "You've come through danger relatively unscathed. Don't be fools, now that it's almost over."

Ashur and I dutifully secured our belts. Dragonette settled on Ashur's shoulder.

Kitten sat in my lap. "It all seems a bit anticlimactic," she said. "Is that normal, for adventures?"

"It is," said Gennady. "Maybe that's why people keep going on them. They start to feel disappointed with *normal.*"

I did *not* feel disappointed. I felt tired.

Our limo began to roll. Behind our seat, a barrier rose between us and the driver. Once it had sealed, Baba Yaga said, "You have done well, *Olympians*. You woke the sleeping giants *just a little*. And *you*, Oichi, had the good sense to back off at the right time."

Well, I had the dumb luck and the foolish doubts, but if those look like good sense, I'm happy to go along with it.

"I suspect you will find the Three behave more sympathetically toward you when they have limitations," she continued. "I don't have a lot of limitations myself, so bear that in mind."

"Yes, ma'am," said Ashur.

"Your Sunken Cathedral program was good, by the way." Baba Yaga gave Ashur a short nod. "It reminds me of the sort of thing Andrei Mironenko used to do when he was very young."

Gennady winked at me.

"Did it turn out the way you wanted it to?" I said.

He shrugged. "It turned out the way Grandmother wanted it to, but I agreed with Lady Sheba. It should have been *you*, Oichi. The *power* you would have commanded! We would have become supreme."

"Except for one minor detail," I said. "The southern gods."

"True." He shrugged. "There's something to be said for Ashur's interface. He got the entire graveyard to agree on something. That's a first."

Kitten sat up. "It's only a first if you experience linear time. We didn't."

"That's an excellent point." Gennady gave her a measuring look, then turned back to me. "You know, Lady Sheba reminds me of Medea."

I frowned. "Jason's girlfriend? From the movie?"

"Well, yes," he said, "but that story is from the early part of their lives, when they were happy. Later, he tries to dump her so he can marry another princess, and Medea murders their two young sons and his new bride-to-be to get back at him."

"That does sound like Lady Sheba."

"And you, Oichi—at first you reminded me of Elektra."

I brightened. "The superhero gal? That lady with the red costume and the tridents?"

"Those weapons are actually called *sai*," offered Dragonette. "I looked it up."

Gennady grinned at her. "Well, yes, that's the movie version, but there's a play, too. You should ask Nuruddin to find it in his collection. Now, I believe you've moved past Elektra. I'll have to wait and see who you have become."

"I'm not so sure I can give up the *sai*."

He didn't smile. "I'm not so sure you should."

There was very little conversation for the rest of the drive, which was a shame, because that was a luxurious spot—so comfortable, it threatened to put me to sleep. I may have nodded off a few times on the way to Port One.

At last, we drove through its gates. Our limo pulled up next to *Merlin*, whose silver hide gleamed in the morning sunlight. Gennady pushed a button, and the window next to Ashur rolled down.

Teddy and Rocket came bounding out of *Merlin* before we had even come to a stop. They were followed by Captain Thomas and Representative Lee, Mirzakhani and Narm, Wilson and Cocteau. It felt like years since we had last seen them.

It felt like centuries.

For them, it was just a few hours, and that was reflected in their happy expressions. Only Cocteau seemed to have some inkling what had happened to us. She winked at me as she walked up to the window.

"Success," I greeted them. "Everyone is alive, with all our limbs intact."

Captain Thomas regarded us with her hands on her hips. "I thought that was going to take you a lot longer. We haven't even been to the bars yet."

I decided not to tell her that it *had* been a lot longer. "If you'd like to wait until tomorrow to leave, that's okay with us."

"We *have* to wait," she said. "They want twenty-four-hour notice of any flight plan."

"Splendid!" said Kitten. "There's time for karaoke."

Narm groaned, but when Dragonette flew out the window, he welcomed her back to her perch on his finger. "For anybody else?" he said. "I would not make that sacrifice."

She gave him her most charming smile. "You won't have to learn line dancing, though. We'll let you sit that one out."

The driver slid the door open, and Ashur got out. Kitten followed, but before I could move, Baba Yaga said, "Wait, Oichi."

I froze.

"Tell them to go inside. I want to speak with you privately."

Cocteau motioned to the others. "Inside, my friends. Oichi isn't quite done yet." She used a tone I hadn't heard before. Everyone obeyed her without question.

"Watch them as they go," said Baba Yaga. "See them, Oichi."

I did, until the final one had passed through the outer lock: Kitten, who stretched her neck until the last possible moment.

"You risked their lives," said Baba Yaga. "It was a calculation I've made many times. They survived. But someday you will take that risk again, and you won't be so lucky. When that happens, *see them.*"

I wasn't quite sure what she meant until she added, "That sere Lady who saved your life, because you were useful, does *not* see the lives she expends. She has lost her perspective. I don't tell you to be *kind*, Oichi. I tell you to be aware, so you will make good decisions, because now your decisions will have an impact on all of us."

"Then," I said, "I will strive to be aware."

Her hand tightened on the head of her cane. Its iron teeth peeked through her fingers. "I believe you. So I'll leave you with one last warning. Remember that powerful entities do not have compassion, innately. They have to learn it. You and your Ashur may have taught it to the Three, but when I encountered their avatars, millennia ago, they were not like the denizens of Ashur's Sunken Cathedral." She paused, her black eyes fixed on mine. "They were death gods."

I had seen their true forms when I confronted them in their Gorge. If they could adapt and change, their choice of death gods for avatars told me as much about the ancient people of Earth as it did about the Three.

She seemed to read that in my expression. "They were lonely. They looked for people who were like the ones they lost. They learned we weren't enough like them; we were too cruel, too destructive. To make them happy—we had to make *you*."

What kind of creature was Baba Yaga, that she could patiently hatch a plan over tens of thousands of years?

"Goodbye for now." She dismissed me before I could ask. I climbed out of the limo. Once on my feet, I turned to get a last look at Gennady, but the window rolled up before I could see him. When Baba Yaga said goodbye, she meant business.

The limo drove away. As I watched it go, the hairs on the back of my neck stirred, and I turned to see who was behind me.

Dagger loomed over me, his crest in full display. "No rest for the wicked," he declared, and he placed his clawed hands on either side of my face.

I had a moment of absolute terror.

Then I felt something stir inside my implant, as if someone were uploading a new program. Once it had finished, Dagger touched the icons for the Three. "Working," they replied, their voices a chorus.

See? I wanted to tell Nuruddin. *The Chorus can ride in the God Machine.*

"We'll fetch Medusa," said Dagger, "and then we'll pay a visit to the people who made you."

My new program executed an action. The Three provided coordinates. A Gate opened. Dagger and I went through.

I emerged inside Lock 212.

From my perspective, Medusa had said, *I'm going to see you a lot sooner than you're going to see me.* She must have gone through that Gate in Birdie's wall just after Kitten and me. Medusa stood just under the spot where we had seized Ryan Charmayne.

<I know you have fond memories of this air lock,> she said. <I harbored them, too. It's time to put them aside, Oichi. This lock has a grander purpose now.>

I studied her face. Her expression still held no affection, but I thought I saw hope there. <Medusa, who invited you to Graveyard?>

<Cocteau,> she said, confirming my suspicions.

<She represented the Sentinels?>

<Yes.>

I had got that right, at least. Now I had to figure out what else was expected of me. Searching, I turned a full circle. "Dagger?"

He didn't respond, yet I sensed he wasn't as far away as he might appear to be. Perhaps he waited in the space between the Gates. I returned to Medusa. <I don't know what to do next.>

<I think I do.>

She flowed over me, and we merged. As soon as we linked, she explored the new program, and the icons the Three had placed inside my directory. <This is interesting,> she concluded. <A much better arrangement, though the permutations could be dangerous. All in all, you did well, Oichi. You did the right things when the chips were down.> She took a moment longer to accustom herself to the presence we could both feel inside the Gate.

<Are we partners again?> I asked.

<I think we've earned some together time. Do you mind if I drive? I've figured out how to work this thing.>

<Be my guest.>

Medusa opened the Gate. We flowed through it. Once *between*, we felt Dagger's presence, though his shape was unclear.

He reached into our link to speak in the voice he had used on Jigsaw and Graveyard. <The *me* you have seen is not the *me* you observe between the Gates. It is a useful manifestation.>

Medusa said, <You are an entity who lives between Time and Space?>

<That explanation is suitable, if incomplete,> replied Dagger.

<Where do you want us to go?>

<There is a ship called *Itzpapalotl*.> Dagger showed us where it was.

<Bingo,> said Medusa. <Let's roll.>

We stepped through the Gate, into a room so magnificent, I wanted to ask if there were some mistake. This was not a room one would find on a spaceship.

Unless the ship was *Itzpapalotl*. There were elements in the design and the furnishings of that room that reminded me of the finest things in the homes of the Executives of *Olympia* and *Titania*. Vaulted ceilings, wooden screens, tapestries, ink-and-watercolor paintings, and exquisite ceramics decorated a space that evoked an ancient palace. The low dais in the center of the room could have come from the House of Clans. I addressed the man who knelt there, pouring tea from a set decorated with flowers and bees.

Here was the man who had almost destroyed us, though that hadn't been his intention. As much as he blamed Gennady for the losses we had suffered on our journey, Bomarigala had been in charge. He was the most responsible. If he had earned every syllable in his long name, he had also earned my vengeance. Yet even as we stood over him, I had a feeling that payback was not in the cards. I wasn't even sure I wanted that anymore.

"Bomarigala," I said.

He looked up, but didn't drop his cup. "Join me. Have some tea."

We stayed where we were.

"You just *had* to wake them," said Medusa. "With no second thoughts about the consequences."

Bomarigala lifted one eyebrow. "Oh, I assure you, there have been *plenty* of second thoughts about the consequences of waking the Three. We committed ourselves long ago, and we can't afford to have doubts."

That would have been the right moment for me to lay down the law, but I felt so intrigued by this person who moved people as if they were pieces on a chessboard. I wondered if he grieved for his missing clone, or if there were plenty more where he came from.

"Tell me, Oichi," he said. "What are *your* doubts?"

"I had plenty, going in," I admitted. "Now I have just one question, Bomarigala. How do you expect to move forward? The Three have not awakened the way you wanted them to. They've made their choice. Your best gambit failed."

"You sound very tired," he said. "Please, do have some tea." Once again, he indicated that we should sit.

Medusa and I knelt in the spot he indicated. "No poison, please," I said.

"No poison." He handed me a cup.

Medusa sampled the contents with the tip of a tentacle. "Trust in Allah," she said, "but tie up your camel."

Bomarigala raised an eyebrow. "What is Allah's verdict?"

"No poison in the *tea*." Medusa's tone implied she wasn't sure where else a toxin may hide.

He sipped his tea, studying us over the rim. Medusa raised our cup to her lips—we drank it together. "Bit of a fruity undertone," I decided. "Maybe a hint of honey. That would explain the bees on your charming cups."

He seemed pleased with the compliment. "This conversation is turning out much better than the last one we had. I believe negotiation may be possible."

"You understand our terms?" Medusa said.

"You expressed them succinctly. The Weapons Clan has always adapted to new circumstances."

Medusa and I took another sip. "What do you expect of us?" I said.

"For now, simply that you should not regard us as enemies."

When we didn't answer that, he gave us a grim smile. For a second, I could see the ancient man who watched behind the young, perfect face. "I know—that's easier said than done."

"I wouldn't count on it being done anytime soon," I agreed.

He nodded. "We did not order the destruction of *Titania*. We would have stopped it, had we known what the Charmaynes were planning."

"No one is to blame," I said, "yet everyone is responsible."

"Fair enough. It may interest you to know that we have been contacted by Union representatives. They are sending an ambassador to *Olympia*. They are seasoned negotiators, and we don't oppose their participation in this matter."

<True,> Medusa said. <A man named Argus Fabricus. He is thirty-seven hours out from *Olympia*, according to his last communication.>

"Not all negotiations require an ambassador," I said. "For instance, we have a demand that can't be negotiated."

He didn't smirk at me. He didn't frown either, but he seemed overconfident when he said, "Everything can be negotiated."

"We want the survivors from *Titania*."

Bomarigala poured more tea into his cup, and offered the pot to me.

"No, thank you," I declined.

He didn't make us wait while he sipped, but set his cup on a low, carved table that smelled of cedar. "Do the *Titania*ns have a choice in the matter?"

"Sure," I said. "They can choose whether they want to live on *Olympia*, on Graveyard, or with the Belters. They don't get to choose you. They don't get to choose *Itzpapalotl* and the Weapons Clan. If they do, they will become my enemies, and I will treat them accordingly."

He raised an eyebrow. "Well, now. It would seem you learned quite a lot from your Executive oppressors."

I felt grateful Medusa's stern visage covered mine. "Count on it."

Bomarigala picked up his cup and took a sip, watching us over the rim. He looked almost proud. "I do count on it, but I'm curious—how will you pry them out of here? We are the Weapons Clan. It goes without saying that we are well defended."

Medusa stretched her tentacles, then drew them in again. "Were your defenses in full effect when we arrived?"

His heart rate remained admirably steady, and he managed to return Medusa's fathomless gaze with one of his own. "Good point. Still, I feel compelled to point out that you are two, and the *Titanians* number in the thousands. Together, you could do quite a lot of damage, as you roamed this ship in search of people who don't wish to be rescued, but damage isn't what you're trying to accomplish—is it?"

Diplomats have methods for getting past an impasse in negotiations. At least, I hope they do. I was new at that game, and I was beginning to feel flummoxed at Bomarigala's circular reasoning. *You can't make us, and they don't want to leave anyway.* I wondered if he knew how close he was to finding out how much damage Medusa and I could do. That was no small measure— and we had a new means of transportation that could tip the balance.

We hung on that precipice for a few seconds. Then I felt the program in my head activating a Gate. Moments later, an overwhelming presence emerged, and I did not have to confirm the arrival with our eyes.

Bomarigala looked past us. His face became supernaturally still.

"His name is Dagger," I said.

"An entity from the graveyard, I presume," said Bomarigala.

"Yes . . . ish."

"And the agent of your sudden appearance in this room?"

When Bomarigala hadn't been surprised to see us, I had presumed he knew something about the Gates. That he hadn't, yet had still been so calm, said quite a lot for the relative steeliness of his nerves.

"The very one," I confirmed.

Bomarigala stared for a moment longer, then nodded. "I'll take you to your people."

"Understand"—Dagger's voice reached every corner of that space—"I know where they are. All of them."

The implication was clear. Bomarigala couldn't keep any of my people secretly.

"I understand," said Bomarigala. He set his cup down and stood. "We'd better get started."

<You're exhausted,> worried Medusa.

<Utterly.>

<Let me do most of the work.>

Yet a certain amount of energy still had to be expended. I had to speak coherently to people, to stand upright when I wanted only to fall into my comfy bed back home, to activate the program inside my head, to see and feel where I put people. Despite Bomarigala's claim that the *Titania*ns didn't want to leave, few expressed displeasure at the idea of going to Graveyard or *Olympia*.

We found each *Titania*n, in groups or singly, spread throughout the vast chambers of *Itzpapalotl*. We transported most of them to *Olympia*. The rest went to Graveyard, with credits in their new bank accounts, thanks to Bomarigala.

"Thank you for that," I said sincerely if not humbly.

"I hope it will pave the way to friendly negotiations in the future," he replied.

Medusa said, "It is an excellent start. Have we retrieved all of them?"

"You have," he said. "Oichi—I regret that your parents did not survive."

I suspected he did, but it hadn't stopped him from holding their possible existence over my head when he had thought it might gain him leverage.

I doubt it would have stopped me, in his place. "By the way," I said, "did your missing clone ever show up?"

Bomarigala didn't bat an eyelash. "Which one?"

Perhaps he expected some parting bit of verbal diplomacy from us, but we opened the Gate without another word and stepped through.

I expected we would emerge on *Olympia*. Thoughts of my bed loomed large in my mind. Our suspension *between* stretched. I felt Dagger there with us, and others of his kind, watching us. Each of them had a different form.

<Dagger,> I pleaded, <I'm so tired.>

<You recall I mentioned a price,> he replied.

I had tried to forget it.

<Take off Medusa's mask.>

Medusa withdrew her face from mine. It hovered where she could observe his actions. Through her eyes, his *between* form almost made sense. He touched my face.

<The Old One of the Weapons Clan reminded you of a loss,> he said.

<My parents.>

<Show me that loss.>

Did he want to see it the way the ghost of my mother had revealed it to me? Should I provide the same soundtrack, the *hayashi* flute, shoulder drum, hip drum, and stick drum, as chaotic scenes patched together from Security cameras all over *Titania* showed me the bulkheads tearing apart, people and objects being dashed against surfaces as the parts of their ship were wrenched in different directions by the gravity bombs?

I felt a tiny spot of moisture on my face. I had mustered a tear. Dagger collected it with the tip of a claw. <There,> he said. <That will do.>

Understanding dawned on me. <You wanted my DNA?>

Dagger's almost-sensible form loomed in the *between*. Others seemed to peer over his shoulder at me. <That, and your grief.>

My sanity was beginning to fray. I could feel Medusa trying to hold me together. She respected my need for answers. <May I ask why?>

<One morning,> said Dagger, <the people in the North woke up and the people in the South were gone.>

<On Jigsaw?>

<Yes.>

<Because you took the people of the South?>

<Yes.>

I tried to focus. He had told me more, and it should make sense, but *between* and my weariness were having their way with me. <And—you tweaked them.>

<Yes.>

<With my DNA?>

<In part. There were other contributors. Afterward, we put them back— for the balance.>

<Then why get it from a tear?> I said. <Why do you need to analyze our pain?>

<So we don't inflict it,> he said, <without understanding the conse- quences.>

The southern gods watched my struggle for understanding. I couldn't grasp their physiology, but my instinctive reaction was awe. I tried to question that. I tried to gain a different perspective, but that struggle prolonged my presence in a place that made me want to unravel.

<It's because of your God Machine,> I said. <That's why they—that's why . . . >

<Time for this one to go home,> said Dagger, just as the lights went out.

26

It's All Downhill from Here

I felt my bed under me, long before I woke—or at least, before I woke all the way. <You're home,> Medusa said when she sensed me stirring. <Rest.>

You'll notice she didn't say *you're safe*, but it was enough to reassure me, and let me drift back to sleep.

My dreams were crowded with the people, and things, and places that had consumed me since *Merlin* shuttled Ashur and me in-system. I dreamed of the luau on Maui, but a wider cast of characters sat at the table. Kitten danced down the center, singing "I'm Gonna Wash That Man Right Outa My Hair," and Baba Yaga declared, "Send him on his way!"

Lady Sheba frowned at the spectacle. "This nonsense has gotten out of hand."

Across from her, the Second One, her twin in appearance if not in character, declared, "On the contrary. It hasn't gone far enough." They eyed each other across the table in a clash of titans.

Gennady Mironenko speared a bit of meat and vegetables from his plate and offered them to me. "Try this combination. They enhance each other's best flavors."

I longed toward the bite, but Bomarigala touched my elbow. "Trust in Allah," he warned, "but test the tea."

Commander Lana tried to coax Security Chief Schnebly to eat more. "You're too skinny!" she chided.

He shrugged. "My work is my life. I still haven't found Nemo's head."

"You're all wearing me out," I complained. "I just want to relax!"

I felt Dagger's clawed hand on my shoulder. "It's all downhill from here," he assured me.

Downhill proved to be a good description of the rest of my dreams, since they seemed to careen in that direction. Landscapes shifted around me, from the dim, narrow hallways of *Olympia* to the red sandstone of the Ernie Formation to the white seashell ships of Seaside and the dead buildings of Ever-night. I ran into the big poacher again, but I still had no knife, so I snatched up a piece of unsorted apocrypha and threw it at him. I hit him right between the eyes, and he burst into tears. When I stumbled away from him, he sat down among the Misfit Toys and continued to cry.

After what felt like a century, I found myself on that same dusty road that had led me to Jigsaw. No one called to me from broken overpasses. I closed my eyes, wishing for it all to just end. When I opened them again, I saw a spire in the distance.

Not *three* spires. This time only one. I knew her.

What remained of her engines lay at her feet, their rims black and corroded. Her colossal bulk had been rammed into the earth so far, perhaps a third of it must reside underground. Her communications array disappeared into the clouds. No lights burned anywhere on her skin, or from any of the view windows that were still intact.

I could make out some of the letters on her flank:

LYMPI

Someday, she would be placed in the graveyard, along with the other not-so-dead marvels. Ten thousand years from now? Thirty thousand? As soon as tomorrow? We *Olympians*—would we be dead then? Or moved on to other stations, other worlds?

I heard an inhalation, and turned to see Dagger sitting beside me.

"Destiny is not a road," he said. "It's a junction."

That's what woke me up.

Sleep is a good thing, but there are times when waking up is preferable. I hauled myself out of bed, got into a nice, hot shower, and then ordered breakfast.

Ah, the comforts of home.

As I plowed through a second helping of waffles, I got a call from our captain, who used to be called Second. <Three ships have been granted permission to dock by the Security Council. *Tawhiri* has been directed to Lock 238. She carries a delegation from Maui.>

<Dear me,> I said with some dismay. <I haven't had a chance to speak with Ogden Schickele yet, and we need to throw them a party.>

<I'll do it,> she volunteered.

<Thank you. Who's on their roster?>

She recited a list of dignitaries, including Commander Lana and Ambassador Argus Fabricus. <The second ship is from people identifying themselves as Woovs. It's called the *Korvarrk*.> She stumbled a bit over the pronunciation, so I assumed a Woov would say it quite differently.

<Is *Merlin* the third?> I hoped.

<Yes. Carrying Ashur and the Minis. You have a special message from Engineer Cocteau. She says to save her some wine.>

<Don't put *Merlin* in Lock 212,> I said. <Put them in 217.>

<Medusa has declared Lock 212 off-limits,> said the captain, and she signed off to make arrangements with Ogden.

I still had waffles to finish, and coffee. My guests in *Tawhiri* would be going through decontamination, and the scrubbers had to clean toxins off their vessel. If the captain of *Olympia* followed the usual protocols, that would take twenty-four to forty-eight hours.

On the silk screen across the room, my painted tiger eyed the waves lapping at his feet with a worried expression. "Why are you still troubled?" I asked him. "Things turned out remarkably well."

"They did, didn't they?" Crow appeared in the chair across from mine. His carved eyes glowed with warm light.

"Hello, Graveyard," I said.

His mouth moved stiffly, but he spoke clearly. "You understand us."

"I understand that you conspired together to create a particular outcome. I don't blame you for it. If I were an entity in your community, I wouldn't want the Three to regain full consciousness."

"Even *they* didn't want that," said Crow, "but there was something in you that could have made them do it, something very different from what Ashur had to offer."

I waited for him to say what that something was—after all, the Three had once created avatars based on human death gods—but apparently the entities could be tactful when necessary.

"You had to risk letting me in so I would find Queenie," I said.

"Anyone else who tried to talk to Queenie in her previous state would have died. She is vital to our defense. We were reasonably confident the southern gods would decide to intervene if you made the wrong decision about the Three."

"By killing me?"

"The Three are the most powerful entities in the graveyard," said Crow. "They could have upset the balance."

"Fair enough." I added sugar to my coffee and stirred.

He watched me, one stick leg crossed over the other, his pointed elbows propped on the armrests and his twig fingers laced together. He looked dapper in a red jacket, white-collared shirt, and fawn trousers. His blue shoes had buckles.

"I suspect our business isn't finished," I said. "We'll collaborate again?"

"Yes," said Crow.

"Not today, I hope."

"Not today. I think you'll be ready, when the time comes."

I sighed. "Then I hope you don't mind if I ask your opinion about something."

"Not at all."

I pointed over his shoulder. "What do you think of my tiger? Is he worried?"

Crow inspected the screen for a long moment. Then he turned back to me. "We think he's just getting ready to sneeze."

It's interesting that Crow presented himself as a scarecrow. They're supposed to frighten scavengers off. They're protectors.

We enjoyed a pleasant visit. I stuffed myself full of waffles and drank too much coffee. He had a few more bombshells to deliver. "The Rock Elves are the ones who invited Sheba to Graveyard."

I had no idea how to respond to that.

"The Earlies declined to interact with her," he continued. "They believed she wouldn't see them as intelligent people. The Earlies are very, very smart, and very, very kind, but even they have a limit to their patience."

I was out of coffee by then, so I couldn't nurse a cup while I pondered what to say. Something in his demeanor warned me I hadn't heard all of it. "The Rock Elves are still talking to Sheba?"

"It's for the best, don't you think?" He steepled his stick fingers. "She rallied the survivors of *Titania*. Her fast thinking kept them alive until they could be rescued."

"Her fast thinking got them blown up in the first place."

"Yes," he admitted. "It's easy to misunderstand the Rock Elves. Many of their actions seem whimsical on the surface. They're anything but."

"Fair warning," I said.

"Indeed. Are you feeling well rested and recovered now?"

"Well fed and scrubbed, too."

"Good," said Crow. "Because there's one more detail you have to attend to on Graveyard."

<Medusa,> I said. <Will you meet me in Lock 212?>

<Coming,> she replied.

Medusa had been in Lucifer Tower when I called her, but we arrived outside Lock 212 at the same moment.

<I thought we should have this discussion in person,> I said. <I've gained some perspective. I need your help.>

We entered Lock 212 and closed the pressure door behind us. I told Medusa what Crow had told me. She listened thoughtfully.

<You're still linked with the Sentinels,> I said. <Could they put me where and when I need to be, even though I'm using Dagger's Gate?>

<Yes,> she said. <But I'm concerned that you want to do this alone.>

<Do you think it's the wrong decision?>

Her tentacles swirled overhead, moved by the tide of her thoughts. <No,> she said at last. <My presence would complicate things. You need clarity for this. Does she still have that knife?>

<Yes, but I've got this.> I reached into a pocket and withdrew a blade.

Medusa's eyes gleamed when she saw it.

<Is that . . . ?>

<A gift from Timmy. She decided to turn down the contract on Graveyard. She left a gift with Baba Yaga—for me. The grandmother witch gave it to Crow.>

<And he just gave it to you.> She smiled. <That's better. Very well, Oichi. Are you ready to do the Last Thing?>

<I'm ready,> I said. It was mostly true. I hadn't opened a Gate entirely by myself yet.

I remembered how Medusa had done it, and I had thought up a few permutations.

I studied the three new icons in my directory. The symbols were unfamiliar, yet I knew whom each one represented. Was this something like Birdie's visual virus, downloading a new language into my brain? Was it some kind of racial memory?

Maybe neither, but it worked. When I activated the Gate, I used the ocean of information behind those icons to select a destination. <Working,> I told Medusa, and she linked me with the Sentinels. Through them, I could see the loops. Together, we found Lady Sheba in the proper time.

<Now,> they suggested, and I stepped through the Gate.

Between, I felt the presence of the southern gods. They watched me, but they had no comment as I passed through their realm.

I emerged in a section of Joe's Salvage Yard we hadn't seen on our way in. This one had narrower aisles, stranger apocrypha, and a sign that said JOE'S SPECIAL BINS. It seemed deserted, save for an automaton leaning in one corner, making muted mechanical sounds, as if it were talking to itself.

At the far end of the row, people and movers passed along the main drag. None of them were close enough to see the arrival of a form made of light, who unfolded her wings like a bird of prey and dropped a passenger from her claws, then went on her way to a former time, where Ahi's younger self would find her.

See you later, Queenie, I thought. *Or sooner.*

Sheba stumbled a little as she got her bearings, but her recovery was quick (and downright admirable). She straightened her shoulders and set a resolute pace down the row toward the main aisle.

"Sheba, wait."

She froze, then turned to see me near the bins. When she recognized me, her face twisted in contempt. "I have my invitation into the graveyard," she said, her hand on the hilt of her knife. "Attend to your own expedition, young woman."

I touched Timmy's knife, but didn't draw it. "I'm not that Oichi. I'm from the future."

The contempt leaked out of her face. "I see."

I was careful to maintain the same distance from her that she had kept between us in the yard of Misfit Toys. "You were right to shove me away," I said.

"Of course I was," said Sheba. "I don't do anything for trivial reasons. When I catch up with the future, I expect to find that the Three have awakened—as they should."

"Right," I said. "About that . . ."

She frowned. "I don't believe they ignored you. Your mere presence agitated them."

"Yes, it did, but I wasn't the only one in the graveyard, Sheba."

She thought that over. "Young Ashur."

"His interface is a lot safer. When all is said and done, we made the right deal with them."

She might have agreed. Or she might have told me I was a fool. Before she could do either, she saw something flash past our row, a wheeled cart carrying passengers. Sheba was one of the passengers.

Suddenly she looked very tired. "I've missed my window of opportunity."

"Yes, but there will be plenty of new opportunities to go around."

Sheba lifted her chin. "You've figured that out, at least. Tell me your terms, Oichi. I have my own."

Apparently we weren't going to stand around reminiscing. That was probably for the best. "If you set foot on *Olympia* again," I said, "you will die. Consequences be damned. Believe that."

My warning made her more confident. "Do you think I won't *prosper*, wherever I live?"

Prosper. That word generated echoes in my head.

"I think the opposite," I said. "I expect you to be our partner on Graveyard."

Give her credit—she wasn't so surprised by that as you would expect her to be.

"A fine conundrum, wouldn't you say?" Sheba's smile was devoid of humor—or at least, the sort of mirth *I* wanted to understand. "*Olympia*ns think I crafted that wretched Music in Education initiative, and *Titania*ns see me as their strength and inspiration. If you disavow any of that, you destroy your own credibility."

"It's not useful to disavow any of it," I said. "The narrative works well the way it is."

She understood me. If I'm going to be honest, the woman my mother had called the Iron Fist had more in common with me than anyone. Sheba is the person I could become if I don't heed Baba Yaga's warning about *seeing* the people I utilize. She blew Terry Charmayne's mother out an air lock. *I* held Ryan Charmayne while he suffocated. Sheba destroyed *Titania*, but that wasn't personal. That was collateral damage. I killed twenty-seven members of one Executive family in one night—that *was* personal.

Seeing her in that state, so tired, so old, so sure that every murder and every ruthless move was the right thing to do, I remembered that Sheba loved music, too. She had favored one piece of music above all others: Pachelbel's Canon in D, which she felt exemplified her existence. That music still plays inside my head every time I think of her.

Prosper! the Sentinel had cried. Then, *Oichi, where is the cannon?*

I had mistaken two sound-alike words. The ghost hadn't meant *cannon*, as in tubular metal gizmo for firing big projectiles at things. She meant *canon*.

As in Pachelbel's Canon in D.

"You're not going to believe this," I said, "but it really *is* for the best."

Sheba gave me a grudging smile as I stepped back through my Gate.

Medusa waited for me on the other side.

<It's done,> I said.

<I have a confession,> she said. <I tweaked your arrival time, just a bit.>

It's foolish that the idea hadn't occurred to me. <How much?>

<Forty-eight hours. You seem to be in the proper mood for negotiating. I thought we should take advantage of that.>

I nodded. <I don't disagree. Think of all the waffles we've saved, in the meantime.>

She waited. I tried to muster something clever, and failed.

<Kitten has played me the footage,> she said at last.

<All the stuff she recorded in the canyon?>

<Yes.>

That would make one hell of a documentary.

<Terry Charmayne has invited our guests to stay in his compound,> Medusa continued. <Ogden Schickele is coordinating with him for party arrangements.>

<Perfect,> I said, relieved not to be doing any of that myself. <Well. Do we have a little time before we greet our guests?>

<Yes. Why?>

I took a deep breath, even though I wouldn't be speaking aloud. <Because I owe you an apology.>

<Really?> I don't think she expected that. I don't think I did, either. I wasn't quite wired for it, but if anyone was worth the effort, it was Medusa.

<You have been my conscience,> I said. <I was expecting you to do that heavy lifting for me instead of learning it for myself.>

<I'm as much to blame for that as you,> said Medusa.

<I know we can't go back to the way we were. It wasn't good for either of us. I hope we can agree to stay partners. We can keep working on the communication.>

Even at that point, I thought she might reject my offer. Or make another searingly objective observation.

Instead, she hugged me.

We stayed that way for a long time. I said, <You saved me. You made me real.>

<Dagger asked me, too.>

<He . . . what?>

<He asked me what price I have paid.>

Did you meet an entity named Dagger? she had said. *And did he ask you about a price?*

<What did you tell him?>

<I told him I had to give you up. It was the only way I could save you. The only way you could become—real.>

I thought about that for a long time. Finally I said, <You did the right thing.>

<You, too,> she said.

<Do I get credit even if I did the right thing by accident?>

<Maybe,> said Medusa. <We'll have to wait and see how it turns out.>

EPILOGUE

Fate favors the prepared mind. That explains how a worm like me can manage to make the right decisions—by accident.

One of my best decisions was *not* an accident. I gave my pain to Dagger and the southern gods, so they could understand the suffering of we who have limitations. In return, we got the Gates. I may not be a genius at negotiating trade, but I think we came out ahead on that one.

Olympia is near the end of her journey, and I have my own equilibrium to pursue. Our new situation involves ambassadors and semi-mythical crones, Belters and Woovs, Bomarigala and all the rest. Commander Lana has started negotiations by pitching us a curve ball.

"We have heard you intended to establish orbit around Graveyard, but there is a halfway point in between, a world called Almost. There are mining colonies on the surface, and the people live partly underground, with big domes over their habitats."

She said all that as if it were a wonderful endorsement. "There were intelligent races who lived there long ago," she continued, when I failed to look enthusiastic. "Mysterious beings. Some say they may still be there, but that's not the reason you would want to establish orbit around Almost. Right now, there's a space station orbiting that world, but it's not very big. *Olympia* could become a hub on that trade route. A very *prosperous* hub. If you settle around Graveyard, you'll still have a lot to sell, but your location won't be as advantageous, for any of us."

As Kitten likes to put it, "Location, location, location." That matters a lot in the Charon system. It matters so much, I'm glad I won't have to make that decision by myself. I'm happy to share that with the leaders in the House of Clans.

Olympia is no longer a microcosm. We have exited the Children's Caverns, and those of us who survived must remember how we suffered and profited from the deaths of our kin. I have to tell you, it sounds like a lot of work—but no rest for the wicked, right? Even if she means well. *Especially* if she does.

I do. We'll see what comes of it.

I'm a bit concerned that all the loose ends haven't been tied up. Will Bomarigala's clone ever emerge from the graveyard? Will I have cause to use the knife Crow passed along to me?

If Baba Yaga is really one of the Titans, is she the only one still surviving?

I received a letter from her, shortly after my talk with Commander Lana. Like all her communications, it began abruptly:

> You should accept the Belters' offer and park your ship around Almost. You'll find it has more to offer than just commerce. I've done some investigation on my own, and I believe those dead races that lived here are not so dead. Not that I've spoken to them—but you might, Oichi Angelis. They could become exceptional allies.

Notice she said *exceptional*. Not *wonderful*. That's probably no accident.

> Regardless, you'll see me again. Maybe Timmy, as well. You and she have something in common. You could learn from each other. I don't promise you'll learn anything from me, but we may find ways to help each other. Perhaps my greatest fears will not come true, after all.
>
> Be careful of Bomarigala, and of Gennady. Trust Argus Fabricus, and those *Merlin*ers. Keep the door open with the Ancient Races, too.
>
> Speaking of Gennady, you might consider marrying him. It would be an advantageous match for both of you. You would have to watch your back, but so would he.
>
> See you soon, Oichi. Probably when you least expect it. Don't take that personally.
>
> —B.Y.

Marriage to Gennady? Which Greek tragedy would that be? Would I become Medea, after all?

No—I think I'll stick to Elektra, and her three-pronged weapons. What did Dragonette call them? *Sai.*

I have a feeling they're going to come in handy.

About the Author

EMILY DEVENPORT's short stories have been featured in various esteemed publications such as *Asimov's Science Fiction, Alfred Hitchcock's Mystery Magazine,* the *Full Spectrum 5* anthology, *The Mammoth Book of Kaiju, Uncanny, Cicada, Science Fiction World, Clarkesworld,* and *Aboriginal Science Fiction,* whose readers voted her a Boomerang Award. She currently studies geology and works as a volunteer at the Desert Botanical Garden in Phoenix.